DEDICATION

FOR MUM AND DAD – I've always thought that raising a child must be one of the scariest things in the world. You never know when they're going to live on ketchup, run away to America or badmouth you on television. Well, in case I ever try that last one, you can display this to the world: I'm happy, I'm healthy and I love you. I wrote a book!

You didn't do so badly. (And the ketchup was delicious.)

SARAH REES BRENNAN

SIMON AND SCHUSTER

First published in Great Britain in 2009
by Simon and Schuster UK Ltd
A CBS COMPANY

First published in the USA in 2009 by Margaret K McElderry Books,
an imprint of Simon & Schuster Children's Publishing Division.

Simon & Schuster UK Ltd
1st Floor, 222 Gray's Inn Road
London WC1X 8HB

A CIP catalogue record for this book
is available from the British Library.

ISBN 978-0-85707-357-0

1 3 5 7 9 10 8 6 4 2

Printed by CPI Cox & Wyman, Reading, Berkshire RG1 8EX

www.simonandschuster.co.uk

www.mistful.livejournal.com

1

Ravens in the Kitchen

THE PIPE UNDER THE SINK WAS LEAKING AGAIN. IT WOULDN'T have been so bad, except that Nick kept his favourite sword under the sink.

He rescued it, wiped the steel, and absently tested the edge with his thumb while water flowed out onto the kitchen floor. Once he'd laid it aside, he realised the knees of his jeans were already soaked through.

Alan brought Nick his toolbox.

"Care to lend a hand?" Nick inquired without much hope.

"No, I'm too busy cooking," Alan said. "You do the heavy lifting around here. I'm more the sensitive intellectual type."

Nick raised his eyebrows. "Oh, get in the kitchen and bake me a pie, woman."

He peered into the cupboard again. The pipes made an ominous gurgling sound, and the bottom of the cupboard became the site of the world's tiniest waterfall.

"I can be a sensitive intellectual type as well," he said at length. "If the other option is drowning under our sink."

"Save us all from a watery grave or cook your own dinner. It's entirely up to you."

It was a compelling point. Nick could cook his own dinner, but Alan actually worked at being a good cook. He made everything from scratch, and the sizzling sound of food hitting the pan and the sudden rich smell of frying vegetables made his argument for him.

Nick glared, which was effective when dealing with everyone but his brother. Then he took the knife out of his wrist sheath, laying it carefully alongside his sword, rolled up his sleeves, and got to work.

Aside from the sink, this house was pretty good. It was small, the colour of cardboard that had been left out in the rain, and exactly like every other house standing in the military lines of the housing estate. Still, each house was separated from its neighbours by a decent distance. There was nobody complaining about strange noises in the night. That was worth any amount of leaks.

On the whole, Nick liked Exeter. There was a statue on the high street that reminded him of a knife, and he was learning to map the city out from that point. It was rare for them to stay in one place long enough for the landmarks to become familiar, but they had been here two months with no danger signs yet. They both had jobs, he was just about getting by at school, and Alan had even had time to find a new crush.

He would be sorry when they had to leave.

The pipe gave a long metallic groan, like an ancient robot about to fall to pieces, and Nick gritted his teeth and twisted the wrench hard. It was too old to be properly fixed; all he could do was try and hold it together until it could become the next tenant's problem.

"Someday we're going to live in St Leonard's and get away from all this."

"Oh, sure," said Alan easily. The chilli was simmering and he was leaning beside the sink, arms crossed over his thin chest, watching Nick work. "When I win big on the lottery. Or when we start selling your body to rich old ladies."

"If we start selling my body to rich old ladies now," Nick said, "can I quit school?"

"No," Alan answered with a sidelong smile, warm as a whispered secret. "You'll be glad you finished school one day. Aristotle said education is bitter, but its fruits are sweet."

Nick rolled his eyes. "Aristotle can bite me."

Over their heads the floorboards creaked in a sudden, sharp sound, like boughs breaking. Nick looked up on reflex, but he knew what it was: it was Mum, pacing the floor in one of her bad spells. By the sound of it she was just getting started, and Alan would spend all his time up there with her.

Alan must have noticed Nick's glance at the ceiling, because for some idiotic Alan reason he reached out with the obvious intention of ruffling Nick's hair. Nick shied away.

Alan sighed, then Nick heard him reach for the radio instead, the small click as it went on, and the music that poured out and drowned the sound of Mum restlessly moving in the rooms above. Alan limped over to a cupboard and began to rummage around for something, singing softly under his breath. Nick ducked back in under the sink and let the sweet sound of the singing rush over him, let his mind relax while his hands were busy with practical work. Dinner smelled almost ready. Maybe his stupid brother would sit down and eat his own food before he saw to Mum, and maybe this would be an okay Thursday after all.

There was only an instant's warning.

The talisman Nick wore always hurt him. It was a

constant irritation, an anchor hung around his neck that hummed and stung, but now pain flooded through him like an electric shock with the talisman as its source. The bird bones built around the talisman, woven into a web of crystal and net, shifted to form a new pattern. It felt as if the new pattern were being slowly burned into his skin.

"Alan," he ground out between his teeth.

Then the window exploded inward, a sharp burst of glittering shards caught in the fluorescent lights. Nick dropped the wrench and shielded his face with his arm, turning and glancing under his sodden sleeve to check that Alan had already hit the floor.

In through the window came an unkindness of ravens.

Their enormous iridescent wings were crammed against each other, the kitchen suddenly packed with feathers and the birds' deep, hoarse cries. The air of the room seemed to be nothing but the wind caused by their wingbeats, and they sounded hungry.

Nick crawled along the floor until he could grab his sword. The hilt was slick against his wet palms, and he hefted it in one hand and reached out with the other to grab Alan by the scruff of his neck and drag his brother behind him.

Alan lifted his shirt and took his gun out of its holster.

"Don't pick me up. You're my little brother, and it's shameful."

"You're a beanpole, and it's too easy," Nick returned, watching the birds carefully. They were starting to settle on the kitchen surfaces, the curves of their folded wings hunched forward like shoulders, apparently watching him back. "I can't believe you're still using that stupid gun."

"I like my gun," Alan protested.

"They don't always work!"

"Well," Alan conceded, "that's why I've got three knives on me."

There were ravens between them and the door. Nick hefted his sword and swung, feeling a rush of fierce joy when the blow connected and cut deep. One raven fell to the ground with its chest bleeding, and the rest screamed and wheeled on them. Nick hit the floor again, rolling towards the wall with one arm over his head. Alan was beside him, and Nick figured that he could be more or less shielded between the wall and Nick's body.

They stayed down, panting, and Nick tried to think through the blood pounding in his temples. These birds were obviously under the control of a demon, and there would be a magician watching to make sure the demon did its job.

Demons almost never possessed animals. They hated being trapped in bodies with such limited brains. Nick wondered how many human bodies the magicians had offered this one in return for the favour.

"You get the magician," Alan whispered. "I'll take the demon."

"I'll get them both," Nick said roughly, and shoved Alan for emphasis. "You stay down."

Nick rose and for a moment felt like he was out in the night and in a storm, except that the storm was made of feathers. He had to throw up his left arm to beat away two ravens that went for his eyes. The talons of one bird scored burning lines down his cheek, and Nick knocked it away, forgot all about strategy, and brought the sword around in a brutal circle through feathers and flesh.

This time none of the ravens screamed. Four more

descended on Nick, their talons sinking into his sword arm, and cloth and skin came away in strips. When Nick tried to shake them off, more skin tore away, and when he lifted his face so he could see what he was swinging at, a bird hurtled down towards him. Its curved beak was aimed directly at his eyes.

He got a sharp elbow in the back from his idiot brother, pushing him to one side. He recovered his balance, then spun and cut two birds down, sending the other three in mad, croaking flight to the ceiling.

By the time Nick turned back to his brother, Alan was already advancing, and Nick saw he had the leader in his sights. He went to Alan's side with his sword at the ready, in case the gun didn't work. Alan's eyes narrowed behind his glasses. He took aim and fired.

He didn't miss. At this range, the demon didn't have a chance.

The body of the raven went down, and the demon that had been possessing it went up through the ceiling, its body an insubstantial black plume, rising like glittering smoke.

Now that birds were not trying to claw Nick's eyes out, it was easy enough to spot the illusion. He was good at spotting magic. He'd tried to explain to Alan once that illusions were sharper, more real than the real world, more real than they had to be, but Alan had never been able to see it.

There was one bird now that was not milling about frantically like the others, but making directly for the broken window.

Nick pointed. "There!"

Alan fired again, and where a bird had been was a man falling.

As the body fell to the ground, the door leading to the hall opened and Mum stood in the doorway, her magicians' charms shining with power, her hair falling like shadows over her face.

Alan was checking the man's pulse, so Nick was the one who looked over at her and said, "It's dealt with. We don't need you."

Mum stood in the darkened hallway, watching him with pale eyes, and said at last, "I didn't come for you."

She closed the door, and Nick heard her slowly climbing back up the stairs.

They both looked around, panting a little, in case there were any more surprises to follow. But after five minutes nothing else happened. Nick let his sword point drop and touch the floor.

It was over. They were left with about fifteen confused ravens, a dead magician on their kitchen floor, and the sound of their mother's footsteps fading away.

While Alan salvaged dinner, Nick leaned against the kitchen counter and tried to keep out of the birds' way. They might no longer be under the sway of a demon, but they were still animals with great big go-to-hell beaks and claws, and Nick had never really been much of an animal person. Animals could tell, too. Alan'd had a cat once, and he'd had to give it away after it bit Nick a few times.

They didn't have to discuss it: this meant moving. Great. Nick had only just got Alan's bookshelves up the way he liked them.

The cuts along his cheek and arm stung. Nick fingered the gash on his cheek and tried to judge how deep it might be.

"Don't touch that," Alan said, slapping his hand away without looking at him. "It'll get infected. Dinner's done, I

7

think – let me patch you up and then we can eat. We'll clean up afterwards."

Nick saw Alan shiver. The night air was blowing in cold. At least some of the birds were noticing the enormous space where the window used to be. A few had already left.

His cheek hurt and he was starving. Nick fingered his talisman and scowled.

"Jump up," Alan said, sweeping broken glass out of the way with his sleeve pulled down over his hand. Thank God the saucepan lid had been on their dinner.

Nick rolled his eyes and slid into a sitting position on the counter. Alan got down the first-aid kit, tilted Nick's chin up, and started to pour the disinfectant carefully into the wounds. Alan always tried too hard to be gentle, which made everything worse. Nick set his teeth.

"Am I hurting you?"

"No," Nick said. "That was the stupid birds."

"They're very intelligent, actually," Alan told him as if he was under the impression Nick cared at all. He squinted and pinched the lips of the wound, taping them together. Then he set to work on Nick's arm. "If you catch them young, you can teach them to talk."

"I don't see what the big deal about that is," Nick said. "I can talk."

Alan pushed him gently; he still apparently hadn't absorbed the fact that Nick was twice as broad across the shoulders as he was, and that Alan would really have to try to hurt him. "Well, I caught you young too. Anyway, I think a raven might've been easier—"

There was a noise outside.

Nick placed his hand over Alan's mouth, cutting off all

that fond reminiscing nonsense, and slid off the kitchen counter. He pushed Alan aside, put a finger to his lips, and bent to scoop up his sword in one swift motion.

Then he walked quietly to the back door. Alan could not follow him. Alan was not very good at stealth, because of his leg, but Nick glanced behind him before he nudged the door open with his sword point. Alan had drawn his gun.

The door swung all the way open, and there was a sharp movement in the darkness. Nick lunged.

"Don't hurt her!" yelped a boy's voice, and Nick caught himself just as Alan flipped a switch and light flooded the little garden.

Nick stopped with his sword poised against a girl's throat.

She and her friend had obviously been hiding under the kitchen window. Chances were good they'd seen everything.

To her credit, the girl did not draw back from the blade. She did not even flinch. She just looked at Nick, her dark eyes large and calm in the sudden light, and Nick realised how all this must seem to her: the window frame with only jagged edges of glass left in it, the ravens winging through the air around them, the dead body on the floor. The boy with the sword to her throat.

All she did was swallow very gently against the blade and say, "I heard this was the place to come if you had a problem that was . . . out of the ordinary."

She looked familiar.

"Obviously that wasn't true," said the boy standing at her shoulder, taking a nervous step away and then back to her. "Obviously this is the place to come if you want to get murdered by lunatics. Um – we're sorry to have bothered you! Is there any chance we could just leave?"

There was something a whole lot more familiar about his

9

voice, which was light but wavered at crucial points where it was meant to be lightest and airiest. He was standing in the girl's shadow, but the light caught his earring.

Nick recognised that before he recognised the boy's worried face, the spiky blond hair that the darkness had turned into a pale crown.

"Wait," Nick said.

"O-okay. Is there any chance we could get off with a flesh wound?"

Nick shifted his stance so he could look back at Alan, and saw the girl brace herself and the boy grasp her shoulder, fingers going white. Alan was standing in the doorway with his gun drawn.

"I know this guy," Nick said. "He's harmless."

"Sure?" Alan asked, squinting behind his glasses.

"Sure," Nick said. "James Crawford. Trust me, if he was a magician, he'd be able to defend himself at school. He's harmless. He's useless."

"He's not—" the girl began furiously.

"Let's not argue with the crazy person holding the enormous sword!" James Crawford said. "And – did you say school?" He stepped away from the girl to look at Nick properly. "Oh my God, Nick Ryves."

Nick still hadn't lowered his sword. He was a little bit intrigued by the fact that the girl hadn't moved away either. She was still looking up at him, still determinedly calm.

He knew her now. She was the weird girl in the class above him, who dyed her hair pink and always wore a lot of pentagrams and crystals. Right now she was also wearing giant chandelier earrings and a violently pink T-shirt that bore the words ROMEO AND JULIET WOULDN'T HAVE LASTED.

He avoided people like her. He avoided anyone who tried to be noticed. That had been one of Dad's first lessons: try to act just like everyone else. If you failed to blend in, the magicians would find you.

"You know him?" she asked James.

"Well, yes," said James. "He hangs around with a pretty rough crowd at school, Seb McFarlane and that lot, but they're smoking-behind-the-bike-shed-rough. This is different, there were gunshots. My life was going to flash before my eyes, but it decided to hide behind my eyes and quake with terror instead. I think we should just go."

"I'm not going anywhere," the girl said. "I saw that bird turn into a man! You saw it too, Jamie. You must have."

"I don't know what I saw. It could've been a hallucination. You get those from sniffing glue."

"You've never sniffed glue!"

"I've smelled glue," Jamie said after a pause. "In art class."

Nick was about to tell them exactly what he thought of their babbling and exactly what he would do to them if they didn't go away at once and never breathe a word of what they'd seen, when Alan moved from the doorway into the light.

"Mae?" he said, his voice incredulous, and then quickly, "Nick, put that sword *down!*"

Mae said, "Bookshop Guy?"

Nick looked at her, tilting his head and recalling Alan's wistful speeches on the subject of the pink-haired girl who liked the Beat generation. He put two and two together and came up with the fact that this entire situation was ridiculous.

This was Alan's latest crush, then.

Nick drew the sword slowly away from the girl's throat and lowered it until the tip almost but not quite touched the ground, holding himself ready just in case. He let his gaze follow the blade, towards the ground and away from Mae.

"Whatever you want," he said softly.

Jamie was staring at Alan. "You helped me find *Catcher in the Rye* today and now you *shoot people?*"

"He only shot one person," Nick remarked. "But the night is young."

Alan glanced at him reproachfully, then turned back to Jamie and smiled his slow smile. He'd tucked the gun away under his buttoned-up shirt, along with his talisman, and all trace of the boy who fired to kill and never missed was gone.

The smile spread just a little bit at a time, coaxing and sweet, persuading Jamie to smile with him. Jamie was wearing a shy, crooked grin before Alan was done.

"Forgive him, he has no manners."

"I get by on good looks," Nick said.

"I know all of this is pretty strange," Alan continued, "but you came here for a reason, didn't you?"

"We came here because – something really strange has been happening to Jamie," said Mae, her voice hard. "I was expecting someone who could give us real occult help, though, not a guy who works in my bookshop and a school thug younger than I am. I wasn't expecting birds that turned into men and weapons and weird necklaces. I don't know what the hell is going on!"

"If you're so disappointed," Nick said, "get lost. We're busy."

The evening was getting colder and colder, as was Nick's dinner, and he had to board up the window and call the garage to tell them he was quitting. He did not care what these people wanted, or what was going on with them, or why anyone would use the word occult when they didn't have to.

He just wanted them to go away.

"No, no," Alan said at once. "I know all this must look strange, but we can help you. We want to help you."

Nick felt himself bound to correct this misapprehension. "I don't. And we've talked about this, Alan. Don't you think we have enough going on without opening up a charity shop for people who think they need occult" – he let his lip curl – "help?"

"Dad would have wanted us to help people," Alan told him, and then addressed the others. "Look, please come in. I can explain everything."

It was a testament to Alan's powers of persuasion that they did not laugh in his face. It was a testament to Alan's powers of looking non-threatening that he could manage it with the door open on their destroyed kitchen, with a corpse on the floor. He rumpled his red hair and adjusted his glasses in an anxious sort of way, and he took a couple of steps back to the kitchen. He let them see the limp: he used that, the same way he used everything.

Mae and Jamie visibly relaxed.

Nick gave up, shaking his head and following his brother inside. Mae squared her shoulders resolutely and crossed the threshold into their home. Nick was standing in the doorway and stepped back about an inch, so she had to brush by him. She looked irritated and uncomfortable doing it, and he smirked at her. He saw her hesitate, as if she was about to turn and run, but Alan stood before her looking honest and inviting.

She stopped, reached up, and tapped the talisman lying against Nick's chest.

"What's this?" she asked, her voice a little softer.

"It's a talisman," Alan answered gently. "It warns him when magic is being used nearby, and it protects him from smaller spells."

"Protects him," Mae repeated. "So you're talking about black magic, then? The kind that hurts people – that causes trouble."

Nick laughed, looking at the broken glass and black feathers around them.

"There isn't any other kind."

"I have a feeling this is going to be one hell of an explanation," Mae said, and walked into the kitchen and towards Alan.

Jamie still looked wide-eyed and extremely doubtful about what he was doing, but he dashed in after her.

Nick closed the door and found himself wondering what had brought this pair to their house. You had to be desperate to come to them.

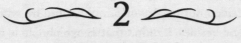

2

Demon's Mark

OF COURSE NICK WAS EXPECTED TO GET RID OF THE BODY.
He always did it, since Alan couldn't be expected to
haul corpses about the place with his leg, but he seldom found
it this irritating. He could've had his dinner first, if Alan hadn't
been worried about what the guests would think.

He twisted the steering wheel more viciously than he
should have, since making sharp turns in the narrow roads
around Exeter was not exactly advisable.

His foul mood might have something to do with the fact
that these two freaks were from his school. People from his
school had seen the way he lived, with the sword and the gun
and with ravens and demons. It didn't seem to bother Alan, but
it should have. There were a lot of things about their life that
should have bothered Alan.

He drove along the river Exe for a while, the low-lying city
lost behind the car, the faint shapes of buildings in the distance
looking like no more than the shadows of a larger city he could
not see. He waited until there had been nobody else on the road
for ten minutes, then pulled the car over to the side of the road
and climbed out.

Nick bundled the body out of the boot. The man had been tall, he noticed idly, and he wondered if he should check his sigil to see what Circle he belonged to.

He decided not to. Anyone could come by while he was doing it, and besides, it didn't matter which Circle had found them this time. All the Circles were after them. It would be a different one next time.

The presence of sigils on the bodies was good for only one thing. It meant that the Circle would check for the tattoos and take back their own, and the police would not come to Alan and Nick's asking questions about discovered bodies and shots fired.

All the same, it was usually a good idea to remove the corpse from their actual property.

Nick looked into the man's slack face. It was also a good idea to get the body into running water as soon as possible. Otherwise the Circle might give their fallen comrade to the demons. A demon could use a dead body for a few days.

The body was easy enough to haul up onto the parapet, and Nick balanced it there for a moment, looking down at the river. The waters were black and quiet before he dropped the man into them, hoisting the flopping legs over the side as he went. The body hit the water with a splash, sinking almost entirely under, dragged down by the weight of a heavy leather coat and innumerable charms and talismans. Nick watched a pale hand bob at the surface, buffeted by the current so it looked alive.

He turned and climbed back into the car. He hoped that their uninvited guests would be gone by the time he reached home. It shouldn't take long for Alan to tell them that there were magicians in the world who could call up demons and set them on people. That there were quite a lot of other things happening side by side with the normal world those idiots pretended they didn't fit into. They had probably just heard the warnings Alan had spread and convinced themselves they needed "occult help".

Chances were, after all, that whatever problem the pair had was imaginary. He turned the engine on. It roared to life, and he pulled away fast from the side of the river where the body was sinking.

Imaginary problems. Must be nice.

By the time Nick had turned the curve past St David's station, he was sure Alan was already finishing the usual spiel. He told everyone who came all they needed to know to protect themselves. If Alan had been less eager to help people and more concerned about protecting himself, Nick would've felt better.

Nick could almost hear Alan's voice now.

There are demons living in another world, he would say, a world side by side with ours, and they are hungry.

They are hungry for the sounds and sights and sensations of our world. None of them can get in, though. None of them can touch you, unless a magicians' circle builds a bridge for the demons. Stay safe. Stay away from the magicians. Stay away from us.

Worked for Nick.

He parked the car, jumped out, and came in angling the door so he could see everything, his sword half drawn, as he usually did.

Alan's voice drifted to him through the open door. "So, Mae – is that because your birthday's in May? Because it's almost May now . . ."

Alan had changed the usual spiel a bit, Nick noticed.

He pushed the door all the way open and slid his sword all the way out of its scabbard. This pair had invaded his house. He could scare them if he liked.

"It's not May like the month," Mae explained. "It's Mae like Mae West."

"Like you *wish*," said Nick.

At the same time, his brother glowed and asked, "Are you a movie buff?"

The sitting room was brightly lit and conspicuous for its ordinariness, unlike their kitchen full of broken glass and dead birds. Alan had obviously made everyone a cup of tea, and he and Mae were sitting in the two big, broken-down armchairs. Jamie was perched on the end of their sofa, his tea untouched, as if he did not trust it. Alan was leaning slightly towards Mae, and she twisted her head at the sound of Nick's voice and looked towards the door.

Nick observed the flicker of appreciation in her brown eyes. He wasn't particularly surprised. She was just the type to like them tall, dark, and carrying a lethal weapon.

He let his lip curl. That kind of behaviour was so stupid, he couldn't bear it.

"You lot still here?" he asked. "When's dinner?"

"We have a serious problem," Mae told him, now looking angry rather than appreciative.

Nick came in, idly swinging his sword, and took a seat on the other end of the sofa. "I'm sorry to hear that," he said. "And I'm still hungry."

"I'm sorry about him," Alan put in, glaring. "He gets cranky."

Nick raised his eyebrows. "I'm only cranky when I'm not fed."

"So he's – he's cranky?" Jamie repeated. "Cranky, and – and he carries a great big sword. Well, that's marvellous, that is."

Alan laughed, and Jamie relaxed again. Alan had a knack for that. Parents, bosses, animals, and children, they all liked Alan.

Girls liked Nick. He felt it was a fair trade.

Nick realised that since Jamie was in his class at school, chances were that they were the same age, but Nick had always looked and felt older than all the kids at school, and Jamie was small and wide-eyed: made to be his teacher's pet and his class-mates' target.

He probably would've been less of a target if he hadn't insisted on wearing lavender shirts and jewellery to school.

Nick didn't blame Jamie for being nervous around him. Lots of people were, and besides that, Seb McFarlane and his lot were always hassling Jamie, and they were technically Nick's friends.

Nick thought the kid was stupid for sticking his neck out when he didn't have to and couldn't protect himself, but he'd never laid a finger on him. It was a waste of energy; Jamie had never done anything to him, and Alan would have been furious.

He understood anger, though, the restless urge to lash out at anyone that made that little group of bored boys tick. Nick always gravitated to those boys, the troublemakers in every school. The other kids avoided Nick, as if they could smell the violence on him. It didn't bother Nick; he could smell the weakness on them. These boys thought every danger sign was a show of strength. They weren't afraid of him, and he needed a group. A boy alone got too much attention.

"So," Jamie said, apparently now under the impression that he was welcome, "you two live together?"

He jumped a little when he saw the expression on Nick's face, then edged so far down the sofa he was practically sitting on the arm.

"Yes," Nick responded, in a voice of ice. "Because he is my *brother*."

"Ah," Jamie said faintly.

"Don't take that tone with *my* brother," Mae said, tilting her chin. "How was Jamie supposed to know? You two don't look anything alike."

Nick looked away from her and Jamie, to the mirror over the mantelpiece. It only reflected the lamp against the wall, the light a low sunset colour inside the ugly orange lampshade. His grip on his sword tightened.

He didn't need her to tell him. He knew that.

Mae and Jamie were not much alike, as siblings went. She was on the curvy side, and Jamie was a skinny wretch Nick could have snapped like a twig in one hand. Jamie was blond, and Nick suspected that under the pink Mae was a basic brunette, but they both had the same big brown eyes, the same heart-shaped face. They shared a few markers of kinship with each other, the small signs of shared blood that Nick would have wanted to share with Alan, and not with *her*.

Alan looked uncomfortable. Nick cleared his throat, and Jamie jumped again, as if the sound was a gunshot. "Alan looks like Dad. I look like Mum."

It was as simple as that. He fixed both of them with a stare that dared them to ask further questions or make further personal observations. His family was none of their business.

Neither Mae nor Jamie spoke. Alan, however, could never be stopped from talking by any power of God or Nick.

"Now that Nick's back, why don't you tell us why you're

here and what you think might be wrong," he said, still smiling. His eyes creased up behind his glasses when he smiled, until they were nothing but gleams of vivid blue.

It was Dad's smile, and Alan used it to the same effect Dad always had.

Mae was apparently not immune to the smile. Her face softened and her back straightened as she smiled back.

"Well," she said. "I'm psychic myself, you see."

Nick snorted. "Oh, of *course* you are."

Mae looked offended. "It's possible that I've grown out of it, but very strange things happened around me when I was younger. Little objects used to smash by themselves, or fly through the air. I didn't know what was going on, but I've researched and I've looked for people who might know something, and I've heard things about magicians and the demons who give them power. And it's true, isn't it? That man you – he'd turned himself into a bird! He was a real magician. It's all real."

Sounded like some of the Market people had been talking. Nick wished they could learn to keep their mouths shut, or at least learn not to take advantage of Alan's soft heart, and stop sending the problem cases his way.

"It's real," Alan said, "but I don't think—"

He looked worried about distressing the lady, so Nick came to his rescue. He leaned forward, looked at Mae, and said, "Let me put things simply so you will understand them. You're not a magician. You're an idiot. A few people in this world are born with a certain amount of magic, but they don't grow out of it. They either learn to control it and keep it a secret forever, or they try to do something with the magic. Which means that most of them become magicians and call up demons. It's the safest and easiest way to get more power, but there're also rituals with the dead, and—"

"Rituals with the dead," Jamie repeated in a faint, stunned voice. Nick turned and looked at him coldly. "I mean," Jamie said, and swallowed, "how interesting and not at all creepy! Please go on!"

Nick was tired of this. They'd been attacked, they were going to move again, and he didn't need these people witnessing what a mess his life was. He hated it that they were from his school: that Jamie had seen him trying to read, and now they were getting an illicit peek into his weird world. Afterward they'd go home, safe and warm, and they would think that they'd had an adventure.

He leaned forward and caught Mae's eyes again, giving her the kind of look that made most people flinch.

"There are the magicians' messengers, and people who can enchant others with music, and people who can make magical objects," he explained, his voice low. "But funnily enough, there are no people who grow out of having magical powers. If you had them, you'd know about it. But you don't know anything, and none of this concerns you. Go home and stop bothering me for no reason."

Mae did flinch and immediately looked furious with herself. "I have a reason!"

Nick was ready to snap back at her when Alan leaned forward and touched his arm. His grip on his sword tightened, but he fell silent, and Alan said in a much kinder voice than any Nick could've achieved, "What's your reason?"

Mae looked at the floor and said, "I told you. It's Jamie."

"It's crazy, is what it is," said Jamie. Nick turned to look at him again. Jamie did not seem overjoyed to have captured his attention. He swallowed and made a face, as if someone was forcing something bitter down his throat, and then continued, "It all started with – these dreams. I thought they were just dreams, strange dreams, of someone beautiful outside my window, asking to be let in."

"A succubus," Mae put in helpfully. Nick raised his eyebrows at the word and made sure she saw him do so. She frowned at him and continued, "Or an incubus, that's the word for the men, isn't it? I've read about them, they're demons who come in the night and basically have their wicked way with you."

"Their wicked way?" Nick repeated. "My, my. What kind of books have you been reading, and does your mother know?"

Mae glared, and Jamie's face went scarlet. So did Alan's. Apparently he'd never heard that there was such a thing as being too sympathetic.

"What happened?" Alan asked quietly.

Jamie looked up from the floor and found something in Alan's eyes that made him square his shoulders and say, in a steadier voice, "I let him in. And then, in the morning, it was real. I mean, someone had really been there. There was—"

"All you need to do is answer the question," Nick interrupted. "We don't need details."

Mae's glare intensified, and Nick smiled, feeling pleased and vicious at once. These people shouldn't have come here. School and home should not overlap. Nick was meant to be normal at school, and this was his place, his brother, his home, even his mad mother rocking upstairs. He did not care about their problems. He only wanted them to leave.

He leaned forward to say something else.

"Nick," Alan said, and Nick reluctantly closed his mouth. Alan nodded at Jamie to go on.

"The next day there was a weird mark on me. When I told Mae, she started asking some people questions."

"When I was asking about magic, I started hanging out with people who have unusual interests," said Mae. "There isn't much of a Goth or Wicca scene in Exeter, but I went to a few places I know and asked around. A lot of people wouldn't talk to me because the Goths think I'm a bit of a baby bat, and the Wiccans think I'm a playgan."

"People think you're – a bat," Nick said slowly. "Well, of course. Many people think I'm a blueberry scone."

She grinned a sudden, unexpected grin, and he almost smiled back at her, but then he recalled that she was invading his home and looked right through her until her smile melted away.

Unfortunately, the rest of her stayed put.

"It means they think I'm just playing around and not serious," she continued in an even cooler tone. "Some of them listened to me, though, and there was one guy – a stranger – who told me that if I had a weird problem, I should come here."

"Considerate of him," Nick murmured.

He was icily furious. Forget the black arts, any magician could find them by asking a few questions down at the local, because the Goblin Market felt the need to spread the word. They said that it was their responsibility to protect normal people from the magicians. Nick thought it was their responsibility to remember that the magicians could be listening anywhere, at any time, and careless words could get them all killed.

Nick gave Alan a dark look, but Alan was not looking at him. His gaze was fixed on Mae.

"*Was* it an incubus?" Mae asked. Nick snorted.

Alan said, "There's no such thing as an incubus. Not exactly. There are just demons, and demons will take any shape and offer anything to get what they want."

A question broke from Jamie. "What did he want?"

Nick shifted his sword, laying it flat against his knees, and smiled when Mae's and Jamie's gazes were caught by the gleam and slid along the blade.

"He wanted what all demons want," Nick said softly. "He wanted to come in out of the cold."

"The demons live in another world," Alan explained. "All the writings I've been able to get my hands on stress how different the worlds are. There are old legends that say humans were made of earth and demons of fire. It's a metaphor, of course, but it's a good one. They are made of entirely different materials from us. There is no description of the demon world available in the books. Maybe it can't be described, but apparently it is so bleak that the demons are willing to do anything to leave it, even for a short time – and that is where the magicians come in."

Mae reached over and took Jamie's hand, lacing their fingers together. Jamie held on tight.

"There are magicians after Jamie?"

"Oh, sure," said Nick. "After him. Or you. Magicians aren't fussy. You're all just meat to throw to the demons."

"You're not helping!" Mae exclaimed.

Nick leaned back against the sofa, crossing his legs and balancing the sword against one knee. He bared his teeth at her.

"I am helping. I'm telling you the truth. You don't like it, that's your problem."

"Meat," Jamie repeated, his voice trembling. "What does that mean?"

"Demons can only enter this world if they are summoned," Alan answered. "The magicians summon them, so they can use the demons' power as their own. You have to understand – people don't ever have much magic of their own, but demons can control the elements. They can create illusions so real you can touch them. And they're willing to give some of their power to the magicians, because they want entry into this world." He looked at Jamie, his eyes wide and serious. "There must be magicians close by who called up a demon and let him go hunting for a body to possess. And you must be older than you look."

"I'm – I'm sixteen," Jamie said. "I was sixteen in October. What does that matter?"

He was almost six months older than Nick, then. Nick found that mildly amusing, since Jamie came up to his shoulder.

Then he remembered his birthday last month. Alan had made a cake and told him to make a wish, and he'd done it because ridiculous things like that made Alan happy. He'd closed his eyes and wished for a long time here in Exeter, safe and undisturbed.

Nick scowled. Look how well that had worked out for him.

"Demons won't go after anyone younger than sixteen, not if they have a choice," Alan explained. "They don't like being in the bodies of animals or children. The brains aren't developed enough to have proper control over their magic."

"Children aren't like animals," said Mae, frowning.

"Demons aren't PC," Nick said. "Imagine that."

Alan reached out and touched the back of Jamie's hand. Alan was a great one for touching people.

"You don't need to worry," he said. "If you have a mark,

we'll bring you to the next Goblin Market and get it taken off. Mae has her talisman, and I can get you one as well. The demons will move on to easier prey."

Jamie shifted on the sofa, as if he was not sure which way to move. Nick had become familiar with that kind of reaction. People were always upset to hear someone like Alan casually saying things like "easier prey".

"I always thought that Mae talking about magic was sort of . . . silly," he said, with an apologetic grimace at his sister. "The first time I found a mark, I didn't even tell her, but—"

Nick's sword point hit the carpet at the same time as he seized Jamie's arm and yanked him to his feet. Jamie twisted in his grip for a startled instant, and then froze when he saw the look on Nick's face.

"Exactly how many marks do you *have*?" Nick snarled.

"Let my brother go," said Mae, who'd stood up at some point. Nick did not bother looking at her.

He caught another movement out of the corner of his eye, though, and did look. It was Alan, getting up with a great deal more difficulty than Mae had. Alan was never more obviously crippled than when he had to climb to his feet. He had to use the back of the chair to lever himself up.

Seeing it never did anything to improve Nick's mood.

"Nick. Take it easy. Put the sword down."

"Yes!" Jamie said, arm trembling in Nick's grasp. Nick could break it now, if he liked. "Yes, that's an excellent idea. Why don't you put the sword down?"

Mae hovered at Alan's elbow, looking defiant but clearly unwilling to do anything that might put her brother at risk. Alan reached out and took hold of Nick's wrist, his grip gentle but firm.

Nick let go of Jamie's arm. He backed up a step, laid his sword carefully on the living room table, and stepped away from that as well. He swept his sword arm wide to display the vast emptiness of his hand, and then he looked expectantly at Jamie.

"Now," he said. "Show me."

Jamie swallowed and glanced nervously at his sister.

"It's all right," Alan told him. "Nobody's going to hurt you."

There was a pause in which Jamie carefully did not look at Nick, though Nick was waiting with his arms folded, promises in his eyes of what he'd do if this boy had endangered his family.

Slowly Jamie undid the buttons of his shirt, starting from the bottom. He fumbled with the buttons, fingers dragging as if weighed down by everyone's stares, and then stopped when the shirt was halfway undone. His chest looked like any boy's chest, any boy who didn't eat or exercise enough. Pale, thin, and then high on his left hip, just above his jeans, there was . . .

Nick swore. "A third-tier mark. You came to us with a third-tier mark."

"What does that mean?" Jamie asked in an agitated voice, which climbed higher with every word. "How many tiers are there? What d'you mean, tiers, like – tiers on a wedding cake?"

The windows of the sitting room showed nothing but blackness, but that was the problem with night. The demons could be on you before you had a chance to prepare yourself, and now there was a boy with a third-tier mark in Nick's house. He glanced at Alan, and Alan looked so sorry. Alan was

28

obviously trying to think of a way to tell the boy kindly, but with news like this it didn't matter how you said it.

Besides, this was nothing to do with them. Except that the boy had brought it into their home.

Nick went and sat on the table beside his sword. He reached out and pointed, his finger tracing the air an inch from the mark on Jamie's skin. The mark looked red at first, but after a moment looking at it your vision would blur, as if the mark was trying to slip out of sight. Even though the heart of the wound was red, the torn edges were black as shadows, black as blood in the night. There were two lines cut in Jamie's skin, and within the two lines were three ragged puncture marks in the shape of a triangle.

Within the lines and the triangle, scarlet and shiny as a burn, was an open, staring eye.

"Three tiers," he said curtly. "The first tier is the two slashes. They form the doorway. Once it's made, the demons are aware there's a weak spot, and they start to gather at the door between the worlds. They can track you once that first mark is made. Second tier is the triangle. Three equilateral points – three equilateral punctures – and once they're made it means that someone has to die."

Mae abruptly sat. She had been standing right behind Jamie, hovering protectively, and then suddenly she wasn't. She had fallen backwards into an armchair, her face white and her fingers gripping the arms of the chair.

"Die?" Jamie echoed.

"Someone has to die," Alan repeated. "Either you or a magician: one of the magicians' Circle that summoned the demon. Their blood could be used to wipe the second mark away."

"That doesn't matter," Nick interrupted. "Because you have a third-tier mark. Inside the door, inside the triangle, is the eye. That's the third tier. Once you have that, they have a fix on you. Eventually they will be able to break down the barriers in your mind, crawl inside you, and control everything you do. The demons are watching you now, and nobody but you will do."

"Wait," said Jamie, his voice trembling, his whole body trembling. "You can't mean that. I thought the two slashes were just tiny cuts. I thought the triangle of puncture wounds were insect bites or something. I didn't even tell Mae until there was a burn mark that looked like an eye. I didn't even know if we should come here tonight, and now you're saying that it's too late already?"

Nick shrugged. "Yeah."

He stopped pointing and clasped his hands loosely together, leaning forward with his elbows on his knees. Jamie was just standing there, shirt crumpled and half open, hands hanging empty and open at his sides. Both he and his sister were wearing blank, blind looks, as if the universe had been rearranged in front of their eyes and the new version hurt too much to look at properly.

It was the look on Alan's face that unsettled Nick. He was obviously feeling something, something softer and more than pity, something that came naturally to Alan and that should probably come naturally to Nick. He felt somewhat at a loss. The doomed ones always upset Alan.

"There has to be something," Mae protested, her voice on a hard edge between rage and fear. "There has to be something I can do, you can't just tell us that there's nothing—"

"I'm sorry," Alan said. "I would help if I could."

"Why would the demon just want him to—" Mae checked herself, clearly unable to say the word.

"The demon will not want him to die," Alan answered. "The demon wants to possess him, but once it does, the strain of the human spirit and the demon struggling for possession of the same body will be too much. It will tear his body apart. It always does: the demon can't make it last. And they won't give a body up."

"First he'll be a demon," Nick said. "Then he'll die. Shouldn't take more than a month."

Jamie appeared to be on the verge of hyperventilating, to judge from his breathing. Nick did not look at him. There was nothing he or Alan could do, no matter how much Alan wanted to help. They had told them what was going on, and that it was bad. He didn't know what these two expected.

It was because he was looking at the carpet that he saw it first.

Creeping from the small unused hearth, over the worn red rug, and spilling onto the carpet, came pale, almost invisible tendrils of mist.

"Mist inside," Nick reported sharply.

Two attacks in one day, and a boy wearing the demon's eye in their house. They were certainly getting a lot of attention.

"Out of striking range," Alan ordered the others. "Get onto the chairs. Get your feet off the floor."

"Striking range," Jamie repeated, clambering onto the sofa even as he spoke, holding fast to the back. He was still trembling. "It's mist. Does mist generally strike in this house? Is it attack mist?"

Nick picked up his sword and prowled around the circumference of the rug, hefting the hilt a little against his palm as the mist spread across the floor. You could hardly see it, and then the slow creep caught your eye, the wavering of the air at the edges of the room, and you realised the room was brimming with mist.

Mae had got up on a chair, but she was twisting where she stood to get a better view. "Mist," she said. "Is it a vampire?"

"No, woman, it's not a vampire," Nick said scornfully. "It's another stupid illusion from stupid magicians who think we'll be too distracted by their first attack to notice it."

He scanned the room from edge to edge, looking for the most likely sign of movement, holding his sword ready. The thin film of mist made the carpet blur a little before his eyes, everywhere he looked.

"Mist is a small magic," Alan explained. "It usually resolves into a small animal that a demon's possessing. Mist's easy enough to deal with."

The usual form the mist took was a rat. Once, though, Nick had been forced to try and stab a large spider. He hoped it would be something big this time; he could use some action. Thursday night had been ruined, his house had been invaded, but he could be calm about this. All he had to do was kill.

The two amateurs were up on the chairs, moving and making a racket. Alan, who knew better, stood perfectly still and never distracted Nick by stirring or speaking at all. Nick stalked around the perimeter of the room. He caught the shimmer of mist gathering and forming a shape the instant before it happened.

He would've had it, but he was not expecting something as long and twisty as a snake. There was just the mist and then suddenly it was there, a thin black stripe against the carpet, moving faster than Nick did, striking faster than Nick did. Nick was only a second behind it.

He sprang forward and brought the sword down hard.

He cut the snake in two bloody halves an instant after it had sunk its fangs into Alan's leg.

For a moment he was not worried at all. Then he saw the expression on Alan's face, and he remembered his brother saying, *Mae has her talisman, and I can get you one as well.*

Nick had not thought to wonder where Mae had got hers. He had not noticed the absence of the telltale bulge under Alan's shirt.

"You're wearing it," Nick breathed, turning his eyes to Mae.

She put her hand to her throat, silent for once. She was smart to stay quiet. There was blood pounding in Nick's ears. There was blood sliding down his sword. Alan knelt, quite calmly, and rolled up the leg of his jeans. Nick saw the mark, saw two red lines just above his ankle, saw the doorway of the demons on his brother.

This had never happened before.

"Nick, calm down," Alan said, his own voice unacceptably calm. "It's only a first-tier mark. We'll take care of it. We'll go to the Goblin Market and have it removed."

Nick's arm ached with the effort of not swinging his sword, not bringing it down anywhere, on anyone. His whole body felt run by cold rage, as if rage was flowing in his veins and the chill was stinging him into action.

"Shut up!" He wheeled on Mae and Jamie. "Get out," he suggested. "Or get hurt. It's your choice."

His teeth ached, he was gritting them so hard, and Mae and Jamie scrambled away from him over the furniture. He had to lower the sword then, because the only target left was Alan.

Nick drew in a deep breath and threw his sword against the wall. It struck plaster with the ring of steel, and he shut his eyes at the sound.

"You gave your talisman away," he said, hunting for words. He didn't want to speak, but he had to; he could do nothing else, because what he wanted to do was hit Alan.

He paced, desperate and silent as an animal. Finally he found words, and threw them at his brother.

"I can't believe you were so *stupid*. Not again!"

3

The Hidden Girl

NICK REMEMBERED THE FIRST TIME THE MAGICIANS HAD caught them.

He had always known they were there, a hunting presence like the sound of trumpets and dogs in the undergrowth must be for foxes, but that time was different. It was the difference between knowing they were there and having the dogs upon you, jaws snapping, with no chance to run.

Nick had been eight years old, and Alan eleven. Nothing had seemed serious then. Mum had always been strange, had never liked Nick, but it was Dad's job to take care of Mum, just like it was Alan's job to take care of Nick.

There had been a lot of moving but always to houses that were warm, places with gardens and lots of room. Nick had never worried where his next meal was coming from, and never worried that someone might try to kill them. Nick had known the magicians were hunting them, and Dad had made sure they knew how to fight. It was just that Nick never really believed the magicians could get past Dad.

Dad could do anything. He could calm Mum in her wildest fits, and he could reassure anyone who ever got suspicious.

He looked just like Alan except big, an enormously adult and comforting presence who could carry a tired boy anytime they had to move in the middle of the night. Nick remembered those midnight moves only as moments when he stirred to find his cheek pillowed against Dad's broad shoulder.

"You're mine," Dad used to say. "And I'm going to take care of you."

Back then wearing the talisman had just been a precaution, like Alan holding his hand when they crossed the road. Nick hated the talisman.

A talisman looked a lot like a dream catcher decorated with bones, which had crystals in the place of beads and salt and spells poured over the weave when they were made. Dad used to buy them both talismans at a stall in the Goblin Market, like a normal father buying his sons toffee apples. Wearing a great big dream catcher struck his eight-year-old self as stupid, and besides that it was uncomfortable.

It was always moving, always burning. It left a faint silvery scar on his chest where it usually rested. Nick understood what that meant now. He took after his mother. He wasn't happy about it.

At the time it was simply a nuisance. Nick was forever leaving it on his bedside table or by the sink in the bathroom, and Alan was forever finding it and bothering him to keep it on.

The talisman was in the back seat of the car on the night Dad carried Nick right into a trap.

The magicians had got there first. They had laid a circle around the family's new house that flared into the three points of a triangle once they'd all passed the threshold. Three equilateral points, like the Bermuda Triangle. The sign for death.

Dad had put Nick carefully down as they all looked at each

other and knew what this meant. To break the circle would mean death. They were caught as neatly as animals in a snare, with no chance to run, and the magicians would be able to come and collect them without a fight.

Dad had not made a fuss at all. Nick had watched uncomprehendingly as his father walked across the floor and knelt down in front of Alan.

"You'll look after your mother and your brother. You'll do whatever you have to do. Swear to me."

Alan whispered, "I swear."

"That's my boy," Dad had said, and kissed Alan once, on the forehead. He took him by the shoulders and looked at him for another moment, and then he rose to his feet and ran at the circle.

His family stood and watched him burn as he crossed the magicians' line, collapsing in on himself like a hot coal stabbed by a poker. There was nothing left of him after a moment but ashes and emptiness.

Dad was the one who gave them a chance to run, but Alan was the one who got them out. He grabbed Mum's hand and asked Nick if he had his talisman. Nick remembered exactly how he had felt in that moment: empty of all words, hardly able to understand Alan's question. He'd shaken his head, and Alan had paused and then tugged the talisman over his own head.

"Take mine."

The magicians were lying in wait. Their demons were ready. The air had been thick with them: attacking birds, ice underfoot, licks of flame like whips leaping at them from empty air. Fire passed right through Mum's wild black hair, and she sobbed and clutched at her talisman in gratitude.

Fire hit Alan's leg and he cried out; he had to lean on Nick to get to the car, and tears had poured down his cheeks as he told Mum what to do and where to drive. They drove to Scotland, not even pausing to sleep, and it was not until days later that Alan decided it was safe to go to a hospital. By then infection had set in, and the muscles were damaged.

Nick never took his stupid talisman off again, no matter how uncomfortable it was.

It was only Alan and Nick from then on. Mum hardly counted.

It had been eight years. They had been running ever since, hardly able to keep themselves fed, hardly able to escape when they were cornered. It had been eight years and Alan, that *idiot*, had not learned that he should never give away his talisman again.

Alan fled upstairs to Mum the instant Mae and Jamie were gone, mumbling something about feeding her and meaning that he was a complete coward. Nick couldn't follow Alan up to Mum. She'd be upset for days if Nick actually went into her room. When she had her bad days, she needed the security of knowing that if she stayed in her room, she wouldn't have to see him.

They had some time to move out, at least. The magicians had lost one of their number and must have used up a lot of power with those ravens and the mist so soon afterwards. Still, Nick knew he should stay inside tonight, stay close just in case of another attack.

Instead he went out and did exercises. He had to practise long hours with the sword, making sure he could move as if it were another, somewhat sharper limb – and besides, the kind of mood he was in, he was almost hoping the magicians would attack him. Let them try.

The night wind swept cool along his bare arms as he lunged and feinted, trying to stab shadows through the heart. The few teachers he'd had told him it was all about the moves, but Nick always had to imagine an opponent: someone he could hurt and whom he wanted to hurt badly. In order to really practise, he had to make a more deadly enemy than he'd ever faced out of the air. He had to be better than anyone he could imagine.

Especially since his stupid crippled brother was apparently determined to throw his life away.

Nick fought the air and thought about the night Dad had died. He only headed back to the house when it was past four in the morning, shrugging his shirt back on as he went. The material was chilled and damp from lying on the grass, wet with a night's dewfall, and it stuck to his sweat-slick skin.

He came inside to find Alan frying eggs.

"Do you remember Mrs Gilman, our neighbour from three houses ago?" Alan asked. "She used to watch you practising the sword with binoculars. I never told you. I'm sorry."

Nick laid his sword down on the draining board with a metallic clink.

"Why did you do it?"

"Well, Nicholas, she was over sixty. I thought you'd be a little disturbed."

Nick said nothing. He stared at Alan, jaw set, and let silence stretch from him to his brother as if it was a red carpet he was unrolling for Alan to talk on.

"Look, they needed help and we were the only ones who could give it," Alan said rapidly. "I can buy another talisman from the Market people tomorrow. I thought I'd just give Mae mine and replace it—"

"Stop lying to me."

The scrape of the spatula in the pan faltered. Nick crossed his arms over his chest and waited.

"I don't know what you m—"

"It was the boy who had the problem. You gave the girl the talisman. Don't try to pretend that you didn't want to give her something. Don't pretend you didn't want to impress her with how magically attentive to her needs you could be."

The tips of Alan's ears were violently red.

"Maybe you're right," he admitted.

"I'm right."

Alan hesitated, then set his thin shoulders. "I wanted to impress her, but I wanted to help them too. The talisman will protect her. If I wanted her to – to like me as well, what does it matter?"

Alan looked tired in the remorseless yellow light of the kitchen. He should be asleep, not up frying eggs and worrying.

"I don't see why it matters if she likes you or not."

Girls were an old subject of argument between them. Alan sighed, and Nick stared out of the window, where the shadows of night were paling slightly, preparing for dawn.

"Don't – I know you're worried," Alan said. "Don't be. How many people with first marks have we seen? How many first marks have you removed? How is this different?"

Nick turned his gaze from the window to Alan.

"This is different," he said. "This is you."

Alan looked terribly pleased for a moment, and Nick realised that his brother had taken this as one of the ridiculous, sappy things Alan was used to saying all the time. Nick had only meant what he'd said. It had never been his brother before.

Thankfully Alan did not make a fuss about it. He could believe Nick had said any stupid thing he wanted, so long as there were no scenes.

All he said was, "Here, have your dinfast. Then we can start packing."

"Dinfast," Nick repeated.

"Dinner and breakfast!" Alan said triumphantly. "Like brunch."

Nick subjected him to a long, judgemental stare. "There's something very wrong with you," he said at last. "I thought you should know."

Undaunted or perhaps just unsurprised by this news, Alan began to do the dishes. He pushed Nick's sword away with sudsy fingers to make room for a wet frying pan.

"Where do you fancy living next?"

"London," said Nick, because he thought that Alan would like it.

Alan looked pleased, and he saw he'd guessed right.

"London, then. We'll find a better house, one with a kitchen window that's not all smashed, and we'll go to the museums. Then come May we can go to the Goblin Market and find someone to dance—"

"I'll dance," Nick said.

The comfortable clink and splash of the washing-up stopped. Alan had gone rather still.

"You don't have to. Someone else can do it. You told me you never wanted to dance again."

For all that Alan was so fond of talking, for all that he could bang on endlessly about nothing for hours, he didn't actually seem to understand words. Nick had said everything quite clearly. He had never intended to go into the circle again, never intended to dance for the demons again. As far as he was concerned, the marked ones could go to someone else for help.

Only this time the marked one was Alan, and it was different.

"I'll dance," he repeated. Alan smiled his embarrassing touched smile, and Nick rolled his eyes. "I'm not going to any museums, though."

It was late when Nick woke, full sunlight pressing against the restraining curtains. He only woke when he did because of a noise below that sounded ominously like someone dropping every one of their pots and pans.

Nick found a clean shirt with all due haste, and came down the stairs still buttoning his jeans.

"Give me that," he ordered.

"Oh, but young sir, the doctor said I could go back to heavy lifting if I was real careful of my poor old heart," Alan croaked.

Nick forcibly removed the box of cooking equipment from his brother's thin arms. "Go pack up your books."

It was a luxury to have time to move out of a house. Whenever Alan had to leave his books behind he got wistful, and when they moved in a hurry they always had to spend their first pay cheque on plates and blankets instead of the heating bill. Nick liked the peace of physical exertion, being useful and not having to think; liked the heft of big boxes in his arms and the sun on the back of his neck as he pushed the final box into the car boot. The air felt like it had rained sometime this morning, and the sky was washed a lighter shade of blue than normal. Nick turned back to the house, cracking his neck, and let one thought form in his mind: they were going to London, and they might have at least a couple of months before all the freakish madness caught up with them.

No sooner had he thought this than a thunder of feet on the tarmac behind him made him spin, going for the knife sheath in the small of his back.

Framed against the pale sky, rushing towards him in a flurry of open flannel shirts and the chiming of about four necklaces apiece, came the odd couple from last night.

Nick let go of his knife, though not without a moment's reluctance, and fixed them with a cold look that was usually effective. They did not run in the opposite direction, but Nick leaned his forearms on the roof of the car and maintained a baleful gaze, just in case they decided to reconsider.

Mae's eyes scanned the filled car and Nick's dishevelled appearance, and realisation swept over her face. "You're running away!"

"You're an investigative genius," Nick said.

She scowled at him, small face twisted into an incongruous expression of fury. It struck Nick as funny that this short, pink-haired girl would obviously have loved to be tall and imposing and have her fury strike fear into people's hearts.

"What about us?" she demanded. "We don't have anyone else to help us!"

"So? I don't care."

Mae seemed momentarily floored, her righteous outrage lost in uncertainty. She glanced at Jamie, who was standing about doing his impression (Nick had to concede it was good) of a wounded deer. She reached out a hand to clasp his shoulder.

"You know what's going to happen to Jamie," she said in a low voice, scraping on her pain. "How can you just leave us?"

"Why shouldn't I? People die all over the world, and I doubt you lose sleep over them. What's so special about you? Why should I want to help you? You two invaded my home and got my brother marked!"

Nick set his teeth lightly into his lip. He'd come close to raising his voice. His arms were tensed, his hands clenched with the longing to reach for a knife or a sword, his insides knotted with the urge for action. He wished sometimes that he could feel angry without feeling the urge to kill, but he never had.

It was different for Alan. He'd asked his brother once what he felt when he was angry since Alan never wanted to kill people – though sometimes he had to – and Alan had looked upset and described feeling indignation and annoyance and a hundred things all at once that he said added up to anger.

Alan was too soft. All Nick felt was the violent desire to cut down whoever was in his way.

"Come on, Mae," Jamie said, his quiet voice a shock. "I told you he'd be too angry to help us. We'll find some other way." He glanced at Nick, eyes sliding apprehensively from him to the safer sight of the car. "I'm sorry about your brother. We didn't mean for him to get hurt."

"Doesn't matter what you meant," Nick pointed out.

He'd be on edge until Alan's mark was gone. He didn't need these people bothering him as well.

Jamie reached up to take his sister's hand that rested on his shoulder, twining her fingers around his and trying to use it to tug her away. He backed up a step and then stopped, like a boat caught short at the end of its rope. Mae stood firm, her eyes boring into Nick.

"Get lost," Nick said, enunciating each word as if she was a bit slow. "There's no help for you here."

That was when Alan came outside, blinking slightly in the bright light. His quickly checked smile at the sight of Mae made Nick feel unwell.

"Hi, Alan," Jamie said in a small voice. "Are you feeling okay?"

"Yes, of course. There's no need to worry about me, I'll be right as rain in no time," Alan assured him, smile fading as he looked at Jamie. This was just how Alan had looked at the sick kitten he'd taken home so it could grow up big and strong and able to bite Nick.

Jamie offered him a little smile as if to call Alan's back. "You'll get it fixed at the – Goblin Market thing."

Mae's and Jamie's faces suddenly changed, as if a shadow had fallen over them. Nick turned to see that shadow was actually Mum's dark form at Alan's shoulder, moving slowly forward until the cold light touched her face.

Mum walked past Alan, her hand lingering on his sleeve for an instant as she went by. Her black flag of hair streamed behind her as she went, as if it wanted to cling to the shadows. When she stopped in the middle of the yard, her hair fell with a weighted swish like heavy curtains around her face. Nick kept his eyes turned to her so he would not have to look at Mae and Jamie. It was always the same, the way people's eyes moved from Mum's face to Nick's, while their expressions moved from recognition to silent horror.

Nick's mother had a face that kept all secrets but one. Her broad, slanted cheekbones made her look catlike, and her wide mouth was constantly moving and always formed a shape at odds with her expression. She was tall, and her black hair made her look even paler than she was. She looked like Mae might have wanted to look, if Mum had not looked insane. The full mouth kept shifting with the spasms of a tic. Past the protection of hooded eyelids that seemed pulled down by heavy lashes, her eyes were icy blue and seemed always fixed on someone who was not there.

Except for the colour of his eyes, Nick looked exactly like her. He hated it when people saw her. They could never look at Nick again without associating him with madness.

"We're leaving again," she said flatly. "I don't know why we bother. He'll find us."

Nick wished he could look away from her. He wished that he could leave her. He wished that Alan would agree to leave her.

Mum smiled dreamily, the rest of her face frozen and expressionless. She said, "He's not the kind of man who fails."

Alan limped forward to stand beside her in the uncut grass of their front garden, and reached for her hand. Nick didn't see how he could bear to touch her. "Olivia," said Alan, voice low, "don't. Let's get in the car."

She turned and pressed her fingers against the curve of his cheek, gazing at him but not quite meeting his eyes.

"You're a sweet boy," she whispered. "You're my sweet boy, but you've got it all wrong."

Mae cleared her throat, pulling absently at one of her necklaces. The movement almost drew Nick's eyes to the tangle of talismans and chains around his mother's neck, but he stopped his instinctive glance. These two knew enough about his family already. They didn't need to see him looking at Mum's charms.

He looked at Alan instead, expecting to find steadiness there, expecting sanity and familiarity.

He saw fear.

He saw Alan draw his gun out in the open, out in their front garden where anyone could see. Nick didn't hesitate. He drew his sword and held that sharp, glittering barrier between his brother and the rest of the world, and then he looked around to see what was threatening them.

She was coming down the road towards them, her high heels clicking on the cement. She looked to be in her forties, with a sleek brown bob and large earrings that caught the sun, shining perfect circles with a knife in the centre of each one.

The knives danced jauntily in their circles as she turned and smiled at them.

"Hello, boys. How are you today?"

Nick strode towards her, Alan a pace behind him. He wheeled behind the woman, and after a moment Alan came to stand in front of her. She swung around, briefly teetering on her heels, unable to keep them both in her range of vision and unsure who to focus on.

Nick claimed her full attention by stepping in to her as if they were about to dance. She stopped, facing him, then looked down to see that he was holding each end of his sword and pressing the length of the blade lightly against her stomach. He gazed down at her and smiled a little.

"All the better for seeing you."

There were as many types of magic user in this world as there were colours in white light. On one end of the spectrum were the magicians, and on the other end was the Goblin Market.

There were a lot of people who wanted more power than the Market offered, and who didn't quite have the stomach for feeding their own kind to demons. There were the necromancers and the messengers, the pied pipers and the soul tasters, and a dozen others, and Market people trusted none of them.

They trusted the messengers least of all. Every messenger wore the sign of a knife through a circle. It was a sign from the magicians. It meant that the messenger was attached to a Circle of magicians, and if you crossed the messenger, you crossed the Circle.

The knife more or less indicated how things would go from there.

Messengers were closely associated with magicians. They carried information back and forth between Circles, and between magicians and the outside world, and in return they were paid with demons' magic. Magic bought in blood.

As far as Nick was concerned, they were magicians without the guts.

Over the messenger's shoulder he saw Mae and Jamie, looking alarmed by the sudden appearance of weapons and a stranger. He saw Mum standing by the car, her face a complete blank.

The messenger smiled, a small, wary smile like a concerned parent watching her child. She looked far more like a mother than Mum. Possibly Nick should hire her for his next parent-teacher meeting.

"You're looking very grown-up, Nick."

"It's true, I'm entering on manhood," Nick said. "You're a stylish, sophisticated, ever so slightly evil woman of the world. Do you think we could make it work?"

She looked much less like a mother when her smile went sharp like that. "Probably not."

Nick adjusted his grip on the sword, held it at the precise point where her ribs ended. "Pity."

Alan interrupted, his face grave and his gun at the small of her back. "What's your message?"

"Oh yes," said the messenger. "That."

She twisted lightly around, ending up with Nick's sword against her spine and Alan's gun against her stomach. Nick met Alan's eyes over her shoulder and watched for any signal.

The messenger's voice was calm. "Black Arthur says that now's the time. He wants it back."

In the silence there was a small, sharp sound. Alan had released the safety catch.

Nick could only see the back of her head, but the messenger sounded like she was smiling. "You can give it to me now, or Black Arthur can come and take it."

There was very little in Nick's life that stayed around long enough to be familiar. There had been a statue in one place, a building in another, but taking his whole life into account, Alan's face was the only reliable landmark he had.

He had never seen Alan look like this before.

"Let me ask you this," Alan said, his voice dangerous and shaky at once, like a knife held in a trembling hand. "What d'you think would be the best message to send Black Arthur? Maybe I should let you go back and tell him that he can come and try? He's been chasing us for years. What makes him think he can catch us now?"

The woman tilted her face towards Alan's, as if they were going to kiss.

"He's serious now," she murmured, sounding as if she was about to laugh. "Hadn't you noticed, Alan? We did send you a sign."

Alan went perfectly, terribly white.

The demon's mark. Nick heard his own voice saying, *They can track you once that first mark is made.*

"Sweet Alan, so devoted, so much trouble. We won't be chasing after you blind now, will we? Wherever your little family goes, you'll lead us right to them."

Nick could see the gun shaking in Alan's hand now, in tight, terrified spasms. "Last night we put a magician in the river," Alan said, his voice low and intense as if he was making a promise. "Maybe we should send you to join him."

"You know the rules," the woman whispered. "Don't shoot the messenger."

Nick interrupted, leaning down to speak in her ear. "Do they say, 'Don't cut the messenger in half with your great big sword'?"

Alan's eyes narrowed. He stepped back and said, "Let her go, Nick."

Nick stepped back too, but he did not sheathe his sword. He held it ready, just in case, and the sun danced along the steel and turned it into a dazzling line of light. He could barely see the messenger's small, polite smile.

"What shall I tell Black Arthur?" she asked.

Even Alan's lips were white. "Tell Black Arthur that no matter what I have to do, I'll make him regret sending that message," he said. "Now *go*."

The messenger looked from Alan's white face to Nick's dark smile, and went. She turned sharply on her heels, balance perfect again, and walked away. Her step was measured and unhurried, her head held high, as if she were walking away from a successful board meeting.

Alan looked as if he was going to collapse or kill somebody.

The two strangers in their world were staring at his pale face and the gun still in his hand. Nick looked at Alan's eyes, sheathed his sword, and strode towards the intruders. Jamie flinched as he came.

"If you'll excuse us," he said, his voice on the edge of a snarl. "We've just had some bad news."

Mae did not back down a step. Under other circumstances that might have impressed him, but just now all he wanted to do was get his brother away from the curious stares of strangers and take that look off his face, and her stubbornness simply infuriated him.

"Who's Black Arthur?" she asked.

"None of your business," Nick barked.

"It is my business," Mae snapped. "It sounds like he's the person you're running from, and once you're gone, who will be left to help Jamie?"

Her voice trembled on Jamie's name, and of course that made Alan look up, soft touch that he was. His face was a nasty grey-white colour, but he looked a little more like himself.

"Mae," he said, and his voice was kind again, "I told you. There's nothing any of us can do to help Jamie. I'm sorry."

Mae surprised Nick again. Instead of bursting into loud fury, her mouth worked for a trembling terrible moment, and he thought she was going to cry. "I'd take his place," she said, her voice rough. "Can I do that? Is there a way?"

The second surprise was Jamie, speaking in a tone of command. "I wouldn't let you!"

"It doesn't matter," Nick told them. "There's no way."

He wanted fiercely to be on the road, to leave Exeter and everyone in it behind them.

"If I could help you, I would," Alan said helplessly, as he had last night. "I swear I would."

Mae's eyes narrowed, reminding Nick of a woman at a stall, trying to make a shrewd bargain. "You're going to the Goblin Market to get help. Can't we go there too?"

"No," said Nick.

Alan hesitated. "I don't think anyone there can help you."

Mae pushed her advantage. "There might be someone, though. There might be some way you don't know about. It's a chance, isn't it? Please, Alan. Please let us come."

There was a long moment where Mae stared at Alan, and Nick stared at his clenched fists.

"All right," Alan agreed at last. "If" – and a note of bashfulness crept into his businesslike voice – "if you'll give me your number, I can – I'll call you. Once I find out where the Market is being held next month."

Compared to the demon mark and the early move, compared to the magician's message, seeing Alan embarrassing himself over yet another girl should not have mattered.

It did, though. It was so pointless, they were leaving, but Alan could still stand with their crazy mother in the yard and their crazy life packed up in their car, all of it in plain sight, and hope.

"So you're getting your way," Nick said, hearing his voice slice through the silence, like the sword he'd wanted to use on that woman. He was furious and he wanted someone to pay, he wanted to hurt someone, and Mae was there. It wasn't fair, but what was? "I'd hate to disappoint you," he went on. "What else did you want to know? Oh yes, Black Arthur."

He threw the name like a missile at his mother, standing in the middle of the garden with her black hair blowing around her face. She had not moved since the messenger appeared, and her expression had not changed. She had simply watched the whole thing, watched Alan, like a ghost watching something that could not possibly concern her.

As he bore down on her, her expression did change. Her lip curled.

"It's a romantic story, really," he said harshly, staring down at her. "He was the man our mother loved. She was one of his magicians, and she fed people to the demons on his orders. He drove her mad, and drove her into Dad's arms. She ran from Black Arthur bearing a powerful charm, and since then every magician in England has been hunting us for it."

He grabbed a fistful of the chains around her neck, and she turned her face away. They had been like this for as long as Nick could remember. He could not forgive her for the lives they had led, for Dad's death. He could not forget the look on Alan's face, and that was her fault as well.

He leaned towards his mother and whispered, "And now it seems that he wants it back."

Which wouldn't have been a problem, except that if someone took away the charm, Mum would die.

Nick'd had his moments of thinking even that wouldn't be so terrible. She had been a magician, after all. If she was gone, he and Alan could have normal lives. If anyone at the Goblin Market had known the truth about her, they would have said she deserved death.

This was not one of those moments. If the thought of her dying made Alan look like that, she had to live.

Nick stood with his mother's chains, heavy and cold, in his hands. They were both breathing hard.

When Alan spoke, he sounded tired. "The Goblin Market will be held on the first of May. Shall I give you two a call?"

They made muted noises of agreement. Even Mae seemed cowed at this point, though it was Jamie who gave Alan his number. Alan looked a bit crestfallen but accepted it, and at least after that they were finally rid of the interlopers.

Nick left to get the last boxes while Jamie was still writing down his number, and by the time he emerged from the house they were gone. Nick went around the car so he and Mum would not have to come within a yard of each other.

He looked at Alan, who was standing gazing into the open boot of their car, at something in one of the boxes. When he noticed Nick looking, he smiled a small, strained smile.

"I think that's it," Alan said. "Come on. Looking forward to London?"

They swung into the car. Nick let Alan have first shift. He was the better driver, but he was only sixteen and it would be a year before it was actually legal for him to drive. It was better to get out of Exeter, where some people knew that, before Nick had his turn.

"Well," Nick said as Alan gave him a stern look over the top of his glasses and Nick rolled his eyes and buckled his seat belt. "Let's examine the events of the past twenty-four hours in Exeter. Ravens in the kitchen, snakes in the living room, demon marks on you, magicians sending us stupid messages, and at the end of it all you got the boy's telephone number."

Alan tilted his head as he considered this and then laughed. Nick leaned his forehead against the car window, and the engine purred soothingly to him.

"Let's get the hell out of here," Alan suggested.

After an hour on the M5, Alan's leg started to ache, and they switched places. There was never much conversation while driving because of Mum, so Nick looked straight ahead and Alan stared out at the rolling green ground, going for miles on both sides of the road. Nick glanced over at him a few times, wondering if that message was bothering him or if the demon mark was hurting him.

"You all right?" he said eventually.

Alan took a moment to answer. When he turned, Nick saw that half his wavy hair was sticking up from being pressed against the damp window.

"Yeah," he said. Nick's amusement was cut short when Alan went on, "I was thinking about Mae and Jamie. It's just – they both seem so great, and we know what's going to happen to them. It's terrible, that's all. I hate it."

Nick frowned out at the road. "Why do you care? You barely know them."

"I know them well enough to feel sorry for them," Alan said. "Anyone would. I mean, don't you feel bad for them? A little?"

He looked at Nick with a testing, expectant air. Nick didn't know what to say.

He felt angry with them. If it hadn't been for them, Alan would not be marked. Nick did not think that expressing this would go over well, though.

"I don't feel anything for them."

That answer made Alan look so unhappy that Nick almost wished he had told him about the anger. Alan said nothing, though; he only turned back to the window, biting his lip.

Nick glanced in the rear-view mirror to check on the distance between them and the car behind, and caught his mother's reflected eyes. In the mirror they looked even colder than usual, as if she was staring at him from under ice. Her lips were drawn tight over her teeth, giving her beautiful face the appearance of a skull that still had eyes to stare. She looked at him as if she hated him, but she always did that.

Nick bared his teeth at her in a silent snarl and turned away from the mirror.

Alan read out the directions Merris Cromwell had given him as Nick tried to work around the London lunch hour traffic. Nick didn't like Merris much, but since Alan had helped her at the Goblin Market last October, they'd never had to crash in shelters or hostels while they looked for a place to stay. Nick wasn't sure if she had contacts everywhere or if problems simply slunk away in the face of her formidable efficiency.

If the Market had been a magicians' Circle, blasphemous though the idea might be, Merris would have been the Circle's leader.

She was connected even though nobody knew where she came from, rich even though nobody knew where she got her money. Nick thought she might be the only person in the Market hiding as many secrets as they were.

Nick looked at a map and took a detour by Westminster so Alan could get a preview of the doubtful delights he would soon enjoy. They passed the square-spiked silhouette of Westminster Abbey, and stone saints peered down at them while Alan began to tell himself interesting historical facts, because Nick didn't care. The spire of Big Ben and the curve of the Circle went by in a smooth line, and as Nick turned the car into less traffic-choked channels, Alan gave a happy sigh and starting talking about dinosaur exhibits in the Natural History Museum.

"I've changed my mind," said Nick. "The demons can have you."

He was glad that Alan seemed so pleased. Nick had not really remembered London, and looking around it now, with old and new buildings jostling each other at every turn and no street empty, he was feeling a distinct sense of foreboding.

Demons liked cities. Cities meant victims, and London was teeming with bodies for the taking. Nick thought he might have made the wrong decision choosing this place, but it was too late now.

Camden Town opened up into a broad grey road, with a small cinema on one side, some restaurants and a grey building that said AMERICAN METHODIST CHURCH in large metal letters outside. A fine drizzle started as they drove up one of the narrow side streets and stopped in front of their new home.

The drab brown front of the house made it look as if it had been built from rusty spare parts. Someone always put lace curtains in the windows of dreary houses, and Nick was unsurprised to see the curtains making their attempts in every window of this place. There was a china garden gnome on the doorstep, wearing a desperate, crazy smile.

"It's not so bad," Alan said.

"You never take me nice places any more, baby," said Nick, and was mildly gratified by Alan's ring of laughter, like a living bell that had been caught by surprise when it was struck.

When he got out, he opened Mum's door without thinking, and she shuddered away from him. Alan knelt on the wet pavement beside the car and reached out his hand to her.

"Olivia," he coaxed. "We're here. We're home."

"For now," Nick muttered, going over to the boot and getting out the first box of Alan's books.

He hefted it in his arms and put the box down only to retrieve the keys. Someone had carelessly put a dark closet where the hall should have been, but the staircase was broad and, more importantly, had a sturdy-looking wooden banister for Alan to lean on. When he got up the stairs he saw there were three bedrooms, which was always good news. Nick allocated the bedroom farthest away from the other two to Mum, and when he went into the other rooms, he saw there was a bookcase built into the wall of one. That room clearly had to be Alan's. Nick put the box down and palmed the knife from his boot to cut the packing tape. He began to shove books on the shelves. It might be a few minutes before Alan got Mum calmed down.

Nick was putting down the last book in the first row when it fell.

There was a white flutter from the yellowed pages of an old book, and then, on the tired-looking carpet, lay a picture of a girl.

The girl looked older than Nick, in her late teens or perhaps her twenties, with curly blonde hair and a bright smile. She was wearing a loose, flowing shirt, in the kind of retro style Alan's girls often affected, and she looked as if someone had just told her a joke.

It occurred to Nick that this picture was what Alan had been thinking of when he was standing gazing into their car boot. As soon as he was alone he'd gone straight to it, as if being near to it – even if he couldn't see it – was his only possible source of comfort.

He hadn't come to Nick.

Alan was sentimental enough to keep pictures. The couple of girls who'd actually been his girlfriends had been awarded a place of pride in his wallet. He had a school picture of Nick and the picture of Mum and Dad on their wedding day framed by his bedside.

It was keeping a secret from Nick that was different. He'd kept only one secret from Nick before: the letters he used to rise early for and collect from the postbox. Nick rose even earlier to cut them up, and eventually they had stopped coming.

Nick wondered if this was a picture of the letter girl. He picked it up and looked her over more closely, but he couldn't see anything special about her. The letters had been more than a year ago. Why should Alan still keep her picture? He flipped it over and looked at the back. TONY'S PHOTOS was printed there in grey, but over that in a black sprawl was the name "Marie".

Nick heard Alan's limping step up the stairs in plenty of time to put the photograph back where he had found it, and when his brother came into the room, he saw Alan look at the shelf in alarm.

There was no innocent explanation, then.

Alan had not forgotten that the picture was in the book. He had not bought a book with a picture already inside it. He had deliberately hidden this girl, this Marie, away from him.

Nick remembered the girl's smiling face and scowled, staring at the floor. He felt intensely uncomfortable. It seemed wrong that this girl should matter to Alan, when Nick didn't even know who she was. What was so important about her, that he had to hide her from his own brother?

Nick planned to find out.

That night Nick slept on the kitchen floor in their new home. The cork tiles were curling up at the edges like pieces of old bread, rough against his stomach when his T-shirt rode up, and he hadn't brought down a pillow because he didn't want to be comfortable. He dozed uneasily, feeling like a guard dog unable to rest because he had to be on the alert for dangers outside.

But it wasn't anything outside that he was waiting for.

He was in one of the dark places between sleep and simply having your eyes shut when he heard the sound of the front door clicking softly open. His body moved before he thought; he crossed the hall in two swift strides, fast and soft as a predator. He always found it easier to hunt than think.

When he launched himself at Alan, he did think; he remembered to strike on Alan's left side. They went tumbling into the grass of the front garden, and Nick landed crouched beside his brother. He'd been careful not to hurt Alan's leg, not to even touch it, and now he felt so angry he wished he'd done it after all.

"You're not leaving," he snarled.

Alan lay flat on his back, looking up at the sky. The full moon caught his glasses and made the edges flash brief silver. "If they can track me," he began, "it's not safe—"

Nick laughed harshly. "When have we ever been safe?"

How safe would Alan be, he wanted to demand, by himself and with a demon's mark? Maybe he would be all right; Alan could take care of himself, but Nick wasn't about to take that chance. Nick wasn't about to let him go.

Nick was breathing fast and his vision was blurred a little, turning the edges of the night hazy and pale. He felt as if he'd been exercising too hard. He was just angry at the thought that Alan could leave, so easily, for any reason at all.

Alan sighed and sat up, drawing his good leg up to his chest and linking an arm around it. Nick knew this look from the days when Mum had her screaming fits, or when a teacher wanted to talk about Nick's reading. Alan looked tired and unhappy, and the expression fitted on his face too comfortably, as if he was used to feeling that way and didn't let it affect him too much. He was too busy being concerned about what other people might feel.

"Nick," he said gently, "it isn't that I want to go. It wouldn't be for very long. Just until the next Goblin Market, just so that you and Olivia would be safe."

Mum was the one the magicians were after, the one they'd always been after. Mum was the one who'd caused all this, and in spite of everything, Mum was the one Alan was worried sick about.

"I'll leave her," Nick said.

The night seemed very still suddenly. Nick stayed crouched and watchful, waiting for Alan to make any movement, willing him to give in. Alan shut his eyes and swallowed, looking so disappointed in Nick and so scared. For their mother.

"I swear I will," Nick said, voice low, threatening and promising, meaning every word. "If you go, I'll leave her. I'll come and find you. What do you think would happen to her if we both left?"

Nick didn't lie. He'd seen Alan lie to people his whole life and every time he opened a book he saw words twist across pages, their meaning slipping away from him. Words were treacherous enough without him telling lies.

When he said something, he knew Alan would believe it.

Alan opened his eyes and looked at Nick. His eyes were bleak.

"All right, Nick," he whispered. "I won't go."

Nick spoke with difficulty. "All right."

He grabbed the bag Alan had been carrying, climbed to his feet, and went to the door without casting another look at his brother still sitting in the grass. He was tired, and he didn't want to think any more about Alan trying to leave.

When he dropped the bag into Alan's room, he saw his brother had left a note on his pillow.

Nick sat on Alan's bed and tried to read it. He needed to concentrate to read, and his mind was all over the place, thoughts wild and tangled, and the words went wild and tangled too. They looked like nothing but inky thorns spreading across the blank white page.

He caught one sentence, which was *I'm going to a place where I know I will be welcome.*

It made him remember the picture of that girl and look across the room. There was only one gap to be seen in the crowded bookshelves. Alan had planned to leave him, but he'd meant to take the book and the hidden picture wherever he went.

Nick stared at the letter and felt that sharp urge to hurt something again. He palmed a knife and cut it up, once, twice, three times until the words were gone and the letter was nothing but tattered white fragments.

A slight noise made Nick lift his head. He saw Alan hesitating in the doorway. He couldn't read his face any more than he could those words. He wondered how long Alan had been standing there, watching Nick slice up his goodbye letter.

They looked at each other without speaking, and in the silence Nick wondered if Alan had told him another lie: if he'd wanted to go to that girl. If he did want to leave, after all.

Alan cleared his throat. "You were right. I was being stupid."

"No kidding," Nick said roughly.

"I panicked when that message came," Alan explained, leaning heavily against the door frame. "I couldn't help it. I don't want to be a danger to you, and I don't know what to do. But if they tried this, they'll try something else. Running away won't solve anything. I have to think of a plan. I have to do something to settle this once and for all."

Alan's voice gathered determination as he spoke. If he thought he was going to change Black Arthur's mind then he was dreaming, but it was familiar and soothing for Nick to see his brother ready to plan their way out of every situation.

Alan picked up the bag Nick had carried upstairs, and Nick crossed the room to take it from him.

"Give me that. I'll put your stuff away."

"Thank you," Alan said, smiling at him. He reached out and took the book with the hidden picture from a side pocket, smoothing his fingers – born musician's hands, Dad had always said, long fingers that touched everything lightly – with absent affection over the cover. "I'll take this. I'm reading it."

He limped over to his bed, still holding the book. Nick was quiet, methodically putting away all the clothes and weapons Alan had packed, erasing any trace of the fact that Alan had meant to leave.

"I'm sorry about this," Alan said softly, surprising him. "I won't let you down again."

Nick didn't know what to say. He didn't know what Alan was talking about; it was ridiculous. Alan didn't let him down. He'd never once done that.

"Stop being stupid."

Nick glanced over at his brother. Alan was looking serious and a little sad, standing beside the bed with the pieces of his letter scattered around his feet and his fingers tracing restless patterns over the cover of that book.

"Yeah," Alan said, and smiled at him with an obvious effort. "I'll try."

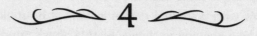

4

The Goblin Market

"STOP SULKING," ALAN SAID AS HE PARKED THE CAR.

Nick was not sulking. He simply did not know why Alan exercised his considerable intelligence to achieve such stupid goals. He'd fabricated enormous lies, he'd pleaded and he'd twinkled energetically at old ladies, all in order to get Nick into school. Where Nick had no desire to be, because school was a waste of time. It meant dozens of teachers hassling him about being dyslexic, and it meant Alan working full-time when Alan wanted to go to college. If Alan would just let Nick work full-time in the garage, then Alan could go to college and Nick would never be saddled with any more reading, and everyone would be happy.

Only Alan was a stubborn idiot who refused to see reason, and he had actually forced Nick into a school uniform.

Nick said nothing. He was trying to rumple his uniform by sitting still and directing the sheer force of his hatred at it.

"You are sulking," Alan said into the vacuum of Nick's stony silence. "You shouldn't be. You need to complete your education and besides, a man in uniform always looks dashing."

Nick gave him the kind of look he felt a word like "dashing" deserved.

Alan frowned and said, "I do wish you'd eaten breakfast."

Nick's view of his new school, a brown institutional building as square and basically uninspiring as a brick, was suddenly obscured by a girl. She was platinum blonde and slim in a schoolgirl skirt.

He supposed there was something to be said for the uniform after all.

"Just to please you, I will," Nick said, and nodded in the girl's direction. "Don't you think she looks like breakfast?"

While Alan checked a smile and began a lecture on speaking of women with respect, Nick snagged his bag and got out of the car. Alan leaned over the passenger seat.

"Remember," he called. "Just be yourself, and everyone will love you!"

Nick rolled his eyes and made a rude gesture, and Alan drove the car away laughing.

Slouching towards his scholastic fate, Nick caught the blonde's eyes while they were sliding over him, and held them. Then he winked.

There were enough pretty girls to keep Nick entertained for most of the day. The last class was computers, and while the teacher was droning on, Nick typed "Tony's Photos" into the search engine.

Luck was with him. He only had to scroll down past half a dozen Tonys who wanted to share their holiday photos with the world before he found a shop in England. Miraculously, it was not a chain. The small website, boasting a chubby and somewhat manic-looking baby, informed him that it was located in Durham.

They had never even lived in Durham – but last year they had lived in Sunderland, thirteen miles away. On the day after Christmas, Alan had disappeared for four days, talking about a Sumerian stone tablet that he'd been called in to examine. Mum had not come out of her room for the entire time Alan was away, and she would not have eaten if Nick had not gone upstairs and forced food down her throat. She'd screamed the entire time Nick was touching her.

Whenever Nick had made a noise in the house, he'd known his mother was listening for it, frozen and panting as if she were a hunted animal. Alan was the one always talking, turning on the TV and the radio, bringing home the weird people who were their only guests. Nick had stopped turning on lights and appliances because it wasn't worth the bother of sending Mum into hysterics. The house started to seem shut off from the rest of the world, darkness and silence pressing all around until Nick felt as if he could not get out. He wanted to leave, he needed to buy groceries, but he sat on the stairs and waited in the dark.

Winter light had come in with Alan as he opened the door. Nick had looked up from his place on the stairs and said, "You can't do this again."

Alan went pale and answered, "I won't."

During the four days of darkness, it had never occurred to Nick that Alan could possibly have been lying, or could possibly have abandoned them for his own reasons.

It was occurring to him now.

Nick took down the address and phone number of Tony's Photos in Durham, and then closed the window.

The next day at school Nick went and found his new crowd. There was a large bike shed at the back of the school, which looked like a concrete block with a sheet of tinfoil on top. He'd seen it yesterday and known at once that this was the place.

Sure enough, there were three boys there already, two of them smoking. One dropped his cigarette on the gravel as soon as he saw Nick. He'd be no trouble. Nick raised his eyebrows, saw the boy's eyes drop in embarrassment, and turned to the boy who'd kept smoking.

"Nick Ryves," he said. "Mind if I join you?"

He threw out the words like a challenge. He'd found that was the best way to start things, since it always ended up that way in the end.

The boy eyed him with what Nick thought was an unusual amount of hostility to start off with. Usually it took Nick a couple of weeks to antagonise people to that degree.

"Carr," he said at last. "Joe Carr."

He was the usual type. He'd be snarling and trying to trip Nick up all the time, like a terrier with a Rottweiler in his garden. Still, much like a terrier, he'd stick around and never cause Nick any real trouble.

Alan had made him promise not to take up smoking. Nick always regretted that on the first day at new schools, when he wished he could smoke instead of talking. He hated talking to strangers. Sooner or later, he always said something that pulled someone up short, and then he had to glare them all into submission.

New schools were always a pain. He could hear Dad in his head all the time on the first days, telling him to blend in, telling him to try and be just like everyone else. All their lives depended on it.

"Nice place you have here," Nick said after a beat. "Love the scenery. Especially that Cathy girl."

"*Cassie* is my girlfriend," Joe snapped at him.

"Whoops," Nick said. "Oh well."

The other two boys snickered, and Nick grinned at them. He'd picked the right group again. When he was little, he'd gravitated towards what was familiar and tried to make friends with people who were like Alan, only without guns hidden under their button-up shirts. People who talked too much and did their homework and who, on reflection, he'd kind of scared.

This was much easier. Dad would've approved.

He sat at the back of their next class with Lewis, the boy who hadn't been smoking. He was still thinking of the picture girl from Durham and he forgot to talk at all, which was a mistake. Long silences made people uneasy.

"You all right?" Lewis asked, shifting as far away from Nick as he could.

"Fine," Nick snapped, and then thought of Dad. "Just girl problems, you know," he added as casually as he could.

The other boy sighed, sounding reassured. "Girls always turn out to be problems."

"Yeah," Nick answered absent-mindedly.

He was still thinking of that hidden picture, that possible hidden trip. He had no problem with Alan's crushes on girls like Mae, girls who weren't interested and who were going to be left behind. A girl who could make Alan lie to Nick, though, that was something he wasn't going to tolerate. He had to know what was going on.

He grinned at Lewis. "She won't be a problem much longer."

They all went out afterwards, hung around a chip shop with a couple of girls. Sadly, neither of the girls was pretty blonde Cassie.

Nick got home after dark, feeling good about the whole group thing being sorted. He thought again that Dad would've been proud.

He found Alan in their tiny sitting room, on the floor by the coffee table. The coffee table was covered with papers, and Alan's head was in his hands.

"Alan," Nick said, in a command for him to be all right.

Alan lifted his head. "Hi," he said, and tried for a smile. "I didn't – I didn't hear you come in."

"What's going on?" Nick barked at him. "What's wrong? Is that stupid mark hurting you?"

The contented feeling of a job well done evaporated. Nick abruptly wanted to hit something.

Alan sighed. "No."

The answer came to Nick, inevitable as the tide coming in. Of course it was all Mum's fault.

"It's that stupid messenger and what she said to you."

"I'm just trying to come up with a plan," Alan told him.

He sounded worn and frayed as an old shirt. Nick hated it; his desire to hit something increased. He walked over to the table instead, to where Alan sat looking tired and rather small.

The papers on the table had magical symbols all over them, drawings of demons' circles and protective amulets. There were papers covered in Alan's scrawling handwriting, and then papers with single lines written on them, which had obviously been tossed aside.

"I like this plan," Nick told him, selecting one of the papers with just one line on it.

The paper read, in large, almost frantic-looking letters: *Kill them all*.

"It's a lovely plan, but it wouldn't work," Alan said, his voice almost amused. He ran his fingers through his hair. "I need to talk to Merris. I've got the numbers of about a dozen people who work for her, and none of them will put me through."

"Can she help?" Nick asked.

"I don't know," Alan said, a note of bleakness creeping in. "God, I hope so. We might have to wait until the Goblin Market; we'll see her then."

Nick nodded, and then hesitated. He couldn't think of a way to say what he wanted to, and for a moment he was tempted to let it go, but he looked down at Alan's bowed head and tried all the same.

"Don't—" he said, and stopped. "You've got a demon's mark on you. This isn't the time to think about—" He thought of Mum and Mae and the girl in the picture. "Don't worry about anyone else. If it bothers you so much, I'll do something about Mum. I'll find a way to help her. Whatever you need, I'll do it. Just make sure that you're all right. Nobody else matters."

Alan looked up at him with dark troubled eyes, blue under shadows.

"I know she isn't good to you, but you've lived with her all your life. Does the idea of her dying—" He swallowed. "Do you care at all?"

Nick wondered why Alan was looking at him with those pleading eyes. Nick had said he would help already.

"You care," he said. "That's enough. I'll help her even if I don't care. What does it matter?"

Alan looked down at his crumpled papers.

"We'll go to the Goblin Market and get everything sorted

out," Nick said forcefully. "I told you. Don't worry about anything but yourself."

At a new school the teachers always took a while to go over Nick's reading problems, and Nick always took a while to go over the girls. At home they spent all their time going for their weapons at every noise, waiting for the magicians to do what they had promised and come after Alan. Given that he and Alan had to find new jobs, too, for the first week in London, Nick had no time to do anything about Alan's mark or his secret.

He thought about both, whether he had time or not, and he could not stop uneasily watching Alan in case he decided to bolt. It came as an enormous relief when Alan informed him that the next Goblin Market would be held near Tiverton in a few days' time.

"It's the closest place to Exeter they could have chosen," Alan said. "We can pick up Mae and Jamie on the way."

Nick rolled his eyes. "Thrill me, why don't you."

Perhaps he would find Mae's hidden picture next. He scowled at the thought, and Alan caught his expression.

"You don't have to dance, you know," he said.

"I told you," Nick answered, still frowning. "I want to."

He would deal with the mark and the threat to Mum, and find out about Marie. His brother would be safe. Everything would be like it was before.

Alan went off to call Jamie.

They arranged to meet Mae and Jamie outside Northernhay Gardens in Exeter, behind the old wall. It was quiet and already growing dark by the time they pulled up. Unfortunately, the headlights of the car were bright enough for them to see Mae's outfit quite clearly.

"Oh my God," said Nick, and shut his eyes.

Jamie gave a small, nervous laugh.

"What?" Mae demanded. "Alan told us that we were supposed to dress as we truly are!"

The mad girl was wearing a pink silk crop top and a long white skirt that was all gauze and frills. Every inch of her was decked with metal. She wore ankle bracelets on each ankle, had an army of gleaming bangles lined up along both arms, and was laden down with necklaces. They reminded Nick of the charms around his mother's neck, a metallic tangle linked into chains by the years.

"And you felt that what you truly are is a Christmas tree with too much tinsel." Nick grinned. "Huh."

"Stop it," said Alan, and then blushed. "I think you look very nice, Mae."

The sudden smile Mae gave Alan was as sweet as it was unexpected. Alan smiled helplessly back, and Nick thought over this new development. On one hand, if Mae was going to start smiling at him, Alan might sink to even greater depths of idiocy. On the other hand, the girl had a nice smile, Alan seemed happy, and soon they would be at the Goblin Market. Alan's mark could be removed, and so could Nick's constant irritable feeling that something had gone terribly wrong with the world.

He was beginning to feel cautiously optimistic about this trip.

Nick drove away from Exeter through the narrow, jolting roads towards Tiverton. Alan's mouth tightened with every bump in the road, and Nick was almost grateful when the tourists in the back started asking questions.

Jamie coughed. "This may be a silly question, but are there, er – goblins at the Goblin Market?"

"No," said Nick. "Everyone at the Market is human, just like you."

"Just like me," Jamie echoed sceptically.

"Well," said Nick. "Probably smarter than you."

"It's named after a market in a poem," Alan explained. "The poem mentions magical fruit being sold in a market. We have magical fruit as well – we just don't sell it."

"Magical fruit? Like . . . lemons of sorcery? What do you do with them?"

Nick tossed a cold look over his shoulder at Jamie. "You'll see."

Jamie pointedly addressed the next question to Alan alone. "So why is the Goblin Market being held in Tiverton? It's titchy compared to Exeter."

Alan spread his hands over the dashboard as if it was a lectern, and as if he could form explanatory shapes out of the air if he gestured enthusiastically enough. He'd have liked to be a college professor or something of that sort, Nick thought, and would have been, if it hadn't been for Mum.

"Tiverton means *twy ford ton* – the town of two fords. The river Exe and the river Lowman meet at Tiverton, and that means it is protected from attack. Possessed bodies do not like to cross running water."

The Goblin Market was not being held in the town centre, of course. People might have asked a few questions about selling amulets and calling demons in the streets.

It would take place in the old Shrink Hills, past the point where Cranmore Castle stood. Nick and Alan had been to Tiverton before, when the Goblin Market was held there nine years ago. Nick had danced in those hills before. It had been his second Goblin Market, and Dad's last.

"It's supposed to be lucky to hold the Goblin Market in a place with some history attached to it," Alan went on happily. "It's one of the Goblin Market mottoes: 'Our world, claimed by our kind.' Cranmore Castle was a hill fort in the Iron Age, and in 1549 one of the battles of the Prayer Book Rebellion was fought here. It was a battle over whether a child should be christened in the new religion or the old."

"Who won?" asked Mae.

"What does it matter?" Nick inquired. "All anyone knows is where the bones were found."

Tiverton was in view on the darkening horizon, a grey mass in the night, dominated by a church and castle that leaned together in a fellowship of crumbling stone and decayed glory in the midst of small streets and tall trees.

They stopped on a dirt road a few fields away from Cranmore Castle, which was now nothing but a mound, grey in the night but green under a daytime sky, a lump in the ground where people had once lived, and lived no longer.

"I expected something a little more castle-shaped," said Jamie.

"Nothing lasts forever," Nick said. "Except demons, of course."

"Has anyone ever told you that you're a charming conversationalist?" Jamie asked.

"No," Nick replied honestly.

"I cannot tell you how much that surprises me," Jamie told him, and Nick gave him a half-smile. Nick's blood was already racing.

There was always a chance that someone had let slip the

location of the Goblin Market. Everyone came to the Market prepared for a fight. Everyone was aware of the possibility that magicians might descend upon them on Market night and try to wipe them all out with one blow.

The air on Market nights was always strung tight with nervous excitement. The Market was always balanced on the edge of destruction.

Nick looked out into the night and let his smile spread. That was why he liked it.

"Where *is* this Market?" Mae asked.

Alan spoke before Nick could tell her to hush. "It's all right," he said. "I've got directions. The Market is left of the crooked tree, outside the beaten path, and straight on to the moon."

Jamie blinked and said, "Thank you for clearing that up, Alan."

His face was pale in the moonlight as they climbed out into the darkness of a country road, fields and trees massed around them on both sides. Nick had not looked at Jamie particularly, except to note with gratitude that he was not dressed up like Mae, but now that he did look, he was sure the boy was thinner than he had been a couple of weeks ago. He and his sister were both shaking, but Nick thought that with Mae it was excitement. With Jamie, it looked like fear.

Of course once Alan noticed that he was drawn to Jamie like a mother hen to the littlest chick in the farmyard.

"I know the way," he said, and offered up the warm, sweet smile that always made people believe he wasn't carrying six concealed weapons. "Walk with me." He paused and added, "I see you're not dazzling us all like Mae."

"Well, I thought – I thought that I usually look like what I really am."

Alan's smile became less reassuring and more genuine. "I've always thought the same."

Nick was glad that Alan felt no need to complement his shirt and jeans with a little earring, but on the whole he approved of Jamie's decision to look halfway normal. His approval must have been obvious, because as he followed Alan up the hill, Mae fell into step with him and spoke in a combative tone.

"You're dressed up," she said. "You're all in black and you're carrying a sword. How is that different?"

"I have a reason to dress this way."

Mae glanced up at him, instantly curious. "And what is that?"

"Oh," Nick said, teasing a little, "you'll see."

He smiled properly at her, looking down into her upturned face, her mouth curved and eyes dark in the moonlight. Then he remembered that this girl was off-limits. He shook his head impatiently and lengthened his stride so she would have to scurry to keep up.

The tree branches overhead were curled around each other like cats leering down at them from the shadows, and the leaves were thick enough to hide the moon. Alan's red hair looked as black as Nick's as Nick drew level with them.

Alan broke off a conversation about the beautiful poetry of Christina Risotto or whoever, of all things, to give Nick a reproachful look. "You left Mae?"

That much was obvious, so Nick didn't bother to answer him. Alan turned and limped back to Mae. When she drew level with him, he offered her his arm.

Nick, left alone with Jamie, felt it his duty to make things clear.

"I realise the fact that my brother talks about poetry is misleading," he said. "But he's not that way, all right?"

Jamie gave him a look, then redirected the look. Nick followed his gaze to Alan stooping over Mae and apparently doing an impression of a lame stork attempting a mating dance.

"Really," Jamie said dryly. "I would never have guessed."

Nick scowled.

They walked on until there was no path, only grass stretching out on all sides until it was blotted out by the dark fringe of the woods. Alan took the lead from the point where the path failed, but it was obvious to them all where to go. Someone had arranged to have cars parked at strategic points along the fields. The car roofs caught moonbeams, and every metallic place where the light fell formed a bright stepping-stone for them to follow.

On the far side of the mound of earth that people still called Cranmore Castle were enough trees to be counted as a wood. Streaming from the heart of the wood, glowing among the leaves and warm against the tree trunks, they saw light from the lamps of the Goblin Market.

Nick fell into step with Alan, leaving the other two to follow them as they chose. He heard a sharp exclamation behind him as they walked into the wood, but he did not know which of them had made it, or why. People were usually taken like that by the Market at first.

It was impossible to see all of the Goblin Market at once. The stalls were placed in a zigzagging circle around the trees, glinting at intervals like secret treasure. There was one stall, and then another, and before they had taken more than a few steps, there were stalls on all sides. The bright drapes over the stall fronts were like flags being flown to declare war. The lamps, hung in twisting pathways up in the boughs, swung in the wind and cast their light on first one stall and then another.

For a moment the spotlight fell on a stall hung with dream catchers, the real kind, bones and feathers and thread formed in the patterns to silence the voices in your head and keep the demons from your bed. Then it swung to a table laden with words, clay tablets tumbled with calfskin-bound volumes, cheap paperbacks lying with scrolls. One stall made its own illumination, since it was hung about with what the Market people called fairy lamps. There were the glow-worm lamps to attract your true love, and the beacon lamps you set in a window to call a wanderer home.

Nick took a moment to scan the swaying lights and the shadows creeping around them, the bright stalls and the dark cleared spaces where the dancers were practising, and then relaxed. There were no gaps in the lines of the stalls and no familiar faces missing. The Market was just as it had been last month, and with luck it would be just the same next month too.

They all had to keep quiet for fear of discovery, so the drums were muffled and the stall owners' voices were like the clear, low sound of chimes ringing from all sides.

"Come buy!" sang out clearly from every stall. "Come buy!"

"We can buy things like this with ordinary money?" Mae asked, her voice half awed and half dubious. "We're supposed to buy help?"

"We may be the only defence against magicians and demons that there is," Nick said. "No reason not to turn a profit."

Phyllis from the chimes stall noticed them first. The Market was in full swing and people were mostly concentrating on business, haggling and comparison shopping. Light glanced on faces without illuminating them.

"Chimes?" Phyllis asked. "Chimes to call a lover? Chimes with the voice of a bird trapped in them? Chimes that play you whatever song you most desire to hear?"

"No thanks," said Nick. "We've got MTV."

She peered among the glinting metal and crystal of her wares, and her face cleared. "Oh, Nick, it's you! Alan, my sweet, come here and kiss an old woman. You get taller every year."

"You get younger every year," Alan said, stooping in among the chimes to kiss her.

The stall owners of the Goblin Market had the same indulgent attitude to Alan as all the teachers, landladies, and shopkeepers. Human nature didn't change, whether you sold love charms or toilet rolls.

"Soothing charms for your poor mother?" asked Phyllis, who had never seen Mum. "Guaranteed to calm an uneasy mind. Special price for you."

"Not tonight, Phyllis," Alan answered. "Nick's dancing, and we need to buy a speaking charm. Have you seen Merris?"

"No," Phyllis said, her eyes suddenly gleaming brighter than her chimes. "Nick's dancing?"

Nick took Alan by the scruff of his neck and dragged him away bodily. Alan made the usual protesting sounds about that, but Nick noticed he didn't try to go back. Nick had forgotten, but he remembered now. He remembered when he was seven and Dad had first asked him to dance, and the way everyone had stared, because he was so young, because the dance came so easily to him. Because the demons came so easily to him.

Alan paused by a stall selling talismans and Nick waited for him, arms crossed over his chest and trying to ignore the rising tide of whispers around him. People who danced in the circle were not magicians. They just had to have enough coordination to keep within the lines of the dance, but their dance called demons. It looked like magic. If people had known Nick's mother was a magician, if they had known how Nick's talisman hurt him, they would have called it magic.

Alan put his thin shoulder supportively behind Nick's and did not say a word, which was how Nick liked things best.

"Fancy a sword forged in lightning? Get your genuine lightning-born blades here! Comes with a free enchanted knife."

The gleam of sharp steel under coloured lights drew Nick like a beacon lamp. Alan moved with him, watching Nick's back, and murmured appreciation at the sight of a beautiful sword Nick had instinctively reached out for. Carl had some gorgeous new stuff in this month.

"You guys have magical arms dealers, too?" Jamie asked faintly.

"We do need weapons," said Alan. "They cost a lot in the outside world. Here in the Market you can barter and lay up credit."

Nick slid the sword out of a sleek leather sheath. It made a faint, seductive ringing sound in the air, as if it was begging Nick to take it home.

It looked expensive, though, and a short sword was really more practical for concealment purposes.

Nick weighed the hilt against his palm; it fitted his hand, the balance of the blade perfect. When he stepped back and made a few passes with it, the movement felt as natural and sweet as that of his own muscles. He looked up from his absorption in the glittering metal and met Alan's warm, pleased eyes.

"Like it?"

"We can't afford it," Nick said. He meant to sound practical, but his voice came out curt.

"Oh, we could—" Mae began.

"No!" Nick snapped.

"No, but thank you," Alan told her, gentle but firm. "It's okay, Nick. I did some extra translations this month and saved up the credit. It's the first Market since your birthday. Did you think I wasn't going to get you anything?"

"Oh," Nick said.

That was why the sword felt like it had been made for him. It had been. Alan couldn't use a sword himself, his balance was completely off, but he knew all about the design of a good blade. Nick looked at the deadly, beautiful thing again, and while he was looking down, he smiled.

"Like it?" Carl asked with a broad grin. He tossed the sheath at Nick, and Nick caught it absently in his free hand.

Nick shrugged. "It's not so bad."

"Think it came out rather well, if I do say so myself," Carl bragged. "Your brother wanted nothing but the best. Wish *I* had a brother."

"Yeah," Nick said. "He's not so bad either."

"Well, I've been thinking we could use an enchanted knife," Alan said, taking the knife that came free with the purchase and sliding it into his pocket. He reached out to pat Nick's shoulder or something stupid, and Nick stepped easily away from him, eyes still on the sword.

They walked on through the Market, weaving through tourists, necromancers with their bone toys and worn teeth, and pied pipers playing instruments that sang with human voices. Nick could not quite bring himself to sheath his new sword and Alan kept by his side, and if that had been all, it would have been a great Market night.

Unfortunately, he and Alan had not come to the Market alone.

Behind them, Mae said, "All this stuff – it's magic, isn't it? I thought you said the magicians were the evil ones. What's the difference?"

"The difference, my dear girl," said a new but familiar voice to their left, "is that we use magical things, but none of us have magical powers."

Nick wasn't so sure of that, but it was a matter of pride in the Goblin Market. Magicians tended to be the ones with the most power, the ones tainted by it. While the Market folk put up with visitors who could do magic, not one would admit to having a drop of natural power themselves.

A long time ago the Market had been set up to provide help for magicians' victims. All the born Market folk claimed they were descended from those who had stumbled upon the magicians' secrets and had sworn to help the innocent and defenceless. Nobody wanted to admit that the people most likely to find out magicians' secrets were magicians' families, or magicians themselves.

Nick thought it was just as stupid to deny the fact that some of the Market shopkeepers had magic as it was to deny the fact that what had started out as using magical objects had become a buying and selling of magical objects: that the Market was not about a crusade any more but about earning a living.

Everyone pretended the world was different than it was. Nick supposed he shouldn't be surprised. After all, most people did not even know magic existed. People were good at being blind.

The voice continued, "Magicians give victims to demons, which means that demons will give them anything they want. The people of the Market can only summon demons in the dance. We would prefer not to summon them at all, but we are desperate. The demons will come because they are desperate too, so hungry for our world that anything is better than nothing, but they will give very little in exchange. So we have to stand against the magicians armed with nothing but the information we can gather from demons and little magic toys. These are not attractive odds, which is why I think we should start giving bodies to the demons for the greater good. We can start with people who ask stupid questions."

Merris Cromwell emerged from the recesses of her dim and crowded stall, her dress sweeping the ground as she came. She wore her talisman as a brooch, crystals and bones and silk threads forming an intricate pattern under frosted glass, and no other jewellery. She was not the type who depended on anything someone else provided, so she had a scarlet-screened lamp attached to the front of her own stall. Crimson-tinted light fell on her face, on the almost rectangular jaw and the grey-streaked hair, scraped back from a forehead the shape of a cathedral dome.

Everyone in the Goblin Market had a speciality. Phyllis sold her chimes, the Davies family told fortunes, the Morrises did metalwork, and the silent twins sold words in every form, all the books and tablets and scrolls you could dream of. Merris's stall was loaded with what looked like specimens from every stall. She specialised in being the best.

"She's joking," Alan explained to Mae. "Merris, this is Mae and Jamie."

Merris unbent slightly. "Alan's young lady, I presume?"

Mae actually blushed. "Er – no."

"Young Nicholas's, then," Merris said wearily. "What they all see in you, I cannot imagine."

Nick leaned against the stall and smirked at her. "You'll never know until you try."

Merris gave him a quelling look, and Alan nobly distracted her. "They're people we're trying to help. Merris, Nick is going to dance tonight. We need a speaking charm."

She thought for a moment, and then leaned over to produce a clay tablet from the heaps of her stall. "I want the translation by next month," she said. "Don't let Nicholas touch it; it happens to be five thousand years old."

Alan glanced at it and nodded, and only then did she press a gleaming white shell on a chain into Alan's palm and close his fingers over it. Merris Cromwell was the only seller at the Goblin Market who never accepted money. She traded in favours. She had enough money, though nobody knew where she got it. Her currency was power.

"Alan, what language is that?" Mae asked, peering at the tablet and looking excited. No wonder Alan's little crush was so persistent. Nick hadn't realised she was a big nerd.

"Sumerian," Alan said.

"The oldest written language in the world, from the world's first civilisation," Merris explained condescendingly. "It was the written language for Babylon as well. Half of what we know about magic comes from Sumerian records. I do not know what they teach you children in school these days."

Mae looked impressed. "You can read Sumerian?"

Nick believed that Merris Cromwell was as fond of Alan as she could be fond of something that was not a magical artifact, but she was a businesswoman. She looked extremely bored by the exchange of Sumerian sweet nothings and turned her attention to Nick.

"Which of your demons do you mean to call?"

"Anzu," Nick said.

People used to laugh at him because he had only ever been able to call two demons, but he was able to call them faster than anyone else, and he never made a mistake.

"Er, excuse me, but how *do* you call a demon with dancing?" said Jamie, glancing from Merris back to her stall. He looked a lot less caught up in the glamour of it all than Mae did, and he was smiling the nervous smile that Nick was coming to recognise. "Do demons have disco fever?"

He was so weird. Nick didn't understand him at all.

Merris Cromwell looked as if nobody had ever uttered the words "disco fever" in her presence before. She did not deign to respond to Jamie. Instead she nodded at the shadows and a man Nick did not recognise took her place at the stall. Merris walked through the Goblin Market, sweeping the rest of them in her wake, until they reached the place of the dancers.

There was a spot where the stalls ended and the Market did not, a clearing full of light and music. There were dozens of little lights in the trees above, bright as stars that had somehow become tangled in the branches, and under the lights the grass looked silver and the night behind the dancers' heads looked like a black velvet backdrop.

There were about six couples already. The women wore bright colours, slashed skirts spinning out like vivid petals as if they were pansies who had come alive after dark. The men were their gliding shadows, all in black, and Nick was aware of Mae's glance towards him.

Nick gave her a sidelong smile and concentrated on the

dancers, on the dark-haired girl wearing poppy red. When the men lifted the girls, she looked like she was flying, her partner's hands trying to pull her back down to earth and him. She was fast the way a swordsman had to be fast and beautiful with it, a twist of crimson in the air like a trace of blood in water, and the tourists gathering began to resemble sharks.

All the girls wore crowns of fever blossoms. The orange and red petals looked like tiny flames set in the swift dancer's dark hair.

If a dancer threw someone a fever blossom, it was a token of special favour.

The crowd surrounding the dancers rustled and murmured as the dark-haired dancer drew a blossom from her crown. A slow smile curved her cherry-ripe, gleaming lips. The dancers all spun in perfect synchronised circles, shadow and light, and as she spun the girl in red blew on the blossom cupped in her palm.

The petals burst into the air like a flurry of multicoloured butterflies, flying to the winds. The crowd sighed with disappointment and the release of tension. The dancing ceased.

The girl in red broke away from her partner and came towards them.

Before anyone else could speak, Mae said eagerly, "That was *amazing*."

Nick laughed a soft, surprised laugh. Girls did not usually react to Sin like that. Mae turned to him with her face bright, her eyes dazzled, and he let her see him smile.

"That was just for the tourists," he said. "Wait until you see the real thing."

5

Dancing Up a Demon

Nick did not smile at Mae for long, because he was busy being kissed by another girl.

Sin Davies, the best dancer in the Market, reached him and leaned up, resting her palms against his shoulders, to give him a kiss. It landed light as a butterfly, as a petal, in the area between Nick's mouth and cheek.

"You're dressed for dancing," she said in her throaty stage voice.

"Being undressed for dancing occurred to me, but I didn't think Merris would like it."

Sin slid a look over to Merris, who did not look any more outraged by Nick than usual, and then laughed. Sin was the hot tip to succeed Merris as the unofficial leader of the Market, and Merris was the one who had looked after the Davies family since magicians had killed Sin's mother; Sin would do anything for her. Merris had been unimpressed when Sin had thrown Nick a fever blossom on a warm night last summer.

Nick seldom cared much about girls, but for that one night he'd thought maybe he could like this one.

Merris pointedly introduced Mae and Jamie, and Sin

flashed a bright, practised smile at them. It warmed into a real smile as Mae enthused over her dancing, and it became an entirely different smile, something secret and tender, when Sin's little sister ran up to tell her the baby was in bed.

"Thank you," Sin said, fingers lingering in the child's blonde hair.

The way she was with her baby brother and younger sister was one of the reasons Nick had noticed her.

"Come here, sweetheart," said Alan helpfully. He knelt with some difficulty on the grass, and the child ran to his arms as all children did, instinctively seeing him as a refuge. He whispered something to her, low and sweet, and Lydie laughed.

"Thanks," Sin said without looking at him, her mouth a thin straight slash of red.

"You're welcome, Cynthia," Alan replied, his voice distant.

The way all the dancers acted around Alan was one of the reasons Nick had stopped dancing and one of the reasons he had not spent any time alone with Sin since last year. It was almost reasonable, Nick supposed. Dancers relied only on their strength, their sure feet, to save themselves from the demons. Even seeing someone stumble made a dancer wince; seeing someone crippled was like seeing their own death.

Nick understood all that and did not care. Nobody was allowed to look at his brother like they did.

He glared at Sin, who looked badly startled. Then he looked away and met Mae's eyes. The excited flush in her cheeks was fading, and she was watching them carefully.

She turned to Merris and said, her voice loud in the sudden silence, "Will you tell me how the real dances work?"

It was such a banal tourist question that everyone relaxed.

Sin turned to a couple of the other dancers, Alan began murmuring to the child again, and Merris gave Mae an approving look. Merris's favourites were always the ones who knew how to manage situations to their own advantage.

Merris reached over and plucked a fever blossom from Sin's shining hair. "These flowers grow on trees that need magic to feed them. The trees bear fever fruit; once dancers eat fever fruit, their perceptions of the world are altered and their inhibitions are lowered. In this state they can share energy with demons. They dance in magical circles and perform exorcisms."

"Exorcisms?"

Merris raised her eyebrows. "Calling demons into this world is usually referred to as an exorcism."

"I thought that meant getting rid of demons," said Jamie.

"Exorcism means naming the demon and commanding it," Merris Cromwell answered. "Often people do try commanding the demon to leave, but once a demon has a human body, it will not leave without destroying the body. Call a demon into the circle and bribe it, though, and it may do what you want. If you offer enough."

The dancers were already cutting the lines for the weaving. Each had already cut their own circle in the ground, perfect circles set about with charms to keep the demons inside. The demons were always trying to get out, but not even a magician would let a demon go free.

Nick knelt on the ground, motioning away the offer of a ceremonial knife. He preferred to use his own weapons, even if he did have to sharpen them afterwards. He took his largest knife from a sheath strapped around his ribs and began to cut his circle. The blade bit deep into the earth and he made a symmetrical circle with the ease of long habit, his hands remembering the symbols and guiding the blade without input from his brain.

First there was the circle itself. Then he cut the lines for walking between the worlds, travelling out from the centre like the spokes of a wheel. He cut two circles intersecting to represent worlds colliding. He cut straight lines through those, the lines of communication that would hang between him and the demon like magical telephone wires so that the demon would be able to understand human speech and the silent communication of the demon would be translated into human words for Nick. Later he would have to walk each line perfectly, in a series of measured steps, or the demon would never come and the circle would remain silent and still.

"A dancer calls a demon into the circle – but a dancer does much more than that," Alan said in his earnest teacher's voice. His arm was still around the little girl, but he pointed out the intersecting lines with his free hand. "This is the weaving. It opens up a connection between a human and a demon, so the demon can feel some of what the human is feeling. A dancer has to follow the lines of the weaving perfectly, even while he takes fever fruit to lessen his control."

"Demons always demand a price," said Merris Cromwell. "That is why magicians are corrupt. A magician is some-one who wants something for nothing – they are willing to let someone else pay the price for what they want. A dancer opens himself up to demons. He lets the demon share a few beats of his heart, a few breaths from his lungs, and Alan's right, the demon can feel what the dancer feels. The dancer shares a part of himself with the demon in the dance, but he has to be careful what he says when the demon comes. If he says the wrong thing or takes a wrong step, then the demon can have all of him."

Merris Cromwell regarded the circles with a slightly wistful air. The story in the Goblin Market was that she had been a famous dancer when she was a girl.

Jamie looked extremely alarmed. His eyes darted from the dancers – some of them already stretching, most lying on the earth cutting the lines of the weaving – to Nick.

"Alan will be the one doing the talking," Nick explained.

"That's what the speaking charm is for," said Alan. "So I can speak for Nick. Demons trick you, and the fever fruit lowers your defences, so—"

"Never been all that good with words," Nick said. "Alan always does it."

"So the dancer in the circle is the one who asks for favours," Mae said in a strange, speculative voice.

"Well, there are always two dancers in two circles," Alan said, and went a little red. "Usually a girl and a guy dancing side by side. It's often couples, because, um – the demons are attracted to strong feelings, and the fever fruit lowers inhibitions, and, er—"

"It's all very Magical Circle Dancers Gone Wild," Nick interrupted, and tucked his knife away. "You'll see."

"We can ask about Jamie," Alan continued, looking relieved to be on a safer subject.

"I'm getting that damn mark off Alan," Nick corrected, so that everyone was clear. "I might get around to Jamie later."

Mae's eyes had a bright, strange look about them. They were fixed on Alan. "So it matters if you care about what the demon has to offer," she said slowly. "That's why Nick is doing it for you."

Nick looked away into the darkness of night and tangled trees. He did not hear Alan reply. It was possible that Alan nodded. It was possible that Mae simply swept on without waiting for an answer.

"And you don't have to be able to do magic?" Nick could look at Alan then, and he saw him nod this time. At Alan's nod Mae went on, her voice gathering determination. "If it's just steps along those lines, I can do it. I want to do it. I want to dance. I can ask the demons to help my brother myself."

Of course it was all about helping her brother, and nothing to do with being a dazzled tourist.

"You can't dance," Nick said flatly.

"I can," said Mae, the light of battle in her eyes. "I'm a good dancer."

"I don't care," Nick snapped. "If you get one step wrong, then calling the demons won't work, and calling the demons is *going* to work. This isn't clubbing, sweetheart. This is my dance. And I say you can't do it."

A moment afterwards Nick knew he had made a mistake. Merris Cromwell did not like anyone besides herself to assume authority. Her face changed as she looked down at the small and defiant shape of Mae.

"If you want to help your brother," she said, in her cool voice, "that might make a great difference. How much do you want to help him? Are you desperate?"

"Mae, don't," said Jamie.

Mae met Merris's eyes. "Yes."

"That's good," said Merris. "The demons will like that."

"I'll do anything—"

Merris made a hoarse, abrupt sound that was almost a squawk. She sounded like a kicked crow. "You must understand,

92

you have to be very careful about what you say. None of that 'I'll do anything'. The demon will be trying to twist any word into a promise so it can possess you."

"I promise I'll be careful," Mae said breathlessly.

"Well," Merris said, with a certain amount of approval. "If you dance with an experienced partner like Nick, it might do."

"She's not dancing with me," Nick snarled.

"Be sensible, Nick," Merris told him. "You always do best with an emotional partner."

"That's true," added Sin over her shoulder. She was looking at Mae with some sympathy.

It was true. Everyone always said it was because Nick didn't have much feeling to share with the demons. It didn't bother Nick. He thought they were right, and it made sense. Why should he care about the strangers dancers were usually called on to help? Their problems had nothing to do with him. When he'd danced before, he'd been doing it for money or favours.

He opened his mouth to say it was different this time because it was Alan, but they were all looking at him, and he couldn't think of a way to say it. He shut his mouth.

"Come, child," Merris said briskly. "We will test your speed and reflexes. We'll see if you would make a dancer."

Sin reached out and grasped Mae's hand. The other girl dancers moved to form a fluttering crowd about Merris, like bees attending the queen, and they moved away from the lights in a group. They all looked coldly at Nick as they went past.

Apparently Sin did not appreciate being glared at. Well, what did it matter? He'd made his decision about her already. Dad wouldn't have approved of him getting mixed up with a Goblin Market girl, someone who might have guessed the truth about Mum, and Sin shouldn't look at Alan like that.

Maybe dancing with Mae wouldn't be so bad, he thought suddenly. At least she was decent to his brother.

His gaze fell on Jamie, who was looking decidedly nervous about Mae's sudden departure.

"Don't mind Merris, she always acts like that around me," he said. He figured jokes were the only language this boy understood, and added, "She tries so hard to hide her attraction. Her mouth says, 'I cannot imagine what they all see in you' but her eyes say, 'Take me, wild stallion'. She'll be back. She can't keep away."

Jamie smiled, looking a little startled.

"You're not allowed to be a wild stallion until you're older," said Alan, but he caught Nick's eye and smiled crookedly at him, looking very pleased.

Alan cared so much about kindness.

The dancers returned, bearing the platters of red and golden fruit to lay around the circles. The fruit formed bright circles around the dancing circles, rings laid within rings. The lights of the Market danced over the fruit and made it gleam.

Fever fruit was grown from small trees carefully nurtured in the caravans of the Market folk. For a long time they looked like nothing but dry sticks in little pots, shrivelled and dead, but every tree had a day of blooming like a butterfly. Then the tree was garlanded with blossoms, their colours bright as ribbons on a maypole, and under the rich colours the fever fruit grew. They were gold and scarlet, like apples to bite into but with a single poisonous stone at the core, and they had the heavy exotic smell of expensive perfumes.

Once anyone tasted fever fruit, it became their favourite food.

Nick gave Alan his new sword to hold, took one of the fever fruit, and bit into it. The skin broke at the first light touch of teeth, and juice burst thick and sweet on his tongue.

"Don't eat those," Alan advised Jamie, stopping the boy's reach. "They're kept for the dancers. The dances used to be called bacchanals once, and nobody measured the amount of fruit they should eat. After the dance was done, the dancers were let loose on the world. Sometimes they killed people."

"I think I've read about that," Jamie said. "The dancers, they were called maenads. The wild women."

The juice of the fever fruit coursed down Nick's throat in a thick stream as he ate, like the blood in his veins, quickening everything, making him feel better about everything. Maybe he'd dance with Mae and like it, maybe she would fail the tests and he'd dance with Sin. One thing was certain: either way, he would cure Alan. He laughed and Jamie looked alarmed at the sound. Nick grinned at him and realised he was not grinning so much as baring his teeth.

He pitched his voice low. "Not just women."

More dancers started to gather around the fruit, taking a piece for themselves. Laughter and a humming sort of energy started to rise from their little group, and a larger group gathered to surround them. Dancing was just another part of the Market, since most of the dancers were dancing for pay, for strangers who needed help or information, but it was also the closest thing to entertainment the Goblin Market had to offer.

Besides, Nick was going to dance again. They all knew it would be a good show.

A lot of the time dancers would dance through their steps,

and no demon would show, but they never failed to come for Nick.

"Who's Anzu?" Jamie asked. "Nick said he was going to call him."

"Two demons have given Nick their names so he can call on them," Alan answered. "Demons can do and show themselves as almost anything, but mostly they have preferred forms and ways of doing things. There are the ones Mae would call succubi and incubi, who try to appeal to people romantically, there are those who show themselves wearing the faces of the dead, there are the ones who favour a particular animal. The demons Nick calls are Anzu, who often takes a bird shape, and a succubus called Liannan who – well." Alan glanced over at Nick, who smiled at him and waved a hand for him to go on. "Demons don't have a very good sense of time," Alan went on. "Liannan thinks Nick is a boyfriend of hers from a while ago."

They were starting to light torches and chant to prepare the circle for opening. Torchlight caught Alan's hair and changed it from the colour of blood in the dark into bright gold.

Jamie looked stunned. "A boyfriend? I thought demons were evil!"

Alan frowned. "Well, it's up for debate. Some of us argue they are, and of course Liannan would have been ready to take her boyfriend's body and his life. You can't trust them, not for a second, because they are so desperate to get into this world, but – some people think that not all their feelings are simulated to trick us. They are very different from us. It's hard to tell, but some people think . . ." Alan's voice softened, and he admitted, "I think – that they can love."

Nick thought that if a succubus ever got to Alan, he would

probably want to take her out to dinner and talk about her feelings before he'd accept any dark demonic delights.

The torches were burning steadily in brackets set on the trees around them. The circles were done and the plates of fever fruit were emptying. Nick felt like he was separate from his body and still trying to keep it steady. Light was brimming and refracting in his vision as if he was seeing it underwater. Girls and boys with sticky fingers and sticky mouths crowded around him, laughing and asking him why he was dancing again. Alan, the fixed point in a whirling world, stayed close and answered for Nick. He would be asking questions for Nick soon enough.

The drums started the dancing rhythm, a low, muffled sound that seemed to begin in his bones. They always had to muffle the drums in case someone heard them, but all the sounds of the night were distinct in Nick's ears suddenly – the sound of a woman spreading her cards on a stall, the sound of small, frightened animals in the wood.

The light step of a girl, behind him. Nick spun and saw Mae.

"Good news," announced Merris Cromwell. "We have found a most promising new dancer."

Nick laughed, and Merris regarded him coldly. "She fulfils all the requirements. She has good coordination, she has a strong desire to call the demons, and she has no fear."

"She'll be afraid enough in a minute," Nick murmured.

"Want to bet?"

Mae strode past Nick to the nearest dish of fruit and seized one as if she was picking up a gauntlet someone had thrown. When she bit into it, the juice ran in a golden stream down her chin.

Her eyes met Nick's, and his hand went to his belt. He

unbuckled his old sword and scabbard, and tossed them aside. He wasn't going to back down from a challenge.

"Let's dance," he said.

As Mae cut her circle under Merris's direction, he turned to Alan, who offered him the shell. It gleamed in pale seashell colours, blue and violet and apricot in the Goblin Market lights, and then it was white once more. Nick kissed it, put the speaking charm around Alan's neck, and then stepped into the circle of summoning.

Nick's talisman flared in a sudden moment of pure pain. Nick tilted his head back and absorbed the shock, let it wash over him like water, and listened through the feeling of pain and rising magic for his brother's voice.

"I call on the demon they called Anzu in Sumer!" Alan said as the sound of the drums came faster and faster. "I call on the demon they called Djehuty in Egypt! I call on the demon the Romans called the thief at the gates and the watcher by night. As they called him, so I call him: I call on Anzu!"

Mae must have entered the circle beside him when Nick had entered his, but Nick had no awareness of her now. Partners or not, she would dance or fall on her own.

The drums surged and pounded in his temples, and he stepped along the lines for communication. The lines of travelling began to whirl as if they really were the spokes of a wheel, and he had to keep up with them. There was a cold, well-known touch all along his side, a seductive and almost familiar voice whispering to him, and in his other ear the call of "Come buy!" spiked into an appeal to stay, a promise of warmth in this world. He sidestepped neatly, never going too far to meet the demons; he twisted and spun in the centre of sound and colour and set lines.

There were thin screams of approval all around him. Arms reached out for him. Some were human, and he let them reach him. They pressed warm hands against his body, against his face, and the fever fruit was pressed again to his lips. He bit down and the world was bright around him, like a glass sculpture on the very edge of a mantelpiece, catching the light before it fell. He put his body between the worlds, threw back his head and put the straining muscles of his shoulders, the twisting strength of his hips, put his heart and his clenched hands at the service of the demon, and then held firm.

Nick always had to wait for his partner to catch up. He waited with his heart slamming against his chest and his throat raw with every breath, the world in a glow from fever fruit.

For a moment all he registered was that Mae was doing well for a beginner. Her steps along the weaving were sure, and she was making the right gestures of offering and appeal. Then he saw the fall of her skirt against her leg, the gleam of the chain around her stomach in the firelight. He saw her hands sliding like a lover's hands down her own throat as she tipped her head back, and he realised that he could want her, after all.

He realised that he did want her.

There was no time to think about that, since at the point where their two circles intersected there was a cold light burning, racing along the patterns of the weaving but growing stronger and stronger at the point where it had started. Until the light gave birth to a dull red bonfire, and at the centre of the red chill a shape formed.

Anzu was taking the shape of a man today, though there was a suggestion of the eagle in the curve of his nose, a glint and pattern like crimson feathers about his golden hair. The fair skin he had chosen to wear was reddened by the dull glow of the fire around him, and when he lifted his eyes to Nick's face, they were enormous, and clear as water.

Nick saw his own face reflected in those eyes, black eyes and black hair, a face far colder and more grim than the demon's face before him. That was Anzu's intention, of course.

"Nick, isn't it?" Anzu asked, pronouncing Nick's name as if it was rather a good joke. "Well, well. Dancing again, are we?"

"Our pair danced for you and you fed off their feelings. You owe us some service, Anzu," said Alan.

Anzu peered out past the circle. "Ah," he said, looking even more amused. "It's Alan, isn't it? The one who knows so much. What service do you require?"

A new voice broke through the sound of drums and the sizzle of the flame.

"I want to save my brother," said Mae, clear and confident. "He has a third-tier mark. How can I do that?"

Anzu laughed. "You can't," he answered. "He's ours now. It's only a matter of time." His great glass-coloured eyes travelled to Jamie's face. "So young," he remarked, smiling wickedly at Mae. "We do like them young."

He turned and grinned at Nick. Nick saw sparks pinwheel around Anzu's head and take flight in the shape of tiny birds.

Alan hesitated, his face grave, but Nick's brother knew better than to leave a pause for a demon to misinterpret.

"I have a first-tier mark," he said quietly. "Can you remove it?"

"Oh, of course," Anzu replied. "Washing you clean would be my pleasure. Can't have you leaving that little family of yours. What would they do without you? Put the mark in the flame."

Alan knelt with some difficulty on the grass and rolled up his jeans. He extended his leg into the circle, making sure it was lifted well above the pattern of the weaving, and held it in the centre of the fire.

The fire did not burn him, but its sullen glow lit up his leg so the first mark stood out dark against his skin, the two slashes forming a doorway. The shadows lurking in them were so deep that it looked like they were welling with fresh blood.

"Hmm," said Anzu. "That's interesting."

Alan's voice was clipped. "Explain."

"Oh – it's nothing," Anzu said. "Only that your mark" – he nodded to Alan – "and the young thing's mark were made by the same Circle. The Obsidian Circle. And they were made by the same demon."

"What does that mean?" Alan demanded.

"A small thing," Anzu told him. "It means that if you agreed, I could transfer one of the young thing's marks onto you instead. That would mean you would both be bearing a second-tier mark, which still means death for someone. If you caught and sacrificed two magicians of the Obsidian Circle, then you would both live. It is the only chance the boy has, but it would be a terrible risk for you to take." Anzu waved a careless hand, fingers blending into the flame. Nick could almost see talons. "Forget I mentioned it."

"Wait," said Alan.

Nick had kissed the speaking charm and given his voice into Alan's keeping a hundred times, and he had never missed his voice. It was almost peaceful, having no words, having Alan speak for them both, but now Nick had something to say. It felt as if smoke had got caught in his throat, or the lack of words was scorching him. He moved his mouth, moved his tongue with a painful effort, and found his whole body empty of words when he needed them most.

Mae had words. She looked at Alan and she said simply, "Please."

Nick knew that while he was within the circle, Anzu could feel a little of what he felt. Even though Nick could not speak, even though he knew that his own face rarely betrayed much emotion, Anzu looked at Nick as Mae spoke and Nick was sure Anzu knew everything Nick could not say. In turn, Nick thought he could feel just a touch of the demon's malicious delight.

No, Nick thought, his whole body thrumming with that single word. He wanted to shout it. *No*.

Alan cleared his throat and said, "All right."

Still looking at Nick, still grinning, Anzu reached out one of those hands that blurred into talons, and with a talon he stabbed Alan three times as deep as he could.

He drew the second mark, which meant death, onto the skin of Nick's brother.

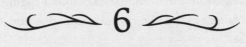

6

The Hunt Begins

As soon as the balefire died and the demon went down in smoke, Nick broke out of the circle in one stride. He was beside Alan in another step, one fist clenched in Alan's shirt and one closing around the speaking charm. He ripped the charm violently from Alan's neck and took a savage satisfaction in seeing the thin red line spring up on Alan's skin when the chain broke.

He stamped on the shell and felt as if he had bitten his tongue and blood was filling his mouth, slipping down his throat. Only instead of blood, it was his voice.

Now that he could speak, he found he had nothing to say. It was done.

Nick shoved Alan away, sending him stumbling back into the ash and the broken pattern of the demon's circle. Alan was easy to throw off balance. If Nick had thrown him back with any more force, he would have fallen, and if he'd fallen, Nick might have kicked him when he was down.

A crowd of people had gathered to watch the dance, and now they were all gaping like the idiots they were. Even those idiots were not stupid enough to get in Nick's way. He stormed forward, and they scattered in all directions before him. He plunged into the depths of the wood, away from the noise and lights of the Goblin Market into a raging darkness. Branches caught in the night wind whipped at him, twigs raking his face.

There was a sharp burn in the corner of one eye and a trail of heat down his cheek. Of course, it was blood.

Nick wiped at his eye and saw the lurid smear of blood on his knuckles, red even in the darkness. He wanted every trace of the fever fruit burned out of his system. The fruit made even this dark wood too bright. It made the wind and shadows into whispers and lurking thorns.

He turned at every sound, wanting to lash out at something, but nobody was stupid enough to follow him. He was surprised when he heard the unmistakable sound behind him, a sound not of wind or branches but of a step, and he realised that somebody had been stupid enough to follow him, after all.

He wheeled around and it was not Alan.

It was Mae, coming towards him with her eyes wide and her whole face luminous with emotion. At first Nick thought she was just happy. She had every reason to be happy, after all, since Nick's stupid brother had removed her stupid brother from immediate danger by risking himself.

Then he remembered the fever fruit.

Mae's eyes were a little too wide, her pupils dilated. Nick remembered how the world was after that first taste, how everything was magnified and glowing, every colour breaking in on you like light, and every thought like a revelation.

"What do you want?" Nick snapped.

Mae's lips were slightly parted and quivering. She licked

them, and with that fevered sharpness Nick saw the place on her mouth where her tongue had rubbed away the lip gloss.

She came closer, put out her hand, and pushed Nick against a tree. Her lips quivered again, and she spoke.

"I want," said Mae, offering up her mouth. "Oh, I want . . ."

She lifted her free hand to pull Nick's head down, fingers knotted in his hair. Nick remembered, with a vividness born of the fever fruit, the curve of Mae's hips dancing. He could want her.

Alan wanted her too. This would hurt Alan, and after Alan's little stunt Nick liked the idea of hurting him.

Nick seldom said no to a girl, and he had never done so in circumstances like these, with the lights of the Goblin Market glimpsed like far-off lightning behind her and her trembling mouth an inch from his.

Nick touched her for the first time.

He took hold of her shoulders and pushed her away. Then he leaned forward and whispered into her ear.

"You'd want anyone right now."

He let his lips touch her ear and when he drew back, she did not look angry, only dazed and uncomprehending.

He left her. He did not want to run, because that would have looked like fear or some other ridiculous thing, so he loped through the woods, going easily, knowing that when he walked fast no girl and no crippled idiot could catch him. He held his hands clenched in fists, but he did not hit out at any thorns.

When black night was touched with the cold, unfriendly blue of coming morning, Nick went back.

The Goblin Market was in the process of being packed away. The remnants of the stalls stood forlorn as their owners stored their wares in boxes, and the few customers left lingered uneasily around the debris of magic.

The others were standing in the centre of the clearing, near a fortune-telling stall. Jamie was looking uneasily around and saw him at once. Mae was leaning against Alan, cheek pressed against his shoulder. As Nick came towards them, she made a determined effort to twine herself around Alan and turned her face up to his.

It seemed that, indeed, anyone would do.

Alan stooped and gave her a soft kiss, light, but enough to show her she was not being rejected.

"No, Mae, I really can't. It would be taking advantage," Alan was saying.

The fortune-teller picked this unfortunate moment to lean over her stall and pluck at Nick's sleeve.

Her crystal ball, left out in forlorn hope, stared up at Nick as if the woman had a huge third eye cupped between her palms. In the crystal depths, luminous points of green spiked like a tiny forest; above the green, streams of iridescent blue were looped like ribbons.

"See the future, young sir?" the old woman croaked theatrically. Merris Cromwell would have coldly recommended a cough drop.

The tightly interwoven blues and greens darkened. The impression Nick received was that of a shadow falling over a lake, a silhouette that grew more distinct, moving from a shadow into the lines of a face.

It was just his own face, his darkly reflected eyes staring out of the crystal. Nick picked up the crystal in one hand and hurled it with vicious force at the nearest tree. The crash made Mae and Alan jump and look around. Nick caught their movement from the corner of his eye, but mostly he was staring at the glittering shards.

"I think I've seen enough," he said.

They dropped Mae and Jamie home, Alan giving strict instructions for Mae to be put to bed and kept there. Jamie made solemn promises and held Mae's hand tight with the air of an anxious nanny.

"You don't need to worry," he said, leaning into Alan's open window. "And, er, Alan?" he added. "Thanks."

He gave Alan a quick kiss on the cheek, and then disappeared through the gate with a struggling Mae in tow. It was rather a fancy gate, loops and swirls wrought in iron creating a picture Nick couldn't quite make out. Through the intricate pattern he glimpsed an ivy-covered house, large and white, looming in the still-dark sky like a big expensive iceberg. The windows in the upper floors cast yellow light on the big garden and the tennis court.

These two had everything. They could have left Nick's brother alone.

Nick crossed his arms over his chest and said stonily, "Quite a night you're having."

Alan said, "I'm not talking to you while you still have the fever fruit in your system."

Not talking was fine by Nick. He stared out of the window as Alan drove.

Usually the journeys back from the Goblin Market were all right no matter how long they were. It was not like moving; it was just the two of them without Mum. Alan played classical or country music and talked for ages about whatever his latest craze was, from vintage comics to philosophy. It was all just insane ranting to Nick, but he didn't mind hearing it, and he always bullied Alan into letting Nick drive most of the way home.

This time there was silence. Nick did not offer to drive at all. He measured exactly where the halfway point was and when it came, he did not speak. Let Alan tell him to drive. Let Alan take care of himself for a change. Nick glanced over at Alan and saw his jaw set. He was not going to ask Nick for help; he was too proud to ask for anything that was not offered willingly.

Nick was viciously glad. It was Alan's own fault. Let him suffer.

They continued to drive in silence, except for the tiny hitches of breath that began to rise helplessly in Alan's throat. Nick listened to every stifled sound of pain.

Alan would never have let Nick hurt himself, no matter how angry with Nick he might have been. Nick knew that, but that was the difference between them. Nick was a jerk, and Alan was a suicidal fool.

The car drove into a lurid yellow morning, the terrible toxic colour of leaden clouds filtering pale, sickly sunlight. There was a fine, continuous rain falling. Nick stared out at the wash of water down the glass and wondered if other people got as angry as he did. He'd seen Alan angry, but he'd never discovered in Alan's eyes any savage urge for blood. He wished he wanted to yell at Alan or slam doors, wanted to do anything but lash out with extreme violence. He sat, fists clenched, too aware of the new sword at his belt and the knife against the small of his back.

When they pulled up outside their house and the purr of the car engine stilled, Alan let his leg relax and breathed out a sigh of pure relief. For a moment there was complete quiet.

Then Alan said, "While you were gone, I talked to Merris. She said she wouldn't be able to help us with Black Arthur, but – I don't know. I've heard stories about the experiments she does in her house. She won't talk about them. What we need is an excuse to get into Merris's house."

That was just like Nick's stupid brother, still worrying about Mum when he was the one in danger. What Nick needed was to get both marks off Alan, and that would be almost impossible.

"We need to kill a magician," Nick snarled.

Dad had been killed by the magicians. They had spent their whole life running from the magicians, and now they had to seek them out.

"We've killed magicians before," said Alan.

"When they came for us," Nick snapped. "They live in magicians' Circles. If we try to deliberately find one, we'll find a nest of them. They have demons, they have magic, and they outnumber us."

These were the facts. Alan knew them, and it maddened Nick to have to enumerate them. He did not add the next fact, which was that Alan was probably going to die.

"It's a chance," Alan said. "Jamie didn't have a chance before. Now we both do."

"Why should he expect you to die for him?" Nick demanded. "What would I do with Mum if you were dead?"

"I didn't realise," Alan said slowly, looking a little pale, "that your concern was so entirely practical."

Nick stared at the dashboard. Alan was choosing now, of all times, to talk nonsense. Nick was in no mood for it.

"You weren't being noble," he informed Alan after a

moment. "You didn't want to give anyone a chance. Don't lie to me. Don't tell me it had nothing to do with that girl!"

Before Alan could tell him anything, Nick had wrenched open the door. He leaped out and slammed it shut behind him. He ran as he hadn't run through the wood at Tiverton, as if he was being chased down the grey side streets of south London.

He ran to the new garage he was working at. Nick found comfort in machines that were either working or broken, and if broken could be either fixed or destroyed. He found the garage as still as a graveyard, cars in various stages of repair like sad metallic spectres.

Nick kicked a box of tools and sent wrenches and spanners flying out onto the cement. He wanted to overturn a car, and he felt sure he could. He was so angry he wanted to kill.

A car, winched up as high as it would go, collapsed with a crash behind him. Nick spun and drew his sword as a loose wheel rolled into the wall, and he noticed for the first time that the lock on the garage door was broken. Somebody or something had smashed it.

Nick was suddenly happy. He hoped this was an attack, that here at last was something he knew how to deal with. He turned in a slow circle, watching for a flicker of movement, for the slightest sound. Another car fell with a thunderous crash as soon as his back was turned.

"Got you," Nick said, turning on the sound with his sword already arcing through the air. All he saw was a lick of flame leaping under the bonnet of the car.

It was a demon. It had to be. The crash had not been enough to start a fire and besides, Nick's talisman was a prickling, harshly humming weight against his chest. There was a demon, somewhere close, and it would not show itself so he could kill it!

He thought for a moment that he needed to go and warn Alan so they could all start packing, but then he remembered. They were chasing demons now. If there were magicians here, they had to stay and hunt them.

He should really go, he realised. He didn't need to be caught and laid off for setting fires.

"So," he said to the dying flame and the empty room, "I'll get you later."

He did not feel like going home, so he took a walk, and then returned to work, where everyone was wondering who the mystery vandals were. Nick nodded at all the theories, and then popped a car bonnet and got down to work. He worked grimly and silently, two shifts, until it was dark and someone told him to get out and enjoy what was left of his night.

Nick just nodded a final time and left. He went home at last and got into bed without seeing anyone. Sleep, black and consuming, swallowed him whole.

He woke late as usual and came downstairs to find Alan playing with a piece of toast. He looked pale and worn as an old bone, after only one night with a second-tier mark. There were violet shadows under his eyes, and he did not look up from his plate as Nick approached. Nick could usually sneak up on anyone but Alan. He went over to lean his forearms on the back of Alan's chair and frowned at the back of Alan's neck.

"Don't," he said, and saw Alan jump at the unexpected word, so close, and then relax. "Don't do anything like this again," he said. "All right?"

Alan reached behind him and grasped Nick's upper arm.

His thin fingers only half closed around the swell of muscle, but he held on.

"I promise I won't put any demon marks on myself for the sake of any fetching pink-haired girls or their brothers ever again."

Nick hung over Alan's chair, uneasy but not exactly wanting to break away, and said in a rough voice, "You'd better not."

Alan offered to run him to school, but Nick said he'd take the Tube. He knew Alan must really be tired when he agreed. Nick had no intention of going to school. He knew what he had to do.

Anzu had given him the name of a Circle. The Obsidian Circle: Black Arthur's Circle. He knew that much, but he did not know how much power they had or where to find them. He did not have time to wait for the next Goblin Market. He could draw a basic circle of summoning. He would dance again and alone.

He needed answers. He needed his other demon.

He needed Liannan.

On one of the bleakest roads in Camden, there was a small grey lot behind the American Methodist Church. It was filled with builder's dust and rubble years old, and there was a large metal dumpster in it that was heaped with an assortment of rubbish.

On a Monday morning Nick didn't think he would be disturbed here.

He drew the circle of summoning and confinement carefully with a white piece of chalk he had stolen from an art shop on the way. He'd taken a few protective charms from

Alan's bedroom, and he laid them carefully at intervals around the circle. The circle had to be secure. He was taking risks, but he would not take that risk. If a demon ever got out into the world, free of a magician's control, it could mean the end of the world.

Nick was planning to take risks only with himself. He had no fever fruit, he had no dance partner, and he had never spoken directly to a demon before. If he slipped up, the demon would have him. If he could not manage to offer something she wanted, Liannan might not even come.

He was betting that she would come. She had always seemed like she wanted to come to him.

She was not a woman, of course. That was only a shape she chose to trick humans, but Nick thought it would be easier if he could pretend she was a woman. He had called girls to him before. There was nothing so easy whether you were walking into a classroom, a club, or down the street. All you had to do was send out the right signals, give her the right look, turn your body the right way, and never for a moment let it cross your mind that she might not be interested.

Nick was not carrying his sword, so he laid down his knives before he entered the circle. It was a gesture. He was surrendering and inviting the demon in.

He could not let himself worry about scuffing the chalk marks that showed the lines of communication, or the lines that meant the boundaries between the worlds. If he got distracted from the dance, she would never come.

Pushing away the reality of a grey sky in London, he thought about night, the taste of fever fruit, and the taste of a girl's mouth. He thought about being in a nightclub and catching a girl's eyes gleaming under the coloured, moving lights.

He thought about Mae's skin under the lanterns of the Goblin Market.

The right words were, as ever, the hardest part. He swallowed and heard his voice come out rough, commanding a girl rather than coaxing her. That worked, sometimes.

"I call on the one who gave me the name Liannan! I call on she who loves water and lives in ice, she who follows men invisible and drives them mad. I call on the face men follow through a winter storm to their deaths. I call on Liannan."

He thought about practising the sword in darkness, his whole mind narrowed into nothing but the movement of steel in the night. He danced and remembered fighting, training his aching body until he knew only the desire for perfection, the perfect kill, the perfect kiss. He threw back his head, arched his back, and called Liannan to his side.

When he opened his eyes, there was nothing but the tarmac, the worn building, and the chalk outlines of what looked like a child's game. Nick waited for a heartbeat, despaired for a breath, and then saw pale fire building from one chalked-in line.

It was a very pale fire, almost colourless, as if water had learned how to burn. Liannan rose from a high flame the colour of a fountain with her head bowed, like a goddess rising from the sea. The fire settled over the circle, lapping gently as the sea at low tide around them, and she stood before Nick and lifted her face to his.

His talisman sent a pang of sheer agony through his body, and he gave a quick gasp. She smiled.

She was smiling; she who was a legend in lands where men would follow her into ice and shadow for a smile. She was dazzling, and she would have been even more beautiful if she

114

had not been so pale. Pallor lay over her like a veil, making the colour of her eyes impossible to distinguish and cooling the fire of her red hair, as if the vivid colour was seen under frost.

"It's been a long time," she said, her voice ringing like the chimes at the Goblin Market.

Nick crossed his arms and stared at her. The less he spoke, the less chance there was she could trick him.

Liannan tilted her head. "Do you like this?" she asked. "I remember you always had a fancy for red hair."

Nick actually preferred blondes, but that hardly mattered. She thought he was a different man, centuries dead, and probably dead by her hand. Demons found it hard to tell humans apart.

"It's all right," Nick said grudgingly. "I have two questions for you. I know I didn't dance with a partner or take the fruit. Tell me your price for answering them."

"My price." Liannan's voice changed to a whisper that sounded like a waterfall. "I will answer one question – if you take off your talisman."

Every dancer always wore a talisman, because a demon could mark you if you were in a circle, as easily as they could take a mark off you, if you did not wear some protection.

If he refused, though, she would go. She had chosen her shape, and it was a shape to seduce rather than to force. He could stop her if she tried to mark him.

Nick nodded, and for the first time in eight years, he took off his talisman and cast it to one side.

Losing the talisman should have made him feel vulnerable, but he felt nothing but relief. He always carried the talisman and thought of what had happened to Alan without one. He carried it and bore with the endless prickling discomfort, the pain doubled whenever a demon was near or spells were performed in his presence. He was free of pain at last, and he felt wonderful.

This new freedom made him feel more confident rather than less. He didn't need any warning. He could deal with demons on his own.

He looked at Liannan and smiled. A smile spread over her face in return, a sad, beautiful smile, with just the faintest gleam of sharp teeth.

She reached out for him, her fingers shining like knives. They were icicles.

"I can touch you now," she said.

If he tried to fight her, Nick might accidentally step out of the circle. He let her touch him. It wasn't so bad, since she looked like a girl. She might have been any girl, with her slim body pressed against his, her eyes fixed beseechingly on his face. One hand was curled around his neck, her fingers sharp and cold.

"Ask me your question."

"Where are the Obsidian Circle?"

She didn't answer him. That would have been too easy.

Nick could see the demon's breath, as if she were a child puffing out warm clouds into the cold air, but her breath against his cheek was icy.

"The Obsidian Circle," she repeated thoughtfully. "That was the Circle that hunted you first. That was the Circle that wanted you most."

"Tell me something I don't know," Nick snapped.

"All right," Liannan said, and laughed. "Did you know that was the Circle that killed a man called Daniel Ryves?"

Nick thought of being eight years old and watching his father fall to ash.

"This Circle has something to pay for, then," he said. "I'm glad you told me. I'll be glad to kill them. Now, where are they?"

"Exeter," said Liannan. "But you won't find them there. They're leaving soon."

How like a demon to give an answer that was completely true and utterly useless. Liannan must have seen some of Nick's fury in his face. It made her laugh.

She had two rows of pointed teeth like a shark. They all flashed when she laughed, and she swayed closer to him. Her mouth was the colour of frozen cherries.

"What is it like, being human?" she asked. "I cannot imagine what it must be like, to feel the blood warm in your veins and the sun warm on your face. Will you tell me that you love me?"

"I don't love you," said Nick. "I don't even know you, demon."

"You did know me once."

"Did I?" Nick asked. "When was that, exactly? A hundred years ago? More?"

"Something like that," Liannan murmured.

"How do you think humans work?"

She had no eyelashes, like any reptile or underwater thing. She only looked like a human at first glance, before you noticed that all the details were wrong.

"I have no idea," she answered, and lifted her free hand to touch his face.

The cold burned and numbed him to the pain. He did not even feel a sting when the icicles cut him, only blood trickling down his cheek. She put her mouth to his face, her lips cold but very soft. When she leaned back, her mouth looked warmer, and she trailed her hand down Nick's chest. His shirt tore under her sharp fingers.

Her clasp around his neck, more palm than icicle fingers, was firm. It was as if she thought he might try to get away.

"Do you think I'm afraid of you?" Nick asked.

"I hope not," she said. "There is something else I think you should know. Anzu is working for the Obsidian Circle."

"Oh, so I shouldn't trust him," Nick said. "In future, I should only summon you."

Liannan nodded.

Nick laughed. "Demons work for anyone who can call them," he said. "Do you think I don't know that? Do you think I don't know better than to trust any demon? Don't try to play your tricks on me. I have another question. Name your price."

Liannan sighed like a tired child and rested her head on his shoulder. He felt her chilly breath running down the back of his neck, making him shiver every time she spoke.

"My dear," she said. "My darling, my beloved. What do these words mean? I suppose you know now."

"I know."

Nick meant his tone to be brutal, meant it to turn the words into an offence, but the demon lifted a face to him that was as radiant as sunlight on miles of snow.

"I want some warmth to take back with me," she whispered, her voice an icy breeze. "Surely you remember – a time when you were warm."

"That's your price?" Nick asked, to seal the bargain.

"That's my price," said Liannan. "A moment of your life."

If he failed to pay the price, she could take anything she wanted.

"Tell me where the Obsidian Circle are going," Nick said. "And you can take it."

The demon nodded and stood on tiptoe to press her soft, cold mouth to Nick's. Nick shut his eyes and tried, as her kiss chilled him and her icicle fingers scrabbled against his skin, to think of a time when he had been warm.

He shivered, struggled against panic, and remembered being cold.

Liannan had mentioned his father. Perhaps it was that which reminded Nick of the time right after they had lost him. They were living in Scotland then, in the smallest, cheapest flat Alan had been able to find. Alan, injured and unable to walk, was not sure how to make Mum go out to work, and their heat had been cut off in the middle of winter.

Through the thin walls, Nick heard Alan crying every night. Nick had not been sure if he was supposed to cry too. He had never cried in his life, and he did not particularly want to do it now. He just lay curled up in bed, his mind ticking bleakly over all these new facts. He was eight years old, his father was dead, his brother was crippled, and he was so cold.

He was huddled under the blankets, thinking about it all, when his brother limped in and carefully heaped his own blankets over Nick's bed. Nick stared silently up at Alan's face, pale and tired, marked with new lines of pain. His glasses were too big for him and kept tilting off. Alan had smiled at him determinedly and crawled in under the covers, sliding his arm around Nick. Alan had been bigger than Nick back then, big enough so that Nick felt a little shielded from a world that had turned unfriendly, and Alan's body and the new blankets made him start to feel warm.

Alan had reached out and smoothed Nick's rumpled hair.

"You're mine," he said, in a trembling young voice that already had a ring of Dad's about it. "And I'm going to take care of you."

It was a memory of warmth, after all.

Liannan leaned back, her lips parted. Her eyes were shining like ice under moonlight.

"Thank you," she said.

Then she put her winter-cold mouth to his ear and whispered, "No need to go looking for them. They'll be in London in nine days. Didn't you guess? The whole Circle is coming for you."

Nick came home afterwards feeling like a gutted fish, limp and neatly filleted. His mouth felt bruised from the cold, and he did not want to tell Alan what he had learned.

Alan took one look at him and shut his eyes.

"Missing school again," he said, putting aside his book. "How am I supposed to bring you up right if you won't cooperate?"

"Dunno," Nick said, and stretched himself out on the couch with his head near Alan's good leg. Alan looked worriedly down at his face and torn clothes.

"So you've obviously had a fight – with some of the hyenas that have been menacing the streets of London. And you got roughed up."

"You should see the hyenas," Nick said, and shut his eyes.

There were sounds upstairs. Mum must be feeling particularly lively today; Nick hoped this would not be one of the times she started to scream and would not stop.

"Er," Alan said, and Nick heard the note of unease in his voice. "Before I bring you antiseptic—"

"And a sandwich."

"There's something you should know."

Before Alan could tell him what he should know, Nick knew. There were footsteps coming down the stairs, and the door to the sitting room swung open to reveal Mae, with Jamie peeping nervously over her shoulder.

Nick rose in one movement, barely checking a snarl. He hated to be caught at a disadvantage at any time, let alone at a time when two people, who had caused him enough trouble already, decided to invade his home.

"They arrived about half an hour ago," Alan explained. "Jamie has to be there for the kill. It does make sense . . ."

Nick did not think having strangers in his home made sense at all, and he was about to say so when Mae stepped forward, lifting her velvety brown eyes to his face.

"What happened to you?" she asked.

"Since you ask," Nick snapped, "I was gathering some information. The Obsidian Circle is coming for us."

Alan looked troubled. The Obsidian Circle had been in Exeter, had been hunting them, and had come close enough to send ravens and snakes.

Part of the reasons that magicians' summoning circles were so powerful was that every group of magicians had a summoning circle built of huge, powerful stones. Every circle they made was a reflection of that one, and if the whole Obsidian Circle was really coming to London, they would have to bring their chunks of obsidian with them. Nick couldn't imagine how any charm of Mum's could have enough power to justify risking the circle the magicians were named after.

The Obsidian Circle was more committed to hunting them than he had dreamed.

"They're coming in full force," Nick continued. "They're hunting us. How are we supposed to hunt them?"

Alan was as pale as he'd been when the messenger came, but he looked calm, and when he answered his voice was thoughtful.

"If Black Arthur is hunting us, his magicians should be easy to find."

"And what's to stop him getting to Mum while we go after his people?"

Nick would have sacrificed Mum to save Alan, every time. That wasn't what was bothering him.

This was . . . all wrong. Less than a fortnight ago, Alan had said that no matter what he had to do, he would make Black Arthur pay, and now it looked as though he wanted to play right into Black Arthur's hands. He should have suggested sending Mum away. He should be telling Nick his plans. He should stop hiding things from Nick!

"I have a plan," said Alan, and did not say what it was.

Nick did not ask. He started to and then stopped, as it occurred to him that his brother might actually lie.

It had always been a comfort to him that Alan could lie so well. Nick could not do it; the world was complicated enough without making up another world of words that weren't even true. He had always assumed that Alan never lied to him, and now the idea that Alan might lie, might already be lying, was like being asked to read in school. He felt panicked, not knowing what to say. He had a picture of words stacked up around him, caging him in, and not one of them could he trust.

He stood silent, feeling like an animal held at bay. Mae and Jamie were staring at him, their eyes travelling over his ripped and bloodstained clothes.

His brother looked sad and kind, but then, Alan never looked kinder than when he was lying to someone. "Will you just do what I ask you to for now, Nick?"

Nick remembered that hidden photograph, those hidden letters, and now this secret plan. He thought of Christmas in the dark, and Alan coming back, opening the door with the light behind him.

"Do I have any other choice?" he growled.

Alan nodded at him, and then let his gaze drop. The shallow gashes Liannan's icicles had left in Nick's shoulders stung, and his mouth ached with cold. He suddenly felt very tired. He'd done what he could, and he had no idea what Alan was doing.

He'd carry out Alan's little plan, even if he was in the dark. This was his brother. He had no one else.

"So – can we stay?" asked Jamie tentatively, as if this was a visit instead of an invasion.

"Stay if you like," Nick snarled, too tired to argue. He strode past them to the stairs, pulling off his bloody shirt as he went, and threw a warning over his shoulder. "Just make sure you keep away from me."

7

The Intruders

NICK WAS NOT USED TO LIVING WITH ANYONE BUT ALAN.
Mum hardly counted, since it was best if she never saw Nick.

He didn't like it, even though Mae and Jamie proved to be quite useful. They were willing to pore over Alan's books and scrolls for hours, trying to get information about the Obsidian Circle. They tried to memorise the few pictures of Obsidian Circle magicians that Alan had drawn from descriptions he'd been able to get from Market people. They chipped in for groceries, and Jamie honestly tried to help with the cooking. Alan offered to give up his own room to them, but Nick insisted that they take his instead. He wanted Alan to keep the bookcase.

Sharing a room was fine by Nick. The second mark meant that demons could send Alan dreams every night. Nick had to watch and wake Alan if he seemed restless.

The cloud of Black Arthur and his message hung over their house. He was coming for their mother, and their mother knew it.

There were small magical incidents throughout the house

these days, lights unexpectedly coming on and strange noises. Alan said that it meant Mum was scared, but Nick didn't care. He didn't need these reminders of his magician mother everywhere in the house; the magic felt like another intruder.

Alan liked the human intrusions. Both of them.

Alan liked reading books with Mae, and he loved that she wanted to learn the Greek alphabet. He fancied her, Nick could understand that, and if it hadn't been for Nick's uneasiness about what idiot thing his brother might do next, he might have been all right with that. But Alan seemed to like having Jamie around too.

He and Jamie watched television and listened to music together, and Alan was trying to teach him the difference between cooking things and burning them.

Nick was not sure why that bothered him, and then he realised that if Alan was this ready to welcome strangers into their home, he must be very lonely.

Nick had no idea what to do about that. He just wanted them to go away.

"Won't your parents be wanting you back?" he asked when he came home from school on the third day, slinging down his bag and pulling his horrible tie over his head.

Jamie, who was attempting chips and something that looked like French toast, gave Nick a slightly apprehensive glance as usual.

"Well," he said cautiously, "they don't know we're gone."

Nick strode over to the fridge, grabbed the milk, and took a swig. Alan would have seriously objected to him drinking out of the carton, but Jamie just kept watching him warily, as if he thought he might have to dodge at any moment.

"How did you pull that one off? If you have an evil twin,

you should send him over," Nick said, leaning against the fridge. "I might like him."

Jamie's face closed down in what Nick could tell was a trained performance, telling a story he'd had to tell a lot and pretending he didn't care. Nick didn't lie, but he'd learned to recognise the signs of lies in others. The world was filled with clumsy liars, amateurs who didn't realise how they looked to other people and didn't work to perfect the act.

Nick could always tell, except with Alan.

"Our parents are divorced," Jamie said with false airiness. "They split up about seven years ago, but it took a while for the divorce to come through. They're both . . . society types; they have a lot of money and it was all tangled up. It was a pretty acrimonious divorce. They both wanted most of the assets and less time with the kids."

Jamie tried to smile. Apparently he made jokes when he was upset as well as when he was afraid. Nick just stared at him, and after a moment Jamie started talking again.

"Mum got the house, Dad got the holiday home, and they got joint custody. They both thought they got ripped off. It's easy enough to call them and say you're spending extra time with the other one. They can't check. They don't talk, and anyway – they're glad to be rid of us. Even if they did find out we were gone, they'd think Mae took me to one of the raves she sneaks off to sometimes. So."

So that explained some things. It explained why the demon had gone for Jamie in the first place. The magicians didn't dare let the demons out often or at random, since secrecy was as important to them as it was to the Market. Demons had to choose victims who were alone and unprotected, whose disappearance would not be noticed soon, and parents usually noticed rather quickly if a child disappeared or turned up possessed. Not these parents, obviously.

It explained Mae's rebellion, created to punish her parents or get their attention, and explained the way Jamie was, caught young in the middle of a domestic war, just trying to stay out of trouble. Look how well that had worked out for him.

Nick could understand it, but he wasn't sure how he was supposed to respond to it.

"So the magicians knew you wouldn't be missed," he said.

That didn't seem to be right. Jamie went very white.

"I suppose they might think that," he said. "Mum's very busy, and I don't think being a single parent is the type of life she had planned. I don't think we're the type of kids she wanted. She never means to be unkind."

When Mum was in her screaming fits, she sometimes hit out. Alan had got black eyes that way. Mum never meant to hurt him, but there it was.

"What is that?" Nick asked abruptly, staring at the pan.

"I don't know," Jamie answered, stirring the unidentifiable mass with a helpless air. "It was meant to be omelettes."

"I thought it was French toast."

"It sort of looks like brains," Jamie remarked sadly.

They both regarded the pan for a moment, and then Nick came to a decision.

"All right, push over. I can fix this. You go and grate some cheese."

Jamie squinted up at him. "You're going to fix this?" he repeated, and looked extremely doubtful.

"Yes," Nick said. "All this and I can cook, too. Get out of my way."

He pushed Jamie aside, lightly enough because Jamie was so little that a rough push from Nick might have sent him through the window. Jamie still looked unsure, but he went over to the fridge and got some cheese in an obvious effort to look willing.

"Can I ask you something?" he asked.

Nick looked up from chopping onions. "In the sense that I won't stop you with actual violence," he said in a guarded voice, "yes."

"What do magicians want?"

"And why would you ask me that?" Nick said, and watched Jamie flinch at his tone. "I'm not a magician."

He refused to think of Mum and how like her he was. He glared at Jamie and was amazed when Jamie did not look away.

"I'm not!"

"I – I didn't think you were," Jamie said, obviously lying. "I just meant – they kill all these people. Why do they do that? What could possibly be worth that?"

It was clear he thought that Nick had some kind of dark insight into a magician's psyche. Nick wondered why he didn't just go to Mum if he was so curious, but it wouldn't do any real harm to answer him.

"Power," he said. "As I understand it, just using the power makes you want more. It's a rush; it's addictive, and it's not just that. Once you have enough power, you can have anything you want. Some magicians are successful politicians. Some are actors. Some are completely normal people, people you see at the bank and the post office, who just happen to have the ability to change shape or control the weather. Some magicians are rich, some are famous, some are stupidly good-looking."

Jamie gave Nick a rather complicated look.

Nick raised an eyebrow. "Some of us manage to be stupidly good-looking on our own."

"Er," said Jamie, and cut himself on the cheese grater.

"I have changed my mind," Nick announced. "You can help cook by standing in a corner and not touching anything. Do it carefully."

He said it without heat. The omelettes were starting to resemble omelettes, and he hoped the subject of magicians was closed. Most conversations he had with people from school went a lot worse than this.

Jamie was quiet, fidgeting with an oven glove on the countertop.

"Don't hurt yourself with that," Nick advised.

Jamie grinned. "Okay." He kept fidgeting while Nick went to the fridge for some peppers, and then asked suddenly, "So – where's your dad?"

Nick slammed the fridge door. "He died."

"Oh." Now Jamie had the look of a deer caught in the headlights, who for some reason was feeling really sad for the car. "Oh, I'm so sorry."

"Why?" Nick snapped, opening cupboards just so he could bang them closed and express his fury at people who did not know when to shut up. "You didn't know him. Why should you care?"

"Um. Empathy?" Jamie suggested.

Nick stared at him silently. The silence stretched on, Nick watching Jamie become ever more uncomfortable, and then a moment before Jamie's nerve broke Mae and Alan came into the kitchen and rescued him.

Alan looked from Nick to Jamie's alarmed face and seemed a little sad, just like he had when they were young and teachers had told him that Nick didn't play well with others. Nick failed to see how it could keep coming as a surprise.

"This is excellent," said Mae, coming and sitting on the draining board. "Carry on. I have always dreamed of having handsome men lovingly prepare all my meals."

"Nick rescued the omelettes," Jamie confessed. "They were going wrong for me somehow."

Mae laughed and tugged him towards her, putting her arms around him from behind and giving him a kiss on the side of his head. "Funny how they always do."

Neither of them was too bad. Mae was good at smoothing over awkward situations, good at dealing with people, and Nick appreciated that, but he didn't need to find himself appreciating anything about her.

Nick made omelettes and Jamie made jokes and Mae and Alan made conversation, but Alan was still marked. All Nick had learned was that Mae and Jamie's parents would not be arriving to remove at least one problem from his life.

On the morning of the fourth day, Jamie tipped a switchblade out of his box of cornflakes.

"I think these promotional campaigns have really got out of hand," he said, freezing with his hand on the milk carton. "One shiny free knife with every packet of cereal bought is not a good message to send out to the kiddies."

He picked up his bowl, tilting it and trying to drop the switchblade back into the box without actually touching it. Nick rolled his eyes, reached over, and took the knife, tucking it into the waistband of his jeans. He saw Jamie's eyes wander to the flash of skin and didn't make an issue out of it; a lot of people liked to look at Nick.

"So – do you have a system?" Jamie asked.

"What?"

"Well, if knives go in the cornflakes, do guns go in the raisin bran? I just wanted to know if there's some kind of system I should look out for."

Even though a system was actually not a bad idea, that kind of thing was a problem. The way Jamie kept making uneasy jokes about their life and Mae kept revealing a disturbing fascination with it made Nick feel as if he was a freak show suddenly on display for these people.

Mae walked in the door at that point. She pushed Jamie's hair out of his eyes as she went by, then took a proper look at his pale face. She stooped and kissed his forehead before she went to get her muesli.

They were always doing weird stuff like that, as if they thought it was normal. It made Nick uncomfortable. He was just glad Alan hadn't seen the latest bit of weirdness. Alan's face went strange every time they did something like this, as if someone had hurt him.

Nick frowned at Mae as she tried to spoon up her muesli while bent over Alan's copy of the *Hexenhammer*, an old German book about witches. Nick was used to having girls over now and then, but it was strange for him to have a girl constantly, comfortably around the house, sitting rumpled and sleep-flushed over a book, white curving flesh showing as her pyjama top shifted with her movement.

That kind of thing was another problem.

Mae's voice was accusing. "Are you looking down my top?"

"Well," Nick said, "it's a new experience for me."

"Oh, *really*?"

"Generally girls take their tops off so fast around me,"

Nick explained. "It's hard to get a good down-the-shirt view. Not that I really complain, under the circumstances. Very nice, by the way."

Mae looked annoyed for a minute, and then a smile tugged at her mouth, drawing her away into amusement. "Well," she said, shrugging. "I grew them myself."

Nick liked the easy, casual way she flirted, comfortable with her body and confident about its appeal. He liked her smile.

He looked away from both of them, scowled, and ate his cereal. A few minutes later Alan came down with damp hair, smiling as if they were a group of friends who had chosen to be here together. He ruffled Jamie's spiky blond locks before he sat beside Mae, and Nick narrowed his eyes.

He hoped that Jamie wasn't getting any ideas about being a little brother to Alan.

They all started talking about their favourite music, Mae talking about rock music and Alan talking about classical, while Jamie put in a few words for country music.

Nick didn't speak. His favourite music was the music of the Goblin Market, the drums that made the air thrum with danger and tried to pierce the silence of the demon world, and he didn't need Dad's voice in his head to remind him that wasn't normal.

Another thing Nick couldn't get used to was that Mae and Jamie knew about Mum. Nobody knew about Mum. Everyone at the Goblin Market, even Merris Cromwell, only knew about Dad. They knew that he had shown up at the Market wanting help for a wife bound with enchantments, and protection for his young family. Dad had taken Mum in when she came running out of the night chased by monsters, and then taken her as his own.

It was like one of the stories Alan used to read to Nick at bedtime, about the perfect knight shielding his lady. Only the lady was a murderer. She'd chosen Black Arthur, chosen to be a magician, and chosen to kill.

Nick thought Dad must have not known what she was until it was too late.

Now two strangers knew that their mother had called the demons and made sacrifices for them. They sat at their dinner table and looked at Nick and saw his mother's cold face. Mae had even started going upstairs to talk to Mum.

"It's very kind of you," Alan said one night at dinner.

Mae shrugged. "I like doing it. Olivia tells a lot of wonderful stories. My mother's never done anything worth talking about in her life."

She'd taken to calling Mum Olivia, in the same casual way Alan did, as if they were all friends.

"Your mother's never fed people to demons?" Nick said. "Poor you."

Mae's eyes narrowed. "I just said Olivia was interesting. I didn't say I thought what she did was right."

Nick leaned across the table towards her. "Tell me," he said, lowering his voice and watching the way his murmur sliced through her, small and sharp as a hook that a fish might swallow without thinking. "Do you find the demon's mark on your brother interesting?"

"No."

Nick talked right over her. "Just think, if it wasn't for the mark, you would never have heard Mum's stories or danced at the Goblin Market. You were thrilled by all that, weren't you?

You think it's all so exciting, so *glamorous*. Lucky for you Jamie got marked, isn't it?" He lowered his voice even more to see her leaning towards him, caught, and then he twisted the hook into her flesh. He smiled at her slowly and whispered, "Bet you're glad it happened."

Mae's face was crumpled and white as a tissue clenched in someone's fingers.

"How can you say something like that?" she said, her voice taut with outrage. "Your brother's marked too. How does that make you feel?"

She glared at him, eyes accusing, and Nick saw that Alan and Jamie were looking at him too. He didn't bother deciphering Jamie's expression; he looked at his brother, and Alan looked back. He didn't look angry like Mae. He looked patient, and a little pained; he looked as if he was waiting for Nick's answer.

Then they all looked away.

Alan glanced from his own glass to Nick's and then to the water jug. When Nick looked around the table, puzzled by Alan's sudden preoccupation, he saw that everyone at the table was looking at their glasses.

All the glass on the table wore a shining spiderweb pattern. Fractures crossed and crisscrossed each other, cutting thin lines that caught the light. Nick's and Alan's eyes met over the rims of their suddenly beautiful glasses.

The glasses burst quietly, with no more noise than someone blowing on a dandelion clock. Then there was nothing but glittering shards and water pouring over the table.

Jamie's plate broke in half.

What was Mum *playing* at?

Nick got up and hit the table with his fist.

"Nick, don't," Alan said. "You'll hurt yourself." He wrapped his hand around Nick's fist and lifted it from the table.

Nick stared at him, for a paralysing frustrated moment unable to understand what he was saying. It registered, and he looked at his hand in Alan's, the skin unbroken. Alan's warning had been in time.

"Relax," Alan said. "You asked Liannan. She said the Circle was coming, the whole Circle. You know how long it takes to move the summoning circles. They can't possibly be here yet. It's just Mum."

He saw the change in Alan's face, and wondered if his own face had betrayed him, shown some of the rage sweeping through him. Alan never liked seeing it, so Nick tried not to show it more often than he could help.

Then he recognised the light in Alan's eyes and realised he'd had an idea.

"What?" he said, hope rising. "What is it?"

Alan smiled at him. "Wait a bit. I need to go and work something out."

He left his dinner on the flooded table, and Nick heard his dragging footsteps going, as fast as he could, up the stairs and away from everyone to work out his new plan. Nick was in no humour to think about all Alan's secrets.

"I can clean up," Jamie offered.

Nick let him, moodily forking up the rest of his dinner as Jamie cleaned.

He was not used to girls coming to his house so they could glare at him. Over broken glass and water, Mae was staring at him, her eyes gleaming and furious. Jamie was hastily moving anything that could have been used as a missile out of her reach.

After another long moment of glaring, Mae got up. They heard her stamping her way up the stairs as if she wanted to grind every stair to powder under her heels.

Nick rolled his eyes. "How long's that going to last for, then?"

"Oh, don't worry. Give her – ten years, and she'll have forgotten all about it," Jamie said, snagging Nick's plate. "Or you could apologise."

Nick scowled. "What?"

"It's a fairly simple concept," said Jamie.

Maybe it was for Jamie, who moved gently and apologetically through life, like a hunted animal trying not to stir the leaves as he passed. Nick wasn't sorry, and he was ready to rip out the throat of anything hunting him. She'd invaded his house; she could apologise.

On the other hand, Nick couldn't deal with any more hassle than he was dealing with right now. Maybe it would be simpler to go and smooth her down.

He left Jamie washing up and went upstairs to the room that Mae and Jamie shared, the room that used to be his, and found Mae on the bed that used to be his.

She was crying.

Nick was appalled.

"I'll get Alan," he said, taking a smart step back.

He had the door almost shut when Mae said, "No, don't!"

With great reluctance, he opened the door again. There she was, huddled on the bed with her arms around her knees, face red under her pink hair, rumpled and ridiculous-looking.

"I'll get Jamie," he proposed, and what he really meant was, *I'll get out of here*.

"No," Mae repeated. "Don't." She was starting to look

angry again; all things considered, Nick found that soothing. She wiped at her face with the back of her hand and added, "I don't want him to see me cry."

"I don't want to see you cry either," Nick said.

Her face softened slightly, and he realised she'd taken that the wrong way. Nick imagined spending the next five minutes explaining to her that actually she could cry all the time if she liked, he just didn't want to see it, and then shut his mouth.

"What are you doing here, anyway?" Mae asked, her voice a little gruff with crying. She scrubbed at her wet cheeks with her sleeve and looked embarrassed.

Nick chose his words carefully. "Jamie said I should come and apologise."

"Oh," Mae said. "Okay. Apology accepted, I guess. It's not really you I'm mad at, anyway. I'm just – I'm scared, and that makes me angry, you know?"

"Not really," Nick answered, leaning against the door frame. "I don't recall ever being scared."

Mae looked taken aback.

"Fear's useless," he tried to explain. "Either something bad happens or it doesn't: If it doesn't, you've wasted time being afraid, and if it does, you've wasted time that you could have spent sharpening your weapons."

Mae stared at him for a while.

"You're lucky you're cute," she said eventually. "Because you're kind of creepy."

Nick grinned at her. "It's a vibe that works for me."

It was much more comfortable to flirt with her than see her cry. He risked a few steps into her room and she didn't immediately burst into tears, so he looked around. Jamie made his bed, he noticed; Mae left her underwear on the floor.

"Hey," Mae said sharply, and he looked away from her underwear and raised an eyebrow.

"I've never been scared," he said, conceding her something. "But I've been angry, all right."

"Oh really," Mae said. "You come across as so Zen."

Nick grinned at her again, standing beside her bed. She smiled back and wiped a final fierce time at any tears still lingering on her cheeks.

Mae took a deep breath and seemed to be done with crying. "It's just – he's all I have. Even before they split up, Mum and Dad spent more time at the tennis club than with us. We used to play dolls together for hours when we were little."

"Oh," Nick said. "Well, me and Alan did too. Obviously."

"Obviously," Mae echoed, smiling.

"If by dolls you meant knife practice."

"Maybe you can understand," Mae allowed. "You do have a brother."

Guarded in case this was a womanly plot to make him talk about his feelings, Nick nevertheless let himself relax a bit more and said, "I do have a brother."

"He's my little brother," Mae continued. "I have to – I should be able to protect him, and I can't. I didn't. And I always did before. He's my little brother," she repeated insistently, speaking more to the universe than Nick, and then she took another deep breath. "I guess you can understand that. Alan must look after you."

"When I was small," Nick conceded, and shrugged. "I don't need much looking after these days."

He almost smiled as he thought about being small, before Alan had been hurt, when he'd never imagined it was possible for Alan to be hurt. Alan had taught him to read and told him pointless bedtime stories and insisted on holding his hand when they crossed the street.

It was different now. They looked out for each other. They were a team. Or that was how it had been; Nick didn't see how keeping secrets was looking out for him.

"What's wrong?" Mae inquired.

He looked down at her and saw her frowning. He reached out, wrapped a strand of that silly pink hair around his wrist, and smiled at her slowly, drawing a smile from her in return.

"What could be wrong?" he asked.

He knew where this was going, and from the calm look in her eyes she did too: It was solid ground in the midst of his home being invaded, Alan lying, girls crying, and boys talking to him about empathy. It was good to be sure of something again.

"So," Mae said, uncurling from the tight ball of misery she'd been in and stretching a little. "You don't get scared."

"No."

"Ever get lonely?" She smiled as she spoke, her dimple showing as she brought out the line.

He stooped towards the dimple, and then remembered Alan.

He let go of her hair, and it fell from around his wrist. "No," he said, his voice cold. "I have my brother."

Mae looked puzzled, as if she was trying to work out what had inspired this change of behaviour rather than getting ready to weep again. Nick was a little relieved, but mostly he just wanted out. He didn't want to see girls cry, and he didn't want anything that Alan might want for himself.

"Wait," Mae said as he headed for the door. He glanced

back at her. "Thanks for coming up," she said. "I thought –
Alan said you might want help with your homework."

She looked at him questioningly, and he was glad she
wasn't making a scene. He supposed he should have predicted
this. It would take more than demon hunting to make Alan
stop nagging him to do his homework.

He shrugged and said, "Sure."

A few minutes later he found himself in the sitting room
and on the floor, hunching over the small table like a grouchy
vulture. The teachers had set him an essay on a stupid book
about some idiot girl whose problems were too small to really
count and whose life had happened too long ago to matter.
Alan usually helped him with this kind of thing; the fact that
Alan was somewhere upstairs, doing God knew what, made
Nick feel even more annoyed by the book girl.

Nick was already wrestling with the girl's love life when
Mae joined him. She came over to the table, sat cross-legged,
and took the book in her hands.

"What are you having trouble with?"

The answer was everything, but Nick decided to be more
specific. "The stupid girl goes back to the man who lied to her.
She'll never be able to trust him. What am I supposed to write
about that?"

Mae leaned back thoughtfully, arching her spine a little.
"Maybe she doesn't want to completely trust him. Maybe she's
looking for an element of danger."

"Maybe she's stupid," Nick said. "Still doesn't give me
much to write about."

"You might find things slightly clearer if I read out some
important bits," Mae suggested, and did so. Her voice was
calm and sweet.

She obviously had very specific ideas about which were the important bits. She'd worked out, after three days, that Nick didn't like to read. She might run away to raves all the time, but she was smart, in the same way Alan was smart.

When the low light fell on her ridiculous hair that way, it looked a pale rose colour. She lifted her gaze from the book to meet his, and shadows quivered in her dark eyes.

"Right," Nick said. "Thanks."

Mae smiled slowly. "You're welcome."

Nick had never really wanted to get to know a girl, but here she was, in his house. He felt as if he was being forced into it.

Mae walked towards the door and as he watched her go, she turned her head to look at him. The light went out, and the curve of her neck and fall of her hair were suddenly swallowed up in darkness.

Her voice was even. "I suppose this isn't a power failure."

Nick did not bother to answer her. They both knew what it was.

Nick had excellent night vision and acclimatised himself quickly to the darkness. He palmed a knife from the sheath strapped around his arm and walked with a soft tread towards Mae. He could see her shape clearly, but he knew that to her there was nothing but black night and then the sudden touch of his hand on her waist. He held on to her with one hand and his knife with the other.

She stayed still. She had not even flinched when he grabbed her. Nick did like her courage.

"Don't move," he said. "If I see something move, I will stab it."

Her voice was a whisper. He did not even see the movement of her lips in the shadows. "I understand."

They waited a while, standing close, the curve of her hip pressed against his thigh, until it became clear that there was nothing stirring in that still night. Light brimmed for a moment, a faint flicker caught between shadows and brightness, and then flooded the room. Now that she was safe and could see, Mae moved. She put her hand on his arm, her fingertips five warm points against his skin, and he remembered her trembling lips close to his on the night of the Goblin Market.

"I have to make sure Alan is okay," said Nick.

"I'll check on Jamie," Mae responded.

Nick sheathed his knife instead of watching her go. It would be better if she and her brother both left, as soon as possible.

The sudden descent of darkness had only moved Alan to light a candle so he could see the map of England he had stretched out on their floor.

"If demons had attacked under cover of darkness, were you planning to roll that up and hit them with it?" Nick inquired.

"No," said Alan, and waved his gun to prove it. Then he used the gun to trace a line along the map from Exeter to London. "Tell me what you see."

"I think it's called a map."

Alan gave him an expressive look over the top of his glasses. "The Obsidian Circle's coming for us," he said patiently. "Liannan said they'd take nine days. It doesn't take nine days to get from Exeter to London, even with the summoning circle. They'll want to make a stop, find a good place to set up their circle so they can arrive in London with a full complement of demons. They'll want to be at maximum strength. They'll be calling up every demon they have."

Nick was glad that Alan wasn't keeping the plan a secret. He felt he could wait to see why his brother clearly considered this good news.

Alan's eyes were gleaming with triumph. "So where, between Exeter and London, would you stop to do a spot of demon calling?"

His gun traced the path between Exeter and London again, lingering for a moment to give Nick a clue. Nick whistled between his teeth.

"Of course," he said. "Stonehenge."

Alan called Mae and Jamie up to hear their plan, and once Alan had recovered somewhat from Mae sitting on his bed, he was able to explain it.

"Magicians have the same traditions as the Goblin Market people. They'll choose a place with a lot of human history attached to it to call their demons, and there's a six-thousand-year-old tomb on the way." Alan shrugged. "They'll come looking for us here. We can surprise them there."

"We catch them off guard," Nick said. "We catch two of them and bring them back here. Then we kill them and use their lifeblood to take off the marks. You guys can go home, and we can go into hiding."

He thought the plan sounded good, and Jamie seemed to agree with him. Mae and Alan looked faintly wistful.

"You'll have to teach me Aramaic by email," Mae said, and Alan looked embarrassingly pleased.

They launched into an enthusiastic little dialogue about dead languages which Nick, as someone who had failed French, did not pay much attention to. He just noted that this time Alan had picked someone with whom he had a lot in common. That might help him. He was glad, he told

143

himself. It would help them both. Alan could use a girl-friend to distract him from that girl Marie in the picture. Nick wouldn't even think about touching Mae if she was his brother's girlfriend.

Mae shifted on the bed, and a book fell out from under Alan's pillow. Alan moved so fast that he caught it before it hit the floor and shoved it out of sight.

Nick saw Alan's wary glance towards him. He was still try-ing to keep the picture a secret, then.

"We'll go tomorrow," Alan said. "I'll write you a note about going to the dentist, Nick, but you can still make your morning classes. You're not skipping two full days this week."

Normally he would have rolled his eyes and made some comment about Alan being a mother hen, but Nick was still frowning at the pillow. It didn't take Alan long to turn back to Mae and begin talking about Latin.

Later Alan brought up the subject of Mae again. Nick was trying to get to sleep when Alan came in after his shower with his glasses fogged up and his hair dripping onto the shoulders of his I'M A LIBRARIAN, NOT A FIGHTER T-shirt. He tried to towel his hair dry and talk about his feelings at the same time.

"I know that she'd eaten the fever fruit and everything, the night of the Goblin Market," he said. "But she did pick me. I mean, that might mean something."

Nick stared at the ceiling and said, "I guess so."

"It wouldn't be right to ask her while she's living with us and relying on us to help her brother," Alan went on, worried about all the usual little details only he would have worried about. "Afterwards, though, I thought I might ask her if I could give her a call. Sometime. What do you think?"

"I don't know why you always do this," Nick said. "What's the point? You want to get married and have babies and have to run with them all over the country, like Dad had to run with us?"

It sounded more savage than he'd meant it to. When he levered himself up on one elbow and threw his brother a baleful glare, Alan looked a little pale.

"That's not what I meant," he said. "I don't – it'll be years before I start thinking about getting married and things."

"But you do want to," said Nick. "Someday. That's what you're saying. Why?"

His brother flinched. "You really don't understand why someone would want a family?"

"I have no idea!"

Alan clenched his fists around the damp material of his towel, looking like he wanted to throw it in Nick's face. He went dark red and snapped, "I want somebody to love me."

"Oh my *God*," Nick exclaimed, turning violently away.

When he turned around again, which was not for some time, he saw Alan reaching under his pillow to touch that stupid book as if for reassurance. All of Alan's pictures stared at Nick from the bedside table: Mum and Dad on their wedding day, looking as young as Alan was now, Nick a scowling child in the uniform of a long-forgotten school. When Nick closed his eyes, he saw the hidden picture as if it was lined up alongside the others.

"Alan," he said quietly.

"Yes?"

"Do you get scared?"

Alan laughed, a small fraught laugh like something tearing, and said, "I'm scared all the time."

The answer was so unexpected that Nick opened his eyes. He'd never thought of Alan as being scared. Alan always had a plan, always stayed calm and knew what to do. He looked at Alan, and his brother's face looked just as it always did, calm in the low light, but his face lied just as well as the rest of him.

Later that night Nick woke to the sound of Alan talking to demons in his sleep, words Nick couldn't make out broken up with cries. He rolled out of bed as fast as if it was an attack and shook Alan roughly awake. Alan stirred, opened his eyes, and then recoiled violently from Nick, his back hitting the wall.

"Hey," Nick said. "Hey, it's me."

Alan was breathing hard, fresh lines of pain around his mouth and sweat shining on his face. In the moonlight the sweat had a silver sheen; beneath it Alan looked grey. He looked like he'd been fighting, and of course he had. The demons were trying to put the third mark on him. He could only hold them off for so long.

Eventually Alan smiled a bad copy of the smile he used to reassure children, all strained around the edges.

"Right," he said. "Okay, I'm all right now. I'd like to sleep."

But when Nick climbed back into bed and lay silent for a while, listening in case Alan had any more dreams, Alan did not sleep. There was a click, and a circle of yellow light pooled against the wall across from Nick's bed. When he glanced over he saw Alan's thin back, saw the silhouette of his hands. The shadows of Alan's fingers were like long black ribbons in the yellow light, and he knew what his brother was staring at. As if he couldn't get back to sleep without looking at her.

The next morning when Alan got up to make breakfast, Nick stole the photograph.

8

The Capture

THAT DAY AT BREAK TIME, NICK DID NOT GO AND HANG around with his new crowd. He went out into what passed for school grounds in London and, standing behind a sad-looking hedge that had been coaxed into half-life by the coming of May, he made a call. It was to the local paper in Durham, and he asked them to put in a certain advertisement.

"I'll scan the picture and email it to you," Nick said. "Underneath put 'If you have any information about Marie, please call.'"

He gave them his number and the details of the emergency credit card Alan had insisted he should have. He went into the computer room, scanned the photograph, and sent it off, using an email address he'd just made for the purpose. Nick had never wanted to email anybody before.

He did not give the blonde girl's smiling face more than a cursory glance this time around. He'd decided he didn't like her. He would find out what she'd meant to Alan, make sure it was over, and then never have to think about her again.

That done, Nick skipped his last class and went outside to wait for the car. It pulled up, and Nick was enormously unsurprised to see Mae in the passenger seat. He climbed into the back alongside Jamie without comment, and they were off. The journey lasted a little over two hours, though Alan insisted they stop at some place called Andover for sandwiches, in case they missed dinner while they were hunting magicians.

They chose the car park beside the railway station in Salisbury as an unobtrusive place to stop.

"I still don't see why we're going to the city," Jamie said. "If the magicians want to call up demons near Stonehenge, shouldn't we go there?"

"I'll drive up to Stonehenge and take a look around," Alan told him, "but it's most likely the Circle is staying in Salisbury. It's the middle of the day. They're not going to want the tourists to see them conjuring up demons." He hesitated. Silence fell and lingered, seeming embarrassed to be there. "Er, Nick can see illusions, so he'll be going into Salisbury. Who . . . ?"

Now there was a question hanging in the car like very awkward air freshener. Nick saw Mae's hand reaching for the handle of her door.

"I'll take Jamie," Nick said, grabbing him by the collar of his shirt and hauling him out of the car. He kept talking over Jamie's startled squawk. "You have Mae."

Alan looked absurdly delighted, but he kept himself together enough to say, "Let's meet at Salisbury Cathedral in an hour."

"Right," Nick answered. "Where's Salisbury Cathedral?"

"Um," Jamie said, "I think that's it over there."

Nick looked over his shoulder and saw the cathedral, looming against the sky and brandishing its turrets in all directions. The grey, spiky thing reminded Nick of the cathedral at Exeter. There were supposed to be scattered bones under every inch of ground in Exeter Cathedral close. He wondered how many bones were buried around this one.

He nodded at Alan, and the car peeled away just when Jamie had nerved himself to say, "I'd really rather go with—"

Jamie looked somewhat forlornly after the disappearing car. Then his eyes slid uncertainly over to Nick.

Jamie had seen Nick at school, at home, and at the Goblin Market, which meant that Jamie knew him better than anyone but Alan.

It only now occurred to Nick that he was fairly sure Jamie was scared of him, and here they were stranded together in Salisbury.

Well, he was helping to save Jamie's life. Jamie could learn to cope.

"Come on," he said. "Let's go check out the pubs."

Jamie blinked. "Sorry?"

"Magicians like pubs," Nick answered. "Same reason they like cities. Gives them an opportunity to mingle with people and choose a victim. If someone's drunk enough, they can get marked in the bar and never know what hit them."

"I'm on the wagon," Jamie said. "Starting now."

Nick made a non-committal noise and started off down the road. He glanced over his shoulder to make sure that Jamie was behind him. Jamie was, trailing unhappily in his wake, and something else occurred to Nick. The boy had been thin to start with, and now his face was pinched and too pale. There were deep lines on either side of his mouth. The world had taught Nick a lot of things, and one of them was too-certain knowledge of what someone in pain looked like.

"The dreams the demons send you," he said. "They're bad?"

Jamie looked startled. "They're not good. It's cold, cold enough to really hurt, and there are voices whispering all the time. In the dream I can never see anything, but every time it's colder, and every time the voices get closer." He stopped and looked at Nick in that ridiculous, wide-eyed way, and Nick remembered him babbling about empathy. "Alan's tougher than I am," Jamie added softly. "I don't think he lets the dreams bother him much."

It was true that Nick would have noticed Alan getting thinner. Mostly he just looked tired.

"Alan is tough," Nick conceded, and eased his pace so Jamie might have some hope of keeping up. "Don't look so worried," he added. "I won't let anything happen to you."

Jamie seemed more surprised than reassured. "You won't?"

"No, I won't. Alan would kill me."

Jamie blinked. "I'm very touched."

They started at the unimaginatively titled Railway Tavern, proceeding on to places called the Bird in Hand and the Old Ale House. The pubs had all the usual fittings: a bar, a barman, and customers. The Bird in Hand even had a sign that showed a young woman lounging on a gigantic hand, but no magicians.

Nick had never been to Salisbury before. The city seemed mainly residential and comfortable with that. He and Jamie walked down several streets, lined with aged rectangular houses that gave the impression of standing about in cosy groups, to get from one pub to the next. The buildings got older and Nick got more annoyed as they crossed a bridge and found little churches and shops rubbing shoulders, and still no sign of magicians.

They even stopped by some hotels on their quest from pub to pub. Jamie peered too closely at people's faces in the street, searching for any resemblance to the magicians' pictures Alan had drawn from the descriptions of Market folk, and Nick was on constant alert for the sight of something too perfect, too real, which would signal an illusion being used.

They were in a pub called the Chough when Nick returned from his investigation of every corner of the place to find Jamie sitting at the bar exactly where he had left him.

He had not left him penned in by two men, however. Nick's first thought was of magicians, and he reached for his nearest knife before it occurred to him that Jamie's earring probably had more to do with this situation than his demon's mark.

It had been a long and frustrating search already. Nick was itching for a fight.

"These guys bothering you?" he asked Jamie softly, and gave the two men his coldest look. One of them stepped back.

"No, no, no," Jamie said at once, looking wildly around at empty air, as if Nick had started to throw knives.

Nick could throw knives quite well, but that was beside the point.

"If you say so."

"I do," Jamie said. "That is, in fact, what I say. So – I hear there's an antiques fair in town. We should check it out!"

Jamie, who rarely touched Nick, was so overwhelmed by concern for the people who'd been harassing him that he grabbed Nick by the elbow. Nick refused to move for a moment, staying immobile with no particular effort, and watched the men. Time stretched, weighed down with the growing fear and hesitation of the two strangers.

It relaxed Nick. He smiled at them, and the other man stepped back as well. Then Nick let Jamie pull him out of the bar.

He shook off Jamie's restraining grasp and stepped away from him as soon as they were outside.

"An antiques fair," he repeated, almost amused.

"Sometimes I panic," Jamie told him.

"I've noticed that."

They kept walking, and Nick felt his brief moment of cheer fading with every step. They had completed a circuit around Salisbury and ended up where they had begun. There had been no sign of magic from one end of the city to the other.

Nick's gloomy thoughts were interrupted by Jamie, sounding hesitant. "That was – a little scary."

"Was it?" Nick asked.

"Oh, right," said Jamie. "Mae told me. Apparently you don't get scared."

"No," Nick said. "I don't. I don't waste my time with useless fussing around, feeling scared or anxious or what the hell it is you people do. You two may be so complicated you're falling over the knots you've made of yourselves, but I'm very simple."

Jamie slanted a shy glance over at him. "No, you're not."

"Fine," said Nick. "I'm an international man of mystery. Don't fall for me. I'll only break your heart."

"Don't worry," Jamie murmured.

Nick almost liked him for that, even if he and his sister had apparently declared every day Make Nick Talk About His Feelings Day.

"I'm – I don't mean to pester you," Jamie offered after a moment. "I know you're doing a lot for us—"

Nick felt obliged to correct him. "I'm not doing anything for you," he said. "Alan's the one who wants to help people. You're putting my brother in danger, so I don't like either of you much, but it's nothing personal."

"We hadn't endangered Alan when we were at school together," Jamie said. "You avoided us then, too."

"Well," said Nick, "that's because you were weird."

They were just off the high street and getting closer every step to the railway station when Nick saw another pub and headed wearily for it.

"Sorry, I'm taking a moment to process," Jamie said behind him. "I've never been called weird by someone who summons demons before."

"That's something I do," Nick stated absently. "That's not what I am. I have to do all this, but one day Alan and I won't have to any more."

They went into the pub, which was called the New Inn. Nick presumed the wood and stone fittings, not to mention the black-fringed lanterns, were ironic. He prowled across the floor, scanning dim corners, with Jamie still at his heels.

Jamie was also still talking. "See, that's not entirely true. I mean, I don't want to offend you, but it's not just that you summon demons. It's not even about the fact that you've got more knives on you right now than a fancy restaurant has in its silverware drawer. You, um, you don't smile, and you look through people, and you're—"

"Quiet," Nick said.

"Yes, you're very quiet," Jamie agreed, "and I have to say, I find it a little disturbing."

"I mean," Nick said, "shut up. I think I see something."

At the left corner of the bar was a magician. He was buying a bag of crisps.

If he had not attempted to disguise himself, Nick would have passed him by. This man had cast a few simple illusions on himself, to make himself look older and, if Nick was any judge, darker than he was, and the too artistic lines of the wrinkles and too dense blackness of the hair leaped out at Nick. The magician was like a man painted in oils, superimposed on a world drawn in crayon.

Nick's muscles all surged forward at once before he'd even had time to think about it. The hunt was on.

"Get down," he whispered.

"I'm way ahead of you," Jamie said from the floor.

A few people glanced at the suddenly prone boy, Nick noticed in his peripheral vision. Fewer still, with good instincts for where the real danger was coming from, looked at him. He didn't care about them. It did not matter who saw him draw the knife, so long as the magician went down.

Only he had to bring the magician to Alan alive. The thought pulled him up short and he faltered, his easy movements towards the kill lost.

If he had been coming to kill the magician, the man would never have seen him. He'd done it before. He could move smoothly enough, surely enough, to be invisible for as long as he needed to be. When he faltered, the magician's head snapped around.

He dropped his crisps onto the counter and threw up a hand. All Nick saw was a glitter in the air, and then wind hurled sand into his eyes. Nick blinked and the magician bolted, the door of the inn slamming behind him.

The guy couldn't be very powerful if the first weapon in his arsenal was sand.

"Jamie!" Nick snapped. "Can you see?"

"Yeah."

That was lucky. At this range, Nick would've expected the magician's sand to have blinded them both.

"Then follow him!"

"Um," said Jamie, and as Nick tried to see through his smarting eyes, he felt Jamie seize his wrist and pull him outside. "Um," Jamie repeated, sounding even more lost than before. "I can't follow him any more."

"Why not?" Nick demanded, just as he became able to focus and saw the magician lifted by a demon's wind onto the slanted rooftops.

"Because I can't fly," Jamie answered weakly.

Nick narrowed his eyes. The magician did not look as if the wind would be carrying him any farther away. He was running, stumbling on the roof tiles, as if he had only his legs and no more magic to rely on for escape.

He spoke through his teeth. "Nor can he."

There was a shiny black painted pipe on either side of the inn. Nick grabbed the nearest and swung himself up, shoes sliding on the slick paint as he pulled himself up by main force. He grasped for a scrabbling instant at the gutter, and then put all his weight on his arms and hauled himself onto the roof.

The magician was getting farther away. Nick started to run. There was no hesitation now, no thought about what he should do when he caught up with the man, just the clean absence of thought and the ferocious simplicity of the chase. Nick was going to bring him down. What happened next did not matter.

The magician was fast, but not fast enough. Nick would have caught him in a minute if it hadn't been for the terrain he was chasing him over. For the first time he knew why roofs were described as shingled. The jagged red tiles on these roofs were like the jagged sliding stones on a beach that was all shingle. Every tile slipped treacherously underfoot. Every time Nick had to turn during his chase, there was a tinkle of falling tiles.

Turning a corner, he fell hard on his hands and knees. The sky tilted sharply in his vision, but he clung to the roof, jamming his leg against the row of little white spikes at the edge. The tiles left deep impressions in his palms, but after a moment he was able to leap up and run again.

Nick was drawing closer, bearing down on the man. The magician looked over his shoulder for an instant and Nick saw fear in his eyes, saw he knew what was coming. It made Nick want to laugh, but he only ran, so fast that he almost threw himself out into space when the roofs ended.

He looked around to see if the magician's demon had managed to blow him across the street and saw the man veering for an old bridge that spanned over the street to join up with the next set of rooftops. Nick grinned, feeling his lips curl back from his teeth, and hurtled over the curved bridge in pursuit. A gold coat of arms flashed by as he ran, a bright lion below making a face at him. He was several strides past the bridge, onto the next roof and close enough to hear the magician's ragged, desperate breaths. Nick felt the solid weight of his knife handle against his palm, with no memory of reaching for it. He narrowed his eyes, judging the distance, measuring how hard he'd have to throw the knife, and remembered again that he could not kill this magician.

Nick tossed up his knife as he ran and caught it by the blade. Cold steel cut across his palm and he ignored it, aimed, and threw.

The hilt of the knife caught the magician hard on the back of his head, and he went down like a thrown stone, tumbling head over heels. Nick had to throw himself down and seize the man around the middle to stop him falling off the roof.

They were almost at the end of the rooftops. There was nothing ahead but a street and a bridge, this one actually over water. Down below Jamie was running. Nick could hear his voice assuring passers-by that this was a daring rooftop chase scene they were rehearsing for a movie.

Nick sat on the rooftops, cold, breathing harshly, and with his heart hammering a loud, triumphant rhythm in his chest. He'd done it. He'd caught a live magician, and now Alan would be safe.

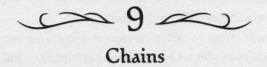

9

Chains

"ALAN," NICK SAID. "DON'T BE A FOOL."

He did not think he had ever been so angry in his life. He'd been the one to catch the magician. He'd carried him over his shoulder through the streets of Salisbury with Jamie on his heels, explaining to anyone who questioned them that the unconscious man was Jamie's cousin and he had fits. Nick had trussed the magician up in iron, mostly bike chains he'd stolen, and thrown him in the boot of the car.

Nick had caught the magician. He should get to decide what to do with him.

Alan ran a hand through his hair as he always did when he was worried, leaving a fuzz of curls in the wake of his fingers as if he felt the outside of his head had to express the turmoil inside. "I'm trying to think of what's best for everyone."

"I don't care what's best for everyone!" Nick snarled. "I only care about what's best for you."

Jamie flattened himself against the wall, and even Mae jumped. Only Alan continued to look tired and unaffected, and Nick was frustrated enough to wish for a moment that his brother would just this once be like everyone else so

Nick could scare him enough to make Alan do what he wanted him to do.

"The Circle may know by now that we have him," Alan said slowly. "They'll be on the alert."

"There were no other magicians around to see us take him. Don't you think I *looked*? Let's kill him now and get the mark off you," Nick argued. "Before they notice he's gone and send something after him."

"We can't kill him yet. We need two magicians, and we won't be able to surprise the Circle again. We need to get information from this one before we kill him."

Nick did not know what to do. Alan insisted on acting as if Jamie's life was worth as much as Alan's, and no matter how much Nick disagreed, he knew with a wrench of furious despair that he was powerless to change Alan's mind.

"Alan," he said at last. "I swear I'll catch another magician. I'll do whatever you want. Only let me kill this one now and get the mark off. Alan. *Please*."

When Alan looked at him steadily, Nick had to look away. Alan knew Nick and knew what Nick was thinking: that he would try to catch another magician, but he might fail, and what did broken promises matter if Alan was safe?

"I don't think we should take my mark off now," Alan said at last. "I think we should take off Jamie's."

"Oh no," Nick breathed. "No."

If Alan thought for a moment that Nick would let Jamie be saved while Alan was still in danger, he was dreaming. Nick opened his mouth to say so.

Unexpectedly, Jamie spoke. He said, "No." Everyone looked at him and his mouth quivered, but he pressed his lips together for a moment and went on. "You wouldn't have a second-tier mark if it weren't for me. We wouldn't have this magician if it weren't for you and Nick. It wouldn't be fair to – I want you to go first."

"Thank you, Jamie," Nick said savagely. "At least somebody is showing some sense—"

"Shh," Mae ordered, speaking for the first time. She was leaning against the wall, studying their prisoner, and now her eyes narrowed. "I think he's waking up."

Everyone fell silent and stared at the magician, who was chained to a chair in the middle of their sitting room and was now stirring.

He was very young, as magicians went. Nick usually only saw magicians in their true forms after he or Alan had managed to kill one, but he did not think any of the corpses had been as young as this. He looked about twenty, but Mum could not have been much older when she joined the Obsidian Circle. Youth did not make him any less dangerous.

It did make him look less dangerous, and he was not a very threatening specimen in any case. The magician had a shock of sandy hair, standing up on his head and then falling into his eyes like the petals on a rather floppy daffodil, and beneath the sandy mop he had a narrow, inquisitive face. There was something about his features, perhaps his long, pointed chin, that vaguely recalled a fox. Apart from that he had a friendly, freckled face, the face of a young man whom old ladies would instantly trust.

He opened wide grey eyes, blinked, and looked dismayed.

"Oh Lord," said the magician. "Now I am in the soup."

Nick was not in the least worried about himself or Alan. They knew what magicians were. He was worried about

Mae and Jamie, and what their reaction was going to be once they got over the revelation that magicians looked and acted entirely harmless, entirely human. Until they didn't.

"We're going to kill you," he said deliberately. "There will be no negotiation. I want to kill you now, but others of the group think you might have information we need. So we're going to have to torture you first."

He added the last sentence so Mae and Jamie could know the worst at once and deal with it however they had to. He didn't want to have to cope with hysterics later.

"I think I could be persuaded to offer you some information without being tortured, if it's all the same to you," the magician said. He had a rueful way of talking, as if inviting sympathy, and a soft Irish accent.

Nick did not often have much use for his switchblade, since the moment it took to flick the weapon open could be a moment that made the difference between life or death. Now he felt he could take his time, and he appreciated the cold, quiet snick the knife made opening, and the way the magician's face paled as he heard it.

"Talk."

"My name's Gerald," the magician said promptly. Again his rueful voice asked them all to laugh a little at the name and see him as a little more human.

His shrewd, friendly eyes travelled over them all, making eye contact and assessing weaknesses. He didn't even look at Nick, which confirmed Nick's opinion of him as intelligent. He looked at Alan for a long moment and did nothing, looked at Mae and smiled bravely, and then let his eyes settle on Jamie.

"We don't care about your name, magician," said Alan.

"Any more than you cared about the names of the people you've killed."

Gerald looked genuinely indignant. "Killers? Is that all you think magicians are?"

"Not really," Nick said, playing with his switchblade. "If I did, I'd think I was a magician."

He knew he should shut up. Mae and Jamie were looking from Nick with his knife to Gerald chained in his chair. He knew they were making comparisons.

"I was born a magician," Gerald said. "It isn't about anything you do. It's in the blood. You're born with the call towards magic, towards power, and one day, no matter what you do, the magic will find you."

He looked from Jamie to Mae as he spoke, Mae who loved knowledge as much as Alan did, and obviously he found enough encouragement in her face to go on.

"People think we can't do much magic without demons, but that's not true. The power that makes calling them easier shows itself in other ways. When I was a child, strange things happened around me all the time. The Obsidian Circle came to recruit me. Nobody had ever understood me before, but I'd always been a magician. One of my ancestors ruled half his country with his power. Magicians see the world differently. Everything is grey and flat and cold, nothing means anything, until you have the demon in your summoning circle and you have some control of the world at last."

"It's nice that you feel fulfilled by feeding people to demons," Alan said mildly. He took a knife from his boot and turned it over in his hand, watching his blade catch the light. "Have you got anything useful to say, or do you need encouragement?"

Nick saw Jamie glance, startled, at Alan's hard eyes. Soft-spoken Gerald must have been looking better by the minute. If they silenced Gerald now, though, they would look even more brutal.

"It's not like your Market is as pure as the wings of a dove," Gerald said sharply. "Do your friends know what it takes to prop up the Market? You're funded by blood money!"

"I don't know what you're talking about," Nick said, bored. "But I know it's not useful."

"It's not always a question of feeding people to the demons, either," Gerald said, still looking at Mae. "Some people want it. Some people ask for it."

Jamie's voice was small but fierce, and it made Mae's intent concentration on the magician waver for the first time. "I didn't."

"Then I'm sorry," Gerald said, and he sounded sorry. "I didn't send a demon after you. I wouldn't do something like that. Surely you know that there are people in this world who hate their lives, who don't seem able to live them, who seem able to do nothing but drag themselves through a succession of endless unpleasant tasks until they die? You've seen people like that. You know them. Don't tell me that you don't."

Mae hesitated, and with hesitation was lost. "I do, but—"

"Don't you think people like that might trade the lives they don't know how to use for what they want? Demons don't come as invaders. They offer people something they want, whether it is money or oblivion or a night that makes these people feel alive as nothing else ever has. And when those people choose to give in, the world gets something in exchange. Demons have lived for centuries; they are wise and powerful, they can give so much back to the world—"

"'They can give you such power," Alan said. "Your Circle marked Jamie and me. Neither of us were willing. I don't think any of your victims would be willing if they understood what they were agreeing to."

Mae cleared her throat. "So sometimes they do agree?"

"Sometimes they do," Alan had to confess.

"I don't unleash demons on unwilling victims," Gerald went on, clearly trying to throw enough conviction into his voice to carry both Mae and Jamie with him. "I'm sorry you were marked." His voice trembled. "Are you really going to torture me?"

He looked directly at Jamie, who looked as panicked as if someone had handed him a thumbscrew and was waiting with an expectant air. "No," he said, almost wildly. "No, I can't. I couldn't possibly."

He turned his face away from Gerald and fixed Alan with a look of appeal. Alan stood, limped over to him, and placed a hand on Jamie's thin shoulder. The gesture might have been more reassuring if Alan hadn't had a knife in his other hand.

"Don't worry," Alan said. "You don't have to. I can do it."

He looked strained as he said it, but he did not hesitate. Nick was sure Alan didn't like it, as sure as he was that Alan would do it if he had to.

When Mae spoke, it caught everyone off guard. "If it will help my brother. If it's for Jamie and – and you," she said, and faltered for a moment on seeing Alan's look of startled happiness. "Then I can help. I can do it too."

It surprised Nick enough to make him smile at her. She looked ill, but she kept her chin up and her shoulders back and met Nick's eyes with an unflinching gaze. The girl might have an unsettling crying habit, but she was pure steel.

"You don't have to do it either," Alan said. "I can handle this on my own. I'll get my things."

As the door shut behind him, Nick knew how things would go: Alan would collect his box of instruments and have a few moments to himself so he could try to deal with what he had to do, and he wouldn't be able to deal with it, and then he'd do it anyway. He would look white and strained and later he'd be sick, but he would never hesitate.

"I *can* do it," Mae said, as the door shut behind Alan. She sounded as if she was trying to convince herself.

Nick had to work fast.

"I know that both of you can do it," he said. Then he strolled over to Gerald, leaned in as if he was going to whisper a secret, and spoke in a perfectly audible voice. "But I want to do it."

Gerald flinched at how close Nick was, and avoided his eyes. He was almost squirming in his chains to get away from Nick, and for the first time it occurred to Nick that he might be as badly frightened as he seemed.

If he was frightened, it was all to the good. He could be scared into telling them what he knew. It would please Alan if he could be spared unnecessary pain.

Nick slid into the man's lap, getting as close as he could so he could scare him worse, listening to the scared hitch of Gerald's breathing. He tossed his switchblade into the air and caught it, near the corner of Gerald's eye, and saw the magician's eyes swivel in an attempt to keep the knife in sight.

All Nick had was a knife. He had to do this quick, and rough, before Alan returned.

"Do you think I won't do it?" he asked, his voice low in the man's ear.

No matter where Gerald looked, he kept his eyes resolutely away from Nick's face. Nick stroked the blade idly down Gerald's cheek and the man shuddered. Nick had been right. He was terrified.

"I'm sure you will," Gerald said, his voice shaking.

"How many of you are there?"

"Twelve!"

That was a good size for a magicians' Circle. There were often fallings-out among magicians, power plays that left a Circle decimated. Black Arthur must be a strong leader to keep eleven others in check.

"The Circle's moving to London. Where are you moving?"

Gerald swallowed, hesitating. Nick slashed a line across his cheekbone and the magician made a sharp, pained sound. Nick intended to show him he meant business, and the cut was deep. Blood welled in the gash and streamed down Gerald's cheek. Nick recognised the gasp behind him as Jamie's, and when he heard the sound of someone rushing to the bathroom and retching he wasn't particularly surprised. Alan hated to see people hurt too. If they had grown up differently, Alan might have been as squeamish as Jamie.

"Central London," Gerald gasped out. "I don't know where exactly, I swear. I think our master bought a house near one of the big parks."

The door opened again. Nick was somewhat surprised that Jamie had been able to come back this soon.

"And Black Arthur's still your leader."

"If Arthur's alive, he's the leader," said a voice behind Nick. "That's Arthur's way."

Nick looked over his shoulder and saw his mother. She seldom came downstairs unless Alan coaxed her, but she was here now, as if she had sensed that something momentous was happening. She was wearing a black shirt and trousers, and she had pushed her hair back from her face. It made her look almost normal.

Gerald was able to look at her. He stared at her with his mouth open, and she smiled at him. The confident, amused smile looked like someone had pasted the mouth of another woman onto her wan face.

"You know who I am, then."

"Lady Livia," Gerald breathed.

Mum kept smiling. "That's what he used to call me. You were after my time, I think."

"Yes. I had nothing to do with what was done to you," Gerald said, bloody but maintaining his calm.

Nick felt his lip curl. "He claims to be innocent of most things."

Mum glanced over at Nick fleetingly. Her odd smile did not leave her lips, though her eyes were suddenly fixed and cold. She made an abrupt gesture of dismissal, as if she still called demons and had one in her power, and then she looked away from Nick immediately.

It was best to humour her. Nick flipped his bloody knife closed and swung lightly off Gerald, moving to the point farthest away from her in the room. Mum approached Gerald, walking lightly, and came to kneel at his feet.

"Innocent?" she repeated, her smile looking more fixed and strange than ever.

She pulled her shirt down, revealing an expanse of dead-white skin and, over her heart, black against the smooth whiteness, the sigil of the Obsidian Circle. It reminded Nick of the sign above one of the Salisbury pubs, showing a woman in a giant hand. Drawn over Mum's heart was a hand, cupping not a woman but the world. There was a suggestion of tension about the fingers of the hand, as if they were just about to clench over the world and crush it.

Mum reached up and drew down Gerald's shirt, stretching the cotton out of shape. There over his heart was the same hand, holding the same world.

"Nobody who wears this mark is innocent," Mum whispered.

Gerald, blood still running down his face, sagged a little in his chair. "You're not going to help me, are you?"

"No," said Mum. "I don't owe you anything. How is Arthur?"

"I don't think he's changed," Gerald said. "He talks about you, often. He never wanted to hurt you. He chose you—"

Mum laughed and leaped to her feet lightly, as if she were young. "I chose him. That's the problem with wanting someone who will change the world for you. Choose a man with that much power over the world, and all he really wants is more power." She turned away and went over to Mae, standing so close to her that she could have slipped an arm around her waist.

"It's probably best to change the world yourself," she added. "Nobody should risk being a sacrifice."

It was strange seeing Mum lean close to Mae, as if she was a normal woman with someone she liked, but Nick didn't have time to think about that. Alan would be back soon. He flipped open his knife again and gave Gerald a meaningful look.

"What else do you want to know?" Gerald asked wearily.

"When does the Circle plan to move to London?" Nick demanded.

Gerald hesitated.

Nick moved forward, relentless as the tide. He leaned down to Gerald and closed his free hand around the magician's throat.

"I've been talking a lot about my feelings recently," he informed Gerald in a conversational tone. "I don't really get scared. Want to know what else I don't feel?"

Gerald's voice was a whisper through the vice grip on his throat. "What?"

Nick trailed his knife down the cotton of Gerald's T-shirt until the blade rested against Gerald's stomach. The magician trembled and closed his eyes. Cut someone in the belly, and they could live for hours afterwards. They just wouldn't like life much.

Nick leaned closer to Gerald, laughed in his ear, and murmured, "Pity."

"Nick!" said Alan from the doorway. *"What are you doing?"*

"Saving you some trouble," Nick answered, and then looked over his shoulder.

Alan had one hand clenched on the door frame, knuckles white, as if only his grip on the door was keeping him on his feet. He looked as if someone had punched him in the stomach.

"Get away from him!"

Nick released Gerald's throat and pocketed his switchblade in one move, abandoning the magician and walking towards his brother. Alan flinched, and Nick stopped.

"What's the big deal?" Nick asked roughly, not sure what words would help and what words would upset Alan more. "I don't – I don't know what I did wrong. It bothers you, it doesn't bother me; I thought I could do it and you'd be – I thought you'd be happy."

Alan closed his eyes and swallowed, and something about his face reminded Nick of the way Gerald had looked as he waited for the knife to come down.

"It should bother you," Alan said in a low voice.

Nick was suddenly furious. He was sick of this whole business. He wanted to kill this man, not chat with him. He wanted Alan to stop telling him what he should do and start telling him the truth; it seemed like his whole life was slipping through his hands and all he had left were lies and rules he did not understand.

He didn't want to look at his brother. He didn't need to be here.

"Fine. You deal with this," he said between his teeth. "You guys have fun. I'm going to go and wash all this blood off."

He watched for Alan's flinch this time, and then shoved past him out of the door. He climbed the stairs wearily, pulling off a T-shirt that had been grubby from the roofs of Salisbury before he'd spilled someone else's blood on it. He was so sick of Alan having this mark, so sick of Mae being always around and always on the verge of becoming a problem between him and his brother. Nick wanted all of this over and the magician dead.

The shower hissed at him like a chorus of snakes when he twisted the knob and set the water running. He got in and bowed his head under the spray.

He was under the water for about a minute when he heard the gunshot.

Nick grabbed for his jeans and realised as he was pulling them on that his knives must have fallen out when he was getting undressed. There was no time to go back for them; he ran down the stairs empty-handed with the shower hissing behind him.

There was a wolf in the sitting room.

It was big and brindled, with thick fur that tufted into white at the places where its hackles rose. Its bared teeth were sharp and yellow. It was circling Gerald's chair, and from deep within its barrel chest rose a long, continuous snarl. It was too big, its teeth too sharp, and the snarl too menacing. It was probably a magician whom some demon had given enough power to make a very convincing illusion. Convincing enough to kill.

Gerald's voice was shaking. "Let me loose! The Circle will kill me before they let me talk. Don't let me die without a fight. I can help you. Let me go!"

Mum was backed into a corner with Mae and Jamie, as if the wolf had herded them there. Alan was standing by the magician's chair with his gun trained on the wolf. Nick edged forward, scooping up a discarded chain from the pile they'd used to truss up Gerald, and saw the wolf's head move a fraction. It fixed its yellow eyes on Alan and snarled.

Nick had already heard a gunshot. Alan did not miss: if the wolf was not dead, then it was bulletproof.

The wolf's snarl became a stuttering, ugly growl that sounded like a dying car engine. Its haunches bunched up for a spring.

Nick wrapped the end of the chain around his fist and lunged forward. He brought the chain down hard against the wolf's back and heard the animal yelp, then yanked the chain back, over his head, and as the wolf swung to face him he dived for it before it could leap at him. They went down together, the wolf's growl reverberating through its body and its body crashing down on Nick's. Its claws scored burning lines down Nick's chest and its teeth snapped an inch from his face.

He threw his chain over the creature's head, caught the

other end and twisted the makeshift choke chain hard in both hands. The wolf choked, the cold weight of the chain hurting Nick's hands. He kept almost grabbing big handfuls of fur and the wolf lunged, trying to find a way to breathe, shoving hard against the single barrier of the chain.

The sound of Alan's gun rang out again, even though he must know by now it wouldn't work. Nick turned his face to one side and felt the wolf's hot breath on his face, felt its teeth graze his cheek. He pulled the chain tight with both his hands and tried to hold the wolf at arm's length while the creature snarled and tried to throw itself at him. Nick pulled the wolf on top of him, rolling with it in a nightmare of claws and straining muscle, trying to wrestle it and strangle it at once. The wolf twisted its head around and sank its teeth in Nick's wrist.

Nick did not have time to scream. He pulled the choke chain closed, a band of iron around the wolf's neck. A howl was choked off in the wolf's throat and the fierce thrashing of its body started to seem less like an attack and more like desperation. It kept trying to breathe. Pain lanced through Nick's arms with the effort of keeping the chain tight and ever tighter, the wolf's eyes were bulging in its head, and suddenly it collapsed forward against Nick's chest.

Instead of a wolf, a woman fell against Nick, her long hair tumbling into his face. He pushed the body off him and sat up with difficulty, his arms suddenly feeling weak, and let the chain slip out of his hands.

It occurred to him when it was too late that if he'd only had his sword, if he'd been able to make her bleed before he killed her, he could have used her blood to paint over Alan's mark. Alan would have been safe.

He climbed wearily to his feet, unsurprised to see Jamie and Mae staring at him with shocked faces. They weren't used to death yet. Mum turned her eyes away when he glanced at her. She looked sick.

Alan grabbed his shoulder and spun him around with one hand. He looked furious.

"Where is it?" he demanded, his eyes blazing. "What have you done with it?"

"What?" said Nick. "What are you talking about?"

"Your *talisman!*" Alan shouted. He was shaking. "Do you know what could have happened? How long have you had it off? Tell me you just took it off now, Nick. Tell me that much."

Of course. His talisman. Now that Alan said it, Nick was completely aware that it was gone. In some corner of his mind he'd known for some time that the small, constant burden had been lifted. Its irritating presence had been an absence ever since – ever since –

"I took it off to call Liannan," he said slowly. "I left it in a building site."

Colour drained from Alan's face, his veins standing out like blue lines struck across white paper. "You haven't worn your talisman for a week."

"You gave your talisman away."

"*I—*" Alan lowered his voice. "I didn't throw it away! I meant it to be for a couple of hours. A week, Nick! Anything could have happened. God."

Now that Nick had killed something, he felt better. He'd done something at last, something useful, and even though his arms ached and his wounds stung he felt calmer; some of his simmering rage had burned away in the fight. Alan was worried about him, and that wasn't bad either.

"Sorry," he offered at length. "I'll get one later."

Alan was hanging on to his shoulder as if Nick had almost walked out into traffic and Alan had only just been able to catch him in time. As Nick spoke Alan breathed out deeply, once, and shut his eyes. Nick slipped out of Alan's grasp as gently as he could and stood watching him uncertainly, wondering what he'd done wrong now.

"You're lucky your big brother learns from his mistakes," Alan said at length. "Come on upstairs. I got some spares at the Goblin Market."

He limped towards the door and Nick followed him for a few steps, then stopped. Alan threw a glance over his shoulder that was more silent command than look; Nick took another step forward without even thinking.

"Wait," he said. "There could be more magicians around. We shouldn't leave this one alone with two tourists and *her*."

Alan looked mildly amused. "We're just going upstairs."

"Yeah, we can handle this," Mae said, her voice calmer than she looked, and Nick felt like admiration was being dragged out of him against his will. "Olivia will stay with us."

She smiled at Nick, and he kept his face chill and expressionless so she would transfer her smile to Alan. She did transfer her smile to Alan, that was the thing: if there had been no hope for Alan at all, it would have been less of a dilemma.

Nick let them smile at each other and leaned back against the wall, examining the claw marks of the wolf. The deepest were on his stomach, on one side of his belly button. Nick looked at the red grooves and was distantly pleased that the wolf had been too busy trying to bite him to claw him open. Intestines belonged on the inside.

The room was a mess. Chains were scattered about the

place, the rug was twisted like bedsheets after his fight with the wolf, and their prisoner seemed on the point of hysterics. The other magician lay crumpled at Gerald's feet.

"We could just kill him now," Nick said, and watched the slow shudder work its way through Gerald's body, from shaking shoulders to trembling lips.

Alan looked impatient. "We can kill him for Jamie."

"*No*," Nick snarled.

Alan looked at him for a long moment, as if by making Nick his single focus he could somehow keep him safe, and then his strained face smoothed out. "We can talk about that later," he said softly. "First let's just go upstairs and get that talisman. We'll only be gone a minute, and – I want you to have it. I don't want you in any danger."

"Good luck with that one. I just strangled a wolf to death five minutes ago," Nick said gruffly. Alan smiled, and they both understood that Nick had given in.

Just on this one thing. He'd come and get a talisman if it made Alan feel better, but he wasn't going to put up with any of this nonsense about Jamie going first. Alan had sacrificed enough for Jamie already.

"C'mon," said Alan, and Nick moved to follow him.

"This is just a thought," Jamie called after them. "But while you're up there, you might see if you can find a shirt."

When they went into Alan's room, Nick could not help casting an uneasy eye over Alan's bookshelves. He hadn't had a chance to put Alan's precious photo back in its hiding place yet, and he had a sudden moment of foreboding. If Alan tried to sneak a look at the stupid picture he liked gazing at so much, he'd find out what Nick had done.

It didn't matter if he did find out. Nick had a right to discover the truth, but somehow he didn't like the idea of how Alan would look at him if he knew.

He turned deliberately away from the bookcase and occupied himself shrugging into one of Alan's baggy old T-shirts, lying slung over a chair. He went to lean against the wall, looking out of the window where the sun was going down, the sky brimming dark blue over the grey roofs of London.

Alan knelt down by his wardrobe and took out the box where he kept his protective charms, beginning to sift through them slowly and thoughtfully as if he was telling rosary beads. Or as if he was afraid to look up.

"I'm serious about taking Jamie's mark off," he said slowly.

"You're being stupid."

"You don't understand—"

"Yeah, I don't understand. I don't understand why you're being stupid!"

Nick's voice rose in a shout, a harsh, flat sound like a whip cracking or a door slamming. If he'd been shouting at anyone but Alan he knew he would have seen the effect of the shout: seen the sound seep into their bones and make them shudder, make them give in.

It was different with Alan. Threatening him wouldn't work; he didn't seem to care about saving himself. He would have to find some other way to make Alan do what he wanted. Nick looked at his brother and suddenly felt icy calm.

He knew what threat to use.

"Here it is," Alan said in a quiet, pleased voice, as if Nick hadn't shouted at him a moment ago. He got to his feet with his usual care, a flash of pain drawing a deep line between his brows, then smiled and limped over to Nick.

The talisman was dangling from Alan's left wrist like a bracelet. There was a crawling sensation of dread in Nick's stomach just looking at it, but when Alan beckoned, he bowed his head and let his brother slip the talisman around his neck. He felt like an animal going back into harness.

The talisman burned where it touched his skin. Nick set his teeth at the return of the dull, constant pain and looked into Alan's face, which showed uncomplicated relief.

"Do you know what I'll do if you don't take that mark off?" he asked. He did not shout this time. He lowered his voice so it was a very private and personal threat, a soft promise of pain.

Alan recognised it. "Nick," he said, startled and a little pleading.

Nick had to make him understand.

"You care so much about Mum? She was an Obsidian Circle magician. She still has the sigil. Her lifeblood would save you."

Alan took a quick, unsteady breath, his thin chest rising and falling sharply. He was trembling.

"I'd do it," Nick swore to him. "I'd trade her for you. I'd do it in a *heartbeat*. I won't let you die!"

Alan's mouth twisted viciously. "Why not? More useful to you than Olivia, am I?"

He was watching Nick in the same hurt, horror-struck way he had when he'd seen Nick with the magician. Nick looked away and out of the window again, to where the sun was sinking, shadow closing its claws over the houses one by one. He fought with black incomprehension: Alan wanted a particular response from him, and he didn't know what it was.

"Well – well, you are more useful than she is," he said haltingly.

"How can you—" Alan began in a furious voice.

He was interrupted by the sound of Mae screaming. It wasn't a scream for help. It was the scream of someone in pain.

Alan palmed the knife from his wrist sheath and held it out before Nick could say a word. Nick closed his fingers around the hilt and ran, taking the stairs three at a time, and bolted into the sitting room, throwing open the door and running almost directly into Mum.

She flung up an arm as if Nick was the threat.

"Don't touch me!"

"I don't want to touch you!" Nick snarled. "What happened?"

Mum didn't bother replying. It was pretty obvious what had happened. Their sitting room was torn apart. Someone had broken the window and shredded the rug. Mae was lying at an awkward angle on the floor with blood all over her face, struggling to get up as Jamie tried to push her down. The chair that had contained Gerald the magician was on its side, the chains that had bound him were a gleaming silver path that pointed to the shattered window.

Outside the window and utterly beyond reach was a huge bird, the curving shape of amber wings outlined in the setting sun, flaring gold as he flew. Nick imagined that its talons were fairly impressive as well, judging by what the creature had done to the rug and Mae's face.

"Mae," Nick said. "Are you—"

Alan stumbled down the last step on the stairs and was almost instantly at Mae's side. Nick fell silent and went for the first-aid kit, passing it to Alan without a word. Alan accepted it with a nod, murmuring comforting nonsense to Mae as he taped the cut across her cheek carefully closed. Mae stopped fighting to get up and bore the taping without a sound, and Nick watched her whisper reassurance back to Alan, watched their shared smiles.

"I'm really okay. Thanks," Mae murmured, low and grateful, Alan's musician's fingers held lightly against the curve of her jaw. "He turned into a freaking bird. I couldn't believe it!" Her voice turned frustrated. "I couldn't stop him. I couldn't do a thing."

"It's not your fault," Alan assured her.

He was right. There was nothing she could have done. If Gerald could transform into an animal, he had a whole lot more power than Nick had thought. He had so much power that it must mean he'd wanted to be captured.

He'd wanted to be brought here.

They'd been played for fools. And that wasn't even the worst part.

Nick gazed with building fury at his brother, bent solicitously over Mae and acting so very concerned.

He said, "You did this."

Alan stood up at once. "Come outside," he said, in that calm, reasonable voice of his. Nick strode forward and grabbed Alan's elbow, dragging him to the front door and only stopping when his brother almost fell on the threshold.

He steadied Alan with his free hand and then stepped back. For a moment his throat was too tight to find words.

"You did this," he repeated at last.

He remembered Alan's face, smoothing into a bland mask when Nick refused to let him take Jamie's mark off. *We'll only be gone a minute. I don't want you in any danger.* He'd been worried, and he'd used that to make Nick do exactly what he wanted.

Once he'd brought Nick upstairs, he'd kept him upstairs with that little line about Jamie. He'd known Nick would argue with him.

He'd deliberately let the magician go, and now he was facing Nick with that careful look on his face, trying to calm Nick down without actually giving anything away, waiting to see what lie would work this time.

"What do you mean?"

"I mean that you got the only two people capable of restraining that magician out of the room! You did it, and you did it on purpose, because you wanted to keep the demon's mark that is going to kill you. I know all that. I just don't know why. And I want to know why, Alan. I'm going to know why."

Alan looked at Nick's face and obviously saw that denials weren't going to do him any good.

"Because of what that messenger said," he answered quietly. "Because I have a plan. Would you rather I didn't have one?"

Nick grabbed the collar of Alan's shirt and pushed him up against the door frame with one hand.

"I'd rather you didn't get yourself killed!"

Alan looked up at him, pale and silent, and Nick realized how this would look to anyone watching. A crippled boy, stumbling and obviously upset, being menaced by a vicious thug. He *felt* vicious; he would've hit Alan if that would have made him stop.

Only he knew his brother. Pain didn't scare him, and nothing could make him stop.

"Mum's not worth this," he snarled. "Nothing's worth this."

"Some things are."

Nick did not shake him, no matter how much he was

tempted. He let go of his brother's shirt and stepped back. He thought Alan looked a little relieved.

"It won't take long for Gerald to report back to the Obsidian Circle," Nick said. "They'll be coming soon. We can't be here. Do you have a plan for that?"

He glared at his brother, and Alan looked back, pained but still calm, still plotting something.

"I do," said Alan. "I told you I needed to see what Merris was experimenting with. She lives on the Isle of Wight. We can go there. We can escape the magicians that way."

Nick looked away from him then, leaning his cheek against the steel door frame and looking out onto the narrow grey street, just another street among the hundreds of streets he had lived on and would never see again. Alan was still thinking about the best way to help Mum, and then it would be the best way to help Jamie, and all Nick wanted to do was take Alan and run. If they kept moving, maybe the magicians wouldn't get a chance to put the last mark on Alan and finish him off. Nick didn't care about anything else.

He opened his mouth and could not find words.

Alan held him in that moment of silence with a look.

"Nick," he said quietly. "I'm going. You can't stop me. If you raise a hand to me I'll shoot you in the leg. I'm going to Merris's because I need her help and nothing you can say will change my mind. You don't have to come with me."

"Yes I do," Nick snapped.

What a stupid thing for Alan to say. They had never been separated for longer than those few days last Christmas; Nick always knew where Alan was and usually knew that he was close. That was how things were and how they were going to stay. Alan was his brother, and if he was set on carrying out his little plan, risking himself to save Mum, then Nick had to be with him to make sure he was safe.

Alan looked almost too worn out to smile but he did anyway, a faint, sweet smile that lingered in his eyes. "All right."

He nodded slightly, as if they were businessmen who had come to an understanding. Then he turned and went back into the hall, limping a little more than usual, as if he was carrying something heavy. Nick followed him. It was clear that Alan needed to be watched. He'd meant what he'd told Alan: He would sacrifice Mum if he had to.

It didn't matter what Alan wanted. It only mattered that Alan lived.

The House of Mezentius

THEY WERE ALL IN THE CAR FIVE MINUTES LATER, abandoning everything that would not fit into the couple of old schoolbags they had in the boot. Nick had secured his new favourite sword at his belt, and Alan had slipped his family pictures, and the book he still thought had the hidden picture inside, into one of the bags.

"What's that?" Nick had said, perversely wanting to see Alan lie to him.

"Just something I'm reading," Alan answered with a wry, plausible smile. Nick was suddenly reminded of Gerald the magician and had to turn away.

Now Camden was passing them by so fast that streets and lights had turned into a multicoloured river, flashing yellow and orange over a smooth stream of grey.

Nick turned the car south towards the M3, hearing a clank as he moved into fourth. He'd have to see to the car sometime, though it was unlikely they would have time for mechanics in the near future.

It would take about two hours to get to Southampton if they were lucky with traffic, and then they could take the ferry to the Isle of Wight.

Nick was still thinking about the traffic when Alan said in a soft voice, "Nick, you get horribly seasick."

"Don't be ridiculous," Nick said.

He didn't remember ever being on a boat. Running from magicians did not leave a lot of time for sailing the high seas, but the idea sounded implausible. Nick was never sick, and even if he had been, they were hardly going to change their plans because of a tiny thing like seasickness. He wasn't letting Alan go off on his own.

"We took you on a boat once when you were little, and it was—" Alan bit his lip. "You coughed up blood. I thought you were going to die."

"I didn't," Nick pointed out. "And if I was little, I imagine I've grown out of it by now." He glanced over at Alan, whose profile was tense and unhappy. If Alan was so concerned about him, he thought, he might try telling him the truth once in a while instead of wasting time protecting him from boats.

Mae, Jamie and Mum were silent in the back seat. After about an hour along the M3 and into the gathering night, Nick glanced in the mirror and saw Mum looking at him, her gaze steady and cold.

Alan seemed so ready to die to save her. Nick couldn't understand it, and he wasn't about to let it happen.

The ferry at Southampton's second terminal was a huge white and red edifice, more like a tin house floating on the water than a boat. There seemed to be a jolly cloud painted on one side, as if they were all off on a day trip to the beach.

There were very few other passengers at this time of night. They waited until everyone else was aboard; nobody was in the mood to deal with strangers, Nick least of all. He strode onboard last, lagging behind even Alan's limping step, and walked towards the railing at the side of the ferry as the whistle blew. He lifted his face to the cold wind and hoped everyone would understand that he wanted to be left alone.

The boat lurched as it set off. Nick felt his stomach tilt with it, and a moment of dizziness passed over him, a disoriented feeling similar to that of standing up too fast and having all the blood rush to your head. He deliberately did not look at the grey expanse of water, leaning heavily against the railing and clenching his hand hard around it. He squeezed the metal so tightly his knuckles went white and his fingers ached, and he concentrated on the pain. Having a focus cleared his head.

He felt the plunge of the hull against the waves in the pit of his stomach. He tried to count the waves but they kept coming, a succession of waves battering the boat, the whole sea nothing but currents under relentless currents.

Mae left Mum's side to come and stand in front of Nick. Her face wavered in front of his eyes, bobbing as if she was underwater.

"Are you all right?" she asked. "We've only been moving for a minute and the sea's calm, but you've gone all green. Do you want to go below deck, or . . . maybe you'd like a basin?"

"Don't be stupid," Nick said roughly, and tried to let go of the railing. His hands felt oddly numb, as if they did not belong to him, and then the boat creaked over another wave and he staggered, almost going down on his knees. Consciousness seemed to be sliding across the deck and away from him.

Alan turned, as if that was a cue he'd been waiting for, and moved towards Nick. The way he limped did not synchronise with the way the boat rocked, and for a moment Alan seemed like the only still point in a world full of endless sickening motion. Nick tried to hold on. Soon Alan could get to him and tell him what was happening.

The world was moving so much it was blurring into a meaningless mess of colour and sound. There was a moment of small centralised pain, someone's fingernails digging into Nick's skin, and someone's voice, high, saying: "Alan, Jamie! *Quick—*"

The world fell away as if the boat had tipped over and left them in the crashing darkness of the sea. There was nothing but darkness and confusion for a long moment, until Nick realised he was lying on the deck and retching, as if he had really been underwater and he had to cough up water to live. He did not taste water in his mouth, only the sharp bitterness of bile.

Bitterness only lasted an instant, though. Nick was used to being in complete command of his body, being strong and able to use all his strength. It was odd now, he thought in a drifting sort of way, to feel so helpless, to be so disconnected from his body. He was only sure that he had a body because of a strange pain that seemed part of the disconnection and because he was so cold.

"Nick," said Alan's voice, compelling and comforting at once.

Slowly, through the chill, Nick felt his hand held tight in Alan's, his cheek pressed against the rough denim covering Alan's knee. He became aware of his head as his own, a distinct shape, because of his brother's hand stroking his hair.

"Nick," Alan said again. "It's all right, Nick."

It was all right. Nick thought about this and decided that what Alan said was true. He'd never been helpless before, not since he could remember, but now he was and everything was all right. He didn't normally let people touch him, but he could not stop it now. He did not have to speak, he was not able to move, all he could do was lie there and have his brother hold him, hunched over and shielding him from the world. His brother's hand was light in his hair, his arm circling Nick's shoulders as well as he could, and his voice in Nick's ear was a warm soothing lifeline in the midst of the cold hissing of all the currents in the sea.

"Hold on, Nick. It's only twenty minutes until we get there. Just hold on."

Nick tried to do what Alan wanted and hold on to his brother's hand, but he couldn't feel his fingers properly. He looked, though, and Alan was still holding Nick's hand, so perhaps that would be enough to make Alan happy. Nick vomited again, too cold and far away to care. He pressed his forehead against the inside of his brother's wrist and let the drowning darkness pull him down again.

When he was next aware of anything, it was of being in a car that was jolting to a stop. His vision was hazy and he looked around desperately, as if by jerking his head hard enough he could make himself see, but then he realised that Alan was still holding his hand.

"Alan," he mumbled, and the orange light of a streetlamp caught Alan's glasses. The flash dimmed and Nick saw Alan's face bending over him in the flickering shadows. "Where are we?"

"We're in a taxi going from West Cowes to Carisbrooke village," Alan answered softly, as if he was talking nonsense words to a child he was very fond of. "We're going to Merris's house. How are you feeling?"

"As if my body doesn't belong to me," Nick said.

"I'm sorry for bringing you onto that boat."

Nick levered himself up on one elbow. "Not your fault. You warned me, I just didn't think I was pathetic enough to collapse because of a little queasiness."

"You're an idiot," said Alan, relaxing enough to smile at him. "But you're not pathetic."

There was a flicker of movement in the corner of Nick's eye. He looked around sharply, dropping Alan's hand, and saw Jamie and Mae sitting on the flip-down leather seats opposite them. He realised properly for the first time that they really were in a cab. He looked beyond the clouded glass to see the tired profile of the cab driver and the black fall of Mum's hair in the passenger seat.

"How are you feeling, Nick?" Jamie inquired, shifting uneasily on his seat. He and Mae looked rather alike just now, both staring at him with wide, frightened eyes. He recognised with a shock the fact that they both looked worried.

"Can you walk?" asked Mae, being more practical. "We're here."

He nodded, and Mae opened the car door. Nick got out, straightened, and did not know what was keeping him up. When he looked down, it was his legs and feet as usual.

There was a high stone wall in front of them and an ornate gate. The stones in the wall glittered with mica. The iron of the gate was shaped into trees and snakes and women. The whole purpose of the walls and gate seemed to be decoration, but this was simply a distraction from the fact that the walls were very high and there were wicked-looking spikes on the gate. There was jagged glass gleaming on top of the walls, almost hidden by the leaves of trees behind them. It reminded Nick of Liannan, with her curtain of hair and sharp teeth.

He had to lean against the cab. He should not have stood up so soon; he tried to move and Alan was beside him. Nick must have been sagging, because he was eye level with the first button on Alan's shirt.

"Mae, help me," Alan ordered, and Mae was suddenly at Nick's side.

Nick dimly approved of Alan's choice. Mae was certainly better able to bear his weight than Jamie, and as for Mum, who was taller and stronger than either of them, she would not have touched Nick no matter who asked. Then his head lolled forward, his neck feeling like a thick tube of spaghetti. He was not going to be sick again; he just wanted to lie down until he remembered how to work his own body.

"Jamie," Alan said, his voice soothing for Nick's benefit, even though he was speaking to someone else. "Go and press the intercom button. Say 'My name is one.'"

"One?" Jamie asked, blinking. "One what?"

"Jamie! Nick is going to fall over!"

"Right. I'm sorry," said Jamie, shaking his head and stepping backwards, almost walking into the tree and turning to scurry towards the gate. Nick heard his voice, seeming much farther away than it should have, saying that his name was one.

The gate swung open stiffly, as if it did not open often. Beyond was a garden with trees weighed down by their late-May green burdens, and crazy paving that stretched on until it was lost from view.

They went slowly down the garden path, Nick's awareness of what was going on ebbing and fading with every step. The garden was a wild tangle that had clearly been left to decay for years; briars formed nightmare patterns against Nick's eyelids as his eyes closed. Alan's voice cut across his consciousness, saying his name, and Nick opened his eyes again with an effort.

In front of them now was a large white house, rising above them like a sheer white cliff. It was so large that it seemed to demand decoration, the decency of pillars and balconies, but here behind the gates there was no such pretence. There was only the severe white building, stretching up five floors. Above the large door were letters raised in gold.

The words swam before Nick's eyes, gleaming fish that wanted to escape and would not form a coherent pattern, and then they stilled. Nick could feel his body now and it felt heavy, so heavy that he could not hold himself up.

The gold letters stayed for a moment, pinned up against the blackness, when his eyelids dropped and he fell forward.

THE HOUSE OF MEZENTIUS, the shining words read, and below that: THEIR NAME IS LEGION.

Nick woke in darkness to the sound of screams.

The darkness he solved by reaching out and turning on the lamp on the table beside his bed, but the screams were different. He sat up, noting with relief that his muscles and sinews now remembered they were his and obeyed him. He slipped out of the tangled embrace of sheets to have a look around. The room had a high ceiling, and little scalloped bits at the corners of said ceiling. His bed was big, with a carved oak headboard.

The screams were faint. Nick judged that they were muffled by thick walls, rather than all that far away.

The heavy door, also polished oak, slid open. Nick reached for a sword that was not there and was glad to see Alan. He was also glad to see that Alan had his sword.

Alan smiled, laugh lines leaping out from the corners of his eyes. "I see you're feeling better." He threw Nick a little heap of fabric, which Nick unfolded and saw was a shirt, the crisp buttoned kind you should wear with a suit. He was about to refuse it when he glanced down at his T-shirt and saw that it was stained with vomit and blood. He didn't want to know if he'd hacked up blood. He just changed shirts.

Once he had done so, he gestured around at the room. "All this is very posh."

"It's Merris Cromwell's house."

Nick supposed that made sense. Everybody knew Merris had money, even though he hadn't known she had this much.

"Where are the others?"

Alan looked pleased that he'd asked. "Nearby. Mum's asleep, Merris gave her something to calm her down, but the others are wondering how you are. We've all been put in the north wing, so we're pretty close together. Do you want to go and see them?"

Nick shrugged, and Alan led the way. The north wing seemed to be mostly corridors so wide they almost qualified as rooms, the walls sleek and white and the wooden floors all dark from years and polish. They found Mae and Jamie in a room reminiscent of Nick's, with the same solemn-looking bed and crenulated ceiling. Jamie was sitting cross-legged on the bed, and Mae was pacing across a fluffy white rug that looked like a decapitated polar bear.

"We should go and check on him," she said as Nick opened the door.

Jamie nodded in his direction. "I think he's probably all right."

Mae looked around and did not blush. Nick liked that, the

way she felt no need to pretend either indifference or exaggerated concern. She just nodded at him.

He was not used to big houses like this. He was used to small, shabby houses and flats, places with so few rooms and such thin walls that he always knew where Alan was. Now he was in wide open spaces under vaulted ceilings, and he was noticing too many things about this girl. The strangeness of it all made him feel irritated and uncomfortable. He slouched against the wall and looked deliberately through Mae. After a few moments she moved away from the coldness of his fixed gaze, towards Alan.

It didn't make Nick feel any better. He felt restless suddenly, and as he tuned out the others' voices and wished for something to do, he registered again the sound that had woken him. Coming to him through heavy doors and solid walls, through all the expensive privacy of this house, were faint but unmistakable screams.

It was obvious that the rest of them couldn't hear it. He should probably tell Alan.

"There is someone being tortured in this house."

Alan gave a guilty start, and it was clear to Nick that he at least already knew.

"That's not entirely true," he said hastily.

"*Tortured?*" exclaimed Jamie.

Nick shrugged. "Sounds like that to me."

"Alan," Mae said, in a tone of command rather than appeal. "Where are we?"

Alan looked defeated already, as if some terrible fate was rushing upon them, something as impossible to reason with or escape from as a storm spilling darkness across the sky.

"This is the House of Mezentius," he said.

"That's what it said above the door," Nick agreed. "Who's Mezentius?"

Alan seemed to be having trouble with the words. "He was an Etruscan king in a legend," he said slowly. "He had living people bound face-to-face with dead bodies and left to starve."

"He sounds a charming host," said Nick. "I thought you said this was Merris Cromwell's house."

"Merris runs the house," Alan answered in a low voice. "It's her job to organise everything here, to keep everything . . . contained."

"Well she's not doing a very good job, is she?" Jamie exclaimed. "If there's someone being tortured in here."

"That person's here of their own free will," Alan told him.

His eyes looked more bruised and sad with every word dragged out of him, and Nick felt the impulse to silence all the questions that were hurting his brother. He'd always trusted Alan to know best, trusted that Alan would sooner or later tell Nick everything he needed to know. He thought of that hidden picture, though, and about him letting that magician go. There were some things Alan never said anything about. He wondered what secret Alan was hiding this time.

He kept quiet, and let Mae and Jamie keep pushing for answers.

"Do you know the person who's screaming?"

"Why would someone come here to be tortured?"

Mae demanded, "Can't you just show us what's going on?"

Alan looked almost grey. "I can," he said. "But you don't want to see. I swear, you don't want to see."

There was another slight movement of unease in Nick's gut. He could still shut them both up.

He hesitated a second too long and gave Mae the chance to make up her own mind.

"Let me decide that for myself. I want to see."

Alan walked down the staircase heavily, as if he was carrying a large burden that he did not expect to be able to put down for some time. Mae walked with a firm step beside him, Jamie was hanging back, and Nick became more and more convinced that he did not like this place.

The staircase was wide, a gleaming marble flight of the kind that women swept down in the sappy movies Alan liked. Only instead of leading to a ballroom, it ended in a hall with the same dark polished floors and severe white walls as the corridors in the north wing. Nick kept trying to work out why this place jarred on him so much, and then he got it. The north wing with its four-poster beds and fancy ceilings was a disguise, and this house was as much of a facade as the decorative gate outside.

This was not a stately home. This place was an institution.

The screaming was getting closer.

After a moment's analysis, Nick decided that it was just one person screaming. It was a woman, and she sounded young, or at least not old. The hall opened into more corridors as they went along, and Nick was amazed that he had not realised before how clinical the corridors were, perfectly upkept, with no pictures or even creaking old radiators to lend them personality. They passed a few simple wooden doors, but Alan kept going, and their little group silently followed him.

Everyone could hear the screams now.

They turned a corner in the winding passageways and the screams suddenly had a definite location. They were coming from a large metal door down the corridor, on the left. There were no other curves remaining in the corridor, and Nick saw it stretching on into dimness. Glinting at intervals in the dimness were other metallic doors, armoured so they bulged out of their door frames, looking forbidding and utterly out of place.

As they drew level with the first metallic door, the screaming stopped.

The scream was cut off so abruptly Nick thought that the person screaming must have died. There was a small window in the door, though, wire forming tiny squares inside two sheets of glass, and when they peered inside they saw no dead bodies.

There were two people in the room. There was a woman kneeling on the floor, and there was a man chained to a wall.

Nick's first reaction was disbelief. This house might be an institution, but it was clearly civilised and organised. It seemed unbelievable that these quiet corridors could lead to dungeons.

Then he looked at the prisoner properly.

At first sight he was a normal man. His face was deeply lined and his body was stooped in his chains, so he looked old even though most of his hair was brown. He wore old clothes, and a beard covered most of his face.

As they all stood staring, the man's flat black eyes darted towards the window in the door. His expression did not change.

His eyes did. They bulged in his eye sockets, bulged until they seemed to bulge *out* of his eye sockets, and then Nick realised they were not bulging at all. The man's eyes had seemed almost like normal eyes at first, but now the pupils expanded as if someone had tipped ink into two saucers and filled them from edge to edge with shiny black.

The black ovals that had been his eyes were lifting themselves out of his eye sockets, showing little legs, and in the space of a few seconds there was a fat black beetle emerging from each socket. They crawled down the man's face like tears.

Jamie screamed, the sound shuddering into a moan, and there was movement in the corner of Nick's eye that suggested he and Mae were clinging to each other. At Nick's side he could feel Alan trembling. Nick was distantly aware that he should be shocked himself, but he'd seen a lot of things in his life worse than this. He kept watching with calm interest, and the man's face sharpened as if he was a dog who had caught a scent. There was a long moment where Nick was sure that somehow the man could see him.

The man winked, his wrinkled eyelid flicking over the raw hollow of his eye socket. Nick hesitated for a second, and then winked back.

One of the fat black beetles reached the man's chin and dropped into the kneeling woman's hair. She looked up and shook the beetle onto the floor with a convulsive tremor, but aside from that initial movement of automatic disgust, she did not seem surprised. She looked to be in her mid-twenties, with thick chestnut hair and brimming eyes. Nick wondered what had made her scream.

"I see you've met Ruth and Thomas," said Merris Cromwell, her voice ringing clear and calm against the corridor walls. She spoke as if she was introducing people at a cocktail party.

"Met Ruth and—? What the hell is wrong with that man?" Jamie demanded, his voice unusually ferocious. He strode towards Merris, and Nick noticed that his shoulders were shaking. He imagined from the way Jamie was behaving that he already knew what was wrong with the man and was doing his best not to believe what he knew.

Merris walked down the corridor as if she could not see Jamie, and at the last moment before a collision was inevitable Jamie stepped aside. "Let me see," she said. "Mute, with no trace of his former personality remaining, and with the ability to manipulate anything in the natural world, including his own body. I shall take a wild leap and say that he's possessed."

Jamie's body snapped back as if he had been punched. "Possessed." He jerked his head towards all the other metal doors, glinting along the corridor until the light was not sufficient enough for them to see and the doors went on in darkness. "Are you saying that behind every door there's someone—"

"Unless one of them has died since yesterday." Merris's wide grey eyes moved past Jamie and looked over them all. She obviously saw something in one of their faces that irritated her, because her lip curled and she demanded in her turn, "Have none of you ever given a moment's thought to what happens to the possessed?"

None of them had an answer for her. Merris waited for a moment so they could all be fully aware of that and went on.

"A mute, magically powerful creature replaces an ordinary person overnight. You can't imagine that passes unnoticed. If the possessed has a family, they soon notice the change. They're horrified, and they have nobody to help them. Except us."

She smiled. "We have these new magical circles specifically designed to confine a demon who has acquired a human body. We have containment facilities. If people come to us with tales of possessed friends and relatives, we do not talk about mental illness and we do not disbelieve in the demon's power. Mezentius House is the only place these desperate people can turn, and of course, we obey the businesslike laws of supply and demand. They pay well for our help."

"They're people in trouble!" Jamie cried, wiping his mouth as if he'd eaten something bad and could not rub away the taste.

Nick thought suddenly of what that magician Gerald had said, that the Market was funded with blood money. This was why everyone obeyed Merris Cromwell. This money was what helped the Market people—helped *them*—find houses and transfer to new schools and jobs quickly.

The money was paid by the families of people who'd been possessed, like Jamie might be. Like Alan might be. He wondered what Sin would think of this.

Merris raised her eyebrows. "So are the people who go to hospitals, and they have to pay. There are a lot of hospitals. There is only one Mezentius House."

Thoughts of Alan aside, it did not sound unreasonable to Nick. Those who dealt in magic had their own private economy, and Merris had worked out how to manipulate it in her favour. There was just one thing he didn't understand.

He cleared his throat. "Why don't you kill them all?"

"The relatives seem curiously reluctant to have the possessed killed. Particularly once I explain to them that their loved one is inside somewhere, unable to regain control of their body. Their friends and family want them controlled but not harmed. They pray for miracles. Sometimes they insist on staying with them, hoping to ease their pain." Merris shrugged. "That costs extra."

"The magical circles you keep the possessed in," Alan said with what appeared to be scientific interest. "How different are they from normal magicians' circles? Can you command a demon in them? Could you summon one?"

"I cannot imagine why we would want to. We have quite enough to do with the demons we have. I consider keeping them confined the most important part," said Merris dryly. "Since you came all this way to insist on answers, I have a few diagrams I can show you that detail how our circles work."

"I'd appreciate that," said Alan.

"They're very basic," Merris said. "You can't summon a demon into them. We haven't even worked out a way to make communication lines work for them. Almost the only thing we can do is keep them trapped."

"What if a dancer was involved?" Alan asked, frowning. "Speaking purely academically, of course."

Nick wondered if Alan had some sort of plan for trapping the demons the magicians sent after them. It didn't sound like it would work.

Mae and Jamie were still staring into the cell with horrified fascination, and after a moment, Mae spoke.

"Does a miracle ever happen? I mean, if you have them trapped – does the demon ever leave?"

"No demon ever leaves," Merris said. "No matter what happens to them, they prefer our world to theirs. But people keep hoping, right until the end."

She nodded casually to the window in the metal door. They all watched, as if the window was a television and the scene had been designed for them to see, while chestnut-haired Ruth climbed stiffly to her feet. She put her hand to Thomas's face, and Thomas – did not blink, exactly. His eyes flickered as if he had multiple eyelids, like a cat, and when his eyes were open they were normal eyes again. He watched the woman with his flat gaze and under his eyes a cut opened on her cheek. She moaned and held her hand to her face, and he looked at her arm. Another gash opened there, as if his travelling eyes were knives.

"Don't worry," Merris told them. "The demon's using all the magic he can think of to make her let him out, but he won't damage her permanently. He knows she's the only one who will feed him."

Moving like an old woman, Ruth replaced her hand against the possessed Thomas's face. She stroked his cheek briefly, and Nick saw her lips move, though he could not make out what she was saying. It had never occurred to Nick before that communication lines could not be drawn for a demon possessing a human. He'd known that possessed people did not speak. Now, watching the possessed body watch the woman with reptilian blankness, he realised that the demon really could not understand.

The woman kept talking, even though it was pointless. Nick thought he made out the word "love" when she spoke, but he could have been wrong.

Mae said, trying and failing to repress a tremor in her voice, "Is she his daughter?"

"Oh no, my dear," Merris said absently. "The man's young. His body's tearing itself apart trying to fight the demon; he didn't look like this a week ago. She's his wife."

The demon who looked like Thomas smiled at his wife, and then his tongue darted out and caught the other beetle that had once been his eye. It made a soft, sickening sound between his teeth. The woman gagged, and he kept grinning.

"He's just trying to scare her," said Merris, her voice still clinical and uninterested. "A demon will try to manipulate a human any way it can. Don't worry. She knows better than to be fooled."

Ruth put a hand to her own mouth and started to cry.

Nick rather expected Jamie to turn and bolt, but it was Alan who did so.

One moment he was by Nick's side, still and quiet as he was when he was upset and turning in on himself, but in control. The next he was limping as fast as he could down the corridor, back in the direction they had come, away from the metal doors hiding the demons.

Nick should have looked at Alan; he should have made sure he wasn't upset. Alan could usually handle himself, but this was different. Alan was carrying a second-tier mark. Alan was thinking of his future.

Nick considered waiting for Mae to offer to go after him. That would please Alan, he thought, but Mae did not offer. Nick glanced at her and saw her standing close by Jamie, feet planted apart as if she was going to wrestle someone, looking furiously concerned. She did not want to leave her brother.

That was fine by Nick. He didn't want to leave his brother either.

"Don't come after us," he said curtly, and spun around and after Alan.

Mae would probably be better at comforting Alan than he would. Jamie would probably be better at it. Nick did not have the slightest idea what to do, but Alan was his brother and no one else's, and he would think of something.

He found Alan in a bathroom, stooped over the sink and looking like he was going to be sick. The water was running, and Alan was splashing his face frantically. He looked up and saw Nick at the mirror. Nick looked at his own stone-faced reflection and Alan's almost frightened eyes.

"Alan," he said, his voice rough.

Alan closed his eyes. "What?"

Nick advanced cautiously, wishing this was as simple as creeping up on someone to kill them. "You okay?"

He wondered if other people ever realised how stupid half the things they said were. Alan was shaking and scared and obviously not okay, but Nick had to ask because that was what you asked, and no matter how stupid the usual words sounded, Nick had no words of his own to offer.

"I might be okay," said Alan, who told lies.

He looked down again, into the basin of the sink and away from their reflections. There were dark circles under Alan's eyes, Nick saw in the cold, uncompromising picture the mirror gave him, and deep lines around his mouth. He was so much paler than he had been even a week ago. It made Nick think of the demon they'd left behind, in a body that had looked young last week.

"Don't," he said, and cleared his throat. "You don't need to worry." He had to drag every word out. "It won't happen to you. I won't let it."

"That's not why," Alan said, but his shoulders relaxed.

This encouraged Nick to go over to him, but once he was there he could only hang uselessly over his brother. Alan was the one who was good at this stuff, who was always hair ruffling or shoulder patting. Gestures like that did not come naturally to Nick, any more than comforting words did.

"Sure it's not," Nick said, trying hard to make his voice gentle. It cracked and came out sounding harsh.

He sat on the floor with his back against the wall, and after a moment Alan gave a sigh that was either tired or resigned. Nick kept his head bowed as Alan's hand settled on his neck, palm gun-callused, and rested there.

Nick had never seen the point of just touching people, but if this made Alan feel better, he supposed it wasn't so bad.

"Why did we come here?" he asked.

"I wanted to see the possessed patients," Alan answered, his voice low. "But I didn't want you to see them. I didn't want any of you to see."

"It's all right," Nick said, trying to be comforting. "They didn't bother me."

He glanced up at Alan, and Alan did not look comforted. He looked as if he was exhausted and in pain.

Nick felt a sharp pang of frustration, like when he'd been younger and teachers had asked him to read aloud or girls had expected some sort of gesture from him, but a thousand times worse because this was his brother and it mattered.

"I'll protect you," he said at last, awkwardly. He felt stupid saying it; Alan already knew that he would.

Alan looked a little steadier, all the same. "I'm counting on it."

"Good," said Nick. "You'll be okay. I'll protect you. Don't – don't be upset any more."

Alan made a soft sound, trembling between a breath and a laugh. "I'm not upset."

"You liar," Nick mumbled.

Alan stroked his hair just once, and then drew his hand away. "I'm okay now," he said. "Really."

It sounded true, sounded like something Nick could believe. He remembered feeling peaceful on the boat, just trusting Alan, and it seemed like something he could do again.

Nick's mobile rang. He cursed and half rose in order to fish it out of his jeans, and then looked blankly at the number that appeared on the screen.

"Who the . . . ?" He shrugged and made to cut them off.

"Probably one of your many admirers," Alan said. "Go ahead, answer it. I'm all right, I promise. I'll be out in a minute."

Nick had been busy lately. He didn't remember giving his number out to any girls, but if Alan wanted a moment, he should have it. Nick scrambled to his feet, lingered for an instant wondering if he should say anything, and ended up just nodding at his brother. Alan smiled at Nick as he went out of the door, and he answered the phone in a good mood. Whoever the girl was, he'd pretend to remember her.

"Hey," he said easily.

There was a brief pause, and then a sharp inhale, and a woman's voice. "Hello," she said. "Is this the person who put Marie's picture in the paper?"

"Yeah. Who's this?"

Nick spoke automatically, so she wouldn't go away before he had a chance to think.

"My name is Natasha Walsh," the woman said. "Marie was my sister."

"She's dead?" Nick rapped out.

He felt nothing but satisfaction at the thought. She was dead then, that smiling blonde girl, and if she was dead she could not lay claim to his brother. He had what he wanted. He almost hung up on her then.

The woman spoke an instant before he did. "Look," she said, and then her words tumbled out, so fast they all rolled together. "Is this about Alan? Is he all right? I haven't seen him since last Christmas."

The way she talked about Alan sounded personal. Nobody whom Nick had never heard of before in his life should be able to talk about his brother like that.

"Last Christmas," Nick repeated.

So Nick's half-suspicion had been true: Alan had gone away and left them for that dead girl. He'd lied about having to do a translation; he'd left Nick in a cold, dark house that felt abandoned, with Mum rocking upstairs. Nick wanted to know why he'd done it. He wanted to know exactly what this girl had been to Alan.

He put a hand to the back of his neck, his own grip stronger and rougher than Alan's, and thought about trusting his brother.

"Look," he said abruptly. "This isn't a good time. Can I – I'll call you back."

He turned the phone off before she could speak again. Then he weighed it, small and stupid-looking in his big hand. He didn't know why he even had a phone, he thought; he never wanted to call anybody.

He did know why, of course. Alan had given him the phone, and he'd kept it because he knew it made Alan feel better to know that he could get in touch with Nick whenever he wanted and check that he was safe.

Nick slid the phone into his pocket and came to a decision. He'd go to Alan and tell him everything. Nick had been hiding things too, but he'd tell Alan that he knew about Marie and what he'd done to find out more. Alan would understand that the secrets and lies had to stop.

He wasn't in the bathroom where Nick had left him. Nick frowned and began to retrace their steps, going slowly back towards where they'd left Mae and Jamie. He was only halfway down the corridor when he was caught and held by the sound of his brother's voice behind a door.

"I knew he'd be sick," Alan said. "That didn't matter."

Nick had been about to open the door, and now he found himself staring at it instead.

"It seems a lot of things haven't mattered to you," said the voice of Merris Cromwell.

There was a small pause, and Alan replied, "I don't regret anything I've done."

Alan had been set on coming here, and Nick had been set on following him. He would have done it no matter what, but the thought that Alan had cold-bloodedly accepted that Nick would be ill made him feel an uneasy shift in his stomach, as if he was still sick. He couldn't connect the image of his brother Alan – who'd raised him, packed his school lunches, and used to sit on the edge of Nick's bed like a small, ferociously patient owl, waiting for him to fall asleep – with the dispassionate voice behind the door.

"You may not regret it, but the Market will resent it," Merris Cromwell said, her voice low and cold. "If we had known, we would never have let you come among us. You'll never be welcome there again."

Alan had told Merris about Mum. Nick should have felt something about that, but he didn't. He felt nothing. He stood in the cold, echoing corridor unable to make sense of anything.

"Do you think I care?" Alan demanded. "Can you help me or not?"

"I can't help you, and I'm glad I can't," Merris said icily. "Don't look to the Market for help from now on. Everyone's hand will be turned against you. You're on your own."

Nick heard Alan make a sound he recognised, a soft, shaky breath; hurt but pulling himself together. "I thought I would be. I know what I have to do, then. Thank you."

"Don't thank me," Merris said. "Don't do this." There was

a real note of pain in her voice suddenly, as if she'd thought she knew Alan, as if she'd believed in Alan like Nick had. "Take my advice, Alan. Nobody ever needs to know about this. Hand it over to the magicians. Walk away."

It was good advice, Market advice. Nobody from the Market would have shielded a magician, or been suicidal enough to openly defy a Circle. Nick wished Alan would take it. If he'd just give up on Mum and give away the charm, Mum would die – but she'd been a magician, and she deserved to die. With the threat of a whole Circle after them lifted, he could protect Alan. They could get that mark off.

But apparently he didn't know Alan any more than Merris did.

"Take my advice, Merris," Alan said in a voice twice as cold as hers. "Don't ever suggest anything like that to me again."

Merris's voice was a low hiss. "Get out of my house."

"No," said Alan. "First I want you to arrange somewhere else for us to live."

"And why should I do that?"

"Because I still have contacts in the Market," Alan told her. "You may spread your stories about me, and some will believe you, but I'm the sweet, studious boy that everybody likes. You're the mystery. Nobody knows where you get your money from, and I don't think many people will approve of you leeching money from the helpless victims of magicians and using it to gain power in our Market. Because that's the way I'll spin it, Merris. And people will believe me. I can make people trust me; you should know that. Even you did."

"Believe me, I'm regretting it now." Merris's voice snapped into her usual tones, cool and bargaining. "A house is the price of your silence? So be it. You and yours will be out of my home by morning. And you'd better keep your part of the bargain, or I'll have you killed."

"Done," said Alan, in the exact same tone. Then his voice softened. "I'm sorry I have to do this."

There was no hint of yielding in Merris's voice. "You don't have to do this. You should give it up."

"I'm sorry," Alan said, his voice kind but firm, "but I've already done this and I'll do a lot worse. I will not give up. And if you can't help me, Merris, then get the hell out of my way."

Under any other circumstances, Nick would have found it funny: his brother blackmailing Merris of the Market and not turning a hair. He would've approved. Only now it was more proof of what Mum meant to Alan.

Mum and Marie, the girl in the picture. Alan wouldn't tell him his plans for saving Mum, and he hadn't even told him that Marie existed. Alan wouldn't tell him anything, but that didn't matter. Nick could find out the truth on his own.

He walked away from the door, back towards Mae and Jamie, and as he did so he took out his phone and rang the last listed call.

The same woman's voice answered, breathless and anxious. "Hello?"

"Can I come and see you?" he asked abruptly. "I know where Alan is. I'll tell you all about him. Give me your address."

Alan's blackmail must have been very successful indeed, since Merris not only found them a new home in London but provided them with her own boat back and gave Nick herbs to make him sleep through the voyage.

"Such concern for me," Nick said on the dock. His voice

was meant to be bitter, but it simply sounded cold. "I'm touched."

The others were standing in a little knot, trying to keep warm by staying close. It was not yet dawn, and the sea air hit Nick's face like a series of slaps with icy hands.

Alan was holding Mum's hand. She still looked groggy from whatever Merris had given her, and she stood leaning against Alan, the billowing black veil of her hair caught by the wind, flying and settling over them both. Alan was watching Nick, his face to all appearances honestly puzzled and hurt.

Nick was standing as far away from the others as he could without actually standing in the sea.

"There's a bedroom you can sleep in," Alan offered, his voice tentative. "I'll sit with you in case you need help."

"I don't need your help," said Nick curtly. He looked away from Alan and Mum, and his eyes settled on another face.

The sight and smell of the sea was already making him feel a little ill, that and the dread of being completely and humiliatingly helpless again curdling in his stomach. The sound of the wind was like the freezing shout of a hundred angry ghosts. Looking at his family only made him feel worse.

Looking at Mae made him feel a little steadier. She had her face tipped up to study his, determined dark eyes and a stubborn mouth. The way she looked was familiar to him by now, and the better he knew her, the better she looked. He smiled at her, a slow, deliberate smile that made an answering smile curve her lips.

"I'd rather have Mae nurse me," he drawled.

Even if he hadn't been able to see her, he would have heard the smile in her voice. "Yeah, all right."

That was when Merris's skipper, Philip, a man with the

close-clipped hair and charcoal-coloured suit of a business-man and the worn teeth and yellow tongue of a necromancer, gestured them aboard. The herbs Merris had given Nick were already making him feel a little dizzy, but that was almost a relief; his dread of coming aboard and his fury at Alan both felt distant, wrapped up safe until he could deal with them.

Soon he would be back on land and he would know all Alan's secrets. For now he could only stagger down the steps to reach the bedroom below deck, his hand fumbling at the doorknob. The room was circular at one end, the bed white and plain with shackles at each corner.

So this was how they transported the possessed. Nick went and lay back on the bed, thankful that he did not have to keep his feet any longer. He stared up at the wooden ceiling and heard Mae come in and shut the door.

"You don't need to use the restraints," Nick told the ceiling. "I'll be good."

Mae laughed. "But I was planning to do terrible things to you once I had you at my mercy."

"Oh," said Nick. "In that case, go right ahead."

"No, you've spoiled the moment now."

"Yeah," Nick muttered. "I do that a lot."

So many girls had started off looking at him all shiny-eyed and breathless, and then they'd all been disillusioned. Most had ended up scared. Mae had already been around longer than any of those girls, and she didn't scare easily, but of course it wasn't like that between them.

"Nick," Mae said, and hesitated.

It was rare enough for her to hesitate that Nick was intrigued. He levered himself up on his elbows and looked at her. She had her back up against the door, her pink hair mussed by the wind and her cheeks flushed. Which could have been another effect of the wind.

"I was wondering," Mae continued. "That girl at the Market. Sin. Are you going out with her?"

"No," said Nick. He didn't really have much else to say, but Mae was staring at the floor and looking embarrassed, so he went on. "I've never really gone out with anyone."

It had never particularly bothered him either. A night or two with a girl, and then having her go away and the next one come along: it had always seemed like an all-right way to do things.

Nick was surprised that she'd asked; not by the directness of it, because that was her style, but he was surprised that she'd wanted to know.

Since she had, it must mean – he was pretty sure that it did mean – that she preferred Nick. And if she really did . . .

Mae's eyebrows had come up. She was smiling a bit.

"Oh really," she said, her voice amused and incredulous. "A complete innocent, are you?"

"Definitely," Nick assured her, letting his voice slide low. "You can try corrupting me if you like."

Mae dimpled. "It's no fun if you're asking for it."

"No, no," Nick drawled. "Release me, you monster. Your wicked ways shock me to my soul. And yet I find you strangely attractive."

The boat purred into life, lurching away from the dock and swaying between one wave and the next. Nick shut his eyes in a brief flash of nausea.

"I feel I should warn you," he said after a moment. "I may be about to get sick or pass out."

"Uh," said Mae. "Sexy."

Funnily enough, it was this exciting news that peeled her off the door Nick had been starting to think she was glued to. She came to stand by the bed, pulling her iPod out of her pocket and fiddling with it, unwinding the earphones coiled around it.

"Maybe what you need is a distraction," she began.

On impulse Nick reached up and pulled her down to the bed. Mae made a startled sound, half breath and half laugh, and he rolled her over and under him easily, using his strength the way girls sometimes liked him to.

He looked down at her, then leaned in close, feeling her shiver at his breath on her ear, and murmured, "Maybe."

The morning sunlight was turning the cotton sheets into hot gold; he saw the flash in her eyes under suddenly heavy eyelids and smiled down at her. He was braced over her, his arms supporting his weight, and a sway of the ship and a breath lifted her hips against his. Her breath turned into a shiver, travelling slowly along the length of her body, and she lifted her hands and ran her palms along the tense swell of his arms.

He probably shouldn't be doing this. Alan liked her, and he might be angry with Alan now but he wouldn't be angry forever. Alan was his brother, and he shouldn't be doing this, but Alan had let him get sick and Mae preferred him.

It was all warm, white and gold and that absurd pink, the curves of her and the rumpled lines of the sheets, all blending and blurring together because he was starting to slip out of consciousness.

Mae pushed him gently backwards onto the pillows, and he went, throwing an arm over his eyes.

"I'd hate for you to get the wrong idea about me," he said.

"Under normal circumstances, I swear, I would have copped a feel."

"I was about to suggest that some music might be in order anyway," said Mae, valiantly pretending that she was not out of breath, her voice warm and trembling as she had been under him a moment ago.

She put one of the iPod earpieces in his ear, and the other presumably in her own, and settled back down on the pillows. The boat rocked them gently back and forth in a way that Nick might have found soothing if he hadn't felt so ill, and he fought to stay awake as he heard music that sounded in a faint far-away fashion like the drums of the Goblin Market.

"That's kind of nice."

"Maybe we can go and listen to them sometime," Mae murmured.

"Maybe," said Nick.

Mae was a warm weight that tilted him slightly to her side of the bed, possibly less because of her weight than because that was where he wanted to be. The sunlight painted dusty gold streaks against the blackness before Nick's closed eyes, and the drums beat in a rhythm with his heart. Mae had one foot tucked under his leg, and as he finally lost consciousness he felt her hand lightly pushing back a strand of his hair. It was pointless, but like the music, it was kind of nice.

The last thing he wondered was whether this counted as her asking him out.

11

Answers

THE STREET IN DURHAM WHERE MARIE'S SISTER LIVED
felt familiar to Nick. He was aware that he'd never been to
Durham before. He didn't recognise the city, but as he pulled
his battered car in line with the shining clean vehicles at the
pavement edge, it occurred to him that he knew the street.

It reminded him of Mae and Jamie's house, of the houses
belonging to school friends or girlfriends whose names Nick
did not now recall. There were neatly tended gardens, fresh
paint on the doors, and a general sense of well-being about
the whole area. Here, suggested the blooming flowerbeds,
people were comfortable, families were secure, and above all,
children were sheltered.

Nick knew it was an illusion. These people hurt each
other as much as all families did, and if magic ever invaded
their lives, they would be helpless.

Maybe it was an illusion Alan wanted, though. This
place was certainly a contrast to the shabby house Merris
had found for them yesterday, close to their old house so
they could hunt any magicians whom Gerald might direct
there. It was squeezed between a Chinese takeaway, bearing

a broken sign with letters that sizzled and flickered, and a derelict house, its boarded windows staring and blank as dead eyes.

Alan must have wanted more than the girl. He must have wanted a home like this. Nick looked at the house in the same way that he would have sized up an enemy. Then, instead of attacking, he went up to that brightly painted door and leaned heavily on the bell.

If it had not been for her anxious eyes, Nick would not have thought this was the right woman. Natasha Walsh was blonde, thin in an attenuated way, and much older than he had expected her to be.

"Are you – who are you?" she asked.

Nick said curtly: "Nicholas Ryves," and was amazed to see this slim, pastel-cardiganed housewife blossom into a tentative welcome.

"Oh, you're one of Daniel's family! Do come in. Please."

Nick stepped into a hall, carpeted brown with great pink flowers, and wondered what Alan had told this woman about Dad.

"So you – you said you knew something about Alan," the stranger said, twisting her hands together.

"You said you saw him last Christmas."

She pushed open a door and led him into a little sitting room, with cream silk fittings and picture frames glinting brightly on every surface. Nick hovered in the middle of the room, feeling like a clumsy animal who should not be allowed in here, and who would break something in a moment.

"Yes," she answered. "He spent Christmas here with us. It was so lovely – we were so happy to have him. He played with the kids. They loved him." She tilted up her chin, almost defiantly, as if to face pain. "We all loved him, and then he stopped answering my letters."

He did not stop answering your letters, Nick thought. *I threw them away. He thought you had stopped caring.*

Alan had come away to this place. He'd left him. He'd wanted to leave him.

Nick didn't even know how to feel about this. It was like the fact that Alan had made him sick. His mind kept shying violently away from the idea and the unfocused pain it promised. It was better to be angry. He hated this woman, hated this whole family. They were weak and stupid and they couldn't have his brother and that was all there was to it. He didn't *need* to feel anything else.

He felt a treacherous twinge at the thought of Alan with kids. Alan loved kids. He'd pick them up and a soft, wondering expression would come over his face. No wonder Marie had been such a temptation, with a home like this.

Natasha turned a beseeching face to his. "Do you know Alan?"

"Yeah," Nick said curtly. "He's my brother."

She stared at him for a long moment and then said, quite simply, as if anybody should know it was the truth, "Alan doesn't have a brother."

The little room felt suddenly cold, frozen in its horrible cream and silver, like a wedding cake left in the freezer. Nick found his voice, and it sounded a long way away.

"He may not have mentioned me," he answered, putting a stone wall of denial between himself and the possibility that Alan had lied about him, had wished him out of existence, "but I've been his brother all my life."

"Do you mean you're his stepbrother?" Natasha Walsh offered, looking perplexed.

People doubting his relationship to Alan was nothing new, but on top of everything else it seemed like an insult he could not bear.

"No, his real brother," Nick growled.

She frowned, her expression reminding him of a dozen mothers who'd looked as if they wanted to call the police on him for daring to touch their daughters.

"If this is some kind of joke—"

"I'm not laughing. I'm his brother."

"You can't possibly be his brother," Mrs Walsh snapped. "My sister Marie only had one child. I think I should know."

Nick stared at her silently, unable to find words. He could only see images, running together in his mind like a slide show. Of Alan's face. Of the face of that smiling girl in the picture, and the mad, cold face of the woman he'd always thought – he'd always *known* – was their mother.

Something about his own face made the woman stop frowning and pick up a picture to display to Nick. It was one of the photographs in silver frames. It showed Dad, big and smiling and wearing a ridiculous moustache, standing next to Marie, who was small, smiling, and wearing a wedding dress. They were holding hands, and Nick, who was used to jealously scanning people for signs of a family resemblance, was held by the sight.

Dad's hands were big, the knuckles large and square, the backs dusted with hair. The girl Marie had hands that were smaller, more feminine, but unmistakably Alan's thin sensitive hands.

It was an enormous relief.

No wonder she'd been wearing old-fashioned clothes in the hidden picture. No wonder Alan had lied. He would not have wanted Nick to know they had different mothers. He would have been afraid Nick would be hurt. He'd been looking out for Nick.

Nick didn't like it, but he understood. Alan had always called Mum Olivia. It made sense that Alan had nothing to do with her really, that he was not tainted by her madness in the least.

"You know who you do look like," Mrs Walsh said suddenly. "You look like Olivia. Daniel's first wife. She—" the woman hesitated. "I think they married very young. They were childhood sweethearts and – I didn't know her very well, but she always seemed restless. She ran away with someone else, and after a few years, Daniel and Marie got married. Is – is something wrong?"

"Nothing's wrong," he snarled. "Everything's fine."

Nick looked at the picture in Mrs Walsh's hands and thought of the wedding picture Alan kept by his bedside. Mum and Dad looked so young in that picture, he remembered. They looked younger than Dad in this picture.

Furious panic fragmented the images in Nick's head for a moment. He tried to piece together all this new information until it made sense. It felt like fitting the shards of a broken glass together with his bare hands, but he didn't care if it hurt as long as he could force the world into a pattern he could understand.

So Mum and Dad had been married and separated. That didn't mean anything. Mum had come back to Dad, then, and he'd taken her in because he'd loved her once. That explained why he'd protected a magician. That made sense. It did not mean that anything in Nick's life had changed.

"She came back," he said, trying to sound calm. "Olivia. She and Dad had me—"

"Marie died fifteen years ago," Mrs Walsh blurted out. "I was with her. I was with Alan and Daniel the whole time. You must be about seventeen! I don't know who you are, but I know you're not Daniel Ryves's son."

She looked upset and suspicious at once as she threw the words in his face, but Nick abruptly ceased to care. She'd told him everything she knew now. She didn't matter any more. Dad used to keep a lot of pictures, but he'd never seen a picture of Alan when he was younger than four, or of himself when he was younger than one. Mum had returned to Dad – to Daniel Ryves – traumatised, scared, carrying an amulet and a baby.

She'd run away with someone else, and that someone else was Black Arthur, who fed people to demons, who had tortured the woman he was supposed to love until she ran again.

I know you're not Daniel Ryves's son.

Everybody always found it hard to believe that he was Alan's brother, because he was not Alan's brother. He'd never had a brother.

"Do you really know Alan?" Mrs Walsh asked, her voice trembling. "Can you tell me how he is? Daniel and Alan simply disappeared one day, and I always wondered what had happened to them. And then Alan found me. He called and he wrote and he visited. He was so polite; he was so good. I didn't see my nephew for fourteen years and he came back crippled and saying that his father was dead, and then he vanished. I just want to know if he's all right."

She looked as if she was going to cry. Alan would have cared.

Nick stared at this woman, Alan's aunt, and realised that this stranger had a better claim on Alan than he did.

The small sitting room and its decorations did not seem frozen any more. Nick wanted to smash it all. He'd been cold before, but now his blood felt too hot. He was burning up, he was shaking with rage.

The horrible woman's voice changed. "Are you all right?" she asked. "Do you – do you need to sit down? Would you like a glass of water?"

Natasha Walsh moved forward, and Nick grabbed hold of her upper arm. She recoiled from the look on his face.

He'd always known that he scared people sometimes. Clearly it was a talent he'd inherited from his father.

The woman was suddenly breathing hard, in small gasps weighted by fear. "Don't hurt me."

He hated her. She'd told him that everything he'd ever known about his life was a lie, and he hated her almost as much as he hated that liar Alan. Alan, who belonged in this place, with this woman and her family, and not with him.

Nick put his lips to her ear and whispered, "Why not?"

He shook her hard, and she gave a thin, small scream and tried to break away. She didn't have a chance.

"Let me go," she pleaded.

"Why?" Nick demanded, his voice rising to a shout. "I don't feel sorry for you. I don't feel anything for you. Why should I?"

He shook her again, her shoulders impossibly thin and frail in the grip of his hands. She stared up at him with terrified eyes that were washed-out copies of Alan's deep-blue eyes and for a moment he couldn't bear it; he didn't know what he was going to do.

Then the picture slipped out of her shaking fingers and clattered onto the rug.

Nick looked down and saw Dad staring up at him.

He let the woman go and bolted out of that warm, comfortable home into the rain.

He had not heard when it started raining, but now the drops pounded against his skin and rattled the roof of the car. He stood with his arms braced against the roof, the rain pulling a slick black curtain of hair over his eyes, and wondered why he didn't just get into the car and drive. It occurred to him that he was not sure where to go. Home had always been an uncertain concept, attached to no particular place and centred on someone who he now knew did not belong to him.

There was no home to go back to. He pressed his forehead against his wet forearms, against the slippery metal of the car roof, and tried to think. It could not be true, not really. There would be no way to live if it was true.

He drove back to London eventually, because he could not stay outside that house and he could not think of anything else to do. He was not panicked or running for a bolt-hole like a wounded animal. He felt strangely empty of feelings or ideas, as if someone had slit him open and removed them. He just kept driving.

Alan called this kind of rain cats' paws, and this rain seemed to mark the passing of a nightmarish army of cats. Nick could barely see to drive, and the grey of a pouring sky seemed not to change but to bleed into the grey of a city. He only really noticed that he was in London when the car coughed to a stop on Tower Bridge, and he realised that night had been closing in behind the rain.

Nick got out and went to the front of the car, intending to check out the engine, but the rain hammered all thought from his mind. He stood staring at the car bonnet, the rain distorting the road and the passing cars into a river of ink, the flow broken occasionally by flashes of metal.

He turned away and left the car amidst the indignant honking of other motorists. He started walking through the rain. Within minutes he felt numb with cold, the relentless lashing of rain against his skin becoming as personal a rhythm as his footsteps.

The towers on the bridge loomed like enemy fortresses against a sky gone slate grey with rain clouds and the approach of night. Nick stared up at them and then at the London skyline, the buildings spiky and glittering as stiletto knives. He bowed his head and walked through the driving rain.

He had to walk for a long time to get home. The sky had turned dull, dead black, and his legs had the heavy feeling that meant every muscle would be aching tomorrow. The rain had not stopped falling. As he approached the flickering sign of the Chinese takeaway, the light turned the raindrops silver, and Nick had forgotten what it felt like to be dry.

He came into the house and leaned against the door. The rain drummed outside, and he wondered if he should just go back out and keep walking. He'd known what to do when he was walking.

"Nick!"

He looked up, more because of the light being switched on than at the sound of his name. At the top of the stairs stood Mae, limned by the pale yellow light of a naked bulb.

"Where have you been?" she asked. "It's three in the morning. Alan's going crazy with worry."

He flinched at the name like a kicked dog and hated himself for doing it. Mae's face changed from inquiry to suspicion.

"Nick," she said. "What's going on?"

He wanted to snarl at her that it was none of her business; he wanted her to shut up and get out of his way. He wanted to tell her that he'd never liked her. When he'd thought that he liked her, he'd been wrong.

He couldn't seem to find any words, just a hollow feeling where words should have been. He opened his mouth and an odd sound came out, like a croaking bird, and he stared up at her blankly.

Mae came running down the stairs, and he moved forward. He wanted to tell her to stop, not to ask him any more questions, but he did not want to open his mouth and find nothing there again.

"You're soaking wet," Mae said. She spoke kindly, and Nick wished she would stop. It reminded him of Alan.

She touched his shoulder, pinching the material of his shirt between two fingers and peeling the drenched material away from his skin. Nick knew he was drenched; he didn't need her to prove it to him, but it was only when she touched him that a look of real alarm flashed over her face. He stood dumb, wondering why, and she pressed her hand flat against his shoulder.

Against her steady hand, he realised he was shaking.

"I'll get—" Mae began, and Nick stopped her.

It was easy to catch her and hold her trapped against the banister. She was small and he was strong, and he pinned her with one hand.

Her breath started coming a little faster and he could see a pulse at her throat jumping even in the low light, but she did not struggle. She stayed perfectly still and raked her eyes carefully over Nick's face. He could practically see her mind ticking over the possibilities, trying to form a plan, trying to guess what Nick would do next.

He kissed her.

He moved in and pressed her hard against the banister, holding her soft and small and trapped against him. He kept her face tilted up, her chin cupped in his palm and his fingers against her jaw. His arm around her waist was tense, unyielding as an iron bar.

She could not get away, and she did not try. After a moment her arm slid around his neck and she kissed him back.

Nick was only aware of how miserably cold he had been when he felt the chill, settled into dull pain in his bones, finally ease. He grabbed the dry, warm material of her T-shirt in his fists, pushed it up until he felt the smooth, warm skin of her back under his hands. Mae curved her mouth against his and against his shut eyes the swinging light bulb became the dancing lanterns of the Goblin Market, and he thought with savage satisfaction of how hurt Alan would be by this.

He and Mae heard the dragging sound of Alan's footsteps at the same time. She pulled back and Nick tried to follow her mouth but did not push the issue when she turned her face away, her breath wavering against his cheek.

Alan was standing at the top of the stairs, his curly hair sleep-ruffled and his kind face startled, about to be hurt. Nick had not realised how much he hated him until now.

"*You*," he said. The word came out thick, as if he were snarling through a mouth full of blood.

Alan had stopped looking surprised. His eyes travelled from Nick's face to Mae's, and he began to look angry. Alan didn't have a clue that Nick had ever, for even a moment, liked Mae. The way he saw it, the only reason Nick had for doing this was to hurt him.

"Sorry to interrupt," he said quietly. He was far too good at lying and keeping secrets to reveal anything in front of Mae. "Can I ask where you've been?"

"Where I've—" Nick abandoned Mae and started up the stairs, slowly, moving as he did when he was stalking something for the kill. "Where did you go," he asked, "last Christmas?"

Alan looked shocked. Of course he looked shocked. He'd thought his lies would never be discovered; he'd thought Nick would never suspect. Nick had always believed that Alan did not lie to him, that he was the exception, but why should Alan make an exception for him? He was nothing to Alan.

After a moment Alan's ordinary, gentle face was in place, a mask that Nick hated and wanted to break into a thousand pieces. Nick kept advancing.

Alan said carefully: "What do you know?"

"I know *everything!*" Nick shouted. "I know that Black Arthur is my father. I know that you've been lying to me all my life. You're not my brother."

Alan bit his lip. "It's not that important," he said in the lying, soothing voice he always used with people who might suspect them. "It's like being adopted. It doesn't mean a thing."

"If it wasn't important, then why did you lie? Why did you keep lying?"

Alan glanced down the stairs to Mae, and Nick saw he was too hurt to be calm about this. "Because I knew you'd go mad!" Alan snapped. "And you're not exactly proving me wrong, are you?"

"Shut your lying mouth," said Nick softly. "It isn't like

being adopted. That's not why you lied. You hid the fact that your own mother existed; you didn't even dare tell half a lie and say we were half-brothers. You tried to tie me to you and that dead idiot Daniel as tightly as you could. You were scared to death that I'd grow up to be a monster!"

"Don't talk about Dad like that," Alan said sharply. "And you're not a monster."

"Why not?" Nick asked. "I'm much better at killing than you are. I can call the demons with a piece of chalk and a word. Did you ever think about what that might mean, Alan? Were you ever scared of me?"

Alan flinched, and Nick saw the truth written clearly on his face for once. He'd been scared, all right.

Nick wanted to make him scared now.

"You thought I might grow up to be a magician like Black Arthur," Nick said slowly. "After all, both my parents have a taste for blood."

"I didn't," Alan told him in a thin voice. "I never thought you were anything like Black Arthur. You're not his son, he didn't bring you up, he didn't die for you—"

Nick reached Alan at the top of the stairs and roared that thin voice down.

"Don't try a guilt trip on me. It won't work! Stop thinking that you can manipulate me the way you manipulate everybody else. It makes me sick. Who says Daniel Ryves died for me? Why should he have done anything for me? It was her he wanted. I was something she brought with her, I was something that belonged to the man who stole her from him. What did Daniel Ryves see when he looked at me? Do you think he liked it?"

Nick was telling the truth. He didn't feel guilty, and he

didn't feel sad. It wasn't hard to stop calling another liar Dad and start calling him Daniel. All he felt was black, twisting fury, the desire to hurt someone, and the knowledge that there was nothing to stop him doing it. Not any more.

He saw the shadow pass through Alan's kind eyes. He saw, quite clearly, Alan's decision to lie again.

"I'm sure that when Dad looked at you," he said, "all he saw was his son."

Nick drew back his fist and punched Alan in the face.

There was an outraged scream from Mae, whom Nick had entirely forgotten. She exclaimed, "Nick, don't," and began charging her way up the stairs when the deed was already done.

She didn't have a hope, but Alan was no clumsy amateur. He'd rocked back when Nick's fist connected, and he was falling when Nick glanced at Mae. There was a twist of movement in the corner of Nick's eye, and that was all the warning he got before Alan pulled a gun on him.

The barrel was cold against Nick's jaw. Alan's grip on it was steady.

"Don't do that again," Alan said, blood blooming from the broken corner of his mouth and trickling down his chin.

Mae hesitated on the stairs and did not come any closer.

Nick turned his face in towards the gun and spoke into the barrel as if it was a microphone.

"If it was adoption," Nick sneered, letting his mouth brush the steel, "why didn't you tell me about Durham? Why didn't you tell your precious Aunt Natasha about your adoptive family? We could have all gone to stay with your real family at Christmas – you, your crazy new mother, and a murderous magician's son make three."

"Nick," Alan said, and made a small sound of frustration. "You're my real family. It was just that – please try to understand. It was just that I wanted to remember how things were when Mum was alive and everything was all right. I just wanted to have a few days of pretending. I never wanted to drag my aunt into this nightmare with me!"

"Too bad," Nick said. "She got dragged in."

Alan's hand did tremble then. For a moment Nick thought he was going to faint, but he just stood there trembling, with his face the whitish-grey colour of ashes. Nick let his mouth curve upward so that Alan would see him smiling, see that he didn't care. Alan's hand tightened on the gun, and for a moment Nick thought that he might use it. Then he lowered it, slowly, as if he thought that he might use it too.

"Nick," he said, his voice wavering badly and making him sound very young. "Nick, what have you done?"

"I didn't do anything," said Nick. "You think I'd care enough to do something to her? Don't flatter yourself."

"Did you hurt her, Nick?" Alan asked.

Nick made himself keep smiling. "Maybe a little."

There was a door standing ajar down the corridor, a silhouette tracing a slightly different darkness onto the shadows. It was either Jamie or his mother, Nick could not tell and did not care. Whoever it was, they were breathing rapidly, as if they were afraid, and standing halfway up the stairs, Mae was breathing too fast as well.

Nick did not glance over to see if she looked afraid. He would not have seen the shadow at the open door, if the door had not been directly behind Alan's head.

He kept looking at Alan who was not his brother, standing there with a gun hanging limply at his side. Alan's face was still that terrible colour, his eyes avoiding Nick's, but his thin chest was rising and falling evenly enough. He didn't look scared. He looked heartsick.

"Listen to me," Nick said. "Everything's going to be all right. You don't need to stay in this nightmare any longer. Your father took me and my mother in. You saved our lives. I'll pay you back. I'll get that mark off you. Then it will be even between us, and once it is, I don't ever want to see your face again."

12

Blood Calls to Blood

EVERYTHING SEEMED UNNATURALLY CLEAR TO NICK IN the days following his discovery, and he seemed to have lost the ability to attach meaning to particular things. He would look at Mae, who was apparently unable to meet his eyes now, and he would look at Alan trying to eat with one side of his mouth bruised and swollen, and he would not feel anything at all.

He'd never been like Alan, never been able to take an interest in people, never had a crush or even a real friend. He'd just thought he was more sensible than Alan. Now he thought that perhaps this easy detachment was what allowed his father to offer people up to the demons. Nick sat on the couch, a lumpy brown affair covered in fluff that seemed to be shedding with age, and thought about sacrifice.

The idea of strangers dying didn't matter much to him. He could do it, he thought. There was nothing the demons could give him that he wanted, but if there had been, he could have done it.

He realised distantly that this should frighten him, but fear, like pity, was something that never came. He didn't want to talk to the others. He didn't even want to look at them.

He'd slept on the shabby brown couch since he found out, not that he was sleeping much. He spent the best part of most nights outside in the garden, practising with the sword until he was exhausted, his skin slick with sweat and his mind mercifully empty, and even after that he didn't sleep well.

The third night on the sofa he'd almost managed to get to sleep when he heard Alan screaming. Nick rolled automatically off the sofa and was at the top of the stairs before he realised what he was doing.

The door to Alan's room was open. Someone had reached him before Nick.

Alan was sitting up in bed. He looked haggard and drained, eyes too dark in a face that was too white, but Mae was sitting with him in the tangle of sheets, and she was holding his hands. Nick couldn't see her face, but he could see Alan's. More than that, he could hear Alan's voice, talking in a low, warm rush that sounded worried and desperate and just a little comforted already.

Mae murmured something, her few words lost in the flood of his, and Alan stopped talking for a moment to smile. It wasn't one of his calculated smiles; it was something helpless and shy. He ducked his head for a moment and then looked up at her again, eyes shining with hope.

Alan would probably go back to Exeter with Mae and Jamie, Nick realised. He'd been thinking that Alan might return to Durham once he was free, but the way he was looking at Mae, he would want to be wherever she was.

Mae leaned forward, one of the strings on her string top sliding down the curve of her shoulder, and gave Alan a kiss that landed to one side of his smile, lips brushing the bruise there as if to make it better.

Maybe she'd want that too.

Nick slipped back downstairs, footsteps falling as softly as a shadow falls, making sure that nobody saw.

If he'd stopped to think, he would never have gone to Alan in the first place. Alan was nothing to him.

It seemed like either Alan or Jamie woke screaming every night now. Time was running out.

Nick went to school because it seemed like a good way to avoid them and spent a day wandering the halls silently, thinking about how many schools he'd gone to and had to struggle through because Alan wanted it and Daniel Ryves would have wanted it. He'd tried to be normal, tried to follow his father's advice, but he wasn't normal and Daniel Ryves wasn't his father.

It all seemed very pointless now.

"Hey," said Carr, that annoying little terrier snapping at his heels, the last in a line of people he had put up with, had pretended to be like. "Where've you been, man?"

Nick looked right through him for a long, cold moment, waiting to see him flinch. When he did, Nick turned away, and Carr grabbed his elbow again.

"*Hey!* What's got into you?"

Nick whirled around and punched him. He fell hard, cracking his back against the floor and sliding to hit the wall. Nick stood over him and curled his mouth, watched fear creep over the other boy's face.

"Nothing," he whispered. "I've always been this way."

He went home. It had occurred to him that there was a magician to talk to there.

When he came in the door he climbed the stairs, and then climbed another narrow, creaking flight to the attic room where Mum was. It was so rare for him to come to his mother's room that for a while he simply stared at the worn wood of the door. It wasn't a barrier. It was nothing but a cheap, flimsy plank of wood. Eventually, since he could come up with no other way to suggest he was on a mission of peace, he knocked on the door.

His mother's voice, calm and pleased, called, "Come in!"

When Nick came in, she was sitting on a stool, straight-backed, dealing cards for herself on her bed. She turned a smiling face to the door and saw him. The cards slipped out of her hands. Her face shut up like someone securing every door and window so their house would be safe from attack.

Nick realised that he always thought of her at her worst, during the screaming fits or the times she had to be medicated. She was always at her worst when Nick was there.

She'd been able to hold down a job when they really needed it, though. She got on well with Alan, who was not her son any more than he was Nick's brother, and she seemed to be friendly with Mae. She was not as mad as he had always told himself, and if she were, it was his father's fault.

"Do you want me to get those?"

Nick meant the words to be polite, but they came out abrupt. Well, it was no use pretending. He and his mother had always been enemies, and now he knew why.

"No," his mother said. Nick looked at her and remembered staring into the pale eyes of the wolf he'd strangled, knowing that there was human intelligence behind the wolf's eyes, and also knowing that she would kill him if she could.

He walked towards her, and Mum scrambled up from her stool, her movements awkward as if panic had wiped away control of her own limbs, and Nick discovered something else.

Mum was afraid of him. It had never occurred to him before, since she had no reason to be frightened of him, but he knew her reason now. He wondered what Black Arthur could possibly have done to her to make her so scared that fifteen years later here she was, backed up against a wall and trembling.

Nick held up his hands in surrender and did not move any closer. "I wanted to talk to you."

She had her face turned away from him, a strand of black hair fanned across her cheek. "I don't want to talk to you."

"Look," Nick said. "I know about my father. I mean, I know that Black Arthur is my father." He stopped, but she did not respond to the name, just kept her face turned away and breathed in little gasps, snatching air as if he was about to take it away from her. "Am I like him?" Nick continued. "Do I look like him at all?"

Mum made an obvious effort and looked at him. The one window the attic contained was set in the slanted ceiling, and in the space between them was a square of light where dust motes drifted and sparked. Their eyes met across it.

"Yes," Mum answered. "You look like him."

It was strange to think he looked like someone he had never seen. He was not used to looking like anyone but her; he was used to her being the worst part of him.

"I'm leaving Alan," Nick said. "He has no part in this. I want you to come with me."

"I'll die before I go anywhere with you."

He had not expected understanding Mum to make everything harder. He could not hate her any more, and he certainly could not feel anything warmer for her, but he'd thought that if he understood her, she could understand him. He'd expected logic, but there was no logic to be had from her. Black Arthur had seen to that.

"What did he do to you?" Nick asked suddenly.

Her eyes went from ice to fire. "I don't talk about that!" she spat, and he watched the saliva fly from her lips, gathering in tiny bubbles at the corners of her mouth. "I don't think about it. I don't want to remember anything that happened before."

She was trembling, her hands grasping the air as if she had to get a handhold on it or fall. Nick moved towards her instinctively.

Her voice cracked like ice breaking underfoot. "Don't touch me."

Nick looked at her grasping hands and thought of Alan's hands, and the way Alan's mother had hands just like his. Mum's hands were small, very thin at the wrists, and Nick stared at them and thought about his own hands, large hands with long, brutal-looking fingers made to curve around a sword hilt or a neck.

He knew who he'd inherited them from. He felt for an instant like the assembled pieces of some weapon Black Arthur had built.

He turned away from his mother and towards the door. He should not have come.

"I'm not him, you know," he said over his shoulder.

"I know," said Mum. "I loved *him*."

That night, when he was practising with the sword in the garden, Mae came to speak to him.

Alan had been pleased by the garden that first morning in the house, when they were still brothers. It was small but the wooden fence was high, hiding them from all the world, and in this hidden place was a weeping willow.

Nick did not care about trees or gardens or anything but the clean cut and thrust of his sword and the ache in his muscles that sang through his body as a relief from thought. He pivoted, sliced darkness across the throat, and came within an inch of beheading Mae.

He caught the downward swing of his sword and stepped back. He did not speak.

Mae ducked under a branch of the willow, its green fingers trailing through her hair. The May air was warm, but it had a bite to it, and she leaned against the tree and hugged herself.

Nick curled his lip and turned his back on her, executing the next movement in his exercises. His sword went glancing through the points of an invisible opponent, throat, chest, thigh, and then he turned and caught one behind him, putting the power of his wrist behind a solid thrust. He let the easy physicality of it take hold of him, that flashing point of steel in the night becoming his single focus in the world, the sustained effort a slow burn through the muscles of his back and arms.

Mae's voice was an unwelcome intrusion in his thoughtless world. It cut through the tactile sensations of effort and exhaustion and pulled him up short.

"When are you going to start talking to your brother again?"

Nick turned the sword hilt between his hands, making the blade jump like a fish. He watched Mae jump as well, and wondered if Black Arthur liked to see people squirm before he sacrificed them.

"You must've mistaken me for someone else," he told her. "I don't have a brother."

"You do have a brother," Mae said. "And I'm worried about him."

"Oh?" said Nick, and lunged forward to slash the air above her head, to her left, to her right. He cut a door in the air for her to walk through and, panting slightly, demanded, "If you're so worried about him, why don't you go and comfort him?"

A trickle of sweat was running between his shoulder blades, the cool current in the air washing down his back and making him shiver. He saw Mae notice, and let her see him smile.

"Or maybe you'd rather comfort me?"

Mae looked up at him silently, eyes dark in the pale upturned oval of her face. The willow was casting long shadows on her skin, like the stripes of darkness cast by a shutter. Her eyes were not like pools, but there was something trembling under their surface.

Nick sheathed his sword and leaned in.

He reached out with lazy intent to touch her hair, and she grabbed his wrist an instant before he touched her.

"Think a lot of yourself, don't you?"

Nick blinked. "I thought—"

"You think you can use me as a way to punish Alan," said Mae. "I noticed."

"That wouldn't be the only reason," Nick told her, leaning against the willow by her side. The bark was rough against his bare skin.

"Oh, no?" asked Mae. "What's the other reason?"

Nick smiled a small smile that someone watching them would not have been able to see. It touched his lips and lingered for a moment, private and promising. "Might be fun."

"I don't think so," said Mae.

She stepped away from him. Her eyes were narrowed.

"I'm not stupid," she said. "I'm attracted to you, I could be attracted to Alan, but what does it matter? I've been attracted to people before. I'm not looking to settle down, and I'm not territory to be fought over in your little war. I won't let myself be used, and I won't let whatever crisis you're having hurt my brother's chance to live."

Nick raised his eyebrows. "Your brother's chance? Who says he has one?"

"I say he does!"

"I'm not interested in charity work," Nick informed her. "If you want to save your brother, you'll have to rely on Alan."

"I trust Alan," said Mae, "but I don't rely on anyone. If I have to, I can kill a magician myself."

"Really?" Nick drawled. "Didn't you let one go just the other day?"

"That was stupid," Mae said. "I should have killed him before he could escape. I won't be that stupid again." He saw her hands clench into fists. "And I'm not afraid."

Nick's eyes travelled over her face. "I believe you," he said, and watched her relax. "You're brave," he added honestly.

When she almost smiled, he leaned in again, and she hesitated, her breath coming fast against his lips. She didn't move.

"You're brave," Nick whispered into her mouth, "but that's not enough."

It had been too easy to palm a knife and hold it to her throat when he went in for a kiss. When she swallowed, the edge brushed her skin.

"They'll surprise you," Nick continued, looking down into her outraged face. "They'll use magic; they'll use demons. You don't know what you're doing, and they will get to you before you can get to them."

Mae tipped her head back because of the pressure of the knife against her throat. He'd been telling the truth. She was brave. She didn't look scared at all. She looked furious.

"Carry a knife from now on if you plan to kill," Nick continued in a thoughtful, detached voice. He grinned at her and added, "Make sure to catch them by surprise."

She glared silently up at him.

He drew the knife across her throat, lightly, not cutting her, but making sure she could feel the edge slide against her skin. "Slash across the throat or" – he trailed the point down her body – "under the ribs. Don't even try for between the ribs. Amateurs always hit a rib, and if they try for the heart, they always hit the breastbone. Across the throat or under the ribs for a killing blow. Do you understand that?"

Mae drove her fist into his stomach, at a point under his ribs. "You're an ass," she said, between her teeth. "Do you understand that?"

He ignored the pain and smiled. "You'd better pray Alan will protect you and Jamie," he said. "As far as I'm concerned, you're on your own."

He touched his knife, and the blade withdrew into its hilt with a soft snick. He slipped it into Mae's pocket, then turned away and stooped to pick up his sword, unsheathing it and beginning to execute a few more passes.

If anything, his return to routine made Mae angrier. When he turned to face her, bringing the sword up and around in an overarm pass, she was trembling with fury.

"You're the one on your own," she said.

Nick swung and ducked an imaginary enemy's swing in return, legs bent and thighs braced. "*I* can take care of myself."

"You're going to be miserable," Mae told him, and stormed back to the house.

He watched her go, squaring her shoulders. Before she opened the door, he saw her touch her face and wondered if she was crying.

Nick stepped backwards, spun, and parried another imaginary blow. He silently congratulated himself on the way he'd made her angry enough to forget all about discussing his so-called brother.

He swung again. These exercises with the sword were nothing like real fights; they were just a way of keeping ready for real fights, making sure his reflexes were still fast and the weight of the sword did not tire him.

Eventually he did get tired. He felt as if the heaviness of steel had been shot through his bones and had settled cold in the pit of his stomach. He was exhausted and chilled and he had to force himself not to think.

Across the dark, ragged patch of garden the window of their kitchen shone a square of orange light. The curtains were open and through the glass Nick could hear faint music playing. Jamie was dancing around like an idiot, and Mae was leaning against the door looking at Jamie, her face smoothing out into calm. Alan was cooking something, and when Jamie pushed the wooden spoon he'd been singing into like a microphone over Alan's shoulder, Alan turned to

Jamie, and Nick glimpsed Alan's smile. Over the strains of the radio came the sudden deep, sweet sound of Alan singing. Mae looked startled and impressed, and she started to smile too.

Nick could have gone in, but he couldn't go in and be one of them.

He turned away from the ordinary people laughing in the warmth and wondered if magicians felt this empty and cold all the time. He raised his sword, on guard, and launched himself into the murder of shadows.

The morning sky was paling after the sunrise into an indeterminate white that would be followed by blue, and when Nick opened the door, the inside of the house looked grey. He went into the little kitchen with the usual worn-thin cork tiles and stopped dead at the sight of Alan.

Alan was sitting at the kitchen table. He looked as worn as the cork tiles, the circles under his eyes looking more like bruises than ever, deep purple and spreading like stains. They matched the real bruise at the side of his mouth.

"I wondered when you were going to come in," he said, his voice weary.

Nick said nothing. He went over to the kettle and flipped it on, then rifled through the cupboards to find instant coffee. The door of one of the cupboards was hanging lopsided, he noticed, and the cork tiling was curling up in one of the corners of the room. They had lived in grimly poor places like this since Dad had died, and Nick had not thought about it much beyond being relieved that they were not hungry or cold.

He remembered Natasha Walsh's house. Alan had been born into a different kind of life.

"I want to talk to you," Alan said, and Nick turned round and fixed Alan with a cold stare at the precise moment that Jamie walked into the kitchen.

He was still in his pyjamas, one cheek marked with the lines from his pillow, and for a second all he did was look bewildered. Then he seemed to take in the situation and backed up a step. His eyes swivelled in all directions, looking for escape, and they lit on the jar of coffee and the boiling kettle.

"Oh look, coffee," he said weakly. "Excellent."

"You don't like coffee, Jamie," Alan said.

"It was just a random burst of enthusiasm for – the general concept of coffee," Jamie told him, and he gave Alan what was clearly meant to be a reassuring smile. "Is everything all right?"

Jamie and Alan were both white and terribly wasted, as if the demons were going to wear them away to pallid ghosts who wandered the house with their eyes huge and imploring in their thin faces. Alan seemed worse hit than Jamie, battered and strained by the demonic assault, but Nick had no doubt as to who would give in first. Jamie looked frail as a single flame in a blast of wind, a trembling thread of light that was about to go out.

In spite of that, he was looking from Alan to Nick and back again, and he looked protective. As if Jamie could possibly do anything to protect Alan.

"Everything's fine," Alan replied, but he looked grateful.

Nick crossed his arms over his chest and asked Alan, "What did you want to talk to me about?"

He was rather glad that Jamie was there. It had always been him and Alan in the past. It would have been too familiar, too easy to fall back into the habit of acting as if they were a team, but Jamie's presence made it clear that everything had changed. Alan belonged with Jamie and other normal people, and Nick was one of the magicians. They were not family.

"There's a spell," Alan said slowly. "It's just a small spell. The magicians' name for it is the blood calling spell. It means your family can always find you."

"Explain further," Nick ordered.

He was talking in the way he always talked to people he didn't know well and didn't like much, every word the equivalent of throwing a stone. He knew Alan recognised it.

Alan did not rise to the bait. He kept his eyes on the plastic sheen of their tablecloth, and he explained. "Say the name. Say the spell. Spill a little blood, and then you can follow the trail of that blood."

"Follow the trail of my blood," said Nick, because Alan didn't want to say it and Nick wanted him to hear it at least. "To my father's."

"Yes."

"You knew Black Arthur was my father all along," Nick remarked thoughtfully. "You could have done this spell at any time. Why didn't you?"

Alan did look up at him then. His eyes looked hurt, but his whole white, bruised face told a story of pain, and a little more could make no difference.

"I didn't want you to know. I didn't ever want you to know any of it."

"Your concern is very touching," Nick sneered. "And you risked your own stupid life because you couldn't bear to tell me something so horrible? How noble. Only, wait – you risked Jamie's stupid life as well. That's not very noble."

He gave Jamie a deliberate, amused look from under his eyelids, seeing how the boy received this news. Jamie's face betrayed nothing, but his hands were shaking as he made himself a cup of tea.

"I put you first," Alan said in a tired way. "I always have. And no, it's not very noble at all."

Nick threw a kitchen knife at him.

Jamie almost dropped his tea, and Alan caught the knife by the handle with no fuss, looking thoughtfully at the serrated edge. Nick didn't want to waste one of their hunting knives on himself. The kitchen knife would do if he stayed still.

"Very thoughtful of you," Alan said, laying down the knife and drawing a blade from his belt. "But actually, I've got one of my own."

Nick recognised the knife, the wickedly sharp point and the signs for power and protection carved in the steel hilt. He remembered weapons glittering under the lights of the Goblin Market, being happy about his brother's present and hearing Alan say so casually, *I've been thinking we could use an enchanted knife*.

He wondered how long Alan had been planning this.

He asked, "How much blood do you need?"

"Jamie," Alan said, "could you fetch me a saucer?"

Jamie put down his mug, tea slopping onto the kitchen counter, and mutely fetched down a saucer from the cupboard with the door askew. He put it in the centre of the table. Nick strolled over to the table and took the chair opposite Alan. He had his gaze fixed at a point beyond Alan's ear at first, but then Alan flinched, so Nick looked directly at him. Alan blinked, looking exhausted and owlish and a little stupid, and Nick put all the chilly distance he had been feeling these past few days into his eyes. He made his stare long and cold as winter.

"Come on, then," he said in a low challenge and held out his arm, elbow on the table and hand half curled into a fist, as if they were going to arm wrestle. "What are you waiting for?"

Alan's gaze was steady now and entirely blank. "Take off your talisman."

It was so strange that Nick paused. Alan had always stressed how important it was for Nick to keep his talisman on if he wanted to be safe.

Well, Nick had always hated the thing, and he wasn't particularly interested in being safe any more. He drew the talisman off and put it down on the table as if he was laying down his stake in a card game. Alan looked at him steadily, recognising and accepting the stakes, and reached out for him. Nick forced himself not to pull away.

Alan trailed two fingers along Nick's arm, the touch light and expert. The blue veins stood out clearly against the dead-white skin, and Alan traced the largest vein until he chose a spot. Nick wanted him to get on with it. He was glad when Alan took his hand away: he preferred the knife.

"Say the name," Alan commanded.

Nick said, low, "Black Arthur."

Alan cut swift and deep. There was no hesitation, nor any trying to spare Nick pain which would have cost him more pain. There was just the slice of the knife and the moment of shock.

A line appeared in the knife's wake, beaded with blood, and slowly the line opened into a jagged cut. Blood dripped down Nick's arm and he angled it so that the blood fell into the saucer, which filled drop by drop. A splash of blood on white china looked almost like a flower, but then Nick squeezed his arm slightly to create a steady flow of blood, and the flower was swallowed up in a pool.

"I claim the right of kinship," Alan said. "I claim blood and bone."

Nick saw Alan dip his finger into the blood and put it to his lips, but he was more concerned by the sudden stir in the blood still in his veins, as if the iron in it were being called to by a magnet very far away.

"I claim the right to follow you," Alan continued. "I claim you for my own."

They were silent then, waiting for enough blood to flow, loosing the blood so it could call out to another body. Nick lifted his eyes from the blood snaking down his arm and met Alan's eyes, closer than he had expected.

"You didn't have to include yourself in that spell. You didn't need to taste the blood."

"It makes more sense this way," Alan said casually. "Now both of us can trace him."

The cut in Nick's arm was starting to throb dully with the pressure he was putting on it. He kept looking at Alan. "How many times have you lied to me?" he asked in a soft voice.

Alan replied, equally softly, "I've lost count."

The saucer was brimming with blood by now.

Alan leaned forward to inspect the cut. "That's enough," he said, and produced their first-aid kit from under the seat. He was unrolling a bandage when Nick snatched the kit away.

"I can do it for myself."

As he wrapped the bandage ruthlessly tight around his

arm, he began to feel a tingling sensation. It was like the time Alan had persuaded him to donate blood, the tightening of his veins and the pull at his blood. Only this time there was no point where the blood could drain away, and the tug was not only in the veins of his arm but in all the veins running through his body, as if the tide of his blood had turned and was roaring towards a strange shore.

He was at one end of a line. The line stretched out somewhere in this city and connected him to his father.

Jamie's voice rang out, sounding all wrong in the tense silence, like a discordant note played on a taut string.

"Did it work?"

Nick nodded slowly, not taking his eyes off Alan.

"I'll get Mae."

Jamie dashed out, and they heard his headlong rush up the stairs. Alan rose abruptly.

He must have been sitting on that chair for hours, getting his leg stiff. He must have been more tired than he knew. Nick rarely saw Alan stumble.

He stumbled now, and would have fallen, except that Nick leaped up and caught his elbow. Alan's weight hit Nick's palm hard, and a bolt of pain shot up Nick's arm. He realised that he had reached out thoughtlessly and caught Alan with his injured arm.

He kept his face impassive. Alan righted himself in the space of a breath, but when Nick let go of him, Alan grabbed his wrist.

"Don't leave me," Alan said.

Nick tilted his head to look at him from another angle. No matter how he looked at him, Alan still made no sense. "I hurt you," he said slowly. "Why would you want me to stay?"

"Oh God, Nick!" Alan said, his voice cracking. "Can't you even understand that much?"

Nick didn't understand at all. It made no sense until he remembered how big Alan was on kindness. Nick wasn't his brother, but he would let Nick stay out of pity, the same way he'd adopt a stray kitten.

He fixed Alan with his coldest look, the one that made everyone back away, and promised, "If I stay, I'll hurt you again."

Alan did not back away. He did not even look away.

In the end, it was Nick who let his eyes drop. His gaze fell on his talisman, and he picked it up and slipped it on over his head almost automatically, and then felt furious with himself for doing so.

He went to the door, still not looking at Alan, and added over his shoulder, "But I won't stay."

He walked into the hall, and Mae, from the top of the stairs, ordered, "Don't go anywhere!"

"Beg pardon?" said Nick.

She ran down the stairs looking flushed and purposeful, her jewellery jingling as she went. "What's the address?"

"We did a spell – we didn't leaf through a Tourist's Guide to the Magicians of London," Nick snapped.

Jamie, standing behind Mae, said tentatively, "Maybe if you visualised yourself walking through all the possible stages that the – the spell wants you to, that might help finding a location."

Nick was about to growl at Jamie to shut up and stop talking to him like a teacher, but the spell tugged at him particularly strongly for one sharp, sweet instant, and he closed his eyes and did envision taking every step the spell wanted him to take, going through a rich neighbourhood he'd never seen before. A street sign hung in the darkness behind his eyes for a moment.

Somewhat to his amazement, Nick opened his mouth, and in a voice that did not sound like his own, gave her an address off Royal Avenue. He was still standing stunned when Mae grabbed her coat.

"I mean it, Nick," she said. "Stay put."

She was gone in a whirl of green coat and bright jewellery. Nick heard the sound of her shoes drumming on the pavement outside. She was going somewhere at a dead run, and he couldn't imagine that she was taking a taxi to go and see the evil magicians.

Nick shook his head and went upstairs. He was going to try and sleep a few hours in a proper bed so he could be fresh when the time came to kill.

When he came downstairs, it was past noon and Mae had returned. She, Jamie and Alan were clustered around the kitchen table, talking loudly. Spread over the table was a floor plan of Black Arthur's house.

"Where did you get this?" Alan asked. "Did you go to the Market people?"

Mae blinked. "I went to planning information at Kensington Town Hall and pretended to be Arthur's niece doing a school project."

"Oh," said Alan. "Yeah, I guess that might work too."

Jamie was beaming at his sister with fond proprietary pride. Nick looked down at the cork tiles.

"Soon she may draw a graph. She gets the businesslike practicality from Mum," Jamie said. "I got the blond genes. Clearly, I win."

"Shut up, I'm nothing like Mum," Mae said, scowling. "Though speaking of business – this floor plan does come with a price." She lifted her chin. "I'm coming with you guys."

"You're not," Nick snapped. "You'll just get hurt."

Mae started rolling up the floor plan. "Did you have a plan?" she demanded. "Besides 'go in there and kill everyone I see'?"

"I only plan to kill two people," Nick said. "Killing everyone isn't part of the plan. Though it would be a nice bonus."

"Oh, now you're planning to kill two people?" Mae asked. "I thought Jamie and I were on our own. So I had to make my own plan." She glared at him, and Jamie, amazingly enough, looked all sad and betrayed. This was ridiculous.

"My plan was just to get in," Alan confessed. He was looking at Mae with appreciation. Nick could tell he was ready to let her have her way.

"This is about my brother," Mae said. "I thought of the floor plan. I might be able to do something else when we're inside. I don't want to be safe. I want the chance to be useful." She looked around for argument, and when it did not come she squared her shoulders, rolled the floor plan out again, and smiled. "This place is big," she continued. "There are four of us; if we split up I think we could cover it more quickly."

"Good thinking," Alan said. "A group of two is quieter than a group of four. If we split up, we have a better chance of catching and killing two magicians before they realise we're there."

He and Mae had their heads bowed close together over the plans, talking about what Market charms Alan could bring with him.

Nick was trying to think. He should've considered Alan's obsession with helping Jamie. Alan was never going to let his mark be taken off without Jamie's being wiped away too.

Alan was right about splitting up as well. They would have a much better chance of surprising the magicians if they went in pairs. Only Mae and Jamie couldn't be a pair. In spite of Mae's bravado, they would be totally helpless without Nick and Alan. Those two weren't fighters. Nick and Alan were the ones who knew how to kill.

Nick would kill a magician for Jamie first and get that out of the way, then. The whole house would be full of them. It shouldn't be too hard. After that, Alan wouldn't be able to put any more obstacles in Nick's path. He could get Alan's mark off, and once he did that it didn't really matter what happened.

"I'll take Jamie," Nick said loudly.

They had no car because Nick had abandoned it on Tower Bridge, so they had to take the Tube to go hunting for magicians. None of them talked much. Nick stood braced as the train rattled through tunnels with a sound like bones shaking in a drum, and tried to ignore the feel of his blood pulling at his veins like a child tugging his sleeve to get his attention.

This way, his blood seemed to be whispering to him. *Faster*. He was going as fast as he could.

They changed from the Central to the Piccadilly line because Nick thought that was right, and Alan did not argue with him. Nick missed driving. Strangers were pressing all around him, and he had to be careful to keep his back to the wall. If anyone was pushed against him and felt the shape of his sword, fastened in a sheath along his spine, there would be trouble.

He just wanted to get to the magicians. He did not think beyond the relief of that, of ending this restless search, calming the new urgency in his blood, and making a kill.

When they reached Knightsbridge station, his blood tingled as if his whole body was a limb that had gone asleep and was now being punished with pins and needles. He saw Alan look up and swing the bag in his lap onto his shoulder.

"Here," Alan said, and Nick nodded and started shoving his way through the post-lunchtime passengers. The others followed in his wake.

Once on the platform he felt a metal point brush his neck and he palmed his switchblade before he realized he was being threatened with the tip of a woman's umbrella. The woman passed by indifferently and Nick smiled grimly after her.

They came out at the entrance near Harrods and stood staring up at the heavy stone buildings with their white-casemented, rectangular windows, letting the flood of shoppers go by. Then they walked along the streets until they were past the biggest shops and moving by the hotels, stately white buildings with gilt fittings to mark the fact that they were not homes.

Nick's blood pounded in his temples, urging him on. It took them twenty minutes until the rows of hotels and office buildings slowly turned into houses.

They were not like the House of Mezentius, hidden behind deep gardens and high gates. Along these streets, the houses were on display. They walked past houses more than five floors high that had darkened chandeliers in the windows and pointed roofs. Some houses had large carved doors with circular windows above them like crowns.

None of them were the house Nick wanted, until they turned a corner onto another wide west Knightsbridge street and saw before them the first house in another row. It had deep, polished-looking stone steps leading to the white front door, which had a shining knocker. All the windows were big, the wide expanses of glass reflecting the morning sunlight, except for one small window at the peaked top of the building.

There was nothing about this house to set it apart from all the rich houses surrounding it, except for the singing in Nick's blood.

This was the lair of the Obsidian Circle. This was the house of Nick's father.

13

The Trick

"NICE PLACE," NICK DRAWLED. "MUST BE GOOD MONEY IN feeding people to demons."

He climbed the steps and found his smallest knife. He'd learned how to pick locks when he was nine. It had come in handy at times when they had to run and sometimes found themselves with no money and nowhere to go.

There was a difference between breaking into a deserted house so you could sleep for the night and breaking into a house full of magicians. Nick tried to be very quiet. He didn't glance behind him; he knew that Alan would have the others casually arranged in front of him so nobody could see what he was doing.

After a while, the lock whispered a soft surrender and the front door swung open. Alan was beside Nick with his gun already out, but the hall was empty. Alan took an amulet out of his bag and rolled it into the magicians' hall. The amulet was a minor one, meant to neutralise all small magics, such as an alarm set to warn the magicians of intruders.

With the door to the magicians' lair wide open and the wards neutralised, they turned and walked away. They went around the side of the house. Nick put his shoulder to the garden gate and broke it with ease.

Inside was an overgrown garden. This one had no willow, only high grass and the dry, tangled branches of dead rose-bushes.

"That's magicians for you," Jamie said, his voice wobbling. "Everyone gets all caught up in the demon summoning. Nobody mows the lawn."

Alan knelt with a moment's difficulty in the high grass and began to rummage in his bag. He took out a climbing rope with a grappling hook attached. It had been Daniel Ryves's once.

He passed it to Nick silently, and Nick whirled it over his head and caught the iron gutter of the house first try. He pulled at the rope a few times, testing the strength of the gutter, and then nodded.

He could've made the climb without a rope, but none of the others could.

Rope secured, they waited. Mae and Alan had planned this out. They had to give the magicians enough time to notice that the door was open and their wards were down. Once the alarm was raised, the magicians should start combing the house from the ground up. It would be the perfect time to enter from the roof.

There were bound to be lone magicians shut up studying or summoning on the upper floors. With luck and speed, they should be able to pick two of them off.

It would take a lot of luck, and first they had to manage to get up there.

They counted ten minutes before Nick climbed the rope. It was as easy as he'd thought it would be, and once he was on the roof, Alan attached the harness to his belt and Nick drew the rope up, doubling it around his fists and drawing Alan up along with it. That was easy too. Alan had grown thinner and thinner in the last month, and now he hardly weighed anything at all.

He hauled Jamie up as well, and then Mae did not put on the climbing harness. She gave Nick a look that said she was still angry about last night in the garden, and began climbing up the rope herself. Nick looked away over a sea of pointed slate-grey roofs.

He didn't see her lose her grip on the rope and fall. He heard Alan cry out, looked around sharply, and saw her suspended in midair, looking confused and terrified. He saw Jamie, braced on the edge of the roof, looking terrified as well.

Jamie pulled on the air as if it were an invisible rope, and as his hands moved, Mae was tugged upward, inch by inch, until she reached the gutter. She grabbed it in a convulsive movement and scrambled onto the roof tiles, and Jamie let out a deep breath and let his shoulders relax.

Then Jamie cast a deeply apprehensive look around at them all.

"Well, well," Nick said. "What have we here?"

He thought of Mae when they'd first met, talking about the weird things that had happened when she was young and saying she was psychic herself. He thought about how easily Jamie had believed everything they'd told him, and about Jamie's plate breaking when all the glasses broke. He remembered Gerald and how he'd looked at Jamie, how Jamie hadn't been blinded by the magician's sand in the bar in Salisbury, and he thought about the timid air Jamie always wore, deliberately receding into the background, purposely camouflaged.

He thought about his own voice back in Exeter when all of this had just begun, saying, *A few people in this world are born with a certain amount of magic, but they don't grow out of it. They either learn to control it and keep it a secret forever, or they try to do something with the magic.*

He cursed himself for a fool.

"You," Mae said in a shaking voice. "It was never me at all. It was you. Why didn't you *tell* me?"

"I—" Jamie said, and stopped. "I didn't want you to know," he said softly. "I didn't want you to – feel any differently about me. I wanted it not to be true."

"I'm sorry," Alan said in a quiet voice. "But we don't have time for this. We have to move."

Mae looked as if she was about to snap at Alan, but she controlled herself with a visible effort. She rose on trembling legs and went over to Jamie, pushing his hair back the way she did every morning at breakfast.

"All right. We'll talk about this later, but – it's all right."

"Let's go," said Nick, and carefully, one by one, they lowered themselves to slip in through the attic windows and into the house of the magicians.

It was a very fancy attic. There was an expensive-looking carpet on the floor, royal blue and goldenrod-yellow, and the ceiling was full of curves and shadows. They all stood looking at each other, panting in the silence, all a little uncertain now that the plan was about to be put into action.

Mae grabbed Jamie in a sudden hug.

"Don't worry," she said, holding his thin shoulders in a death grip. "I'm not worried. It's all going to be okay."

Jamie patted her on the back, looking shaky but enormously relieved, and said, "Okay."

"All this time wasting is very touching," Nick observed. "Shall we go?"

He turned his back on Alan without a word; next time he saw him, Alan would be unmarked and free to go and live in the world he had been born into. Nick did not plan to bother him again.

Behind him, Alan said, "Nick. Don't – if you see Black Arthur, don't talk to him. Don't listen to a word he says."

"Why?" Nick asked. "Will he lie to me? Imagine that."

Twisting the knife worked. There was a significant pause before Alan was able to say, "I'm sorry."

"For which lie in particular?"

Alan stood silent for a moment, and then he said, "You'll see."

Nick made a disgusted sound and jerked his head sharply in a summons at Jamie. Jamie swallowed again and followed Nick as he made his way down the stairs.

He hadn't said much while the others were planning, but he had insisted on leaving the attic, and access to the roof, to Alan and Mae. That would give them the best chance of getting out.

The magicians' Circle must have owned this house for some time. There were no signs of a rushed and recent move, and now that they were inside, it was obviously a magicians' house. The place was filled with charms that would have fetched a good price at the Goblin Market. There were protective symbols cut into the glass of some windows. There was a chandelier in the shape of a dream catcher, feathers and net carved out of crystal and catching the pale noon light. Nick walked under it and along the corridors softly as a cat, glancing occasionally backward to make sure that Jamie was close behind him and not about to cause any trouble.

Once when he turned around, Jamie was not behind him but a few paces back, studying something on a table.

"What are you doing?" he snapped, but quietly.

"What's this?" Jamie whispered.

He picked up the little glass shape in his hands, turning it over, and the glass, which had shown a flurry of golden autumn leaves, suddenly burst into green leaves and bright sunlight.

"It's a season tetrahedron," Nick said. "Like a snow globe, but depending what side you look at, it shows a different season."

"It's beautiful," Jamie murmured. He turned the season tetrahedron again and got drifting white snowflakes.

"Yes, it's lovely," Nick agreed flatly. "And completely worth being killed because you were too busy looking at toys to keep an eye out for magicians. Don't get left behind. Don't think I will not leave you to die."

Jamie put down the season tetrahedron in a hurry, the glass chinking against the marble tabletop. He took a step backwards, towards Nick, and shoved his hands in his pockets.

"Don't worry," he said. "I know you would."

Nick was mildly startled by Jamie's tone. As they walked on, he glanced over at Jamie, whose face was pale above a dark hooded sweatshirt. Nick took a moment to be annoyed by the flash of his earring. He'd never blend into the shadows if they had to hide. That little glint would catch anyone's eye.

"I can't work you out," Jamie felt the need to inform him, because he was an idiot who never stopped talking. He seemed determined and was speaking low enough, so Nick didn't even try to stop him. "You've been okay to me sometimes, but I can't tell if that means you like me. I don't know if you like anyone, I don't know if you *can* like anyone. I thought at least there was Alan, but then you hit him."

Jamie was furious with him, Nick realised. He supposed it made sense. Jamie hated violence so much.

"I've never thought about you enough to dislike you," Nick said. "I just think you're useless."

"And I think you're scary," Jamie snapped. "So we're even."

There was not a sound, not even the creak of a floorboard, but Nick popped the knife from his wrist sheath all the same. He felt more comfortable with a knife in his hand.

"We're not even. You're causing me a lot of trouble, and I am saving your pointless life."

"You wouldn't have lifted a finger to help us if Alan hadn't insisted. Alan's the one who wants to help people. You don't want to help people. I don't think you even see most people as people. You remind me of – someone I used to know." Jamie bit his lip. "He was terrifying as well."

There was a moving shadow down the hall, but after a moment of observation, Nick saw it was a tapestry fixed to the wall only by the top. It was fluttering in a breeze and covered with symbols to attract wealth and power.

"You only do the right thing because Alan wants you to," Jamie continued, still sounding furious. "Without him, I'm pretty sure you'd be a monster."

Nick bared his teeth at Jamie. "So I'm a monster," he murmured. "Are you scared?"

Below them came the sound of running footsteps, sudden and clear. Jamie jumped and grabbed for Nick's arm, making a small, startled sound. Nick whirled and pushed Jamie up against the wall, a hand over his mouth.

"Shh," he hissed. "Try to remember there are monsters here. Besides me."

Jamie nodded. Nick could hear his own heart beating far too fast as they waited, both tense, for another sound, for a door to open or a voice to speak.

Nothing came. After a moment he released Jamie.

"Sorry," Jamie whispered. "I just wanted to talk to you. I wanted to say – that I think you should forgive Alan. We all have our secrets."

"You certainly do," Nick sneered, and Jamie bit his lip again.

He almost wanted to talk to Jamie about that. It was obvious that Jamie had as much potential to be a magician as Nick did. For days all Nick had been able to think of were images of Black Arthur and demons and death.

It was impossible to think of Jamie in those terms, though. Nick could ask him, perhaps, how he controlled his power. If Nick could find some way not to be like Black Arthur, Alan would be pleased.

Except that it would be impossible for Nick to be harmless and well-meaning, to be like Jamie. And Alan was a liar.

"I don't want anyone to talk to me," Nick snarled. "What difference do words make? He's not my brother."

"What does that matter?" Jamie demanded. "Don't you understand—"

"No," Nick growled. "I understood being brothers. I understood that word, but now I don't understand anything and— Shut up and get behind me!"

Jamie went white and ran to obey him. Nick now had an unobstructed view of what he had seen bearing down on them over Jamie's shoulder. He sheathed his knife, reached behind him, and drew his sword. Then he stood waiting.

Jamie's voice quavered behind him. "Is that a magician?"

"It used to be," Nick said.

A demon could animate a corpse. They didn't like to do it. They preferred all the sensations that went with the living, and besides, the living lasted longer.

When there was no body but a dead one available, though, a demon would make do.

Nick recognised this one. She was the woman he'd killed last week as a wolf. Now her eyes were black and turning to fluid, her yellow hair was tangled, and the smell was worse than the sight of her.

Behind him, Jamie said, "I'm not all that accustomed to the walking dead. Is it all right if I cry with terror?"

Nick kept his eyes on the body. He stepped back a few paces, Jamie thankfully having the sense to step back with him, so he could get a proper look at her. She was shuffling rather than walking, hands limp by her sides even though her face was intelligent and purposeful. She was being careful, because this body was almost at its limit.

This was going to be almost too easy.

Nick grinned and waited, shifting the sword hilt in his hands. The body advanced, feet dragged forward by willpower alone, and as she did, her discoloured lips twitched into a grin back.

Nick stepped backwards again and took one hand off the sword hilt to beckon her on.

She lunged and he swung at the same time, the blow connecting powerfully with her neck. The body spasmed, and Nick had to swing and hit twice more, hacking at the neck, until her head came off. It rolled down that solemn, picture-lined corridor. Her hands clawed feebly at the air, trying to get to Nick, and then stilled.

Nick turned to Jamie before the body hit the floor. "They're not hard to kill," he said. "It's just that most people panic, seeing the dead."

"Oh, they panic, do they?" Jamie asked in a hollow voice. "I can't imagine why."

Nick knelt and wiped his sword clean with the charmed tapestry. Blood was much easier to clean off than the stuff that you got on your sword after killing the dead, and he was rubbing vigorously when he heard the voice.

It came from behind the nearest door.

It was a man's voice, and it sounded like he was alone. Mae's plan had worked. They'd caught a magician studying.

"Hellebore and belladonna in a true lover's knot," he said, as if he was reading aloud from a book.

This was a magician, all right.

"Get behind me," Nick ordered again.

It was too good a chance to miss, but it could be a trick. He sheathed his sword and felt in the sheath at his belt for his throwing knife. A throwing knife was tricky; he might have only one shot, and that one from a distance. For a moment he wished for one of Alan's guns.

The voice went on, quiet and familiar. Nick wondered where he knew it from, and then supposed it might be Gerald. He hoped it was. He wanted a chance to get even with Gerald.

"A child's tear and a drop of running water blended. All these things make—"

Nick pressed his hand flat against the door, and the heavy slab of oak went back easily, its hinges moving smooth as silk. The swift glide of the door opening showed Nick an enormous room with a vaulted ceiling and a wide, polished expanse of wood floor.

Across the floor a dozen summoning circles were drawn, as if someone had decided to create designs rather than laying down a carpet. The lines for communication and the borders between the worlds cut the floor into gleaming slices. Walking on that floor would be walking into a minefield of magic.

In the centre of the minefield was an indoor bonfire. Flames rose high from every line inside the summoning circle at the middle of the room and arched to meet up near the ceiling in a great golden dome.

Under the golden dome was Anzu, looking far more bird-like than he had at the Goblin Market. He had a pair of heavy, dark wings that made him sit hunched forward in the flame, and a sharp, curved beak on a human face. From that predator's beak a quiet voice issued, sounding as if he was reading from a magician's book.

"All these things make a trap," finished Anzu, his beak stretching impossibly into a smile.

Nick stared and then, under the hiss of the fire, he heard a tiny stifled gasp. That was when he realized the trap was behind him.

He spun around, but a magician already had one arm locked around Jamie's throat and a knife pressed against his jugular vein. He was standing directly behind Jamie, and he was no taller; all Nick could see was the greying top of the magician's head. Nick hoped for a moment that Jamie would do something magical, but then he realised that Jamie had probably used all his magic getting Mae to the roof.

Magicians didn't have much power on their own. That was why they used demons.

Jamie was helpless.

If Nick tried to throw the knife at the magician, he would hit Jamie.

Fortunately, there was another option.

Standing beside Jamie and smiling was another magician. This one was familiar. This one was Gerald.

He looked as pleasant and foxy-faced as before, his arms folded and his eyes wide. He looked like the perfect target.

Nick badly wanted to throw the knife, and he would have done it, if the talisman against his chest had not stirred into sudden restless life. The talisman burned, and suddenly the world looked different.

Gerald's harmless look was another trap. The way Nick's talisman was reacting, Gerald was already working a spell, something building in the air and ready to be unleashed. It was obvious he had a lot more power than someone his age should. Enough to have hidden all of it before. Enough to make it clear beyond a shadow of doubt that he'd been captured on purpose before. Enough not to bother hiding any of it now as Jamie's breath came too fast and Nick gripped his knife too tight and the talisman warned him about danger he could not escape.

Nick lowered the knife slightly and the burning of his talisman eased.

Gerald ducked his head and smiled, for all the world as if he wanted to make friends.

"Should I cut the boy's throat?" asked the strange magician, who turned out to be a woman.

Nick noted her cool, upper-class voice. He wanted details to remember her by.

"No, Laura," Gerald ordered. "Wait a minute. I want to see something."

So Gerald had authority as well as power. Interesting.

"Nick?" Gerald said in a careful tone, as if talking to a pet who showed signs of turning savage. "Would you put down your weapons?"

The magician called Laura snorted. "You must be mad. Why would—"

Nick smiled slowly. "What?" he drawled. "*All* my weapons?"

"Yes. Put down all your weapons," Gerald confirmed, in his mild, patient way. "Or we cut Jamie's throat."

He'd never liked Jamie all that much anyway.

That was Nick's first thought. His second thought was that Alan did like Jamie, that Jamie made him laugh, and that there had always been more to Alan's protectiveness of Jamie than a desire to impress Mae. Blond, sunny Jamie was probably Alan's idea of a proper brother, a real one, the one he could've had if his mother had lived. Alan would want Jamie safe.

Besides, Jamie was Mae's brother. Nick found he did not want to think about how Mae would look if she learned that he had let her little brother die.

Nick would have preferred not to see Jamie die, given the choice, but he hadn't been given a choice. It was not as if the magicians would let Jamie go if Nick put down his weapons. They would only kill Nick too, and then he would have committed a very noble and totally pointless suicide.

"We won't hurt you," Gerald promised.

"Oh, really? On your honour as murderous magicians?"

Laura made a choked-off sound of surprise or indignation, but Gerald kept his eyes trained on Nick's face.

"Black Arthur doesn't want you hurt. Do what we ask and the boy won't be hurt either."

"Gerald, this is ridiculous," said Laura sharply.

It could be true, Nick thought. Even if Arthur had been hunting them for Mum's charm all this time, he might not want Nick killed. He was Arthur's son.

He could use that.

It was a risk, though. The magicians might just want two intact bodies for the demons to possess. Nick looked down at the reassuring gleam of his knife and then over at Jamie.

Laura the magician had tight hold of Jamie, one hand in his hair, pulling his head back to bare his throat for her blade. The knife was so close to his skin that he could not even tremble in case he opened his veins against the edge. Jamie was keeping still, with his back arched taut as a bowstring and his eyes wide, scared and hopeless.

"All right," Nick said. "I'll put down my weapons."

He knelt and put down the knife, then unsheathed his sword and laid it the ground, looking warily up at Gerald as he did so, ready to snatch the sword back up if he made any sudden movements. Gerald just smiled like a king well-pleased with the tribute laid at his feet.

He rose slowly, and Gerald murmured, "All of the weapons, Nick."

Nick snapped one knife from his wrist sheath and threw it down. Then he reached into his pocket for his switchblade, and drew that out too. Gerald's gaze was fastened on him, watching every movement, and Nick regretted putting any of his weapons down. Anything would have been better than this slow, enforced stripping of Nick's defences under the eyes of the enemy.

He let the switchblade fall out of his open palm. He made sure that every weapon he dropped landed within easy reaching distance.

He left the knife in his boot and the knife fastened inside his belt and jeans, against his thigh, where they were. What Gerald didn't know might end up hurting him, if they were lucky.

"Now take three steps back," Gerald said quietly.

That would put Nick across the threshold into the room where Anzu waited, and a safe distance away from the weapons. Nick checked over his shoulder and saw that three steps would not bring him anywhere near Anzu, waiting in his simmering flames.

He looked back at Gerald and nodded. He took three deliberate steps back.

He immediately felt the difference, a sudden sensation as if walls had slammed down all around him. Claustrophobia seized him, the feeling pressing on his chest and squeezing his lungs so he could only breathe in short, shallow pants. He looked around and saw that there was a circle of imprisonment chalked onto the floor around him.

Nick looked up sharply at Gerald and saw his eyes flash with triumph.

He wondered when magicians had learned how to trap a human in an imprisonment circle. This wasn't one of those where you would die if you crossed the line; it did not even offer you that choice. Nick could feel the barriers in place. He risked it anyway, tried to step forward and simply could not do it, any more than he could have walked through a wall. This was a genuine imprisonment circle, and he was trapped inside as surely as Anzu was trapped inside his.

Inside his, Anzu was laughing.

The magician Laura had loosened her hold on Jamie. She had one arm looped casually around his neck, and it would have looked like a gesture of affection if she had not still been gripping the knife. Nick could see her properly now, a small middle-aged woman with an intelligent face. She looked surprised that Nick had put down his weapons, although not half as surprised as Jamie did.

"How did you know it would work?" she asked Gerald.

"I guessed," Gerald replied, his voice as soft as ever, belying that hard, triumphant gaze. "I was assigned to watch them, remember? I wasn't sure it would work, but I wanted to test my theory."

Nick did not care what Gerald's theory might be. He was busy calling himself a hundred kinds of fool for putting down the sword. It was becoming more and more obvious that they were outmatched. The magicians had tricks none of them were prepared for. The magicians had clearly planned this. Nick should have let Jamie be a casualty and got out of there. Jamie didn't matter at all, not compared to what else Nick might lose.

He felt something colder and sharper than regret turning in his belly as if he'd swallowed a needle, when he heard the footsteps coming down the stairs and down the corridor towards them.

There were at least four people, and one set of steps Nick knew by heart: fast as anyone's step but with that slightly dragging foot. When the magicians came closer, he saw that one had a knife to Mae's throat, and Alan's hands were tied. The magicians had done just the same as they had with Nick and Jamie, targeting the weak one and using them as leverage. Of course it had worked on Alan, but it should not have worked on Nick.

Alan looked at Nick. His eyes widened slightly when he

saw the imprisonment circle. His gaze travelled from Nick to Jamie. Nick saw him putting together what must have happened and he wanted to say he was sorry but then, incredibly, Alan smiled.

His eyes were shining as he asked, "Are you all right?"

Nick nodded. It wasn't a lie. He was going to be all right. He was going to get out of this circle and he was going to kill every magician in this house. He looked at Alan, and Alan seemed all right too, wrists bound tightly but unmarked. After a moment he looked at Mae and saw that she, unlike Jamie, had clearly struggled. The knife must have just grazed her. Her throat was bloody but not bleeding too much, and she looked steady on her feet.

Nick kept cataloguing these details, all the while hollowly aware that he could see no way they were going to survive this.

"Let's all go inside and talk, shall we?" said Gerald, making an inviting gesture to the room of circles and pentagrams. "Black Arthur will be here soon."

His eyes moved from Jamie to Mae to Alan, as if taking a survey, and then they turned to rest on Nick.

Gerald smiled and added, "He's been waiting a long time to meet you."

14

Black Arthur

THE SOUNDS OF LONDON WERE COMING IN FROM AN OPEN window. Cars were purring mechanically down the streets, and the evening sunlight was cresting the tops of the tallest buildings, crowning them with gold. The rest of the city was in shadow, miles of uniform grey stretching out and interrupted by the glittering lines of rivers.

It might as well have been another world. In this room there was no sound that mattered but the hiss of fire in a demon's circle and Gerald's quiet, pleasant voice.

The rest of the Circle had filtered in by now. There were ten magicians in the room with them, far too many to fight. Alan, Jamie and Mae were in a small knot, guarded by Laura and the other magician with the knife. Alan had unobtrusively placed himself between the others and the knives and he kept edging forward, trying to see Anzu, trying to see more of the room. The magicians fell back as he moved, which meant they did not want to kill him yet.

Nick could not move from the circle of imprisonment, but he absorbed all he could. The room was panelled and dim, all light coming from Anzu's fire and light bulbs in faux candlesticks attached to the walls. The room was large, and it looked even larger because of the circles and pentagrams and amulets forming a crazy pattern that tricked the eye. The chalked lines and deep shadows stretched Nick's vision until the floor seemed about to tilt into another world.

There was nowhere to hide in this room. Even if Nick could get out of the circle, it would be pointless. They had to wait until there were fewer magicians, but there seemed no prospect of there being fewer magicians anytime soon. Everyone was gathered here expecting Black Arthur, the leader of them all.

That was bad news, of course, and yet Nick could still sense the singing, tugging feeling of the call of blood in his veins. His heartbeats were pounding to Black Arthur's approaching footsteps and, evil or not, spell or not, he could not help it: he wanted to see his father.

Then he looked at Alan, who had tasted his blood and who must be feeling the same things Nick felt, and as the door creaked open he saw Alan turn pale and sick with dread.

He wished his father a thousand miles away as Black Arthur came into the room.

The spell of blood to blood sang in Nick's veins, as if there was a kettle somewhere bringing his blood to the boil. For a moment all he could hear was that singing victorious sound, and all he could feel was the tug of connection between himself and this man, the link formed of shared blood.

Its purpose accomplished, the spell ended. The link snapped.

In the sudden silence, Nick found himself staring at his father. He felt the same thing he had felt since he found out the truth. He felt nothing.

There should have been at least some feeling of connection, Nick thought, but instead he was left staring at his father as he would have stared at the page of a book, trying to make sense of what he saw.

Black Arthur did not look as much like Nick as Nick had imagined he would.

He looked a lot like Mum, as if they had chosen each other because they wanted to see themselves in each other's faces and not just their eyes. He looked enough like Nick that Nick could see the markers of shared blood he'd never been able to find in Alan's face. They were clear on the face of this stranger.

Arthur was tall and pale and had black hair. He had Nick's broad shoulders and his strong hands, but something about his muscles looked too sleek and civilised, as if he had built them up for display rather than earning them by fighting. He wore his black hair longer than Nick wore his, and unlike Nick's, it was curly. The ends almost touched his shoulders, and the effect was that of a mane.

He had Nick's flat cheekbones and his brutal, full mouth, but the one thing Nick had expected, Arthur did not have. He did not have Nick's eyes.

Black Arthur had eyes an even paler blue than Mum's. They were pale enough to remind Nick of that dying wolf's eyes, so pale that even the blue looked like an illusion, a trick of the light cast on ice.

When he spoke, he did not have Nick's voice. He had the warm, easy voice of a leader, someone comfortable using words and through words, using people.

"Well done, Gerald!" he said, giving due credit to his lieutenant, but he did not glance Gerald's way.

His big, black-maned head was thrown back to survey his prize, and his wintry wolf's eyes were fastened on Nick. They were shining with possessive pride.

Nick folded his arms across his chest and glared as Black Arthur prowled around the circle of imprisonment, eyes running over every detail of Nick's face and body as if he was an art dealer examining a picture.

"Say something," Arthur commanded at last. "Anything."

"Let me and my brother go," said Nick. "Or I'll cut your heart out."

He did not know how Arthur would react to that – whether he would be angry or laugh at the empty threat – but he did not expect Arthur to look delighted. He had the air of a man whose dog had just done a wonderful trick.

Arthur opened his mouth, but Nick never found out what he was going to say, because the moment before he spoke there was a rap at the door.

"Come in," Arthur said irritably.

"Sir, I'm not sure—" said a voice near the door, but the door swung open amid the sound of protests.

Mum stood in the doorway.

There was a magician behind her, but it was hard to notice anything but Mum. She had her eyes fixed on Black Arthur and her face was white, white as a flame that was burning hot as a star.

Nick cursed softly. Alan looked wild with panic.

Arthur said, "Livia!" and held out his hands, and without a moment's hesitation Mum walked towards him and took both his hands in hers.

He stood with his head bowed down to hers, their

black hair mingling, and they looked like brother and sister in each other's arms, like twins. Nick saw in that moment how they must have been together, before he was born: two magicians who did not care about anything but themselves and each other, beautiful and brilliant and cruel. Mum's face looked older than Arthur's now, marked by lines of care and pain, but there was nothing on her face that looked anything like fear.

"Arthur," she said, running her fingers through his hair. Nick had never seen Mum show affection like that to anyone.

Arthur smiled down at her. "I knew you would come back to me one day," he said. "I knew it." He paused, and when Mum kept her silence, Arthur said, "You have come back to me, Livia, haven't you?"

"Yes," Mum said slowly. "Yes, I have."

"You've forgiven me," Arthur prompted her, as a stage director to an actress who seemed to have forgotten her lines.

Mum looked at him for a long time. "No," she said. "No, I haven't forgiven you."

Arthur caught her hands in his again, pressing them as if Mum's were cold. "But you will," he said confidently. "Everything's all right now. It's all turned out exactly as I told you it would. You should never have run, Livia. You should have known you couldn't change anything."

"I always knew this would happen," Mum said. "I used to sit alone in a hundred different rooms and think of how it would be, standing face-to-face with you again. And then I heard the children talking about going to find magicians – and I knew the day had finally come."

Arthur laughed. "You never loved him?"

"Who?" Mum asked. "Daniel? No, but he was very kind

to me. I owe him something. He tried. No man ever tried as hard as he did."

Her gaze moved for the first time away from Arthur's face, travelling in an unconcerned way from the panelled wall to the demon in his flames, until she found Alan. Alan stood there with magicians around him and his hands tied, his face a naked plea. Mum's expression did not change.

Nick was not surprised that Mum never looked at him.

"He tried to interfere," said Arthur. "He failed, and you were always mine. Forgive me, Livia. You'll see that it was worth it. I will give you anything in the world."

"Give me just one thing," Mum said, smiling into his eyes. "And I'll forgive you."

"Anything," Arthur told her, and kissed the top of her head, tucking her against him. They looked as if they were posing for a picture of the perfect couple.

Nick said loudly, "I have a question."

Mum did not look at him even then. She was doing her trick of pretending not to know Nick was in the room, even though her whole body was tense with awareness of him. She had her eyes turned away, and he could see her schooling her face into blankness in case he spoke to her.

Arthur's gaze fell on Nick and absorbed him to the exclusion of all the world.

"Of course," he said. "You only have to ask."

"Are you—" Nick said, and did not look at Alan. "Aren't you going to take her charm?"

Arthur reached to touch Mum's neck, and metal links slipped like sand through his fingers, one chain followed by another, as if he was telling rosary beads. Magic symbols gleamed against his large, capable hands, hands Nick had inherited from him, hands with the strength to kill. At last there was only one charm left, lying cupped in his palm. It was a simple silver disc with a black symbol carved onto it.

"This one?" Arthur inquired. The chain was taut in his hand. If he closed his fingers around it and pulled, it would snap in an instant.

"I guess so," said Nick, not daring to look at Alan. "That one. Don't you want it?"

Arthur lifted the chain and dropped a kiss on the symbol, then let the charm fall back to Mum's breast. "I want her to have it," he said mildly. "It is keeping her alive."

Nick strode forward in a fury and then found himself pulled up short by the confines of the imprisonment circle. It was like being a savage dog kept on a chain so he would not fly at throats. He felt like flying at throats. He made a sound that was almost a snarl.

"If you didn't want the charm, why were we hunted all over the country?" he demanded. "What did you want? Was it her? You killed Dad because you couldn't find yourself a different girlfriend?"

There was a stir around the room. There was Anzu laughing quietly at the spectacle of Nick, unable to escape the circle. Some of the magicians had actually drawn back when Nick moved, and now Alan was standing at the front of their little group.

Alan had not moved. The grey, worn look of dread on his face had not changed.

"I love Livia," Arthur said calmly. "But you wouldn't be able to understand that, now would you?"

He let go of Mum, left her standing by herself and staring almost thoughtfully out of the window. She made no move to stop him leaving, just lifted her hand to her charms and began to thread them through her fingers, telling them as he had moments before, as if she were praying.

Black Arthur walked towards Nick, coming so close that his shoes almost touched the outside of Nick's circular chalked prison. They stood face-to-face, Nick only a shade smaller than Arthur, their eyes almost on a level. Nick knew they were father and son, but he felt as if Arthur was a spectator at the zoo, and he was a tiger in a cage. Arthur looked at him with gentle interest, and Nick only just stopped himself from snarling again.

"We weren't hunting Livia," Arthur said softly. "This was never about Livia. This was never about a charm. Who's been telling you lies?"

Nick looked at Alan and kept his mouth shut.

Arthur went on, his voice soft and smooth, as if with words alone he could reach through cage bars and stroke a tiger into tameness. "You wouldn't understand lies, obviously."

"You assume a lot about me for someone who just met me today," Nick observed coldly.

Arthur smiled at him, a private and particular smile, as if he was about to let Nick and only Nick in on a joke.

"Hunted all over the country," he said, repeating Nick's words with an echo of Nick's flat inflection. "Not just the Obsidian Circle, but every magicians' Circle in England went hunting. Do you know what they wanted?"

His father was close but not close enough to kill, and they were all in danger. The sense of being trapped was worse than anything. No matter what came, Nick could not fight. He could not even run.

"Do you want to tell me?" Nick asked in a rough voice. "While I'm young?"

Arthur smiled again, almost fondly. "They wanted you," he murmured. "Just you."

Nick's mind raced. He didn't know how much other magicians might have wanted Arthur's son as leverage. He didn't know what he meant to Black Arthur.

The intensity of Black Arthur's gaze made Nick think that he must mean something.

"You don't know how often my magicians have watched you," Black Arthur said. "I know so much about you, so much you don't know. So much you need to know. After all, you thought the Obsidian Circle were causing all the little incidents in your house, didn't you?"

Nick nodded guardedly, waiting for Arthur to drop a hint.

"There was the car that dropped in your garage," Arthur reminded him. "There were all those strange things happening in your house, glasses breaking and lights going out. Why would we do any of that? Didn't it ever occur to you that your house was flooded with magic for the week when you were *not wearing your talisman?*"

Nick remembered the lights going out so he could be left in the dark with Mae. He distanced himself from the memory so he could view it at a remove, so he could think about what he had done and what he'd meant to do.

He had been angry before those glasses broke. He had been angry before the car fell. He had been angry, and the world had started falling apart around him.

After all, what did it matter? He had suspected he was a magician already. Now he knew why Arthur had wanted to find him, and perhaps why the other Circles had wanted to get him first.

"No," Nick said, "it never occurred to me – but it makes sense."

"All the other Circles wanted you," Arthur murmured to him, "but you're mine. My greatest achievement. Do you want to know why?"

"Yeah," Nick said. "I'd like you to explain your entire evil plot in detail. Don't forget the bit where you tell me your one weakness."

Black Arthur laughed. "We're not enemies. I'm going to explain all of this to you, and then you'll understand. We're going to be partners, and I, unlike some people—" He spared Alan a dismissive glance and then leaned forward, all his attention on Nick. "I will never lie to you."

His eyes looked as pale as the demon Liannan's and almost as hypnotic. Nick could feel Arthur's breath on his face.

"Nicholas," said Black Arthur. "I'm going to tell you everything."

"Don't bother," Nick said. "I already know everything. Thanks."

Arthur's words, Arthur's caressing and commanding voice, seemed to indicate that Nick, or at least the prospect of a magical heir, was worth a lot to him. There was something a shade off about him, though, something a little too detached about his perfect act, that made Nick doubt everything his eyes and ears told him.

Maybe it was the fact he was still trapped in a magical circle that made him doubt Daddy's affection.

"Do you?" Arthur asked, and his glacier-coloured eyes went to Alan. "Who told you? Did you tell it, Alan?"

Nick spoke loudly, to wrench Black Arthur's attention away from Alan. "It doesn't matter who told me! Tell me what you want."

Black Arthur smiled. "Oh, I want everything," he said.

"Don't you realise how much power you have?" he continued softly. "Don't you realise what you are – what you could *be*?"

"Look," Nick snapped. "I told you, I know everything. Stop playing games. I know that Alan isn't my brother. I know what you're capable of, and I know what I'm capable of. I know who I am." He took a deep breath. "I know you're my father."

There was a long silence. Everyone had drawn in their breath, and there was nothing in the room but dead air. Nick could not look away from Arthur's face. Black Arthur looked surprised, but after a moment he threw back his head and laughed.

"That's what you know?" he asked. "And why would it matter to you who the father is?"

Nick stared. "What?"

"Why would you care who the father of the body is?" Arthur asked, eyes glittering and lingering on Nick's face. "What does it matter? The body's just a puppet. Don't tell me you haven't felt it."

The room was all shadows as the sun began its long descent, the windows full of greyness. Nick felt for an instant as if they were poised on the brink of a much colder world and perhaps had already started to fall. He looked at his hands in the slanting yellow rays shed by the lamps and saw the chalked lines of the circle below. He remembered the House of Mezentius, and a possessed man trapped in a circle just like this one.

"You are a demon I called into my son," murmured Black Arthur. "You never had a father or a brother. You never had a heart."

His gaze stroked possessively up and down Nick, and Nick

finally understood why Black Arthur looked at him the way he did. He was not staring at a son. He was staring at an object, one that he had created and wanted to use.

Nick knew what he meant to Black Arthur now.

Arthur smiled again, slow, brilliant, and terribly amused. "Did you really think you were human?"

15

Nothing Human

"I ... you're lying," Nick said. "You're lying. Demons can't live in the world that long. The bodies don't last."

There was a clock somewhere in this room, cutting time to pieces with a sharp knife. Nick hadn't heard it before, hadn't been aware of time passing until now. He needed Arthur to speak immediately and tell him that it was all a lie.

"Of course that's true," Arthur said thoughtfully. "That was always the problem. You give a body to a demon and a few weeks later, it's all worn out and you're back exactly where you started. I found that most annoying and so, of course, did the demons."

The demons, thought Nick, and looked over at Anzu. Anzu was already looking at him with a mocking smile, dark wings outlined against the flame. He was a sinister figure, even in this room full of magic, and Nick stared into his night-dark eyes and knew it could not be true.

Then he wondered why Anzu had black eyes, when usually demons had eyes that were water-clear. Demons had black eyes only when they were possessing human bodies. Thomas in the House of Mezentius, and the dead woman in this house, both had black eyes. Nick knew that the possessed had black eyes, had always known that, and he had looked into the mirror a thousand times and never put it together.

Anzu's eyes were a message.

Nick looked at his father's eyes, and then looked at his mother's, and saw nothing but blue, blue, blue. Nick's own eyes were an endless, cold black.

"The problem with the bodies was that the souls were always in there fighting. The soul and the demon tear the body to pieces, like two dogs fighting over the same bone," Arthur said. "I knew there had to be a way around that. Have you ever heard the superstition that a child's soul enters its body with its first breath?"

Nick looked away from him and found he could not look at Alan. He looked at Mae and Jamie instead, standing behind Alan, and saw that Mae's face wore an expression of horrified disbelief. When she met Nick's eyes, she flinched.

Jamie looked upset, but he did not look surprised. Nick recalled Jamie saying that Nick reminded him of someone. Of course. He should have remembered that Jamie had looked into a demon's face before.

He wrenched his eyes away.

"The demons only grant us so much power because we can only grant them so much time in this world," Arthur went on, as if telling his son a bedtime story. "I knew that if I could give a demon a lifetime, the power I received would be unimaginable. I knew it was worth any sacrifice."

Nick's mother, the sacrifice, seemed unmoved. She was still staring at the floor and playing with her charms. Nick was surprised to see a shimmer of power running through the chains.

"I started to collect pregnant women," Arthur said calmly. "I had them taken and kept here, but you cannot understand how difficult it is to open a way from the demon world inside a woman's body. Too many of the women became possessed and died. I had to invent a charm to keep them safe from possession."

Mum twirled the charm Arthur had kissed around one finger, and this time Nick saw a symbol on the silver disc as it whirled and caught the light. It was the symbol of a circle with a line straight through it, the meaning clear. It marked Mum as forbidden territory to the demons.

"The women kept dying," Arthur said. "Opening their bodies to the demon world gave them terrible dreams. They went mad. They got sick. None of them survived to give birth. It was then that Livia became pregnant and I realised what I had to do. I knew how strong she was."

Nick remembered the days when Mum screamed all the time, her eyes fixed on something far away, something nobody else could see. He knew every line of pain on Mum's face and now he knew what had caused them.

"At first Livia did not realise what was happening, and when she did, she was . . . rather distressed. But I knew I couldn't stop. I knew what was at stake. I kept on, and Livia survived, and then on one long day of blood and madness, you came into this world. You were a beautiful baby," Arthur said, and his smile flashed again as if all this was irresistibly funny. "You had blank black demon's eyes, and you never cried. You never made a sound."

It was a straw to a drowning man. Even when he grabbed it, breathless and desperate, he knew it would not save him.

"That's right," Nick said. "Demons don't – they don't talk. I can talk."

"I know," Arthur breathed. "I couldn't believe it when Gerald told me. I think that's amazing."

"It's not amazing," Nick bit out. "It's not true. I can talk, so it's not true."

"Do you find words difficult?" Arthur asked. "I can't imagine that you're any good at reading or writing, and as for lying . . . Words are so alien to your kind. They can't come easily to you."

Nick remembered the night he had come back from Natasha's house to confront Alan and had been confronted by Mae. He had tried to talk and nothing had come out but hoarse croaking, a sound that could never have been language, that did not belong in a human throat.

"Do you know what you remind me of? There are children in this world brought up by animals. There were once two girls brought up by wolves, who thought they were wolves. They howled and they walked on four legs and when people captured them, for a long time they were unable to speak. A baby's mind is a small, blank thing, and too impressionable. You couldn't remember what you were; the baby mind was too limited. And then as you grew, the same mind was flexible enough, young enough, to actually take in human speech. The wild girls could howl, but that didn't make them wolves. And you can speak, but that doesn't make you human." Arthur's voice was almost tender. "Nothing can make you human."

Nick thought about animals. They had never liked him. Even Alan's kitten had bitten him. The animals had known.

Then he thought of the boat, and the way he had felt as soon as he had walked onto it: as if his body did not belong to him. He should have remembered that running water was meant to keep the body safe from demons. He should have known.

"I understand that this is difficult for you. It's a lot to grasp all at once. I knew you wouldn't remember everything when you were put in the child's mind. I meant to bring you up and tell you everything. I meant you to be aware of your power. I meant us to have the world, but – well." Arthur shrugged. "Livia was strange, after you were born. She was so quiet, I thought – we all thought her mind had broken. We thought she was neutralised. We left her alone with you, and one day she was gone. She took you from where you belonged, and then that man and his son tried to take from you what you are."

Nick opened his mouth and then shut it. He was suddenly and desperately unsure of what would happen if he tried to speak.

Arthur smiled. "They all failed. You're here now, and you're mine. I made you. What do you think you owe me for that?"

Nick swallowed. There seemed to be barbed wire in his throat, and he thought that if he spoke, the words would come out mangled and torn.

If he didn't speak, Arthur would win. He would just be a demon standing imprisoned in his circle, silently waiting for his magician's command. He had to say something.

"Nothing," said Nick, and was surprised to hear his own voice. "I owe you nothing," he continued, and actually listened to his voice, flat and cold as a sheet of ice. He did not sound human. "I owe you nothing," he insisted. "Because I don't believe you."

A car horn screamed outside in a long cry for help that went unanswered.

"That reminds me," said Arthur. "Those girls who thought they were wolves? They had a mother. The people who found the den had to shoot the wolf before they could get at the girls. An animal might make that sort of mistake, but a human should know his own kind!" He raised his voice. "Wouldn't you agree, Alan?"

Alan lifted his head. The last colour had drained away from his face, leaving it a terrible stony white. His eyes were dark with fury, so dark that they looked almost black.

"Bring him to me," ordered Black Arthur, and then turned back to Nick. "If you won't believe me," he said, "will you believe him?"

The male magician with the knife seized hold of the ropes binding Alan's wrists and practically threw him in front of Arthur, with enough force that Alan stumbled and had to put his weight on his bad leg to keep himself upright. Nick saw his teeth sink into his lower lip, but he didn't make a sound.

"Alan," Arthur said in the tone of a warm, welcoming host. "I think I've worked out all that happened once Livia ran, but I'd be very interested to get an insider's point of view. Go on, don't be shy."

Alan tilted his chin up to meet the magician's eyes.

"Go to hell," he said, and spat in Arthur's face.

There was instant chaos. Every magician but Gerald moved forward or spoke angrily. Mae shouted Alan's name, and the magician holding her thrust the knife back up to her throat. Black Arthur lifted a fist with magical fire sizzling inside it, and Mum lunged forward and caught his wrist.

"Arthur, no! He's a stupid boy. He's lonely and desperate, and he got fond of it. He had nothing else. Don't hurt him."

Arthur lowered his fist, and Nick slowly unclenched his own. Arthur made a small gesture and his face was clean and smiling once more. He stepped into Alan's space, and Nick looked at the breadth of Arthur's shoulders. He was even bigger than Nick. He could snap Alan in two.

He was a magician. He could do a lot worse than that.

"Alan," Nick said, and on that name of all the words in the world, his voice cracked and emerged as a guttural, inhuman croak. He swallowed and forced out, "I want to know. Please."

Alan's mouth twisted. "It's true," he whispered. "I'm sorry."

His voice broke, but it did not mean he was inhuman. It meant he was crying. The sky outside was such a dark grey that Nick knew there was a storm coming with the night, and no light could filter through the clouds. The lamplight caught the tears clinging to Alan's eyelashes and painted the tears running down his face yellow.

Nick reached out, but the circle stopped him. He let his hand fall; he didn't know what he could have done, anyway.

Arthur reached up a careless hand, bearing a large, elaborately carved silver ring, and wiped a thumb over Alan's cheek, chasing away a tear. That was another thing Nick had never been good at, another way Nick had never been human. He was not good at touching.

Alan turned his face away.

"Don't touch me," he said in a muted voice.

"You were very young when it came. Can you tell me what happened?" Arthur asked, as if he had a right to ask, as if he was a grown-up who had come to save Alan from all this. "Can you tell me how it learned to talk?"

Alan glanced over at Nick. "Do you want me to say?"

Nick nodded, and Black Arthur laughed.

"Of course it does," he said. "What does it know about

mercy? It will take from you until you have nothing left. That's what demons are. That's what they do."

Alan turned his face away from Arthur again, towards Nick, but he didn't seem able to look at Nick. He looked at the floor.

"Olivia came to us hoping that somehow we would be able to do something for the baby. Only we couldn't, of course. And when she realised there was nothing we could do, when she—" Alan shook his head, unable to wipe away the tears with his tied hands. "Dad and I went to our first Goblin Market. I thought it was exciting, I came home laughing, and—"

"And what, Alan?"

Alan's voice was very low. "Olivia was in the bathroom, with – with the baby. She was trying to drown him. Only the baby wasn't drowning. The water was boiling, and Olivia was screaming, her hands were getting burned, and my father had to fight her to get the baby. They were both screaming, and when Dad got the baby out, he wasn't burned at all, and he'd never made a sound. Olivia wouldn't stop screaming. Dad had to stay with her, he had to calm her down. He had to get the baby out of her sight. So he – he gave me the baby. He said that I had to be the one to take care of him now."

"And what did you do then?"

"I did my best," said Alan, his voice raw.

Nick had always known that Alan had practically raised him because Dad needed to look after Mum. He had not pictured it like this. Not Alan, small and trapped in a mad world, as a man and a woman wrestled in boiling water and a demon baby was put into his arms.

Nick had a memory dim enough to be imagination of himself in a little bed, with Alan leaning solemnly out of the darkness, singing something: gibberish. Human words. In the memory Alan's small face looked worried and fond; Nick had seen that expression on his face a thousand times and had never wondered what Alan saw when he looked at Nick.

Turning away from Alan's tears, Nick finally located the clock. It was standing in the shadows behind Anzu's balefire. He saw his own pale face flash for an instant in the fire-lit glass of the clock face, reflection curved in the shape of a scythe.

Even the firelight could not warm those black eyes. The face was made like a man's, but it showed no more feeling than a mask, looked no more human than a doll.

They had given *that* to a child. To Alan.

"So it was you who taught it to speak?" Arthur asked, with what seemed to be genuine curiosity. "How did you do that?"

Alan's face was still averted from Black Arthur, but he did answer him. "I'm not sure. I just— He was my responsibility. I talked to him. I read to him. I took him for walks and pointed things out to him, I told him their names. He started to speak when he was four, and I was so happy. I tried – I tried to raise him right."

"No," said Arthur, in the patient tones of a teacher. "You tried to raise it human."

Alan did not answer Arthur this time. He just kept talking, his voice serious. It reminded Nick of the way he used to tell bedtime stories. "Once he started to speak, Dad started to think – Dad thought there was hope. He tried to teach Nick things, tried to tell him how to behave. The last thing he said before you killed him was that I should look after Nick, and I've done my best."

Arthur sounded truly puzzled. "Why did you even try? Do you think you actually mean something to it?"

"I don't know," Alan snapped. "How could I know? That's not the point. He means something to me. I never wanted him—" He made an effort to lift his eyes to Nick's face. The effort did not succeed, but Alan's next words were directed at him. "I never wanted you to know any of this."

"Why not?" asked Black Arthur, and he looked amused again. "Did you think it would be upset?" He shoved Alan backwards a little, turned his head, and grinned at Nick. "Are you upset? What do you feel?"

Nick stared at his wintry eyes, at his handsome, smiling face. This wasn't Nick's father. He'd never had a father. Demons didn't have fathers. Demons didn't have families. They existed forever, unchanging, in a bleak grey landscape like the endless distance between Nick and all feeling over these past few days.

"Not much," said Nick.

Arthur smiled the smile of a man who had guessed right.

"You never did feel much, did you?" he inquired softly. "You always thought half the things the humans did were mystifying and stupid. You didn't want to save people like Alan did. You didn't want to get close to people. You don't even understand what love is. Do you? Human love. Do you know what it is?"

"No," Nick said quietly.

"Do you know anything about it?"

"I don't," Nick said, and swallowed. "I don't know."

Arthur's voice went even softer, though the softness was too smooth and easy to be kind. "It's all right now. You're free. You don't ever have to pretend to be one of us again. You know the truth, and you know your own power. You know how it works: at sixteen, the body can control the demon magic. You turned sixteen, and I sent a messenger to find you. I promised you I would stop at nothing to get you back, and here you are. Where you were always meant to be."

If Arthur was so concerned about him, it was funny he hadn't put forth his best efforts until the time came when Nick could be useful.

Nick thought of the messenger telling them, *Black Arthur says that now's the time. He wants it back.*

It. Nick. The charm Mum had worn had just been another lie, and the look on Alan's face when that messenger came had not been fear for Mum. He hadn't been plotting and lying to shield *Mum*.

Nick ventured a glance at Alan, but Alan's face was still turned away.

Black Arthur was still talking. "You have what no other demon has ever had: a body of your own. You can do anything you want."

Nick wasn't sure he wanted anything. He just felt cold.

"I gave you the world," Arthur said. "And now you can give me the world – or enough power to swallow up all the other Circles, to become the most powerful magician in the world. That's all I want, and I think that's fair, don't you?"

Nick cleared his throat. "Why should I?"

"We made a bargain when I gave you this body, and now I've explained that I expect you to keep it. You gave me your word."

Had he given his word? He couldn't remember that, couldn't remember any of it, but he did remember Alan's voice saying that the demons would do anything to escape their world.

He looked at Black Arthur's face, his hungry wolf's eyes, and believed him. He had made a bargain.

Blood was pounding in Nick's temples. He looked again at that icy reflection in the clock face and then down at his big hands. He had been right, he thought, looking at the curve of his fingers by firelight as if they belonged to someone else. Black Arthur had given him these hands, that face, and every drop of blood in his veins. Arthur only wanted what he was owed: what Nick had promised him.

He hadn't promised him Alan. Black Arthur had no right to touch his brother.

"My word?" Nick said. "I have words of my own now? I thought Alan gave me all of them. You asked me what I felt. I don't feel like giving you a thing."

Arthur shrugged. "I suppose it would be too much to expect gratitude from a demon. You force me to remind you that you have stepped into a magic circle. If you ever want to get out, you need to cooperate. Come, now. What does it matter to you? You can give me what I want without even trying. You owe me, and I wish to collect, but I won't be your master. I told you this was a partnership. I contributed the body of my son, and now you will contribute the power, and together we will be able to do anything. We will be able to have anything."

Nick did not want to be trapped here for the rest of his life. He wondered exactly how much power Arthur wanted and how he was supposed to give it to him. He suspected that a lot of people would be cut down in Black Arthur's progress towards power. He wondered if that should matter to him.

The air of the room seemed heavy with the weight of all these expectations. Black Arthur was watching him. All the magicians were watching him. All but one.

Mum's voice shattered the tense silence, light and easy, as if she was about to sing.

"What about me?"

Arthur looked vaguely startled. Nick thought he might have forgotten she was there. "Livia," he said, turning his head. "You'll be with me. I will give you anything."

"I told you," Mum said, smiling suddenly. "I only want one thing."

She had her hands clasped to her breast, like a little girl hiding a secret from her elders. Nick remembered that she had been playing with her charms before. He knew that small, mad smile. He was not surprised when she opened her cupped palms a little, and they all saw the shimmer rising from her charms. Mum walked towards Arthur with her fingertips wreathed in gold and blue.

"Yes?" Arthur asked.

Mum was still smiling when she reached Arthur, and she let her charms fall blazing against her chest. She reached up and threaded her fire-ringed fingers through Arthur's hair in the same tender gesture she had used before. Arthur was smiling back at her a little; she cupped his face in her hands.

"Arthur," she murmured.

"Yes, my darling?"

"Give me back my child," whispered Mum.

She caught Arthur's mouth in a kiss. She was holding him close when she burst into flame.

16

Exorcism

"OLIVIA!" MAE SCREAMED, FAR TOO LATE.

The room was suddenly a space confining a riot. Some magicians were rushing to help their leader, throwing out water charms and damping spells into the air. Some magicians, like Gerald, were moving unobtrusively towards the back of the room.

When Mae moved, Nick thought the knife at her throat would cut it, but Jamie looked at Mae and made a desperate effort.

The knife at Jamie's throat never moved. The knife at Mae's throat went flying.

Mae slammed an elbow into the man's stomach and hit his chin with the top of her head. When he let her go, she threw herself at him, and they both went crashing to the ground. The magician holding Jamie moved to help him and Jamie stepped swiftly away. They stood staring warily at each other, eyes locked. The magician twisted under Mae, fingers scrabbling for his knife, but Mae snatched her own knife, the knife Nick had given her, out of her pocket and held the blade to his throat.

Nick heard her pant, "Don't move."

From the corner of his eye he saw Alan move, and he turned away from Mae. Alan was taking advantage of the chaos to pop one of his wrists out of alignment, grimacing as he did so, and slip his bonds. He bent his wrist back into place, glanced at Mae, at Mum, and finally at Nick, and then raced for the door. The door slammed shut and Alan was gone before Nick could blink.

Nick could not move. He could do nothing but watch, and he watched Mum burn.

There was a fire now to rival Anzu's, and this fire was real. Nick could feel the heat of it, could smell Mum's burning clothes and hair and flesh. Arthur was screaming, trying to break free of her embrace, throwing up shielding spells, and still enveloped in flames. Nick saw his pale face remain untouched in the centre of the fire, while his black hair became a streaming torch. Mum put up no defences. She did not even scream. She just burned, skin crackling and going black, hair a sheet of flame. Nick knew she was alive only because the fire was still going, backed up by more power than he had ever dreamed she still possessed, burning with the rage and hate Mum had been saving for fifteen years. Arthur's voice was an inarticulate roar, and the water spells were bouncing off them. For a moment Nick thought that Mum was actually going to succeed.

Then she tumbled against Arthur's chest, the kiss broken, her body reduced to charred skin and bones. Arthur gasped for clean air, his clothes and hair hanging in blackened remnants.

Mae shouted, "Jamie, come here!"

She positioned the knife point above the magician's chest, over the heart, and then hesitated. Nick remembered what he'd told her last night: *Across the throat or under the ribs for a killing blow.*

The magician tried to buck Mae off but she hung on, set her teeth, and slid the knife in under his ribs. Blood flowed out around the knife, spreading across the man's shirt, and Jamie went white.

"Mae," he said. "No—"

Mae was panting, her breaths coming out like sobs. "Jamie," she said, her voice wavering. "Come here."

Jamie stumbled forward and Mae closed her hand around the knife blade. Then she reached up to Jamie, still making those sounds between breaths and sobs, and lifted his shirt. She left a bloody handprint on her brother's hip, over his demon's mark. For a moment the mark could still be seen, black under the smudgy red print, and then the lines blurred, turning into a grey shadow, and the mark was lost beneath a magician's blood.

Laura the magician grabbed Mae by her hair, wrenching her up and away from the fallen magician, and swinging her knife down in a vicious arc aimed for Mae's throat.

"No!" Gerald commanded. He took Jamie gently by the shoulders and pulled him back a step. "Don't hurt her."

"She just murdered Rufus!" Laura exclaimed.

"She might be useful," said Gerald. "Leave her alone."

Laura looked mutinous for a moment, but she contented herself with pressing the blade of her knife hard against Mae's already-grazed throat. Mae stayed still, her eyes closed and her face turned away from them all towards the window.

"Do you know why Gerald wants them spared?" Arthur asked, his voice harsh from inhaling smoke and perhaps from something else, something as strange and human as grief.

Nick looked at him, which meant looking at his mother. She was on the floor now, so much discarded rubbish, and Arthur was approaching Nick with glittering, furious eyes. Even as he walked, his burned hair was growing, writhing like so many black and silver snakes. His shirt was wrapping itself around him, the charred shreds twining like lovers.

"Maybe he likes the look of Mae," Nick drawled.

"Don't be ridiculous."

Nick raised his eyebrows. "Does he like the look of Jamie?"

"He thinks that we might be able to use them as bargaining chips," Arthur snarled. "He thinks that you might prefer them alive. I think Gerald's young and he's being naive. I also think that you'll do what I say without more bargaining. I sold my wife for this; I sold my son, and I will have what I paid for! Do you know how many demons would give anything to be in your place?"

There was a strange sound as Arthur spoke. Starting low, and then rising above the hiss of his balefire, was the sibilant sound of Anzu laughing.

"Oh yes, anything," Anzu said. "Who wouldn't want to be trapped in a pathetic little human mind, unable to remember who they were? Especially since it went so well this time. How many demons volunteered to be put into a squalling brat, Arthur? There was only Hnikarr, and he was always reckless and stupid. Even he almost didn't do it. Liannan advised against it from the start."

"Liannan," Nick echoed.

He remembered her cold kiss and her trembling mouth. She had told him that she had known him once, a hundred years ago or more.

She had told him not to trust Anzu.

"You don't remember her, do you?" Anzu asked, beak-like lips curling and wings forming an almost sardonic curve above his head. "You don't remember me, either. Of course, we knew you wouldn't, but Arthur promised he would remind you of us and our claims. I suppose it slipped his mind."

"What claims?"

"Do you think, Hnikarr," Anzu said, black eyes on his, "that we would ever have trusted a magician with one of our own? You, me, and Liannan . . . we had an alliance. We agreed to your crazy plan, we knew you would be helpless as a child in this world if the magicians failed you. You promised us bodies, and we bound ourselves in service to you. For years you've been calling us up, treating us like slaves, playing the human and remembering nothing! Now you know everything, old friend. When will you be paying your debt?"

It had always been so easy for Nick to call his demons.

Anzu had said the word "friend", but that did not tally with the frosty snap at the end of every word he spoke. He was not looking at Nick like a friend.

"You shouldn't have marked my brother," Nick said slowly.

"How did I know you'd say something like that?" Anzu snarled. "You're disgusting. Of course I marked him. I am going to kill him. We are demons. That is what we do! If you don't understand that, there's at least one thing that hasn't changed. You were always a fool."

"Shut up," Arthur commanded.

"And you're a fool too," Anzu said. "Do you have any idea what a demon is? Do you really think, even for escape, we would exchange everything we know, everything we've learned over the centuries, to become a crawling creature like that one?"

He spat in Nick's direction, a fat spark bursting from his beak and sputtering out at the edge of his circle.

"You humans barely live long enough to know you're going to die! Any of us would rather go on living where we are, snatching escape in a crumbling body, than give up who we are. You'd better come to some arrangement with Hnikarr. The rest of us have all seen what he's become. Nobody will have anything to do with your marvellous bargain."

Nick looked at Anzu, dark-winged in his fiery circle, and thought of a hundred questions to ask him, about the demon world, about Liannan. About what he had meant to Liannan and what he had meant to Anzu.

Anzu's face was filled with malevolent amusement. He'd find it funny, not answering Nick's questions. Besides, even if Anzu had wanted to tell him, Nick suspected he would not be able to. He would not understand what Nick meant if he asked what a demon was.

Nick should know what a demon was. He should know what he was.

"I didn't know you two were so closely allied," Arthur said slowly.

"You don't know much, magician," Anzu sneered.

"Well, if you know Hnikarr, you can clear up the little debate between me and Gerald. You've known it for centuries. Will it care about these humans' lives?"

Everyone looked at Mae and Jamie. Mae still had her eyes shut, blood sliding down her throat, bloody hands clenched. Gerald was whispering in Jamie's ear, and there was a change coming slow as dawn over Jamie's face. He was starting to look angry. Nick knew them both, as he had known very few people in his life. He could remember them in a hundred different ways, Jamie frightened in a bar in Salisbury, Mae supporting him outside the House of Mezentius.

He wondered if that mattered.

Anzu snorted. "Why should he?"

Anzu should know.

"As I thought," Arthur said. "Humanity is not something that can be built." He turned to Nick. "You are not my son. You are not something that can feel," he whispered. "Your own mother is lying there dead. And you don't care."

Nick looked across the floor strewn with magical circles to where what remained of Mum lay. All he could see was a heap of burned clothes and hair. She was dead. He had hated her because he'd thought it was her fault they were being hunted, and that had been a lie. She had hated him for wearing her son's face, which was a lie too.

There was the cold thought in Nick's mind, somewhere in the grey absence of feeling, that he shouldn't waste time with humans. They didn't last.

"Laura," Arthur snapped. "Gerald. Bring them to me."

Laura shoved Mae almost onto the blade of the knife with every step. Jamie followed her without Gerald having to push him at all.

Arthur glanced at them and then turned back to Nick with eyes that had been wilder every second since Mum died.

"I know what you are," he said. "A demon, a creature defined by your actions and desires. I made a bargain with you, knowing what you are. You'll do what I want because it's the best thing for both of us. Don't tell me you care if these two live or die."

Nick thought of Anzu's words. He had sounded certain; sounded as if he knew who Nick was, what demons were.

Nick was not certain of anything except for unavoidable realities like Mum on the floor.

Maybe he never had felt anything. Maybe it was just that Alan had always expected him to feel something, and he had convinced himself that he could.

He didn't get a chance to answer Arthur. All the lights went out and they were plunged into what, except for the dim, unearthly light of Anzu's circle, amounted to total darkness.

Someone screamed and Black Arthur swore. Close by there was movement in the dark, shadows stirring within shadows, and Nick knew that Mae and Jamie had dived for the floor. Laura cursed, and Nick thought he saw a smaller movement: her hands grasping for Mae an instant too late.

Everyone was in motion. Nobody was watching but Nick, so nobody else saw the small slice of paler shadow when the door opened and shut.

Black Arthur's voice struck through the darkness like a whip. "Pull yourselves together! There's no need to panic."

Nick threw his head back and let himself laugh. It was a slow, delighted laugh, rolling cold as the sea and washing through the whole room. He'd used the laugh before to make people shiver and turn pale.

He knew now that his laugh did not sound human.

"What?" Arthur snapped, and then, as the low laugh continued, his nerve broke and he shouted, "*What?*"

Nick leaned forward in the dark and whispered, "You don't know my brother."

He was still speaking when the first shot was fired.

It was too dark in that room, with night and a summer storm closing in, to see a thing. There were too many magicians and they were moving too much, and Black Arthur was shouting orders and causing even more confusion. The weak shimmer of Anzu's balefire only seemed to deepen the shadows in the recesses of the room.

Alan had planned this ambush well.

The first shot sounded like bone cracking, and it was followed by a thump. A man screamed, and Nick started to laugh again. The sound should cover the sound of Alan moving. Besides, it was frightening people, and that might help.

He saw another flurry of movement beside him and strongly suspected that Gerald had pulled Laura quietly to the ground. He could tell Alan where they were, once more pressing threats were dealt with.

"Somebody catch that boy!" shouted Black Arthur, and from his charms and amulets came a sudden low, smoky haze of colour. It was red like the embers of a dying fire, shot here and there with moody purple. The power outlined the shape of Arthur's hands in darkness.

Alan fired again as Arthur threw the ball of light in what Nick thought was the right direction. Arthur leaped sideways at the sound of the shot, and the streak of magic flew off through the air at random. It struck harmlessly against one of the panelled walls.

After a moment the light of Arthur's power faded into darkness, and once more the only light was that of Anzu's circle. Acting from what Nick assumed was sheer mischief, Anzu had lowered his flames considerably, and the dull glow provided hardly any light at all. Nick had excellent night vision. He could not imagine how little the humans could see and how afraid they must be.

"Mae and Jamie got down," he let Alan know. "Kill them all."

The room was too small and the magicians were too powerful. Sooner or later Alan would be caught, but Nick thought it wouldn't do any harm to have the magicians hear that. There was another scream and a burst of frenzied movement. Nick thought that someone had tripped over a body.

In the confusion, even Nick lost track of where Alan was. Then he felt a disturbance in the trap that had closed on him, a sudden living presence in the icy walls around him. There was breathing where there had been only silence, and the first thought that came to Nick, clear and calm, was that a human had strayed into his circle and he should kill him.

"Nick," said Alan, under his breath.

He was standing close to whisper to him. Nick supposed that it was easier in the darkness. Alan had not even been able to look at him when it was light.

"Don't worry," Alan continued, his voice rapid and soft. "I'm going to get you out."

Nick listened with detachment to his own whisper back, about as human and reassuring as a whisper from the grave. "I'm not worried."

He could feel Alan trembling in the darkness, and for a moment he thought that Alan was simply afraid of him. Then Alan stepped in towards him, and he felt Alan's hand, the one that was not holding the gun, gentle in his hair. He turned his face into the touch and Alan, as if he was leaning over Nick's bed when Nick was very small, pressed a warm, swift kiss on Nick's cheek.

Then he was gone, and the circle was cold, silent, and still once more.

"Someone go and see what that wretched boy's done to the fuse box," Arthur commanded. "I'll deal with him."

306

There was a movement in the darkness, and then a silhouette against the open door, providing a perfect target. Alan's gun rang out again, and there was another thump. "Sure about that?" Nick asked, grinning in the dark.

"Who was that?" Arthur demanded, sounding more offended than shaken, as if Alan had dropped a spoon in a restaurant rather than a person with a bullet. "Was that Charles? Charles!"

"I wouldn't bother calling," Nick advised. "My brother doesn't miss."

There was a mess of magic in the air, colours crisscrossing like scribbles of crayon over a black page. Magicians were hitting each other. There was more screaming, and in the light of magic, like the light shed by dozens of fireworks in the sky, Nick saw Mae and Jamie on the floor, Mae with her arm protectively over Jamie's head, and Jamie with his arm around Mae's waist. Right next to Jamie lay Gerald, holding on to Jamie's shoulder.

Against the magic-stained darkness, Alan and Arthur were standing, looking at each other. Magic was coiled around Arthur's fists and arms like bright, living ropes, and Alan had his gun pointed at Black Arthur's face.

Alan's glasses reflected the multicoloured light. His voice cut through screams.

"I want you to know I appreciate this, Arthur," he said. "You've made sure my plan worked out perfectly."

Arthur was standing very still. He'd seen Alan shoot now; he wasn't treating him as lightly as he had before, as a child whose tears he could wipe away while he laughed at him. He was working out how to bring Alan down without risking being shot.

"Oh yes," he sneered. "I'm sure that getting your precious brother trapped in a magicians' circle was your plan all along."

Alan stared at him impassively. "Well, not all along. I was hoping that someone at the Goblin Market might be able to trap him in a circle for me, but she refused to try. So I had to do this on my own. I couldn't let Nick know any of it — I wanted him to be human for as long as he could. We had humans in the house, and I was hoping he'd make friends with them. I knew you wouldn't stop hunting him. I knew I had to make sure that no magician could ever touch him again. I took the second demon's mark because I knew that he'd help me hunt magicians. You took him? I brought him to your damned house and your damned circle. I chose this!"

He took a step closer to Black Arthur, who was just waiting for Alan's attention to waver. He was just one human, alone with magicians closing in on him, and Nick could not understand the blazing, triumphant look on his face.

It seemed to infuriate Arthur. "And why would you do *that*?"

"So I could do this," Alan answered calmly, and continued in a clear voice, "I call on the one I gave the name Nicholas Ryves!"

It shocked the magicians enough so that the magic stilled in their hands, and the room fell once more into relative darkness. That was broken by a crackle of power and light from Black Arthur's hands, magic resting against his palms like two lightning bolts.

"What are you doing?" he shouted at Alan. "You don't call on demons like that. You have to call on them using their true names!"

"You're an idiot," Alan shouted back. "You've worked with demons your whole life, and you still haven't figured it out? Why would demons have true names? They don't even have a spoken language. That's not how you call them. They don't answer because they believe that's their true name. They answer because *you* believe it! I call on the one they called Hnikarr in the west, I call on the one I call my brother. I call Nicholas Ryves!"

Alan was no dancer. It should not have worked, except that Nick was already in a magicians' circle, drawn by magicians, calling on and reflecting the power of the true Obsidian Circle that they had moved from Exeter to London.

Just as Alan had planned.

The magicians' circle tightened, as if the walls that Nick could neither see nor break through were closing in. It was more than that. It felt as if he had been in a trap all along that was formed of a dozen different steel strands, and he only realised they were there now, when every strand went taut. They held him at his wrists and ankles, they wrapped around his head. He felt for a moment as if he was on puppet strings; his throat constricted as if he was held on a choke chain.

He remembered Merris Cromwell's voice, saying, *Exorcism means naming the demon and commanding it.*

The feeling was not entirely unpleasant. Now that his power had been called on, Nick could feel it surging within him. His body was thrilling to it, like a rush of adrenaline, and all along the lines in his circle there was magic rising.

He looked at Alan, and their eyes met over a sea of white balefire, glittering like snow and moving like light.

Soft as the crackle of the fire, Nick said, "What do you command?"

Tell me to kill them all, Nick thought.

He turned his head at the sound of Arthur's voice, hoarse and desperate. "What are you going to do?"

It turned Nick's head because it puzzled him. He did not think Arthur would sound that desperate if he were simply afraid for himself. Arthur was too arrogant for that, so that left the question: what did he think Alan was going to do?

Arthur was moving towards Alan like a hunting cat, deceptively slow and poised to leap.

"I don't care what you think of me," he said, begging now. "Not one of us would do something like this. You don't know what these things are capable of. You would doom the whole world."

There was something everyone knew about demons. Magicians called them into circles or into bodies, kept them trapped, kept their powers limited. Not even a magician would let a demon go free.

Alan's plan was to make sure that no magician could ever touch Nick again.

"Don't do this!" Arthur roared.

Don't do this, Nick thought. *Arthur is right. I don't know what I would do. I cannot be trusted.*

As usual, he could not find the words to say what he meant.

Alan ignored Arthur completely, his gaze fixed on Nick. He looked calm and absolutely determined.

"Nicholas Ryves," he said, making the third time a charm, and then he smiled. "I set you free."

Arthur leaped for Alan an instant too late, knocking him to the ground, his hand over Alan's mouth as if he could stop words that had already been spoken.

The walls of the circle crashed down as if they had always been too light and fragile to hold anyone, and Nick's magic came rushing in a white roaring tide over the floor. The flood covered magical signs and human bodies alike, and Nick found the centre of this unlimited power and threw it at Black Arthur's heart. Black Arthur screamed, and Nick spread his arms and broke free of his last prison. He rushed, complete at last and free at last, out into his new world.

He left the body behind him on the floor.

17

Knowing the Words

NICK WENT RACING THROUGH THE CITY. HE WOUND through the narrow lanes and broad streets of London, insubstantial as smoke, curling around humans, who shivered and looked around with wide scared eyes for the cause of their sudden fear. London at night was a glittering playground full of humans and the shiny toys they'd built around them. Nick could have levelled it all.

He went flying up around the spires of tall, aggressively new buildings and let himself plummet in the sheer, sudden drop down to the parliamentary houses that stood in lines of grey stone. There was a hum of human noise everywhere; Nick wasn't used to understanding it.

He moved to a place higher up and farther away from the humans, to the familiar ground of Tower Bridge. There was a break in the clouds there, with the light of the setting sun still streaming through. Nick wreathed himself like mist around the medieval towers turned into fairy-tale gold by the sinking sun, connected by soaring blue arches. His shadow spread across the sparkling river, turning it into a deep, steady stream of darkness that snaked through the whole city.

It was his city now.

Nick spun, and spun the air with him, whirled sky and clouds around his fist and into a roiling grey mass. He clapped and thunder echoed in his ears; he broke dark holes in the clouds and sent lightning blazing through them. Light and sound crashed in the air around him, as if he were caught in some terrible car accident, and he rolled through the storm and laughed again.

The clouds formed layer upon layer of thick grey blankets, wrapping Nick up warm and safe in the broken sky. He could do anything he wanted. Every moment of fury, every impulse towards destruction that he had ever had, could now be vented on the world.

Thunder struck against the clouds, ringing out in triumph.

He'd taken the gamble and won. No magician had a hold over him now, nor ever would again. Liannan had been wrong to advise caution. Liannan . . . she had seen him when he was helpless and ignorant and bound to that human body. She had tried to be kind to him. He could find her now, do something for her, and tell her that he remembered everything. He did remember everything.

He did not remember ever thinking in words before. He did not remember ever thinking of himself as having a name before. Names were human things, important because humans used names in order to use you. A name was a collar and a chain. Nick didn't have a name.

Nick saw the problem with that last thought almost immediately.

He shook it off irritably, reached down and tried to burn the realisation away with a flash of lightning, burning in the sky over London. It crackled in the air below him and thunder rolled above him, a steady, soothing growl, the storm speaking to him without words.

He had to get rid of all the words. He had to stop thinking like this. He'd been taken and indoctrinated by those humans, but he knew everything and he could do anything now.

He stopped and tried to think of something he wanted to do. The storm had no answers for him.

The human world had been the demons' goal for so long, Nick was not sure what to do with it now he had it. The magicians were their masters, promising relief from the pain as long as you gave them obedience, and every demon dreamed of being a master instead. Being the one with all the power, who could terrify and rule the humans.

Demons did not see that there was any position in the human world but the position of master or slave. Now he was no longer a slave. He could crush the people in this world if he felt like it – but what would he do then? He could create a hundred storms like this one. He owned this night and all those trapped in it.

It was dark and a little cold. He felt tired and chilled by everything that had happened today. He wanted to go home to Alan, eat cereal on the sofa, and sleep in his own bed.

That was what humans did, with the whole world laid out before them every day.

He buried the towers in storm clouds. He could set the river Thames on fire if he chose, reduce it to steam in the riverbed.

He could not go back to a human. Going back to a human would be like a beaten dog escaping its chains and then crawling back to its kennel, whining for its owner.

That was a human sort of comparison, though. He had

to stop thinking like a human. He had to stop thinking in words. He did not remember being taught words. Sometime in the distant past he had learned that a sound meant an idea, a particular sound meant a particular idea, and sound and idea could never be disentangled and independent again. He remembered how they all used to laugh at words, to which humans attributed so much power, as if sound and air could possibly mean an idea, or an individual.

He thought of the name Alan, and what that meant.

It seemed that the word *home*, once learned, was hard to forget.

Black Arthur had been right, though. He had never been human, never felt things in a human way, never been completely comfortable with a language made of words. Nick wondered if the girls brought up with the wolves had ever been comfortable with the wolves or humans. He wondered if they had wanted to go back to the wolves once they were rescued, and what the wolves would have done if they had.

It was easiest to be with your own kind. Nick thought of winking at the possessed man in Mezentius House, and how Alan must have seen that and run away to hide his horror and fear, seeing his demon brother belonging with the demons.

Nick had gone after him. It had been all right.

That had been before he knew. He thought of Black Arthur telling him, *You are not something that can feel.* Nick knew what he meant now. A demon had no capacity for warmth.

Alan had let him go. Nick would never have taken that kind of risk with his own world, with his own kind. The humans were not like they were, not powerful and logical, not barren and bleak like the endless stretches of space in the demon world. He thought of Mae's body heat against him, anchoring him while he crossed running water. He thought of Liannan and her cold mouth, how she had wanted a moment of warmth to take back with her to their world.

Things were what they were. They couldn't be changed. Something eternally cold could not turn himself inside out, turn his face away from everything he was, and should not long for something brief and stupid and senseless and warm.

Everything was changed now. He knew the truth. He knew what he was.

There was no way back, not ever.

He let the storm clouds dissolve and the winds die away, and in the gathering quiet it occurred to him that he had left Alan in a nest of magicians.

He went back faster than sound or light, fled uncaring through a city he could have owned to the one place that mattered, then came in through the roof and hovered over the floor where the bodies lay.

There were people standing. Alan was not one of them.

He was lying on the floor, half covered by Black Arthur's body. Black Arthur's eyes were open and blood was coming out of his eyes, his ears, and his nose. He was dead.

Nick had been angry, but surely not angry enough to hurt Alan. Surely he had struck down Arthur before the man had a chance to touch Alan.

There were other magicians in this room who were still alive, and therefore still a threat. Mae and Jamie were facing them hand in hand, defenceless, and facing them just the same.

Nick was about to whirl on the magicians when he noticed that none of them were actually attacking. The most that seemed to be happening was that Gerald was standing toe-to-toe with another magician, and that man was talking loudly.

"We should kill them all!" he said, and Nick pinpointed the man with his power. It would be easy as pinning a butterfly to the wall and watching it die.

Gerald reached up in his friendly, casual way and took the man by the throat.

"Do you think you give the orders around here now, Mark?" he inquired lightly. "Are you challenging me?"

"No," Mark said. "No, of course not, I simply assumed—"

"Don't," Gerald advised, and smiled his shy smile into the older man's face. "We're going to leave now. We're going to let them live. What do you have to say about that?"

"I – nothing," said Mark.

Gerald let him go and turned him like a child, giving him a solid push between the shoulder blades in the direction of the door. The other magicians took the hint and, even though some cast venomous glances behind Gerald's back, they all started filing towards the exit. Some had to step over the bodies on their way.

Gerald gave a small sigh of relief, as if a potentially awkward situation had been happily resolved, and turned to face Mae and Jamie with his hands in his pockets.

"I gave you your lives," he said. "Remember that. I don't give without expecting a return. I'll be watching you." His eyes lingered on the healing cut he'd made along Mae's cheek, something cold in them surfacing for a moment. Then he was smiling again. "And I will be back to collect."

"What, our lives?" Jamie exclaimed, moving in front of Mae.

Gerald shrugged. "Come now, Jamie," he said, eyeing him with what seemed to be a considerable amount of amusement. "Do you think I would go after one of my own?"

Jamie reached behind him and found Mae's hand again. "I'm not one of yours."

"Sure you are," Gerald murmured. "You just don't know it yet. Are you going to feel safe waiting for everyone else to discover your little secret, watching your sister grow afraid of you, knowing that a demon's on the loose out there? You just might be glad to see me when I come back."

He nodded his head at them in farewell, turning to follow his magicians out into the corridor.

He paused at the door and let his gaze sweep up and down Mae, that glint of coldness appearing again like a knife carelessly hidden by someone who would not mind too much if people saw it and were afraid.

"Of course," he murmured, "you might not be."

He winked at Jamie and shut the door.

Nick did not kill any of them. There were enough bodies lying on that floor for Alan to see when he woke. What Nick did was drift towards one of the bodies, the one lying in the magicians' circle. All the other circles were empty. Anzu had gone when the man who'd called him died.

There was no fire left in the circle, and no life in the body. The chest was rising and falling, but the open eyes looked dead.

They were blue eyes, like the eyes of his dead parents. They were all dead, that magical blue-eyed family. The child had never had a chance to live.

Nick surveyed the vacant body dispassionately. He knew it, could remember the feeling of every muscle and sinew. He knew where every mole was, knew every line of the face. It was just that he also knew he did not belong in it, and did not really need it.

He remembered again that time on the river, and the persistent nagging feeling that his body did not belong to him. It was a hundred times worse now when he tried to force his way inside. The body felt heavy, like the earth humans were supposed to be made out of, and he felt as if he was entirely the wrong sort of material to be put into it. It was as if someone was trying to squeeze too much water into a cardboard box.

For a moment he felt as if the body might burst, but then he seemed to settle back into it, his energy running comfortably along the lines of the body again and finding a way to fit. Then it was just a matter of remembering that he had to move the limbs in order to move again. It seemed such a clumsy way to do things, and he levered himself up with arms that felt like rubber.

Nick squinted and the world came into focus.

Jamie was standing by the window, saying, "The storm just stopped," in a wondering, detached sort of way. He turned at the sound of Nick getting awkwardly to his feet.

At least stepping out of the circle was no problem now.

"Nick woke up," Jamie told Mae as Nick walked, surer with every step, across the floor towards his brother. His body was working well enough that when he got to Alan, he went down on his knees beside him, and nothing had ever been so easy.

Alan was lying on his side and he was still breathing. He

had just been knocked out when Arthur tackled him, Nick told himself. He was all right; he had to be.

What Nick did do was reach out and wipe away the trickle of blood at the corner of Black Arthur's mouth. Then he leaned over, passed his bloody fingers over Alan's leg, and watched the demon's mark fade away.

Nick did not touch his brother again. He just stayed by his side and waited for him to wake up.

After a moment, he slanted a look over at Mae. She had not stirred when Jamie told her about the storm or about Nick. She was standing over the body of the man she had killed. Nick remembered now – she had killed him and taken the mark off Jamie. He made an effort to catch her eye, and when he did he smiled.

"Well done," he said.

Mae looked sick. Nick realised that somehow he had said the wrong thing, and he was just thinking that Alan would have said the right thing when he saw Alan stir.

The first thing Alan's eyes fell on when he opened them was Mae, and immediately he sat up and said, "Oh, Mae. I'm sorry."

For some reason, that seemed to be the right thing. Mae almost smiled, and at the sound of Alan's voice, Jamie stopped looking lost in troubled thought and looked instead at his sister. He went over to her at once, looked anxiously up at her, then reached out and wrapped a protective arm around her shoulders.

She smiled properly then, dropping a kiss on his head. That was good, Nick thought, and then Alan said, "Where's Nick?" and all thought of the others was lost.

For the first time since he had heard the truth, he turned and looked into his brother's eyes.

Alan looked enormously relieved to see him and scared to death. Nick looked at him and knew what Alan was seeing: blank black eyes set in an expressionless face, and no way to guess what was going on behind those eyes. Alan had flinched violently away from him when waking from dreams of demons. Alan had deliberately unleashed him on the world.

Whatever Nick did now, Alan would think it was his fault.

Nick decided it was good that he had not allowed Alan to wake and see that empty body. He could be here. He could do that much.

"Nick," Alan said, and his eyes travelled from Nick's face to Mum's body, lying too close to them. Alan flinched back, as if the sight hurt him. He was shaking a little. "Nick," he said again, and his voice was shaking a little too. "Nick, talk to me."

Nick shook too, but not from horror or grief. He just felt cold, empty of the right words. He knew how to talk, but he did not know what to say. He could not give Alan what he did not have. He could not be human, even for Alan.

He allowed himself to remember Black Arthur's voice once more. Black Arthur had said that a demon was a creature defined by its actions and its desires.

"I won't leave you," Nick said, his voice emotionless as ever in his own ears. "I don't want to."

"Okay," whispered Alan. He reached out, the way humans did, and slid his arm around Nick's shoulders. "Okay," he said again, and Nick could tell by the trembling in his voice that he was crying.

His tears fell warm on Nick's hair, and he slid warm fingers through Nick's hair to follow them. Nick closed his tearless demon's eyes and leaned into the embrace.

"What are we going to do?" he asked.

Alan whispered, "We're going to go home," and Nick nodded, abandoned words for just a moment, and bowed his head as Alan stroked his hair. He was not made human, but he began slowly to feel as if this body could be his again. He felt grounded and at home already under his brother's gentle human hands.

ACKNOWLEDGMENTS

Behind this book was an army saving me (and more importantly, my book) from myself.

Enormous thanks are due to Kristin Nelson, my fabulous agent, for the endless patience and the super powers. Not to mention her lovely assistant, Sara Megibow.

Enormous thanks and bouquets are due to the entire team at Simon & Schuster for taking a chance on me and doing so many shockingly wonderful things for my book.

Especial thanks to my brilliant editor Karen Wojtyla for all the wise words, I totally owe you a glass of potatoes in Ireland one day, and to her lovely assistant Sarah Payne.

To Nicole Russo, for the awesome publicity.

To Russell Gordon and Gene Mollica for their combined hard work on my sparkling cover.

To my copy editor Valerie Shea, for not letting night fall three times in one day.

And thanks to the amazing people at Simon & Schuster UK, among them Venetia Gosling and Elisa Offord, who have done lovely things for me my side of the pond.

To Cassandra Clare and Holly Black, for all the excellent advice, comforting words and basically being the coolest writer friends possible, even if Jane Austen were resurrected and wanted to hang out.

To my family and friends in Ireland, England and America who all had to put up with me during the various stages of this book! Particular thanks to the Irish inner circle, Chiara, Susan, Eleanor, Ashling and Rachael, who put up with more than most.

To Anna who lived with me in New York and taught me about publishing and firemen, Pinelopi who lived with me in England while I wrote the book and was the first Alan fan, and Natasha and Jenny who lived with me (somehow!) in Ireland while I edited it.

To Kingston Uni, my writing group there and my tutor Liz Jensen, and to Guildford Library.

To the Debutantes of 2009, ladies who are indeed a feast of awesome.

Thanks to those who have been so wonderful to me on live-journal all these years, and to all the marmalade fish out there.

ABOUT THE AUTHOR

Sarah Rees Brennan was born and raised in Ireland by the sea, where her teachers valiantly tried to make her fluent in Irish (she wants you to know it's not called Gaelic) but she chose to read books under her desk in class instead. The books most often found under her desk were by Jane Austen, Margaret Mahy, Anthony Trollope, Robin McKinley and Diana Wynne Jones, and she still loves them all today.

After college she lived briefly in New York and somehow survived in spite of her habit of hitching lifts in fire engines. She began working on *The Demon's Lexicon* while doing a Creative Writing MA and library work in Surrey, England. Since then she has returned to Ireland to write. *The Demon's Lexicon* is her first novel and she is currently working on the sequel.

AN INTERVIEW WITH
SARAH REES BRENNAN

Q. When did you start writing?

A: I started writing when I was five years old, having just come to the crushing realisation that I would never be a ballerina, and started telling my grandfather a pack of lies about the books I'd written. At seven I really did write a book about ponies and ninjas, and from that point there was no going back.

Q. Where do you get your ideas from?

A: I remember once hearing another writer say he got his ideas from rifling through Philip Pullman's dustbins. I'd do it that way, but I'm afraid if Philip Pullman caught me at it he might call the cops.

Really no writer knows exactly where their ideas come from. It's like a mixture of ingredients – real life, fiction, the thoughts you don't even know your subconscious has served up – that turns out differently every time.

Q: Why are you writing books for teenagers?

A: Because I think that they're awesome! Ahem. The teenage years are really exciting ones: you're discovering love, and yourself, and a whole other world. If you were discovering magic and risking death as well, think how much more exciting life would be!

Q: Is The Demon's Lexicon *a stand-alone novel?*

A: You don't get rid of me that easily. It's the first of three books: a trilogy. *The Demon's Lexicon* comes out in summer 2009, the sequel in summer 2010, and the third book in summer 2011.

Q: Where did you first get the idea for The Demon's Lexicon?

A: My father was watching a documentary on the Discovery Channel and my head snapped up and I said 'Now *that's* interesting.' It was about a wolf bringing up human children, as Black Arthur discusses in *The Demon's Lexicon*, and I started to wonder what would happen if a human brought up something that was as intelligent as a human, but in many ways quite different . . . So *The Demon's Lexicon* was born. Let it be a lesson to us all to let our parents watch boring television. You know, sometimes.

Q: What is this 'urban fantasy' you say that you write?

A: Lots of fantasy has people stepping into a different world to find magic, like in the *Chronicles of Narnia*. In *The Demon's Lexicon* (and other urban fantasy books - sadly I did not come up with this concept) magic exists in *this* world. You're not swept away, not even to a magical school, like in *A Wizard of Earthsea* and *Harry Potter*. In my book there's a whole lot of: yes, there is magic in the world, but someone has to fix the leaky sink, and the brothers have to worry about paying electricity bills as well as fighting demons. I love writing urban fantasy because it's grounded in reality, so can make you feel like magic is right around the corner.

Q. Are your books going to be made into a film?

A: Not that I know of, but I would have no objection! Round up your attractive actors, people, I'm sure we can find a place for all of them on set . . . It's really the decision of the studios whether they want to buy the movie rights, but if a studio decides they would like to, I for one would be delighted.

Q. Which authors have inspired you?

A. Jane Austen is my very favourite writer – she is tons of people's, of course! I have been inspired by lots of different authors: Anthony Trollope, Dorothy L Sayers, Margaret Mahy, Robin McKinley and Diana Wynne Jones among them, and the one thing they all have in common is how real they make people seem and how immediate their characters' feelings are – whether in the midst of murder, magic or a Victorian drawing room.

On a more personal level, I know some amazing writers whose books inspire me and who I can also call up and have them tell me when I'm talking crazy. (What? – I find that inspiring.)

Q: What kind of music do you like?

A: I like country music! I can often be found dancing extremely badly around my apartment to the strains of Dar Williams or Hal Ketchum. (And since I just admitted that, I have to resign myself to the fact I will never be cool.) I know, it's a far cry from the music of the Goblin Market.

Q: Are you ever going to write a book that's not fantasy?

A: Yes, I think so. I've even got an idea I can't talk about yet, but . . . I love fantasy enormously and hope to write many fantasy books besides the upcoming trilogy!

Q: *What should I do if you have not answered my Very Important Question in this list?*

A: Get in touch! I would love to hear from you.

Contact Sarah at: sarahreesbrennan@gmail.com or visit her on the web at www.sarahreesbrennan.com

THE DEMON'S COVENANT

The sequel to *The Demon's Lexicon*

Sarah Rees Brennan

Mae Crawford always thought she was in control. Now she's learned that her little brother Jamie is a magician and Nick, the boy she'd set her heart on, has an even darker secret. Mae's whole world has spun out of control, and it's only going to get worse.

When she realises that Jamie has been meeting secretly with the new leader of the Obsidian Circle, and that Gerald wants him to join the magicians, she's not sure how to stop Jamie doing just that. Calling in Nick and Alan as reinforcements only leads to a more desperate conflict because Gerald has a plan to bring Nick down – by using Alan to spring a deadly trap.

With those around her torn between divided loyalties and Mae herself torn between her feelings for two very different boys, she sees a chance to save them all – but it means approaching the mysterious and dangerous Goblin Market alone . . .